Francis Tiffany

Life of Dorothea Lynde Dix

Francis Tiffany

Life of Dorothea Lynde Dix

ISBN/EAN: 9783337333386

Printed in Europe, USA, Canada, Australia, Japan

Cover: Foto ©Raphael Reischuk / pixelio.de

More available books at **www.hansebooks.com**

PREFACE.

THE question has very naturally been raised why heretofore no attempt should have been made at an adequate biography of Dorothea Lynde Dix; in fact, why — except for a few brief accounts of her career, printed in magazines, read before private clubs, or inserted in encyclopædias — no real information is to be had about her.

Here is a woman who, as the founder of vast and enduring institutions of mercy in America and in Europe, has simply no peer in the annals of Protestantism. To find her parallel in this respect, it is necessary to go back to the lives of such memorable Roman Catholic women as St. Theresa of Spain or Santa Chiara of Assisi, and to the amazing work they did in founding throughout European Christendom great conventual establishments. Why, then, do the majority of the present generation know little or nothing of so remarkable a story?

It was from no lack of pressure on the part of admirers and venerators of the character and work of so exceptional a woman that this came about. The invincible obstacle lay in her own positive refusal to permit anything to be written of her. Living to the advanced age of eighty-five, and never pausing in her career of beneficent activity till fully eighty, she cherished all the disdain of the heroic soldier setting out on ever fresh campaigns, at the thought of quitting the post of present duty to look after the lustre of past laurels. Not in the winning of laurels, but in the succor of human misery, lay the dominating purpose of her life. A woman of great pride and dignity of character, fully conscious, too, of the immensity of the work she had achieved on two continents, she yet shrank in utter aversion from what seemed to her the degradation of mere public notoriety.

Two equally strong, but totally contrasted, natures lay in her: the one the outcome of a sensitive, suffering temperament, instinctively seeking to shield itself from gall or wound; the other born of the fortitude of a martyr in fronting danger, loneliness, and obloquy, in championing the cause of the friendless and "ready to perish." To all this must be added a depth of self-abnegating religious faith which made her life one long struggle to prostrate a spirit naturally proud and imperious at the footstool of God, in the lowly cry, "Not unto me, not unto me, but unto Thy Name be the praise!"

As far back as in 1851, Mrs. Sarah J. Hale, then engaged on a book to be entitled "Lives and Characters of Distinguished Women," applied to Miss Dix for data from which to write an account of her career. To this, as to numberless like appeals, Miss Dix re-

plied in the following strain, so indicative of her persistent feeling in the matter : —

" I feel it right to say to you frankly that nothing could
be undertaken which would give me more pain and serious
annoyance, which would so trespass on my personal rights,
. . . or interfere more seriously with the real usefulness of
my mission. I am not ambitious of nominal distinctions,
and notoriety is my special aversion.

" My reputation and my services belong to my country.
My history and my affections are consecrated to my friends.
It will be soon enough when the angel of the last hour
shall have arrested my labors to give their history and their
results. This period cannot be many years distant. I
confess that giving unnecessary publicity to women while
they yet live, and to their works, seems to me singularly at
variance with the delicacy and modesty which are the most
attractive ornaments of their sex."

For years following, such ardent friends as Hon.
Alexander Randall, of Annapolis, Maryland, General
John A. Dix,[1] of New York, and Rev. William G.
Eliot, D. D., of St. Louis, importuned her not to suffer
such a life-story to die with her. Both Mr. Randall
and Dr. Eliot themselves offered to write out a detailed

---

[1] Though always beginning his letters to her with " Dear Sister,"
no traceable relationship existed between Miss Dix and General John
A. Dix. Miss Dix's admiration, however, was always great for the
man who united such varied qualities as those of the pure statesman, the brave soldier who made the country ring with his " If any
man haul down the American flag, shoot him on the spot," and the
Christian scholar who gave the world such devout and beautiful translations of mediæval Latin hymns.

memorial of her career, if only she would dictate to
them the leading incidents and supply the needful
papers. But she had no time nor inclination to turn
aside. Years later, however, when extreme old age
had rendered the further prosecution of her labors an
impossibility, both Mr. Randall and General Dix
renewed their entreaties, and succeeded in extracting
a half promise from her to make out needful memoranda and reduce the confused mass of her papers to
some kind of chronological order.

Thus in June, 1878, a letter from General Dix to
Mr. Randall bears witness to the earnestness with
which they were coöperating toward this mutually
desired end: —

> "SEAFIELD, WEST HAMPTON, N. J.,
> *June* 25, 1878.

"MY DEAR SIR, — I wrote to Miss Dix urging her to
make full notes of what she had done for the insane. There
is no record like hers, — I do not except Howard or Mrs.
Fry; and it is due to our country to give a faithful account
of the labors of her life. . . . I have pressed this duty on
her for years, and trust your solicitations and those of other
friends may decide her to perform it.

> "Very truly yours,   JOHN A. DIX."

Still later on, Mr. Randall writes urgently to Miss
Dix to know what progress has been made toward the
fulfillment of the promise given: —

"How comes on the Memoir of Miss Dix? You owe it
to our country properly to attend to it yourself. I know
you will not charge me with flattery when I say that if any

other female in the country had accomplished half as much as you, you would have procured her life to be written or written it yourself. . . . Pardon my plainness and repeated request and urgency in this matter, for I do really think such a life as yours has not filled up its measure of practical good until posterity has the benefit of its example."

Two short extracts from replies of Miss Dix to such letters of Mr. Randall's as the above will suffice to show how baffling to her mind was this whole biographical matter : —

Boston, Mass., *October* 13, 1870.

" I assure you of my respect for your opinions, and desire to accept and act upon your request, if I can feel quickened to this burthensome undertaking. . . . There is, I think, great difficulty in writing of one's self: it is almost impossible to present subjects, where the chief actor must be conspicuous, and not seem to be, or really be, egotistical. Then, much of my work has been where neglects and omissions demanded remonstrance and persistent efforts for reforms and amended usages, implying much wrong on the part of others, who must be at the least noticed as blameworthy through either habitual negligence or willful wrong."

Trenton, N. J., *May* 10, 1880.

" I have found myself pressed under the obligation of a promise to yourself, at once honorable to fulfill and yet most difficult and oppressive to carry forward. It is impossible for any one to realize how painful it is to rouse from within a half century's painful past, embracing every form and condition of distress, suffering, misery, and adversity. . . . Language seems to lose force and words to define weakly what

has been and now is, in the present hour as in the expired
years. I cannot, my valued friend, bring into order suitably
for a brief memoir any written details that seem to me fitly
to convey to any reader what cannot be realized, because
there is no relative standard of contrast or comparison.
The whole of my years, from the age of ten to the present,
differ essentially from the experience and pursuits of those
around me."

Yet one more ground of reluctance on the part of
Miss Dix to having any record of her life given to the
world must here in conclusion be noted. It was one
frequently emphasized by her, and is too characteristic alike of the pity of her heart and of her habitual
way of looking on her own exceptional history to be
omitted. Such an account, she feared, would exert
an unhealthy influence in inducing romantic young
women to think it their mission to undertake some
work of a similar kind. "No, let them fall in love,
marry, and preside over a happy home," she would
say; "it will be a thousand times better for them."
She who had never known the meaning of home, even
in childhood, who had led a lonely and wandering life,
who had carried ever in her heart an unsatisfied yearning after those closer ties which unite human beings
in the heaven of tender family relations; she, too,
who, in her redeeming career of half a century, had
sounded all the depths of human misery, and knew
how stern the conflict and cruel the wounds inevitable
in a lifelong struggle to secure redress, felt, as none who
had not shared the like experience could feel, that

nothing short of an irresistible call from God should induce any one to embark on such a work.

The result of these persistent solicitations was that toward the very close of her life, when well-nigh helpless with disease, Miss Dix made faltering attempts to reduce her papers to order. She was then too feeble for the task, and they were left in a state of great confusion. Shortly before her death, however, she gave to her trusted friend and executor, Mr. Horace A. Lamb, of Boston, her full consent that, if such remained his final judgment, the papers might be used in the preparation of a memoir of her life and work. Unfortunately, in what must be regarded as a mistaken sense of the duty of self-effacement, she had previously issued positive commands to her many friends to destroy her own private letters. A few of these friends happily refused to obey the injunction, and to their pious care for her memory is it alone due that any vivid picture can at this date be drawn of her.

The writer of her biography would take this occasion to express his sense of great personal obligation to Miss Augusta I. Appleton, of the Boston Athenæum, and to Miss Katharine H. Stone, for their patient and discriminating labor in reducing the original chaos of the papers to any kind of manageable order. Also, to the superintendents of insane asylums in many quarters of the United States and of Canada, especially to Dr. John S. Butler, Dr. John W. Ward, Dr. Charles H. Nichols, and Dr. Horace A. Buttolph; to Daniel Hack Tuke, M. D., F. R. C. P., of Hanwell, England, and to William Rathbone, Esq., M. P., of Liverpool; as well as to numerous private friends of Miss Dix, he would here record his cordial thanks for constant courtesy and invaluable aid.

F. T.

CAMBRIDGE, MASS., *February* 16, 1890.

CONTENTS.

LIFE OF DOROTHEA L. DIX.

CHAPTER I.

BIRTH AND ANCESTRY.

THOUGH by ancestry and subsequent education a Massachusetts woman, Dorothea (christened Dorothy) Lynde Dix was born, April 4, 1802, in the State of Maine. Her birth occurred during a temporary stay of her parents in the town of Hampden, on the Penobscot River; one, in fact, of the very many places in which her father, who was of an unstable and wandering turn of mind, appears for a short time to have lived. Indeed, this instability of character on the part of Joseph Dix, the father, together with the frequent changes of residence and occupation it involved, makes it impossible to trace with any precision the various stages of the early childhood of his later so remarkable daughter.

Glimpses of this childhood are lighted on at various spots in Maine, New Hampshire, and Vermont, as well as in Worcester and Boston, Massachusetts. So painful, however, to the subsequent woman always remained the memory of its bitterness that in no hour of the most confidential intimacy could she be induced to unlock the silence which to the very end of life she maintained as to all the incidents of her early days.

As throwing light on the development of character in a woman of the ultimate stamp of Miss Dix, it becomes necessary to hint, at least, at the peculiar nature of the trials to which she was so early subjected. They were the trials that inevitably follow in the track of a shiftless, aimless, and wandering life, — poverty, lack of public respect, the absence of permanency of relation with schools, churches, and a circle of endeared and sympathetic friends. Among the abnormal tendencies of the father was one of subjection to states of fanatical religious excitement, during which he became wholly engrossed in writing and issuing tracts, the supreme importance of which to the world's salvation outweighed in his mind every question of the material maintenance and needful education of his family. These tracts the little Dorothy, then twelve years old, and for the time being in Worcester, Massachusetts, was, to save expense, set so continuously to pasting and stitching together that, in her revolt at the hateful task — so the seemingly authentic story has come down, — she ran away from Worcester, and put herself under the protection of her grandmother, then resident in Boston. A proud, ambitious, and high-spirited child, — her paternal grandmother living in considerable wealth and dignity, — she appears to have suffered much the same misery of humiliation at being cut off from advantages of education and kept at menial tasks which Charles Dickens so painfully analyzes in the picture he draws of his own boy-apprenticeship in the blacking-factory. Thus the acute sensitiveness of fibre and high sense of personal dignity so characteristic of the mature woman were manifest from the very start.

Very early in life, then, was the self-reliant and indomitable nature of the child rudely awakened to the necessity of resolutely fronting the world and fighting her way on her own resources. In seeking refuge in her grandmother's house, she saw the only chance open to her of securing a fit education. She had at this time a much younger brother, born ten years later than herself, toward whom she felt the duty would surely devolve on her of becoming protectress and child-mother. The first step to the possibility of this lay in achieving independence for herself, a conviction increased in strength when, in the following year, another brother was born. Break through these trammels of poverty and humiliation she must; force her way out to some pecuniary basis she must. Eager for knowledge, ambitious for more refined and intellectual social opportunities, loaded down already with a premature sense of responsibility, thus early had the iron entered her soul, and the conviction been developed in her of the reality and sharpness of the battle of life.

From what ancestral source, then, it is natural to ask, had descended to the child this self-reliant will, this indomitable resolve to open up for herself a career of her own, together with so high wrought a sense of moral obligation? All the more natural is it to ask this question, seeing that her immediate parents were lacking in energetic fibre.

Very common is it to notice that salient family traits overleap one entire generation only to reappear in renewed force in the generation following. Emphatically was this the case in the instance before us. The paternal grandfather and grandmother of Dorothea were persons of very marked characteristics, — characteristics which in a more refined and spiritualized shape, and enlisted in the service of an impassioned idea, took higher though kindred shape in the grandchild. These furnished the vigorous native stock into which evolving Providence was to engraft scions capable of more sweetly-perfumed flowers and of fruit of a richer flavor.

Dr. Elijah Dix, the grandfather, was born, August 24, 1747, in Watertown, Massachusetts. Of sound old New England stock, but poor, as were most children of large families in the colonial days, he had his own way to make in the world. Struggling doughtily for such desultory education as he could secure, his aspirations were none the less high, and to be satisfied with nothing short of fitting himself for one of the learned professions, as, in those days, theology, law, and medicine were — perhaps we should now think somewhat humorously — termed. A college career he could not compass. Effecting, however, an arrangement with Dr. John Green, an eminent practitioner in Worcester, he spent with him three years, engaged in compounding medicines and studying the theoretical part of the profession; and after supplementing this term with two more years under William Greenleaf, druggist of Boston, he began practice in 1770 as physician and surgeon in Worcester.

The characteristics of the young man eminently fitted him for worldly success. Strong in body, courageous and self-asserting in temperament, ambitious of power and position, nothing daunted him. And yet along with these qualities, whose aggressive excess rendered him highly unpopular, he united a large degree of public spirit and of far-sighted practical judgment. As he rose to position and could make his influence felt, he was the first man in Worcester to advocate by precept and example the planting of shade trees for the adornment of the town, — a remarkable idiosyncrasy of taste, it was thought, at a period in our colonial history when, in the weary struggle of the early settlers with the primeval forests, a tree was looked upon as as natural an enemy of man as a bear or an Indian. He was further a zealous promoter of all means of opening up the country for freer trade and social intercourse, as, notably, in the instance of the Worcester and Boston turnpike. Those were the days when the title of "Pontifex Maximus" meant something, and was not worn as an idle badge of honor by emperors and popes. As an instance, moreover, of his sturdy honesty, it may be stated that, at the end of the Revolutionary War, he crossed the ocean to settle his financial accounts with his former associate in medical practice, Dr. Sylvester Gardiner, and to pay over what he considered fairly the due of his partner. This Dr. Gardiner had, at the outbreak of disturbance with the mother country, taken the royalist side, and so been forced, as a refugee, to flee the colony. As a stanch patriot, Dr. Dix might have felt himself entirely absolved from handing over a penny to one whom it was only needful to stigmatize as a traitor. As an honest man, however, he did not feel himself thus absolved.

Returning home from England with a large collection of books, surgical instruments, and chemical apparatus, Dr. Dix now engaged in the sale of such articles, pursued his medical practice, and projected with great ardor the plan of an academy. In spite, however, of acknowledged ability and public spirit, his dictatorial ways made him so unpopular with his fellow-citizens that a plot was laid to drive him out of the town, or at any rate to subject him to personal violence. Suspecting what was on foot, he, at the first sign of practical action, proved himself entirely equal to the emergency. One evening a man called at his house to summon him to the sick-bed of a pretended patient, living several miles out of town, and on the road to whose house, as later appeared, an attacking party had placed itself in ambush. The sturdy doctor promptly expressed his professional willingness to go, taking the precaution, however, to throw open the window and call out in stentorian tones to his man-servant, " Bring round my horse at once ; see that the pistols in my holsters are double-shotted ; then give the bull-dog a piece of raw meat and turn him loose to go along ! " It is needless to say that the friend of the imaginary sick man " folded his tents like the Arabs, and silently stole away."

With the view of opening up to himself a still wider field of activity, Dr. Elijah Dix, in 1795, seven years before the birth of Dorothea, removed to Boston, where he established a drug store on the south side of Faneuil Hall, and further founded in South Boston chemical works for refining sulphur and purifying camphor. Successful in these enterprises, his indomitable energy next sought vent in large land speculations in the State of Maine, in which State he purchased immense tracts, — buying in one instance twenty thousand acres for the site of a single projected farming village, and becoming founder of the towns of Dixmont and Dixfield, the settlers in which obtained the titles to their farms from him. This diversion of interests on the part of Dr. Elijah Dix henceforth necessitated his making frequent journeys to Maine to see after his property there, on one of which visits he died.

His death occurred June 7, 1809, and his body was interred in the burial-ground near Dixmont Centre. Thus easily is the birth of his granddaughter Dorothea in Hampden, Maine, accounted for. Hampden lies at but a short distance from Dixmont, and was then the only town in the section of sufficient size to furnish decent quarters. No doubt Dr. Elijah Dix had attempted to make his son Joseph his agent for overseeing and disposing of the Maine lands.

The salient traits, then, of the character of Dr. Elijah Dix were indomitable energy and spirit of initiative in new enterprises, fertility of resource, dogged honesty, large public spirit, and a masterful temperament that would ride over obstacles, no matter at what cost of personal popularity. Though but seven years old when her grandfather died, Dorothea always retained a vivid remembrance of what she saw of him in Boston in her childhood, particularly of his fondness for driving her around with him in his chaise, and of talking with her in his strong and racy way. He stood out the one bright spot in her earliest memories, implanting in her mind a life-long admiration for his robust and picturesque qualities. Indeed, of the many great asylums for the insane which she was later instrumental in founding, the only one she ever permitted to be associated with her own name, was Dixmont Hospital, in Pennsylvania, a concealed tribute to her grandfather, as founder of the town of Dixmont, Maine.

After the death of Dr. Elijah Dix, his widow lived on in Boston, occupying the, for those days, quite stately house which went by the name of the Dix Mansion. It was in the large garden surrounding this house that, from some chance seed, sprang the celebrated Dix pear, — one of those Melchisedecs in pomology, without father and without mother, which, like the far-famed Seckel, originated from the start an illustrious family of its own. Here, then, continued to reside the widow of Dr. Elijah Dix, who was destined to survive her husband twenty-eight years, dying only at the late date of April 29, 1837. As one whose personal qualities and peculiar position as head of the house exercised in many ways a marked influence on the development of her granddaughter, it is necessary briefly to speak of her prominent characteristics.

Dorothy Lynde, born May 23, 1746, and married, October 1, 1771, to Dr. Elijah Dix, was the daughter of Joseph Lynde, who, after the burning of Charlestown, Mass., by the British troops, sought refuge with his wife and children in Worcester. Already far advanced in life when, at the age of twelve, her granddaughter became a member of her family, Madam Dix was a typical example of the New England Puritan gentlewoman of the period, — dignified, precise, inflexibly conscientious, unimaginative, and without trace of emotional glow or charm. For generations, indeed, it had been the outcome of the Puritan training of New England to produce a class of mothers unflinchingly nerved, if need be, to die at the stake for their children, but whom no threat of penal fires would have betrayed into the weakness of kissing them goodnight; and as these mothers duly advanced to the dignified stage of grandmothers, the tendency became ever more sharply accentuated.

Indeed, for simple emotional love as a fountain leaping up in sallies of playful tenderness, the majority of the parents of those now far-away days in which Madam Dix had received the earliest stamp of the chilled-steel parental die shared no more sympathetic a response than a mill-engineer for the poetry of the charming cascades of the stream he seeks to utilize for grinding the corn and weaving the cloth of the people. To save waste of available power and to divert the full emotional flow into a strong-banked, prosaic race-way, from which the full head could be turned on to the practical work of making the jackets and knitting the socks of the young, of training them to habits of rigid industry, of exacting iron diligence over the school lessons, and of inculcating the dogmas of the catechism in a way to make them a salutary terror for life, — this seemed the only aspect of the divine quality of love which could be reconciled with a severe sense of duty, and saved from the fatal danger of degenerating into luxurious and enervating sentimentalism. There were good sides to this extreme, and there were very bad ones. It insured a Spartan discipline of education which put bark and iron into the blood. But it steadily atrophied, and, as years advanced, actually ossified, the lovelier and sunnier capacities of affection, opening up an impassable abyss between old age and the sensitive, clinging heart of childhood.

To Madam Dix, then, and to the old Dix Mansion, the child Dorothea owed, on the one hand, a debt of lasting obligation, and, on the other, years of acute suffering and heart-starvation. When she sought refuge from the unendurable humiliation of her life in Worcester, it was to her grandmother's house that she came, and here she secured the advantages of several years of school education. It was a grim and joyless home, but none the less it was a home in which she was trained to habits of unremitting diligence. No waste of time was permitted, no task allowed to be done in a slipshod way. Here was a child, the grandmother felt, who would have her own way to make in the world, and who, as early as possible, would have to become the mainstay of her family. She must fit herself, then, for some occupation by which she could win her bread. It would be cruelty to bring her up with any other idea. In all this Madam Dix unquestionably felt that she was fulfilling the whole law of love, and doing unto another as she at least *ought* to desire that another should do unto her. Still, to the child who was immature enough to crave a little play, a little petting, and a little romance, the process seemed no doubt very chilling and severe.

In later life, people come to be grateful for many things which in childhood looked only hard and cruel. The day was to arrive when Miss Dix, in her watchful supervision of vast institutions for the relief of human misery, — institutions, in which failure in the minutest detail of organization might lead to the most tragic results — was to prove the invaluable benefit of this minute and rigid training.

Stern and unrelenting as it was, the grandmother had, after all, an ideal of her own as to the thoroughness with which every piece of work should be done, which was a true ideal. Indeed, there still lives in Massachusetts a lady, who — after the school was later on established in the old Dix Mansion, as will soon be recounted — describes, as one of the most indelible memories of her own childhood days, how, as an especial reward for excellence in moral conduct, she herself was allowed the unusual privilege of making an entire shirt under the Rhadamanthine eye of Madam Dix. The sense of moral responsibility pre-

cipitated on the poor child was literally crushing, as
now first the startling revelation broke on her mind
of the eternal distinction between the right way and
the wrong way in the minutest particulars. Of the
thousands of stitches entering into the awe-inspiring
structure, not one must differ from another to a degree
that could be detected by a micrometer. The one and
only immutably correct way of cutting and fitting the
neck-band seemed far more out of the range of mortal
possibility than the camel's passage through the eye
of a needle. And yet to this day the lady frankly
admits that, well-nigh fatal as the strain proved at
the time, the benefit was lifelong of having thus been
made to do at least one piece of work thoroughly well.
Indeed, she still speaks of the experience in the same
vein of enthusiastic gratitude in which here and there
a veteran scholar descants on the intellectual bark and
iron put into him by the inexorable discipline of the
classics, in the heroic days when, in the eyes of the
- Latin master, a misplaced particle in a sentence was
as unpardonable a sin as was, in the eyes of Madam
Dix, a misplaced stitch in a shirt.

Meanwhile, the passionate, craving heart of the
child had to get along as best it could. She had her
bread, though it was often wet with salt tears. She
had shelter, education, and oversight ; the oversight
no doubt bestowed in what was felt to be absolute
fidelity to the clearest sense of duty. But as for a
warm breast and loving arms in which to nestle and
confide, this the kind heavens did not grant her. In
bitter intensity of grief would she at times in later
life break out over this irremediable loss in her childhood days. " I never knew childhood! " she would
passionately exclaim. And it was true. To become

independent in means, to educate herself for a position that would command support and respect, to be able to get her two younger brothers under the same roof with her, and enact the part of child-mother to them — this early developed into the indomitable purpose of her life.   There was in those days but one career of independence a growing girl could look forward to, — the vocation of the teacher.   Happily, preparation for this calling was in the line of the deepest instincts of her nature.   These were at that time thirst for knowledge and longing to exert direct moral influence.

The first authentic date of any attempt at teaching on the part of the ardent young girl is her opening a school for little children in Worcester, Mass., in 1816–17.   She was then fourteen years old, and so girlish in look that, as she herself tells the story, she thought it necessary to put on long skirts and lengthen the sleeves of her dress, so as to command due respect by a more adult appearance.   There still lives in Worcester one of these pupils, who vividly recalls the child-teacher as tall for her age, easily blushing, at once beautiful and imposing in manner, but inexorably strict in discipline.   The skirt and sleeves of a grown woman were, this lady thinks, in no way necessary to secure for the young girl absolute ascendency over her pupils.   She bore the stamp of authority from the start.   Herself brought up in a stern school, she had at that date little idea of any government but the government of will.   Indeed, it is always characteristic of very young people, abruptly forced to play the rôle of maturity and experience, that they overdo things.   They show this fault in teaching their younger brothers and sisters at home, and they fall into it in a still more pronounced way when, on taking charge of a school, they think it incumbent on them, as perhaps it is, to assert themselves from the outset. Thus, the impression left on the minds of the little girls and boys in Worcester by their fourteen-year-old teacher, so far from being that of a half-grown girl they could venture to trifle with, was that of one of whom they stood in fear.

In truth, now first manifested itself the instinctive consciousness of a nature born to rule, and seizing the first swift and ready way. Into what a furnace of pain and affliction that nature was to be baptized before it could be duly refined and tempered; through what years of lonely wrestlings, battle with disease, submission of an iron will to the counsels of a Holier Might, it was to pass before she should become fitted to rule as justly, mercifully, and yet imperially as she finally came to rule, — all this lay happily hidden from her in the womb of the slowly unfolding future.

CHAPTER II.

FOR several years after the experiment with the child-school in Worcester, in 1816–17, Miss Dix appears to have lived with her grandmother in Boston, her leisure devoted to carrying on her own studies in preparation for opening a school for older pupils. Though then but a town of forty thousand inhabitants, Boston was already giving signs of an intellectual ferment in theology, philanthropy, philosophy, and literature, which was to inaugurate a new epoch in the spiritual history of New England. The day of provincialism was passing away. Higher ideals of God and of human destiny were breaking in, and young and ardent minds, emancipating themselves from the cramping traditions of the past, already felt that the long, weary sojourn in the wilderness was over, and that, standing at last on Pisgah, they could overlook a veritable Land of Promise. None entered more earnestly into certain phases of this spiritual rebirth, or hailed more rapturously its prophets of the type of Channing, than did Miss Dix.

Not, probably, before the year 1821 did she resume the actual work of teaching, beginning with classes of day-pupils, in a little house of her grandmother's in Orange Court, and only by degrees, raising the standard, till the modest beginning finally developed into a combined boarding and day school in the Dix Mansion itself, to which children were sent from the most prominent families in Boston, as well as from towns as far away as then was Portsmouth, N. H. Later on she was to have her younger brothers with her under the same roof, and was to become practical mistress of the Dix Mansion. The increasing infirmities of the grandmother now kept her largely confined to her own room, an added care of no slight nature. Thus by degrees were devolved upon the never strong young woman the duties of housekeeper, teacher, motherly elder sister, and matron of the boarding-pupils, together with the necessity of carrying on her own as yet imperfect intellectual training, — duties which she assumed with unflinching spirit. Fond of responsibility, ambitious of success, and on fire with an ideal of what a teacher might prove, for time and for eternity, to the children committed to her care, she took no thought of flesh and blood.

Seemingly, responsibilities so arduous as these would have been enough to satisfy the most exacting conscience. In Miss Dix's case, however, there was one imperious element of her nature which they altogether failed to content. More and more evident will it grow, as this narrative proceeds, that the sense of pitiful compassion for the ignorant, degraded, and suffering was the strongest element in her being. She would work for herself now, for work she must; she would work for her younger brothers till they were ready to go forth and do for themselves; but the moment she should stand free, then beyond all things the nearest and dearest of God's privileges to her would be the championship of the outcast and ready to perish. Soon, therefore, besides the school already taxing to exhaustion her strength, she establishes another in a room over the stable of the Dix Mansion, for poor and neglected children. How pitifully she had to plead for permission to do this comes out touchingly in the following letter, so full of the spirit of merciful humanity then first beginning its struggle with that older inflexible temper of Puritanism, which had submissively waited on adult conversion to repair in an hour the results of years of indifference and neglect. The letter is without date, but belongs early in the school-keeping days.

"MY DEAR GRANDMOTHER, — Had I the saint-like eloquence of our minister, I would employ it in explaining all the motives, and dwelling on all the good, good to the poor, the miserable, the idle, and the ignorant, which would follow your giving me permission to use the barn chamber for a school-room for charitable and religious purposes. You have read Hannah More's life, you approve of her labors for the most degraded of England's paupers; why not, when it can be done without exposure or expense, let *me* rescue some of America's miserable children from vice and guilt? . . . Do, my dear grandmother, yield to my request, and witness next summer the reward of your benevolent and Christian compliance.

"Your affectionate Granddaughter,   D. L. DIX."

Like the feeble beginnings in another "upper chamber" in Judæa, this early attempt at stretching out a helping hand to outcast children, was to lead on to far-reaching results. The little barn-school proved the nucleus out of which, years later, was developed the beneficent work of the Warren Street Chapel, from which, as a centre, spread far and wide a new ideal of dealing with childhood. There first was interest excited in the mind of Rev. Charles Barnard, a man of positive spiritual genius in charming and uplifting the children of the poor and debased. With all the love of St. Vincent de Paul in his heart, and a fund of originality in devising happy ways and means, the words of Jesus, " Suffer the little children to come unto me," were the very breath of his life. And when the children gladly responded, it was not to find themselves tormented with rigid catechising and a cast-iron drill, but to be taken into open arms of love, and to be ushered into a new world of beauty and freedom.

In the year 1823, Miss Dix began a correspondence, to be continued at intervals for fifty years, with a dear friend, Miss Anne Heath, of Brookline, Mass., but for the preservation of which no adequate picture could be drawn of the early womanhood of the young teacher. It is to an endeared few alone that personalities of the inborn reticence of Miss Dix are ever able to reveal their inner life. And yet so very great is oftentimes the contrast between the maturer bearing of characters marked by commanding practical ability, and the life of the same persons in the romantic period of youth, that but for some such revelation the hidingplace of their power would go unsurmised. Indeed, the standing marvel of psychological history lies in the imperceptible steps by which so often the sighs and tears of sentimental feeling lead on to the masterly self-control and disciplined strength of advancing years. These letters furnish, then, but one more illustration of the fact that a certain even perilous excess of sensibility will be found at the root of all natures that ever achieve anything high and heroic in life.

Emphatically did all this hold true of the youth of the subject of this biography. Self-repressed and self-mastered as later on she outwardly fronted the world, inwardly her soul was in those days full to the brim of passion and heart-break, of poetic enthusiasm and religious exaltation. In truth, for some years to come, the chief faults of her character are directly traceable to this. Her demands on herself, her demands on her friends, her demands on her pupils, were out of all bounds. She herself must be pure spirit, taking no counsel of flesh and blood; her friends must be incarnations of every attribute of intellect and every grace of soul; in her pupils she must detect, in embryo at least, the prophecy of the coming ideal mothers and saintly helpers of the world. And so the inevitable reaction from such overwrought expectations was subjection to hours of bitter disillusion and even of passionate, unjust censure of average, commonplace mortality.

As tending to foster excess of sentimental feeling, it is here of importance to note the habit, in those days indulged in by young women, of voluminous, effusive correspondence with one another. Their letters, without date and without distinct reference to anything in time or space that would enable a future bewildered biographer to affix to them " a local habitation and a name," wandered off into realms of purely subjective poetry, philanthropy, philosophy, and religion. And yet what intensity of inward life these letters reveal! Anything was enough to start one of them, — the death of an infant, a peculiarly beautiful sunset, a new volume of poetry, an inspiring or heart-searching passage in the sermon of the previous Sunday; and then would they roll on through literally continental sheets of paper, to all the length and with all the volume of the Mississippi.

Far easier is it to give an idea of the character of these letters by example than by description. The method of illustration by extracts is of course exposed to the danger of conveying entirely erroneous impressions of brevity. None the less it may impart a sense of the spirit of these copious interchanges of thought and feeling. First, then, let the following serve as a commentary on the intensity with which poetry was in those days read by passionate young women, — those days of comparatively few books, in which a new poet was a fresh visitant from the celestial sphere. The L. E. L. to whom reference is made is Letitia Elizabeth Landon, a young Englishwoman, whose strains of tender melancholy and romantic sentiment were marked by a degree of real power, which under severer training might have given her a permanent place in literature. The letter from which the extract is made was written to Miss Heath, near midnight, presumably in 1823 : —

" DEAR ANNIE, — You say I weep easily. I was early taught to sorrow, to shed tears, and now, when sudden joy lights up or any unexpected sorrow strikes my heart, I find it difficult to repress the full and swelling tide of feeling. Even now, though alone and with no very exciting cause of joy or grief, I am paying my watery tribute to the genius of L. E. L. Oh, Anne ! she is a poetess that expresses all the genius and fire of Byron, unalloyed with his gross faults ; all the beautiful flow of words which fall like music on the air from the pen of Moore, without his little less than half-concealed consciousness ; all the simplicity of Wordsworth without his prosiness and stiffness ; finally, in the words of her reviewer, ' If she never excels what she already has written, we can confidently give her the assurance of what the possessor of such talents must earnestly covet, *immortality*.' The ' Improvisatrice ' will soon be published in this country and then, Anne, prepare for the enjoyment of this rich feast.

"I worship *talents*, almost. I *sinfully dare mourn* that I possess them not. . . . It is not that I may win the *world's* applause that I would possess a mind above the *common sphere*, but that I might revel in the luxury of those mental visions that must hourly entrance a spirit that partakes less of earth than heaven. . . . I shall try to *feel* and to *act* better, but I *cannot* cease to *lament*.

"Good-night,   THEA."

No one can read a letter like this, crude as it is in expression, a letter written at midnight, her only hour of leisure, by a young woman who, in ill health, was bearing so exhausting a burden, without feeling the fierce pulsebeat of an aspiring nature, which read poetry not for pastime, but for dear life; not for the diversion of an idle hour, but for refuge in a realm of ideality, and for solace to its passionate yearning after a wider, richer experience.

Again and again, in this correspondence with Miss Heath, there breaks out the cry of loneliness and heart-hunger. The strain of each day's work, in itself severe enough, was made all the more exhausting by the additional tasks a mind incapable of rest was forever imposing on itself. Rising before the sun and going to bed after midnight, steadily bent on supplementing the defects of an imperfect early education, at work on text-books like her "Science of Common Things" (which ultimately went through sixty editions, and the fundamental data of which she had to learn as she wrote them down), inevitably there set in that physical exhaustion of body and brain out of which no further response is to be had but by plying whip and spur. There was no joy in the house, no refuge

in a merry, loving home circle, no leisure from ever-
pursuing cares. Thence the hungry void in her heart
which led her often to write in a strain like this : —

"Anne, my dear friend, if ever you are disposed to think
your lot an unhappy one or your heart desolate, think of
her whose pathway is yet more thorny, and whose way is
cheered by no close connections. . . . You have an almost
angelic mother, Anne ; you cannot but be both good and
happy while she hovers over you, ministering to your wants,
and supplying all that the fondest affection can provide,
Your sisters, too, they comfort you. *I* have none."

As early as 1824 it was becoming doubtful whether
the young teacher would have health enough to permit
of her carrying through the scheme on which she had
embarked with such energy. Symptoms of lung con-
gestion, with tendency to hæmorrhage, were becoming
marked. Her voice, remarkable through later life for
purity, sweetness, and depth, was growing weak and
husky. She was fast contracting a stoop of the shoulders, and her frequent attitude, as she stood to conduct
her classes, was that of supporting herself with one
hand holding on to the desk, and the other pressed
hard to her side as though to repress a sharp pain.
" Over the future hangs a veil which mortal eyes may
not essay to penetrate," she now writes her friend
Miss Heath, "but we may trust in the Lord, and be
of good courage."

Of good, of heroic, courage she always was. It was
never her will that flinched, but only the body that
from time to time dropped prone to the ground. Indeed, it is scarcely without a half-pathetic smile that
one can read such self-reproachful goadings of an already overtaxed mind and body as this : —

"There is in our nature a disposition to indulgence, a secret desire to escape from labor, which, unless hourly combated, will overcome and destroy the best faculties of our minds, and paralyze our most useful powers. Protracted ill health is often suffered to become the ally of this hidden disposition, and there is hardly anything so difficult to contend with and conquer. I have often entertained a dread lest I should fall a victim to my besieger, and that fear has saved me so far."

None the less even she was before long forced to yield, and for the next two or three years to spend her time largely in efforts to establish her health. The sharpest pang of this necessity lay in the separation it involved from the charge of her younger brothers, of one of whom she writes to Miss Heath: —

"Oh, Anne, if that child is but good, I care not how humble his pathway through life. It is for him my soul is filled with bitterness when sickness wastes me; it is because of him I dread to die. I know I should have more faith; 'the spirit is willing, but the flesh is' the betrayer."

Happily for the future of Miss Dix, she had by this time won the respect and love of several very influential people in Boston. Chief among these was the celebrated divine, Dr. William Ellery Channing, who evidently clearly understood alike the admirable and the dangerous points in her nature, and frankly counseled her.

"I look forward to your future life [he on one occasion wrote] not altogether without solicitude, but with a prevailing hope. Your infirm health seems to darken your prospects of usefulness. But I believe your constitution will yet be built up, if you will give it a fair chance. You must learn to give up your plans of usefulness, as much as those of gratification, to the will of God. We may make *these*

the occasion of self-will, vanity, and pride as much as anything else. May not one of your chief dangers lie there?
. . . The infirmity which I warn you of, though one of
good minds, is an infirmity. . . . It is said that our faults
and virtues are sometimes so strangely interwoven that we
must spare the first for the sake of the last. If I thought so
in your case, I would withhold my counsel, for your virtues
are too precious to be put to hazard for such faults as I
might detect."

One fortunate outcome of this relation with Dr.
Channing was an invitation to undertake the education
of his children for six months of the spring and summer of 1827. This happily removed her from the
bleak climate of Boston to the softer air and charming
scenery of Narragansett Bay, where in Portsmouth,
R. I., at the distance of a few miles from Newport, his
birthplace, Dr. Channing had a country-seat. Her
duties were light, she could be much in the open air,
and at last her passion for hero-worship found satisfaction in close intimacy with an actual human being
so exalted in intellect and saintly in character that
the more nearly she came in contact with him the
deeper grew her veneration.

Already no mean proficient in botany, and with a
lively interest in all departments of natural history,
the flowers, seaweeds, shells, and general marine life
of the beautiful region exercised a fascination over
her that drew her away from inward conflict and gave
a healthier objective tone to her mind. When the engagement terminated, in October, Dr. Channing wrote
her : —

"You have no burden of gratitude laid upon you, for we
feel that you gave at least as much good as you received.
We will hear no more of thanks, but your affection for us

and our little ones we will treasure up among our precious
blessings. . . . I wish to say to you that if you should think
another summer's residence on Rhode Island would be
beneficial to you, Mrs. Channing and myself would be glad
to engage your services for our children. I dare not urge
the arrangement, for I have an interest in it."

For several successive winters, now, pulmonary
weakness compelled Miss Dix to seek refuge from the
severe winter climate of New England in Philadelphia, and in Alexandria, Va. She kept herself busy
with reading of a very multifarious kind, — poetry,
science, biography, and travel, — besides eking out the
scanty means she had laid by from her teaching by
writing stories and compiling floral albums and books
of devotion.[1] The effect of illness was rarely to depress her spirits. Indeed, it must here be emphasized

---

[1] The following list of the various books written by Miss Dix,
either while actually at work teaching, or while away seeking health,
has been kindly furnished by Miss A. I. Appleton, of the Boston
Athenæum : —

1. *Conversations on Common Things.* Boston, Munroe & Francis,
1824. In 1869, this book had reached its sixtieth edition.

2. *Hymns for Children, Selected and Altered.* Boston, Munroe &
Francis, 1825. Rearranged, Boston, 1833.

3. *Evening Hours.* Boston, Munroe & Francis, 1825.

4. *Ten Short Stories for Children*, 1827-28. Afterwards published
under the title *American Moral Tales for Young Persons.* Boston,
Leonard C. Bowles & B. H. Greene, 1832. Contents: John Wil-
liams, or The Sailor Boy; Little Agnes and Blind Mary; Robert
Woodard, or The Heedless Boy; James Coleman, or The Reward of
Perseverance; The Dainty Boy; Alice and Ruth; Marrion Wilder,
The Passionate Little Girl; Sequel to Marrion Wilder; George
Mills; The Storm.

5. *Meditations for Private Hours.* Boston, 1828. A number of
subsequent editions.

6. *The Garland of Flora.* Boston, S. G. Goodrich & Co., 1829.

7. *The Pearl, or Affection's Gift; A Christmas and New Year's
Present.* Philadelphia, 1829.

as a marked characteristic of her at once heroic and devout nature that suffering not only rallied to the front her powers of resistance, but actually induced a state of high spiritual exaltation. Throughout her whole future career, this will be strikingly apparent. Very interesting is it, then, to read, in the two following extracts from letters written while away in the South to Miss Heath, her own clear recognition of this constitutional trait: —

"DEAR ANNIE, — I am never less disposed to sadness than when ill and alone. Sometimes I have fancied that it was the nature of my disease to create a *rising*, elastic state of mind, but be that as it will (I speak solemnly), the hour of bodily suffering is to me the hour of spiritual joy. It is then that most I feel my dependence on God and his power to sustain. It is then that I rejoice to feel that, though the earthly frame decay, the soul shall never die. The discipline which has brought me to this has been long and varied: it has led through a valley of tears, a life of woe. . . . It is happiness to feel progression, and to feel that the power that thus aids is not of earth."

Again, as presenting a vivid picture of how quickly any vision of sublimity or beauty, whether in the physical or the moral world, would lift her above bodily suffering into a state of transport and adoration, the·following extract from a letter of this period is highly characteristic: —

"Last night, dear Annie, I could not sleep, and after several restless hours rose at one o'clock, wrapped myself warmly in my flannel gown, and was in search of my medicine, when the remarkable clearness of the sky drew me to my window. There was Orion with his glittering sword and jeweled belt, Aldebaran, the fiery eye of Taurus, Saturn with his resplendent train of attendants, and the sweet Pleiades; there, too, flamed Canicula and Procyon, beneath whose rival fires the beautiful star of evening had long since sunk from view; Leo with his glorious sickle followed in the train, and thousands on thousands of starry lamps lent their brightness to light up the vast firmament that canopied the silent earth, — silent, for sleep had exerted its restoring influence upon all save the sick and sorrowing. I turned reluctantly again to seek my weary couch. With feelings of gratitude to my God for all his past goodness and humble trust in his future care, I laid my head on my pillow, and though I could not sleep could meditate."

A more striking piece of unconscious self-portraiture could hardly be quoted than this. The image of that frail young woman rising on a cold winter night from her bed, exhausted with coughing and the sharp pain in her side, to seek her medicine, and suddenly finding relief in the sublime pageant of the midnight heavens, and in the adoration of the God whose glory it declared, — this image indelibly stamped on the mind will give the keynote to a life that was destined to be a perpetual rising from pain and weariness to the beholding of a vision so transcendent in promised blessing for humanity as to inspire her with fairly supernatural strength. But not yet was her day of stern training over. Still farther must she learn to endure hardness as a good soldier of Christ; still farther to school an impatient and indomitable will to wait on the ordination of a Higher Power.

CHAPTER III.

IN alternation between summers spent with the family of Dr. Channing in Portsmouth, R. I., intermittent attempts at teaching, as in the then famous Fowle Monitorial School, and winters passed in more southern latitudes, the years went by till, in the autumn of 1830, Miss Dix was invited by Dr. Channing to accompany his household, as instructress of his children, to the tropical island of St. Croix, in which he was himself to seek the recuperation of his greatly impaired health. The party sailed in the schooner Rice Plant from Boston, November 20, 1830, reaching their destination after a short and prosperous voyage. St. Croix, one of the West India Islands, belonging to Denmark, enjoyed in those days such repute for salubrity of climate as to be much sought as a refuge by delicate and consumptive patients from the United States. Twenty-three miles long by six in width, and crowned by the eminence of Blue Mountain rising to a height of eleven hundred feet, the proportion of land to the surrounding extent of the ocean made residence on it almost like being at sea.

A visit to the tropics had been looked forward to by Miss Dix with intense delight. Now she would see with her own eyes an utterly new flora and fauna, a literal paradise of trailing vines, palms, bananas, rare birds, shells, and marine plants. Indeed, it seems

here the most fitting place again to call attention to
that vivid interest in all the branches of natural history, which unquestionably would have asserted itself
as the dominant passion of her mind, had it not been
overmastered by the still stronger passion for conse-
crating herself to the relief of human suffering. All
through life, the prospect of snatching an hour from
pressing cares for the criminal and the insane, to devote to studying in its native habitat a new plant,
new seaweed, or new shellfish, or for observing anything before unseen in a Bay of Fundy tide, or a remarkable geological formation, excited in her an enthusiasm nothing could call her off from but the cry
of human misery. What she might have achieved,
had her indomitable energy been permanently turned
in the direction of natural science, it is impossible to
say. Certain it is, there would have been no crater,
however deep and sulphurous, into which her courage
would have shrunk from descending; no marsh, however malarious, that would have hidden from her the
secret of its most secluded moss or peat-flower.

Arriving now in the actual tropics, and with all her
Northern energy on the alert for fresh achievement,
Miss Dix unexpectedly found herself brought face to
face with a lesson in human nature, which began a
modification of character in her it took years to work
out. So far in life the uncompromising champion of
the power of the human will to rise superior to circumstances of every kind, great was her dismay and
mortification at finding herself for a time the passive
victim of a purely physical environment. Before this
date, indeed, stern experience had forced her to admit
the indisputable fact that the lungs might become inflamed, and a sharp, burning pain transfix the side.

But this only meant that one could no longer use the voice for teaching. One could still study, write, master fresh knowledge, meditate, and pray. But now she had to succumb utterly to an invisible and intangible foe on which she could get no purchase, — to simple, tropical climate. Pain could be fought, but languor, an utter languor of desire and will, which blunted every weapon she had been used to wield and made the arm nerveless to grasp it, — here was something which baffled her utterly.

Indeed, of this entirely new phase of experience Miss Dix speaks feelingly in a letter to her friend, Mrs. Samuel Torrey, to whom she writes: —

" Another letter from you, my dear friend, impels me to take up my pen. I think that this incitement would not have been needed, had I been under any other influence than this before-named *languor.* Our darling Mary says, ' How changed Miss Dix is ! She used always to be busy, and now she only says, Don't talk to me ! and throws herself on the bed twenty times a day.' I am also the unfortunate subject of Dr. Channing's jests. ' My dear,' he says to Mrs. C., ' where can Miss Dix be ? But I need not ask, — doubtless very busy, as usual. Pray, what is that I see on yonder sofa, some object shrouded in white? Oh ! that is Miss Dix, after all. Well, well, tell it not in Gath ! How are the mighty fallen ! ' All this I bear, but I am rising above it in more than one sense. I am really getting well, — or well over this vexatious *no-disease* that does nothing, thinks nothing, is nothing."

It is of interest here to ask what was the impression made on a mind so sympathetic with human suffering, and so resolute to champion its cause, by this her first actual contact with African slavery. Judging from her letters, it was an experience not at all uncommon with persons of her peculiar type of character. Arriving in the tropics from the bleak North, with a mind long strained to the highest tension in the pursuit of moral ideals, the abysmal gulf that opened up between the careless, dancing, morally irresponsible Africans, and any class of human beings she had up to this time ever fallen in with, seems to have dizzied her in all her previous standards of judgment. Like Northern people in general on their first acquaintance with far Southern life, she too was completely carried away with the fascination of a spontaneity, grace, and spirit of pure, physical light-heartedness, of which the North affords scarcely a trace. The rigid New England school-mistress element in her nature is for a time thawed and dissolved away, giving place to an opposite extreme. Morality is still to her the glorious crown of humanity in Massachusetts, but as for St. Croix and among the negro slaves, is it to be rationally looked for there?

"You have no idea [she writes to her friend Mrs. Torrey] how interesting the negroes are here. They have not, what we are used to seeing in the descendants of Africans at the North, coarse features and clumsy gait and rough voices. They are, in general, handsome, much above the generality of the whites, with very fine figures, and graceful beyond anything I have ever seen. Their voices in conversation are musical and their manners respectful. Sometimes their accents, especially those of the children, are soft and plaintive, touching the heart. For all this they are in reality cheerful and happy. . . . They are the most graceful dancers imaginable. They never make a false step, and there is a heartiness, simplicity, and ease with which they sustain their favorite amusement that draws the spectator into the most lively enjoyment of the exhilarating scene. . . . I cannot regard these subjected beings as *re-*

sponsible for *any* immoralities. Taking into consideration all the circumstances in which they are placed, I would by no means teach them the distinctions of right and wrong. I should not enlighten them, only to insure a tenfold wretchedness *here*, and perhaps not make any progress in aiding them to be happier hereafter. They are not *free agents*. Their managers, overseers, and too often their owners are very corrupt, and the slaves are within and under their control."

Later on, however, it is clear from Miss Dix's letters that this peculiar fascination exerted on tense New England minds by their first contact with pure physical gayety of temperament is fast wearing away, and that her old moral standards are again powerfully reasserting themselves. She is manifestly triumphing, as she said she soon should, over "this vexatious no-disease that does nothing, thinks nothing, is nothing," and now writes in the following strain to Mrs. Torrey : —

"Your view of slavery corresponds with my own. 'Disguise thyself as thou wilt, still, Slavery, still thou art a bitter draught,' and human nature will not wear thy chains without cursing the ground for the enslaver's sake. 'His gold shall perish with him,' would seem to be the mildest language of Justice ; but whatever be the form, or however remote the time, sure am I that a retribution will fall on the slave-merchant, the slave-holder, and their children to the fourth generation. As I regard the hundreds around me for life subjected to bondage, I am tempted to ask, when they commit a fault, 'Do these men sin, or their masters?' . . . These beings, I repeat, *cannot* be *Christians*, they cannot act as moral beings, they cannot live as souls destined to immortality. Who, then, shall pay the awful price of their soul's redemption? Who but those who have hidden from them the bread of life and sealed up from them the fountains of living waters, who have darkened the dark mind

and obscured the clouded powers of thought? Oh for
a Jeremiah to cry, 'Woe! woe!' ere total destruction
cometh! Oh for the inspirations of an Isaiah to pierce
the hardened with the arrows of timely repentance! No
blessing, no good, can follow in the path trodden by slavery.
No door of mercy opens for him whose soul is stained by
unnumbered sins committed by *others* through his agency."

It has been of importance to dwell on this personal
experience of the enervating effect wrought by tropical languor on the most exceptional energy of Northern will, because it is very evident that the winter
spent on the island of St. Croix, and the full year
or more of languishing illness she later on was to
go through with in Liverpool, England, wrought in
Miss Dix a gradually developing modification of view.
These were the first great experiences that fixed her
attention on a class of positive phenomena lying
largely outside the control of the human will, through
the clear recognition alone of which it became possible to her to allow more largely for physical and
moral imperfections and infirmities. Her standard of
judgment was rendered by them less an absolute and
immutable Procrustes bed, on which all alike must be
stretched and cut to a uniform pattern.

Toward herself, indeed, and the demands she through
life made on her own flesh and blood, she remained
inexorable. But she came finally to see that she
"differed from others," and that she was a being
apart, with a law of her own to obey. Gradually,
though only gradually, the disposition lessened in her
to insist on her own almost superhuman standard of
self-sacrifice as the rule, or even possibility, for
others. And so at last, when she had sounded the
awful depths of her own great mission of mercy, and
paid the full tribute of the blood-money exacted, it

came to be with her as with that kindred spirit Elizabeth Fry, whose daughters have recorded in the biography they wrote of her:—

" She would have shrunk from urging the same course on
others. She feared her daughters and other young women
generally undertaking questionable or difficult public offices.
She laid great stress on the outward circumstances of life :
how and where providentially placed; the opportunities afforded; the powers given. . . . She did not consider this
call to be general, or to apply to persons under an administration different from her own."

How complete, however, was, in Miss Dix's own
case, the triumph over tropical languor there is ample
evidence in the journals and notebooks she brought
back with her to New England. They show an ex-
haustive study of all the physical features of the isl-
and, and embrace full catalogues of its native and
cultivated plants, trees, and crops, of its marine flora
and fauna. So valuable were, moreover, the collections of specimens she laboriously made that presents
of portions of them to such scientific men as Professor
Benjamin Silliman, Audubon, and others brought her
the most cordial letters of thanks and praise. Besides,
while at St. Croix, she evidently did a large amount of
reading. Very characteristic is it, as one turns the
pages of these notebooks, now yellow with the time-
stain of sixty years, to see how diligently she wrote out
full extracts from the saints and sages of all periods
and all lands, whose words bore on the right conduct
human life. These extracts are from Hindoo, Per-
sian, Greek, and Christian sources. Though herself
the most orthodox of the earlier type of Unitarianism,
her inner life was of too genuine a strain to resist the
witness of the spirit, in whatsoever land or under
whatsoever dispensation it was breathed abroad.

In a letter to the writer of this biography, Mrs. Mary C. Eustis, the daughter of Dr. Channing, records in the following words her own recollections of Miss Dix at the time of the winter in St. Croix, and of the summers at her father's country-seat in Portsmouth, R. I. : —

"She was tall and dignified, but stooped somewhat, was very shy in her manners, and colored extremely when addressed. This may surprise you who knew her only in later life, when she was completely self-possessed and reliant. . . . She was strict and inflexible in her discipline, which we her pupils disliked extremely at the time, but for which I have been grateful as I have grown older and found how much I was indebted to that iron will from which it was hopeless to appeal, but which I suppose was not unreasonable, as I find my father expressing great satisfaction with her tuition of her pupils. . . . I think she was a very accomplished teacher, active and diligent herself, very fond of natural history and botany. She enjoyed long rambles, always calling our attention to what was of interest in the world around us. I hear that some of her pupils speak of her as irascible. I have no such remembrance. Fixed as fate we considered her.

" We all became much attached to her, and she was our dear and valued friend, and most welcome guest in all our homes. She was a very religious woman, without a particle of sectarianism or bigotry. At the little Union Meetinghouse which adjoined Oakland, our place on Rhode Island, Miss Dix always had the class of troublesome men and boys, who succumbed to her charm of manner and firm will. Later on, after the death of her grandmother, she was a constant visitor 'at our house. She delighted to drop in unexpectedly, and then suddenly receiving a letter from a poor soldier at Fort Adams, would start off at a moment's notice to right his wrong and persuade the government to improve the arrangements for the comfort of the men."

CHAPTER IV.

RETURNING home from St. Croix in the late spring of 1831, Miss Dix, in the ensuing autumn, entered seriously on the work of establishing the kind of model boarding and day school for girls which should satisfy the high-wrought ideal that filled her mind. Once again she found herself settled in the old Dix Mansion, her now well-grown brothers with her, and health sufficiently improved to warrant, she felt, any degree of prodigal expenditure of precious life-force.

Flinging herself with her old intensity into the work, rising before the sun and rarely in bed till after midnight, no long time passed before she made her mark, and secured from prominent families in Boston and from distant places as many pupils as she could take in charge. Health or no health, there were two grand objects she was now indomitably set on effecting.

First, she would achieve pecuniary independence. To the full she appreciated the value of a moderate competence to any one who would be free to carry out self-chosen plans in life. The misery and humiliation entailed by impracticability and shiftlessness had been from childhood burned into her soul. Thus from the outset she showed herself a superior business manager. Generous to the last extreme in giving away money, — her school containing always a number of non-paying pupils, and a charity school in addi-

tion being largely maintained by her, — she none the
less held tenaciously to the idea that the money she
gave away should be her own money. To the end of
life she entertained a sovereign contempt for people
who got their living out of benevolent enterprises,
and selfishly foisted themselves, in the holy name of
charity, as an added burden on the community.

Along, however, with this determination to secure
personal independence there went the resolve to sub-
ordinate every desire for leisure and exemption from
pain to working for what she deemed the highest good
of her pupils. No heart of the day shared more fully
than hers the enthusiastic faith of that great awakening in Massachusetts, which, fostered especially by
the glowing visions of the future for humanity, of the
preaching of Dr. Channing, was prophesying the advent of a new day in education and reform. "The
dignity of human nature," its power, under God, to
rise to heights never before dreamed of but in the
visions of saints, — this had been Dr. Channing's inspiring battle-cry. In all this, her own ardent aspirations had been still farther stimulated by the flaming
eloquence of Dr. Channing's colleague, Rev. Ezra
Stiles Gannett, a man equally ready with herself to
trample the body under foot, and live a daily sacrifice
in infirmity and pain to the cause he fervidly cherished.

For the realization of these prophetic hopes, the
place of all others for work now seemed to Miss Dix
the school. She did not yet know herself or the commanding powers that were slumbering in her. Coming events alone were to reveal these. But in the
school could be gathered together the children un-
spotted from the world, and in the susceptible soil of

their natures could be sown the seed of the coming glorious harvest. None the less it must be frankly admitted that she could never fully enter into the experience of average children, — their exuberance of purely animal life, their suffering under concentration and restraint, their utter immaturity of intellect and conscience. To themselves, they seemed here on earth to enjoy the fun life was made for; to her, to prepare to become the mothers, teachers, daughters of charity of the world. Alas! she had never been an average child herself. She had been premature child-mother, premature battler with the stern problem of life. And so, out of the lack of this essential experience was to grow the one grave drawback to the character of the influence she exerted in the school, — great and salutary as was that influence, and as it is, even to this day, recognized to have been by the decided majority of her pupils who are still living.

"The arrangements of the school," writes a former pupil of it, "were very primitive, — no desks for the girls, only a long table through the middle of the room, at which we sat for meals, and at which it was very inconvenient to write." The studies — as was common in those days — embraced a rather limited range of subjects. Spelling, arithmetic, and composition were rigorously and accurately taught, as well as geography and history, while a French teacher gave the only instruction in any other language but English, unless exception be made in favor of a little elementary Latin. Perhaps far more than in most schools of the period, attention was paid to the teaching of physics and natural history. The main stress, however, was laid on the formation of moral and religious character.

Here lay the overpowering consideration with the
teacher. No more acquisition of knowledge was of
any value in her eyes in comparison with a longing to
dedicate it to the service of humanity. In this respect, the conduct of the school was well-nigh monastic. Unceasing effort was paid to leading the children
to the formation of habits of introspection. The
kingdom of good and of evil within, the probing its
depths and the recognition of the eternal distinction
between the two, — this was to her the one shape of
knowledge that made the turning point of the soul in
time and in eternity. And so on the mantelshelf of
the study room there lay always a certain shell, a
kind of ear of God, into which, daily if possible, letters were to be dropped, recording the results of careful self-examination, — letters to which Miss Dix
would sit up till after midnight writing answers.
Moreover, to this was later on added a Saturday evening provision for private interviews of the most sol-
emn and searching nature between pupils and teacher,
a kind of Protestant version of the Roman Catholic
system of the confessional.

That too great strain was thus put on the sensibilities and conscience of the more earnest children by
this close spiritual touch with so morally exacting a
nature, there can be little question. And yet in reply
to minute inquiries from the writer of this biography,
the majority of the still living pupils insist that, while
overstimulated at the time, they were none the less
spiritually revolutionized by these seasons of close
personal contact, and that to her they owe the best
they have ever done in life. Others, however, seem
to retain none but painful and even bitter memories
of their early relation with one the stress of whose

immense demand was farther accentuated by the inevitable bodily penalties of exhaustion, sleeplessness, and pain entailed on her by overstrain.

Among the miscellaneous papers left behind after the death of Miss Dix, there are large bundles of child-letters of this period, which throw a varied — sometimes amusing and sometimes pathetic — light on the working of this system of education, the shell post-office department of it especially. These letters are but straws indeed. But straws show how the wind blows or the current sets, and so have a value greater than their own. Here, then, is one of them, from a little girl, highly pleased, evidently, at the prospect of spiritual treasures in store for her. The Italics so freely used in these letters are retained as too indicative of emphatic states of mind to be spared.

"Please write me a note, dear teacher. I send you the paper in hopes that you will : do, please! The *casket* is ready, please fill it with *jewels.*

"Your child,   MOLLY."

Next comes a letter from a youthful aspirant manifestly bent on putting bark and iron into a flagging will : —

"You know, dear Miss Dix, that I told you just now that I could not do my composition, and is n't it singular I just read in Martha's letter Borridill's quotation from Mr. Gannett's sermon, 'An iron *will* can accomplish *everything.*' Dear Miss Dix, I *will have* this 'iron will,' and I *will do* and *be* all you expect from your child."

A third example summons vividly before the mind a little girl so actually seething with ambition to succeed that the power of language fails, and has to be eked out with a bristling abatis of exclamation points.

"AUNTY, SWEET, VERY DEAR, SWEET AUNTY, — You asked me just now who I was Writing to. I did not Ans' you on purpose. Aunty! Aunty!! do you think I shall! shall! get my Bible!!! I want to be a good girl so!!! Don't you want me to! I know you do, do, do! Aunty!!! Now, Aunty, I want to be good very much, and i 'l tell you what, let 's you and I never speak together, but write little notes all the time. Tomorrow morning I want to find a little note on my pillow, if *you! are not busy.* Goodbye, dear Aunty."

Surely, this last letter gives evidence of a child-nature much more enthusiastically stimulated than overawed by the shell post-office system. The two next, however, are characteristic specimens of the more pathetic ones, of which there were many : —

I.

"You wished me to be very frank with you, and tell you my feelings. I feel the need of some one to whom I can pour forth my feelings, they have been pent up so long. You may, perhaps, laugh when I tell you I have a *disease*, not of body but of mind. This is *unhappiness*. Can you tell me of anything to cure it? If you can, I shall indeed be very glad. I am in constant fear of my lessons, I am so afraid I shall miss them. And I think that if I do, I shall lose my place in the school, and you will be displeased with me."

II.

"I thought I was doing very well until I read your letter, but when you said that you were 'rousing to greater energy,' all my self-satisfaction vanished. For if you are not satisfied in some measure with yourself, and are going to do more than you have done, I don't know what I shall do. You do not go to rest until midnight, and then you rise very early."

These juvenile effusions sufficiently indicate the varied nature of the effect produced by Miss Dix's personality and methods on children of different temperaments. To them, may be added an extract from a letter written nearly sixty years later: —

" I was in my sixteenth year, 1833 [writes to Miss Dix's biographer Mrs. Margaret J. W. Merrill, of Portland, Me.], when my father placed me at her school. She fascinated me from the first, as she had done many of my class before me. Next to my mother, I thought her the most beautiful woman I had ever seen. She was in the prime of her years, tall and of dignified carriage, head finely shaped and set, with an abundance of soft, wavy, brown hair."

For a period of five years the school continued in full tide of success, the unflinching will of Miss Dix dragging her frail body through the weariness and suffering involved. At last, however, in the spring of 1836, she broke down utterly. Hæmorrhages recurred, the old pain in the side seemed fixed, as though a splintered lance were there, and her exhausted nerves would respond no farther.

She had achieved her cherished ends, though at a fearful cost. Her labors had secured for her the independence of a modest competence ; she had made a home for, educated, and embarked in the world her younger brothers ;[1] she had won a position of dignity and respect as a teacher, and had set a stamp never to be effaced on a large number of young minds. Only it looked as though she had been self-slain in the process.

---

[1] 1. Charles W. Graduated at the Boston Latin School, 1832 ; died on the western coast of Africa in 1843, on board the ship he commanded.

2. Joseph. Became a prosperous merchant in Boston.

She herself, however, looked back with no relentings on the physical and moral excesses of her past. The stake for which she had played seemed to her eminently an honorable one, and to have been necessitated by the stern conditions thrust on her by her lot in life. A spirit of martyr exaltation sustained her in the consciousness that she had never flinched till she fell helpless to the ground.

Summing up, then, the impression left by a careful study of the life of Dorothea L. Dix to the age of thirty-three, it seems inevitable to say that it was at once a life devout and heroic in purpose, and a life marred by willful overstrain. A hectic fever had long been running in her blood, which raised to a perilous intensity the self-sacrificing impulses and the moral and religious ardor of her temperament. She had as yet learned no law of limit. Dr. Channing had put his finger on the very spot when he wrote her, " The infirmity of which I warn you, though one of good minds, is an infirmity." Later she was to learn a very different lesson. But it was a lesson that always came hard to her personally; tenderly and pitifully, as she was brought to recognize its import in the case of others.

Still, even in the midst of these needful strictures, let it in simple justice be borne in mind that we are here dealing with a nature of extraordinary capacity, force, and fire, thus far set to tasks that gave no scope to its splendid energies. The mental and moral powers which, after once they had found their adequate field of action, were to sweep irresistibly before her the legislatures of more than twenty great States of the Union, which were again and again to carry by storm the Senate and House of Representatives of the Federal Congress in Washington, and which, in Europe, were to win a like triumph in the British Parliament, and to revolutionize the lunacy legislation of Scotland, — mental and moral powers of such an order had so far been set only to the petty task of teaching, disciplining, and stimulating twenty or thirty average children. It was like seeking to dwarf into the hull of a little launch a marine engine powerful enough to drive an ocean steamship, in the teeth of the roughest gales, across the Atlantic.

CHAPTER V.

So complete was the state of prostration in which Miss Dix was left by the collapse of her powers in the spring of 1836 that her physicians insisted on the abandonment of every thought, present or prospective, of farther school-keeping. It had become a question of life or death. The immediate necessity was entire change of scene and climate.' To this end a sea voyage to England was prescribed, where she should spend the summer, and in the autumn seek the milder climate of the south of France or of Italy. Provided, accordingly, with letters of introduction from Dr. William E. Channing and other influential persons, she set sail from New York for Liverpool, April 22, in company with Mr. and Mrs. Frank Schroder and Mr. and Mrs. Ferrer, friends who watched over her on the voyage with all care and tenderness. It was' her intention, on landing, to spend several months in England, and, later on, to rejoin the Ferrers somewhere on the Continent.

Once again was all choice of plans taken out of her hands. After her arrival in Liverpool, it became clear that she was in too suffering a condition for either travel or sight-seeing, and forlorn enough would now have been her situation but for the providential kindness of new-made English friends. Fortunately, among the letters of introduction from Dr. Channing was one to the family of Mr. William Rathbone, of Liverpool, a merchant of wealth and high standing, a prominent Unitarian, and identified with every good cause of benevolence and reform. Calling upon the stranger invalid at the hotel where she lay ill, Mr. and Mrs. Rathbone at once insisted on her removal to their own residence, Greenbank, some three miles outside the city, and to this charming place and to the hearts of the family was she now taken.

It was, certainly, with no thought of remaining there longer than a few weeks that Miss Dix became an inmate of the Rathbone household. In reality, with short intervals of change, it was to be for full eighteen months. Frequent hæmorrhages set in, and so great was the exhaustion attendant upon them that much of her time had to be spent in bed or on her lounge. And yet, to the end of her days, this period of eighteen months stood out in her memory as the jubilee year of her life, the sunniest, the most restful, and the tenderest to her affections of her whole earthly experience.

To the strenuous invalid, nursed in the school of stern self-abnegation, there was nothing in the Scripture maxim, "It is more blessed to give than to receive," which she did not thoroughly indorse and gladly practice. By nature, however, it came very hard to her — as always in the instance of overpoweringly active and self-helpful characters — to reverse this maxim, and recognize that the day surely comes to every poor worn and weary mortal when it should with equal devoutness be acknowledged how much more blessed it is to *receive* than to give. But during the whole year of 1836–37 Miss Dix, as her letters show, evidently lived on the mountain-top of this reversed

beatitude.   It was the one only long holiday she ever
knew in life.   She threw off care and ceased to plan,
she lovingly resigned herself and her shrouded future
into the hands of God, while her heart overflowed with
gratitude for the love with which she found herself cherished by the whole devoted household.   The "Storm
and Stress Period" of her life seemed over, and,
spite of illness, perhaps even more on its very account,
the ardent and romantic fervor of affection, so deep-
seated underneath her self-controlled exterior, together
with her native delight in refinement, culture, and
social charm, now found free vent.   It is, accordingly,
in the following happy state of mind that we find her
writing, October 1, 1836, to her friend, Mrs. Samuel
Torrey of Boston : —

"You know I am ill.   You must imagine me surrounded
by every comfort, sustained by every tenderness that can
cheer, blest in the continual kindness of the family in which
Providence has placed me, — I, with no claims but those of
our common nature.   Here I am contracting continually
a debt of gratitude which time will never see canceled.
There is a treasury from which it will be repaid, but I do
not dispense its stores.   I write from my bed, leaning on
pillows in a very Oriental luxury of position, — one which
I think will soon fall into a fixed habit."

Not, however, without the persistent application of
strong counter-irritants on the part of her Puritan
grandmother in Boston was Miss Dix allowed to surrender herself to this blissful state of Nirvana.   The
bare elements of the situation shocked every sense of
propriety in the rigid old lady, who had herself been
brought up in the inflexible early New England creed
that the one and only befitting posture for a triumphant Christian consumptive to die in was sitting bolt

upright in a straight-backed chair, maintaining so long as consciousness survived a clear two inches of space between the person and any terrestrial proffer of support. To her, then, it seemed simply incredible, an outright moral fall, that a granddaughter of her own should actually consent to stay on month after month in a strange household, where she could render no kind of equivalent in service for the trouble and expense to which she must be subjecting everybody. Little could the primitive old lady take it in, that the very reason why the grateful invalid at Greenbank was so luxuriating in her life there, grew out of the fact that now for the first time in her experience her nature was blossoming out in an atmosphere of free, spontaneous love.

Only natural, then, is it to find her writing back to her grandmother in Boston in a strain that shows how deeply her feelings had been hurt.

" I have felt the obligation to my friends in England so exclusively my own that it was not less surprising than painful to know you indulged so much solicitude on that point. . . . There is a danger, perhaps, of my getting a little spoiled by so much caressing and petting, but I must try to do without it if I get better. So completely am I adopted into this circle of loving spirits that I sometimes forget I really am not to consider the bonds transient in their binding."

Likewise to her Boston friend, Mrs. Samuel Torrey, she writes in a similar strain : —

" You know all my habits through life have been singularly removed from any condition of reliance on others, and the feeling, right or wrong, that *aloneness* is my proper position has prevailed since my early childhood, no doubt nourished and strengthened by many and quick-following bereavements."

At the time of Miss Dix's first visit to England, communication between Europe and America was a very different thing from what it now is. The day of steamships lay still in the future, and not yet was the Atlantic turned into a simple ferry, across which boats ply daily at stated hours of departure and arrival. Sometimes eighteen days sufficed to bring letters, while at others two full months must pass without the relief of any intelligence from home. Miss Dix's experience was destined to be the common one of those abroad. Before very long, news of the inevitable changes wrought by death began to arrive. Thus, September 28, 1836, Mrs. H. S. Hayward, of Boston, writes to inform the invalid of the sudden death of her mother, in Fitzwilliam, N. H. : —

" The remembrance of duties so faithfully performed, and the consciousness that you could have done nothing more had you been at home, will be a comfort to you. Your mother's departure was so unexpected that even those in the room were totally unprepared ; no sickness nor suffering, but a sudden summons to go to her rest after a life of suffering from a lingering disease."

The intelligence of her mother's death was the opening afresh of an old wound in the heart of Miss Dix, awakening once more the sense of passionate grief she cherished throughout life at never having known in childhood the blessedness of a happy and loving home, — a grief rendered all the intenser now through daily communion with scenes of domestic joy. For long years, one additional reason for the excessive overstrain she had subjected herself to had grown out of the necessity of contributing to the maintenance of her mother.

He would have been a bold prophet who should in those days have bade the suffering invalid look forward to well nigh fifty years of such extraordinary achievement as to amaze all who came in contact with her. As late as January 25, 1837, nearly nine months after her arrival in England, she writes her friend Miss Heath : —

"I have been very ill from the middle of November till the past week, but have just now less pain in the side, diminished cough, and, on the whole, an accession of strength. This week, for the first time since September, the physician gave me permission to walk about the room several times daily. It is ten days since the last spitting of blood, and altogether I am quite comfortable ; at least, I may say, happy and grateful for the manifold blessings of my condition."

Later on, however, in Miss Dix's stay in England, the improvement of her health grew steadily more marked, and during the last part of her sojourn at Greenbank, as well as on the occasion of visits to other friends, she was able to enjoy a good deal of social intercourse with people of intellectual and moral superiority. Of the privilege of this she writes enthusiastically to Miss Heath : —

"Of my English friends, I should find language too poor to speak the just praise, and the excellence which shines in their characters and lives. Your remark that I probably enjoy more now in social intercourse than I have ever before done is quite true. Certainly, if I do not improve, it will be through willful self-neglect."

Before closing the narrative of this especial episode in the life of Miss Dix, it seems needful to add that an untrue impression would be left on the mind unless emphatic attention were once again called to the

sharpness of the pang it had cost her to renounce her
chosen career in Boston. The thought that any should
suppose she had weakly surrendered when the fiery
test came to her was nothing short of torture. Accordingly, when, as months on months of rest went by
without recuperation, her dearest home friends wrote
to her expressing wonder that she was not already
well, their words seemed to her little short of a moral
insult.

"I wish [she wrote to Mrs. Samuel Torrey] my home
friends expressed and felt less surprise at my not being restored by a mere voyage. I thought they knew me well
enough to count more upon the resolution I could exercise
in *keeping up* when very ill than to have been so deceived
in supposing I would have laid down all my absorbing and
interesting duties so quietly, if the conviction had not been
too clear to admit a doubt that no effort could longer be
sustained. I feel it was right to *go on* as long as I did, and
right to *pause* only where and when I rested."

It is hard, under the actual circumstances of the
case, to read this characteristic letter without recalling
Browning's poem of the heroic boy who, wounded to
death, still clung to his horse's mane till he had dashed
up to Napoleon with the news that Ratisbon had been
stormed : —

> "So tight he kept his lips compressed,
>   Scarce any blood came through.
> You looked twice ere you saw his breast
>   Was all but shot in two.
>
> .   .   .   .
>
> "'You're wounded!' 'Nay,' his soldier's pride
>   Touched to the quick, he said:
> 'I'm killed, Sire!' And, his chief beside,
>   Smiling the boy fell dead."

Before the return to America, the intelligence of
still another death was to reach Miss Dix. It was

that of her grandmother, at the advanced age of ninety-one. This meant, of course, the breaking-up of the only place she could look upon as home. "I feel the event," she wrote in reply, "as having divided the only link, save the yet closer one of fraternal bonds, which allies me to kindred."

Miss Dix returned home some time in the autumn of 1837, after an absence of over eighteen months. While her health had greatly improved, it still had not sufficiently to admit of her spending the winter in the severe climate of New England. Happily, through the will of her grandmother, a bequest had now come to her, enough, with the earnings of her days of teaching, to provide a competency for the moderate wants of a single woman. She was thus made mistress of her own time, and could for the rest of her days have consulted simply the exigencies of health in the choice of a place of residence, and have felt free to follow the strong bent of her social and intellectual tastes.

The first necessity now, however, was to find a milder climate for the coming winter. This she sought partly in Washington, D. C., and partly at Oakland, near Alexandria, Virginia. But the winter proved an unhappy one to her. Her mind was in a restless state. The same ill health that had forced her to give up the school in which the chief interest of her life had centered now forbade her even thinking of resuming it. She had parted her moorings, and was adrift on the world. Nor was this all. In England she had tasted the sweets of a new and fascinating experience. She had basked in a sunny atmosphere of sympathy and love, and had shared a life far fuller of charm and intellectual stimulus than any to which she had previously been accustomed. New England, on her return, seemed to her raw, provincial, hard, and ugly, as, indeed, in those earlier days it was. There seemed no place for any one who was not fitted into some regular groove of work. Work was the one and only refuge, and what work was there now for her? All this inward sense of restlessness and pain found poignant expression in her letters at this period.

" I was not conscious [she writes from Washington, February 24, 1838, to her friend Miss Heath] that so great a trial was to meet my return from England, till the whole force of the contrast was laid before me. Then, I confess, it made an impression which will be ineffaceable. . . . Perhaps it is in myself the fault chiefly lies. I may be too sensitive ; I may hunger and thirst too eagerly for that cordial, real regard which exists not in mere outward forms or uttered sounds ; I may be too craving of that rich gift, the power of sharing other minds. I have drunk deeply, long, and oh ! how blissfully, at this fountain in a foreign clime. Hearts met hearts, minds joined with minds ; and what were the secondary trials of pain to the enfeebled, suffering body when daily was administered the soul's medicine and food ! Yes, beloved, ever too dearly beloved ones, we are divided, and what but the deepness of sorrow, what but the weight of grief, would rest on my soul, if the Future, the glorious Future, the existence that knows no death, no pain nor separation, were not seen in the long vista through which Faith and Hope are the angelic conductors ! But there are duties to be performed here. Life is not to be expended in vain regrets. No day, no hour, comes but brings in its train work to be performed for some useful end, — the suffering to be comforted, the wandering led home, the sinner reclaimed. Oh ! how can any fold the hands to rest, and say to the spirit, ' Take thine ease, for all is well' ! "

CHAPTER VI.

THE concluding words of the last chapter, "Oh! how can any fold the hands to rest, and say to the spirit, 'Take thine ease, for all is well'!" proved prophetic. Before very long were her compassionate heart and dauntless will to be brought face to face with an abyss of human misery in the condition of the helpless and outcast insane throughout the land, so appalling in the scenes it opened up that from that day forward till extreme old age had left her helpless there was to be for her no more folding the hands. "Take thine ease, for all is well!" — nay, much is most hideous, a scandal to self-called Christianity, a heartbreak to any one with a trace of pity! Such was henceforth the haunting cry of reality ceaselessly sounding in her ears with its demand: "Woe! woe! if thou dost not champion these outcast and miserable ones." Never was a redeeming work entered on with a clearer, devouter belief in a direct call from on high, or a more unhesitating answer, "Here am I; send *me*."

Great characters never appear isolated from all sympathetic surroundings. They are more than extraordinarily forceful individualities. They are individualities lifted on the crest of some great tidal wave of humanity. Did they come forward as simple innovators, their work would soon be brought to naught for lack of historic backing. It is to their high de-

gree of receptibility, to their sympathetic power of
forecasting and co-working with forces then in the air,
that they owe their power of achieving such seemingly
miraculous results.

All important is it, therefore, before specifically entering on the narrative of the life work in behalf of
the insane, to which Dorothea L. Dix now made haste
to dedicate herself with the self-sacrifice of a martyr and the religious fervor of a saint, to review as
briefly as possible, while yet with needful fullness and
circumstantiality, the exact state of things prevailing
in New England fifty years ago. Thus only can the
reader grasp a clear conception alike of the point of
departure and of the goal toward which everything
must be made to tend. It is a review which must
necessarily embrace the previous condition of theological thought and feeling in New England, together
with the strange, but very practical, bearing of this
thought, as well on the administration of penal law as
on the theory and treatment of a certain type of mys-
terious and awful disease. Such review must further
seek to contrast with all this the growing influence of
a new and different order of ideas, finally gathering
head and making themselves felt with revolutionary
power. In all her rationality, in all her enthusiasm
of humanity, in all her glowing faith in the birth of a
new epoch in human history, Miss Dix was the incarnation of the sanguine and prophetic spirit of her
time.

Throughout the whole earlier epoch of New England history, the two grand forces which had wrought
together for the education of the people had been
politics and religion. The necessity of laying the
foundation of the state in what had been a previous

wilderness, and of fostering its steady progress toward
maturity, had demanded a constant exercise of practical sagacity and devoted patriotism. And yet all this
so needful work had been regarded but as temporal
and material in its nature, and as strictly subsidiary
to something higher. In comparison with the overwhelming realities of the supernatural world, the
claims of the present world were to be weighed but
as dust in the balance. To maintain in the minds of
the community a high - wrought and imaginatively
vivid sense of this eternal distinction had been the
unremitting aim of the powerful theological system of
Calvinism that dominated the great majority of the
people, —a system, moreover, whose dogmas had been
enforced by a class of preachers of commanding intellectual power and rare elevation of character.

Here, then, was an iron-linked system of theological
thought, which embodied elements in it fitted to produce, as it did produce, many and noble spiritual
results. In its favor must it be said that it had disciplined the mind to close reasoning on the profoundest
subjects; it had put energy into the will; it had led
to the scorn of sloth and ease, and had substituted for
these the stern sense of duty; it had developed, moreover, in a select class of finely tempered souls a rapt
and mystic piety; — but along with these great advantages, it had none the less always carried in its breast
other elements, whose inevitable tendency was to narrow, harden, and well-nigh annihilate the tenderer
and more compassionate qualities of human nature.
So vastly more frequently and incisively had the
righteous wrath of God been emphasized than his
redeeming love, that, logically enough, the majority
of men and women had been led to cultivate and

morally approve in themselves the same inverted relation between these two attributes which they worshiped in their Deity.

Inevitably, then, were the penal statutes of such
communities inexorably severe.   The prisoner, an
outcast from the heart of God, became equally an outcast from the heart of society.   The little he might
be called on to suffer in the jail from mouldy bread
and filthy water, from foul air and swarming vermin,
seemed so as nothing in comparison with the awful fate
awaiting him in eternity, as scarcely to be worthy of
consideration.   Nor was it practically different with
the view taken of the condition of the actually insane.
Nay, in certain respects it was worse.   The terrible
superstitions of the Middle Ages, which had always
sought the explanation of insanity in the idea of
diabolic possession, and had seen in its frenzies of
imprecation, filthiness, and blasphemy simply the
masterpiece of Satan, still hung like a lurid cloud
over the human mind.   Slowly, slowly only, were the
conceptions outgrown which, in the days of the Salem
Witchcraft, had rendered possible the spectacle of an
outbreak of superstitious terror powerful enough to
transport to a pitch of frenzy not merely the ignorant
populace, but many of the foremost judges and divines
of the land.   Such crazy fancies of hysteric women
as would to-day be treated with diet, sedatives, and
change of air were in those days treated, spiritually,
with the terrific anathemas of the church, and, judi-
cially or by mob law, with drowning in the river or
the hangman's noose.

Of course, as time went on and enlightenment grew
greater, the virulence of these Middle Age superstitions steadily abated, though ever lingering in the

background. Practical common sense began to make some headway. Still, the real king who was finally to dethrone these imaginary supernatural terrors had not yet seated himself on the throne. The old theory of insanity lingered on, because no new theory half as plausible had demonstrated its divine right of succession. Nor yet had human reason come to the full consciousness of itself, through the study of those physical laws of nature whose immutable dictum is the one and only basis of authority. And so, with the gradual decadence of the power of the old theological conceptions over the imagination, there came at first another theory of insanity, which was but a partial modification of the earlier one, and which preserved many of its worst features. Insanity was pure mental and moral, not physical, perversion. It was the outbreak of the animal, violent, filthy, blasphemous, and murderous elements of the fallen human *soul*, elements which had culpably been permitted to get the upper hand of the higher attributes. It was thus a fury of the mind, not a fury of the inflamed and congested body acting on the mind. One thing, at least, was certain of it: it turned men and women into tigers and jackals; it made it impossible to appeal to their reason, and thus put them outside the category of human beings. Iron cages, chains, clubs, starvation, must still remain the only fit instrumentalities through which to dominate menageries of such wild beasts. Not that a certain amount of crude and barbarous medical prescription — of purgings, bleedings, and emetics — did not go along with all this. Still, the whole realm of the subtler relations between mind and body was as yet a *terra incognita*. And so the insane were inevitably looked upon with a strange and cruel blending of repulsion, personal fear, and despair of any methods but those of physical coercion.

With the beginning, however, of the nineteenth century, and with steadily accumulating force as its years rolled on, a great change began to come over New England, and especially Massachusetts, — a change which was rapidly to put this State in the intellectual van of her sister States of the Union. More frequent and intimate mental communication with Europe brought the minds of aspiring young men and women into contact with the literature, the art, the science, the philosophy, of the older world. An intellectual ferment was thus set on, and, through it, what may accurately enough be entitled " The Renaissance Period of New England " — the transition from lingering mediævalism to rising modern conceptions — now showed vital signs of drawing on. The day came of fervid reformers in theology like Channing and Emerson, in public education like Horace Mann, in practical charity like Dr. S. G. Howe, in the rational treatment of insanity like Dr. Woodward, of Worcester.

Such, then, was the condition of things in New England during the formative period in which the mind of Miss Dix was coming to its maturity. On no one had one especial class of the ideas of the " New Awakening " — not so much its literary and æsthetic as its religious, philanthropic, and scientific ideas — taken a stronger hold than on her. She had drunk in with passionate faith Dr. Channing's fervid insistence on the presence in human nature, even under its most degraded types, of germs, at least, of endless spiritual development. But it was the characteristic of her own mind that it tended, not to protracted speculation, but to immediate, embodied action. Give her a seed thought, and she made haste to plant it,

water it, and watch it grow, flower, and fruit. Though
mummy wheat, buried three thousand years in an
Egyptian tomb, her first instinctive impulse was to
furnish it here and now with soil and sun, and see
what could be made to germinate. In other words,
she delighted in positive forces, and loved to co-work
with them and see them justify themselves in practice.
The harder the conditions under which they were
called upon to do this, the greater the triumph.

As soon, therefore, as Miss Dix's attention became
directed to the pitiable condition of the insane, it was
not mere sentimental compassion over their sufferings
— deeply and tragically even as this affected her —
that engrossed her mind, but the immediate constructive question, What class of positive forces, philanthropic, medical, legislative, judiciary, can be summoned into the field to cope with this awful problem ?
That is, she proceeded at once to master the whole
question of insanity, its origin, its stages of development, its relations of body and mind, its treatment, its
legal and moral rights, and to put herself abreast with
the most advanced thought on the subject. Here was
the shriveled and desiccated mummy wheat of humanity, which, as soon as she encountered it, she yearned
to see raised in resurrection from the tomb in which
for ages it had been buried.

What, then, it now becomes necessary to pause
and ask, was the distinctive character of the new
thought which, at this particular period, was kindling
the humane and scientific enthusiasm of the more
advanced minds of Europe and America on the whole
matter of insanity ? A clear understanding alone of
this will serve to put the reader in possession of the
inspiring creed of which Dorothea L. Dix was now to
become the fervid apostle.

CHAPTER VII.

. In attempting a brief sketch of the history of the treatment of insanity in the past, it is not necessary here to harrow the mind with circumstantial details of the frightful forms of exorcism practiced by the Church throughout the Middle Ages, to the end of driving the devils out of their supposed victims; nor of the medicines, as loathsome as those brewed from newts and toads in the caldron of Macbeth's witches, which were habitually administered; nor of the chains, whippings, bleedings, and duckings which were thought necessary to physically weaken or subdue with terror the more violent outbreaks of fury. The seemingly unaccountable thing is, that it should have been at so late a day in the history of civilization that, except in the rarest instances, anything more rational began to be believed in. Of this let a single example suffice, — that of Bethlehem Hospital in London, popularly known as "Old Bedlam."

Up to so late a date as 1770, this famous hospital was still regarded as the raree show of the city, superior even, in the attractions it offered the pleasure-seeker, to a bull baiting or a dog fight. No more diverting entertainment could be devised by the average citizen for guests visiting him from the country than to take them, for a hearty laugh, to Bedlam, to see the madmen cursing, raving, and fighting. There was to

be had on show St. Paul or Julius Cæsar chained to
the wall, or Semiramis or Joan of Arc ironed to the
floor, while the general throng, left more at liberty,
were guarded by brutal keepers, ready on the slightest
provocation to knock them senseless with heavy clubs.
The annual fees derived from this public entertainment amounted to several hundred pounds. No one
seems to have felt any pity for the poor wretches.
The abyss which opened up between them and ordinary humanity was too deep and wide for any sympathetic imagination to span. A madhouse was a
menagerie, nothing more ; and it was as legitimate to
look through the bars at one class of wild beasts as at
another.

Think, farther, of the system of medical practice
that, at as late a date even as 1815, and then detailed
before the committee of the House of Parliament by
one of the visiting physicians, Dr. T. Monro,[1] was
still pursued at Bedlam. " Patients," said Dr. Monro,
" are ordered to be bled about the latter end of May,
according to the weather ; and, after they have been
bled, they take vomits once a week for a certain number of weeks ; after that we purge the patients. That
has been the practice invariably for long years before
my time, and I do not know of any better practice."
Then as to the matter of simple protection from the
inclemency of the weather : "Even in the new building " (says Sydney Smith, " Edinburgh Review," 1815–
16), " the windows of the patients' bedrooms were not
glazed, nor were the latter warmed." What this must
have meant, throughout the chill fogs and freezing
nights of a London winter, to poor wretches chained

[1] *History of the Insane in the British Isles.* D. H. Tuke, M. D.,
F. R. C. P., etc.

down to their beds for the night, it needs no words to
portray. The wild-beast theory of insanity, which had
succeeded to the diabolical-possession theory, still
reigned unbroken in the great majority of hospitals.

Strangely enough, it was first in Paris, and at the
height of the frenzy of the French Revolution, when
the excitement of the times had filled the wards of
the asylums with the most violent patients, that the
great moral genius appeared who was destined to inaugurate a complete revolution in the theory and treatment of insanity, — a revolution ordained to prove
historically quite as effective in the overthrow of the
old dynasty of force and terror that had reigned in
these institutions as was that of the Jacobins in the
overthrow of the old dynasty of French monarchism.
"Individual liberty!" had been the fierce cry raised
by the Jacobins, who forthwith proceeded to secure it
for themselves and their own ideas by fire and slaugh-
ter. "Individual liberty, the most of it possible!"
was equally the cry of the gentle, merciful, far-seeing
Dr. Philippe Pinel, on receiving, in 1792, the appointment of superintendent of the Bicêtre, the asylum for
incurable insane males. "Off with these chains! away
with these iron cages and brutal keepers! They make
a hundred madmen where they cure one. There is
another and a better way. The insane man is not an
inexplicable monster. He is but one of ourselves, only
a little more so. Underneath his wildest paroxysms
there is a germ, at least, of rationality and of personal
accountability. To believe in this, to seek for it,
stimulate it, build it up, — here lies the only way of
delivering him out of the fatal bondage in which he is
held!"

With unflagging persistency did Pinel now urge

these humane convictions on the Commune, and seek
to get authority to try the effect of his scheme on at
least one fourth of his patients. The idea seemed to
those he argued with as wildly visionary as a deliberate proposal to go out to the Jardin des Plantes and
fling wide the gratings to the jaguars and tigers confined there. At last, however, he persuaded the fero-
cious Couthon to go with him to the Bicêtre, and consider the problem on the spot.[1] "They were greeted
in the gloomy prison by the yells and execrations of
three hundred maniacs, mingling the clanking of their
chains with the uproar of their voices."

Already had Couthon had long and familiar experience in dealing with the most savage elements of society. But before the proposition now made him he
utterly quailed. "After looking over the patients, he
said to Pinel, 'Ah, ça! citoyen, es-tu fou toi-même de
vouloir déchaîner de pareils animaux?' (Citizen, are
you crazy yourself, that you would unchain such
beasts?)" Permission, however, to try the mad experiment was finally given, some of the first results of
which will be found recorded in the following abridg-
ment of a portion of a memoir, read by the son of
Pinel before the Royal Academy of Arts and Sci-
ences: —

"Near the close of the year 1792, M. Pinel, having repeatedly importuned the government to issue a decree per-
mitting him to unchain the maniacs at the Bicêtre, went in
person to solicit what had been refused to his written representations. With courage and resolution he urged the
removal of this cruel abuse. At length, M. Couthon, member of the commune, yielded to the importunate arguments
of Pinel, and consented to meet him at the hospital, to wit-

[1] *Disease of the Mind*, by Charles F. Folsom, M. D., p. 8.

ness these first experiments, as well as to assure himself
that this was not a stratagem to give liberty to political offenders. Couthon proceeded, himself, to question the patients, but received only abuse and execrations, accompanied
by terrible cries and the clanking of clains. Retreating
from the damp and filthy cells, he exclaimed to Pinel, ' Do
as you will; but you will be sacrificed to this false sentiment of mercy.' Pinel delayed no longer : he selected
fifty who he believed might be released from their chains
without danger to others. The fetters were removed, first,
from twelve, using the precaution of having prepared strong
jackets, closing behind, with long sleeves, which could be
used if necessary.

"The experiments commenced with an English captain,
whose history was unknown : *he had been in chains forty
years !* As he was thought to be one of the most dangerous, having killed, at one time, an attendant with a blow
from his manacles, the keepers approached him with cau-
tion ; but first Pinel entered his cell unattended. ' Ah,
well, captain, I will cause your chains to be taken off; you
shall have liberty to walk in the court, if you will promise
to behave like a gentleman, and offer no assault to those
you will meet.' ' I would promise,' said the maniac ; ' but
you deride me, you are amusing yourself at my expense ;
you all fear me, once free.' ' I have six men,' replied
Pinel, ' ready to obey my orders : believe me, therefore, I
will set you free from this duresse, if you will put on this
jacket.' The captain assented ; the chains were removed,
and the jacket laced ; — the keepers withdrew, without closing the door. He raised himself, but fell : this effort was
repeated again and again ; the use of his limbs, so long constrained, nearly failed : at length, trembling, and with tottering steps, he emerged from his dark dungeon. *His first
look was at the sky !* ' Ah,' cried he, ' how beautiful ! '
The remainder of the day he was constantly moving to and
fro, uttering continually exclamations of pleasure ; — he

heeded no one : *the flowers, the trees, above all the sky,* engrossed him. At night he voluntarily returned to his cell, which had been cleansed and furnished with a better bed : his sleep was tranquil and profound. For the two remaining years which he spent in the hospital he had no recurrence of violent paroxysms, and often rendered good service to the keepers in conducting the affairs of the establishment.

" The patient released next after the captain was Chevinge, a soldier of the French Guards, who had been chained ten years, and had been peculiarly difficult of control. Pinel, entering his cell, announced that if he would obey his injunctions he should be chained no longer. He promised, and, following every movement of his liberator, executed his directions with alacrity and address. Never, in the history of the human mind, was exhibited a more sudden and complete revolution ; he executed every order with exactness ; and this patient, whose best years had been sacrificed in a gloomy cell, in chains and misery, soon showed himself capable of being one of the most useful persons about the establishment. He repeatedly, during the horrors of the Revolution, saved the life of his benefactor. On one occasion, he encountered a band of ' *sans culottes* ' who were bearing Pinel to ' the Lanterne,' owing to his having been an elector in 1789. With bold and determined purpose he rescued his beloved master, and caused that life to be spared which had been so great a blessing to the insane in France.

" In the third cell were three Prussian soldiers, who had been for many years in chains, *but how or for what they had been committed none knew ;* they were not dangerous, and seemed capable of enjoying the indulgence of living together. They were terrified at the preparations for their release, fearing new severities awaited them. Sunk into dementia, they were indifferent to the freedom offered.

" An aged priest came next ; he fancied himself to be the Messiah. Taunted once with the exclamation that if in truth he was Christ he could break his chains, he answered with solemnity, ' *Frustra tentas Dominum tuum !* ' Religious exaltation had characterized his life. On foot, he had made pilgrimages to Rome and Cologne; he had made a voyage to the Western world to convert savage tribes. This ruling idea passed into mania, and returning to France, he declared that he was Christ, the Saviour. He was arrested on the charge of blasphemy, and taken before the Archbishop of Paris, by whose decree he was consigned to the Bicêtre, as either a blasphemer or a madman. Loaded with heavy chains, he for twelve years bore patiently sarcasm and cruel sufferings. Pinel had the happiness to witness *his recovery in less than a year*, and to discharge him from the hospital cured.

" In the short period of a few days, Pinel released from their chains more than fifty maniacs, men of various ranks and conditions, merchants, lawyers, priests, soldiers, laborers, — thus rendering the furious tractable, and creating peace and contentment, to a wonderful degree, where long the most hideous scenes of tumult and disorder had reigned."

It was in 1796, only four years after Pinel's first experiment in the Bicêtre, and entirely independently of any knowledge of his work, that a precisely similar reform was inaugurated in England, — this time not by a physician, but by a member of the Society of Friends, William Tuke, a merchant of ample fortune and great benevolence and force of character. In building with his own means " The Retreat " at York, and retaining the absolute control of its policy in his own hands, he prepared a suitable place for a fair trial of the new method he proposed.

It was by no mere chance, as men call chance, that this great reform in England sprang from the mind and heart of a member of the Society of Friends. The leading tenet of the Quakers, faith in the power of absolute reason, and the identification of absolute reason with the immediate divine presence in the soul, was one that logically led to just such an experiment as this, as likewise to invincible faith in its success. No other religious sect in Christendom had accumulated, and transmitted through inheritance to their children, so great a mass of testimony as to the power of gentleness, patience, and inward self-control to evolve rational order out of the chaos of warring human passions. William Tuke had the moral greatness to see with perfect clearness, and to pursue with heroic persistence, one luminous conviction, namely, that precisely the same moral and physical regimen which has proved itself the only power adapted to quicken, mature, and firmly establish the elements of reason and self-government in ourselves and our children, is the sole regimen that can be trusted to do the like for the feebler and more sorely beset elements of the same essential reason in these poor afflicted ones.

"His feeling that something should be done had been strengthened by a visit he had paid to St. Luke's Hospital, where he saw the patients lying on straw and in chains. He was distressed with the scene, and could not help believing that there was a more excellent way. . . . One day, in the family circle, conversation turned on the name that should be given to the proposed institution. 'The Retreat,' quickly replied the good wife. What's in a name? Everything at times. It was at once seen that feminine instinct had solved the question, and the name was adopted, to convey the idea of what such an institution should be, namely, a place in which the unhappy might obtain a refuge ; a quiet haven in which the shattered bark might find the means of reparation or of safety." [1]

[1] *History of the Insane in the British Isles*, p. 115, by Daniel Hack Tuke, M. D., F. R. C. P.

" In person," writes a contemporary of William
Tuke, " he hardly reached the middle size, but was
erect, portly, and of a firm step. He had a noble fore-
head, an eagle eye, and a commanding voice, and his
mien was dignified and patriarchal." Like all pio-
neers in the struggle of human progress, he had to
encounter his full share of ridicule, obloquy, and opposition. In the end, however, he triumphed, and
" The Retreat at York " became a beacon light of the
world, shining through the dark night of one of the
gloomiest chapters of human history.

Philippe Pinel and William Tuke: these, then, were
the two original minds that inaugurated a new epoch
in the history of the treatment of insanity, an epoch as
revolutionary in character within this especial realm
as that of the Copernican system in the realm of as-
tronomy. It implied an absolute reversal of all previous conceptions ; the substitution, in the place of
restraint and force, of the largest possible degree of
liberty ; the abandonment of the whole previous idea
of brute subjection for that of the emancipation of
the reason and the enhancement of the sense of personal responsibility. Each one of these remarkable
men achieved his task uninformed of the action of the
other.

"It is no new thing [says the eminent American alienist,
Dr. Pliny Earle, in commenting on this singular coinci-
dence] for inventions, discoveries, and innovations upon
traditionary practices to originate almost simultaneously in
more than one place, showing that they are called for by the
times ; that they are developments of science and humanity,
necessary evolutions of the human mind in its progress toward the unattainable perfect, rather than what may be
termed a gigantic and monstrous production of one original
genius."

Happily, the most characteristic mark of distinction between the last hundred years and the centuries which preceded them lies in the rapidity with which new ideas, even the most revolutionary, spread, provided only they can justify themselves before the tribunal of reason. Such proved true of the startling innovation, wrought by Pinel and Tuke. By 1838, Dr. Gardner Hill, house surgeon of Lincoln Asylum, England, ably seconded by Dr. Charlesworth, had asserted the principle of the entire abolition of mechanical restraint, and had to a very large extent carried it out, though personally falling a victim to the bitter opposition he encountered alike from commissioners and his own medical brethren. But immediately followed the remarkable career of Dr. John Conolly, who at Hanwell, on a much larger scale and with far greater success, came to the rescue of the cause.

" To Conolly," says the " Edinburgh Review," April, 1870, " belongs a still higher crown, not merely for his courage in carrying out a beneficent conception on a large scale and on a conspicuous theatre, but for his genius in expanding it. To him, hobbles and chains, handcuffs and muffs, were but material impediments that merely confined the limbs ; to get rid of these he spent the best years of his life ; but beyond these mechanical fetters he saw there were a hundred fetters to the spirit, which human sympathy, courage, and time only could remove."

The dire instruments of coercion formerly in constant use Dr. Conolly remanded to a room in the asylum, and there constituted a museum of them, a Chamber of Horrors, which the enlightened physician of to-day contemplates with practically the same feelings which would be excited in him by a visit to the old dungeons and instruments of torture of the inquisition. And yet, so recently had the possibility of such a change been dreamed of that Dr. Conolly relates that he himself had formerly witnessed " humane English physicians daily contemplating insane patients bound hand and foot, and neck and waist, in illness, in pain, and in the agonies of death, without one single touch of compunction, or the slightest approach to the feeling of acting either cruelly or unwisely. They thought it impossible to manage insane people in any other way." [1]

Is it, then, exaggeration to characterize the absolute change of base inaugurated by the labors of Pinel and Tuke as a Copernican revolution in the realm of the theory and treatment of insanity ?

The beginning of the nineteenth century saw in the whole United States but four insane asylums, of which one only had been entirely built by a State government. They were, in the order of the dates of their foundation, those of Philadelphia, Penn., 1752; of Williamsburg, Va. (the first State asylum), 1773; of New York, 1791; of Baltimore, Md., 1797. In

---

[1] " After five years' experience," wrote Dr. Conolly, " I have no hesitation in recording my opinion that, with a well-constituted governing body, animated by philanthropy, directed by intelligence, and acting by means of proper officers (entrusted with a due degree of authority over attendants, properly selected, and capable of exercising an efficient superintendence over patients), there is no asylum in the world in which all mechanical restraint may not be abolished, not only with perfect safety, but with incalculable advantage." (Tuke's *History of the Insane in the British Isles.*) It may be that this is too ideal a statement of what is possible under any but the rarest combination of circumstances. Dr. Conolly was a man of positive genius in his calling, and of a magnetism and spirit of consecration that carried all before him. At any rate, it was in the right direction.

1813, attention was attracted to Tuke's work in England by certain Philadelphia Friends, who, collecting funds, opened in 1817 a hospital in which the insane might see that they were "regarded as *men* and *brethren.*" One year later witnessed the foundation of the McLean Asylum at Somerville, Mass., — the asylum which "established the character and principles of treatment which have become universal with us, and especially the principle of State supervision." Later on, "The Retreat" at Hartford, Conn., opened in 1824, and the asylum at Worcester, Mass., in 1830, became conspicuous examples of the practical application of the new scientific and humane ideas inaugurated by Pinel and Tuke.

"There were giants on the earth in those days," says, in his paper on "Progress in Provision for the Insane," Dr. W. W. Godding, of the Government Insane Asylum for the Army and Navy in Washington, D. C. Dr. Godding had been speaking of the memorable list of men in the United States who at that early date had already been attracted by genius and character to the development of the new system; Brigham, Butler, Woodward, Ray, Walker, Bell, Stribling, Grey, Kirkbride. Here, enlisted with consecrated intelligence and humanity under the new banner, was a chosen band, who were destined before very long to carry the fame of American asylums all over Europe, and, for a time at least, to keep them ahead of any in the world.

None the less, one indispensable spiritual power in the land was still lacking. It was that of a fervid apostle of the new creed; of one animated with the requisite inspiration and fire to lead a crusade against the almost universal ignorance, superstition, and apa-

thy which still reigned over nearly the whole of the
.States of the Union ; of a mind and heart, in fine,
powerful enough to rally thousands and tens of thousands to the deliverance from the hand of the infidel
of what should seem to her no less than the Holy
Sepulchre of crucified humanity. This imperative demand was now to be answered in the person of Dorothea Lynde Dix.

CHAPTER VIII.

IT was on March 28, 1841, that Miss Dix was first brought face to face with the condition of things prevailing in the jails and almshouses of Massachusetts, which launched her on her great career. The story, repeated in so many scattered notices of her life, runs that, on coming out of church one Sunday, she overheard two gentlemen speaking in such terms of indignation and horror of the treatment to which the prisoners and lunatics in the East Cambridge, Massachusetts, jail were subjected that she forthwith determined to go over there and look into matters herself. The occurrence of the incident is perfectly possible; but the important fact of the case is given in the following extract from a letter of Rev. John T. G. Nichols, D. D., of Saco, Maine :—

"While a member of the theological school in Cambridge [writes Dr. Nichols], I was one of a body of students who took the East Cambridge house of correction in charge for Sunday-school instruction. All the women, twenty in number, were assigned to me. I was at once convinced that, not a young man, but a woman should be their teacher. Consulting my mother, I was directed by her to Miss Dix for further counsel. On hearing my account, Miss Dix said, after some deliberation, 'I will take them myself!' I protested her physical incapacity, as she was in feeble health. 'I shall be there next Sunday,' was her answer.

"After the school was over, Miss Dix went into the jail.

She found among the prisoners a few insane persons, with
whom she talked.   She noticed there was no stove in their
room, and no means of proper warmth.   The jailer said
that a fire for them was not needed, and would not be safe.
Her repeated solicitations were without success.   At that
time the court was in session at East Cambridge, and she
caused the case to be brought before it.   Her request was
granted.   The cold rooms were warmed.   Thus was her
great work commenced.   Of course I claim not a particle of
credit.   I was simply the instrument of the Good Providence
to open the door for this Angel of Mercy to come in."

It was thus that, in the East Cambridge jail, Miss
Dix was first brought into immediate contact with the
overcrowding, the filth, and the herding together of
innocent, guilty, and insane persons, which at that
time characterized the prisons of Massachusetts, and
the inevitable evils of which were repeated in even
worse shape in the almshouses.   Her first act, as has
been seen, was the practical one of enforcing mercy by
law, through insisting that, in a climate where in winter the thermometer frequently registers zero and below, a fire of some sort should be provided for shivering wretches who in their frenzy often tore the clothes
off their backs.   Casting about her for help, she soon
succeeded in enlisting the aid of that ever loyal friend
of humanity, Dr. S. G. Howe, and, through him, that
of the afterwards famous philanthropist and statesman, Charles Sumner.   Close beside her, too, stood
Rev. Robert C. Waterston.

At Miss Dix's solicitation, Dr. Howe himself made
a careful examination, the result of which was printed
in an article in the Boston " Daily Advertiser " of September 8, 1841; an article of course fiercely attacked,
as is generally the case when abuses are pointed out.

Later on in the controversy, Dr. Howe appealed for corroboration to Charles Sumner, who had accompanied him on his visit. To this Mr. Sumner replied : —

" MY DEAR HOWE, — I am sorry to say that your article does *present a true picture* of the condition in which we found those unfortunates. They were cramped together in rooms *poorly ventilated and noisome with filth.* . . . You cannot forget the small room in which were confined the raving maniac, from whom long since reason had fled, never to return, and that interesting young woman, whose mind was so slightly obscured that it seemed as if, in a moment, even while we were looking on, the cloud would pass away. In two cages or pens constructed of plank, within the four stone walls of the same room, these two persons had spent several months. The whole prison echoed with the blasphemies of the poor old woman, while her young and gentle fellow in suffering, doomed to pass her days and nights in such close connection with her, seemed to shrink from her words as from blows. And well she might ; for they were words not to be heard by any woman in whom reason had left any vestige of its former presence. It was a punishment by a cruel man in heathen days to tie the living to the dead ; hardly less horrid was this scene in the prison at Cambridge.

" Ever faithfully yours, CHARLES SUMNER."

Was the state of things in the East Cambridge jail an exception, or did it simply exemplify the rule throughout the whole Commonwealth ? This was the painful question now raised in the mind of Miss Dix, to an unmistakable answer to which she resolutely devoted the next two years. Note-book in hand, she started out on her voyage of exploration, visiting every jail and almshouse from Berkshire on the west to Cape Cod on the east. Steadily accumulating her statistics of outrage and misery, she at last got to-

gether a mass of eye-witness testimony appalling in
extent and detail.   With this she now determined to
memorialize the Legislature of Massachusetts.

As this was the first Memorial addressed by Miss
Dix to a State legislature, — long as was the series of
the like that was to follow, — full extracts from it are
needful, alike to reveal the patience, energy, and spirit
of humanity with which she addressed herself to her
work, as well as the actual character of the evils she
was now in arms against: —

" GENTLEMEN: . . . About two years since, leisure afforded
opportunity, and duty prompted me, to visit several prisons
and almshouses in the vicinity of this metropolis. . . . Every
investigation has given depth to the conviction that it is only
by decided, prompt, and vigorous legislation that the evils
to which I refer, and which I shall proceed more fully to illustrate, can be remedied. I shall be obliged to speak with
great plainness, and to reveal many things revolting to the
taste, and from which my woman's nature shrinks with peculiar sensitiveness.   But truth is the highest consideration.
I tell what I have seen, painful and shocking as the details often are, that from them you may feel more deeply
the imperative obligation which lies upon you to prevent the
possibility of a repetition or continuance of such outrages
upon humanity. . . . If my pictures are displeasing, coarse,
and severe, my subjects, it must be recollected, offer no
tranquil, refining, or composing features.   The condition of
human beings reduced to the extremest state of degradation
and misery cannot be exhibited in softened language, or
adorn a polished page.

" I proceed, gentlemen, briefly to call your attention to
the *present* state of insane persons confined within this
Commonwealth, in *cages, closets, cellars, stalls, pens;
chained, naked, beaten with rods,* and *lashed* into obedience ! "

Page after page, the Memorial then goes on to recite the details of a long catalogue of horrors. They do not furnish pleasing reading, but if the life work of Miss Dix is to be practically written out and duly appreciated, it is necessary to brace the nerves and go through with some of them.

"I give a few illustrations [the Memorial then proceeds] but description fades before reality."

"DANVERS. November. Visited the almshouse; a large building, much out of repair; understand a new one is in contemplation. Here are from fifty-six to sixty inmates : one idiotic; three insane; one of the latter in close confinement at all times.

"Long before reaching the house, wild shouts, snatches of rude songs, imprecations, and obscene language, fell upon the ear, proceeding from the occupant of a low building, rather remote from the principal building, to which my course was directed. Found the mistress, and was conducted to the place, which was called '*the home*' of the *forlorn* maniac, a young woman, exhibiting a condition of neglect and misery blotting out the faintest idea of comfort, and outraging every sentiment of decency. She had been, I learnt, a respectable person, industrious and worthy; disappointments and trials shook her mind, and finally laid prostrate reason and self-control; she became a maniac for life! She had been at Worcester Hospital for a considerable time, and had been returned as incurable. The mistress told me she understood that, while there, she was comfortable and decent. Alas ! what a change was here exhibited ! She had passed from one degree of violence and degradation to another, in swift progress ; there she stood, clinging to, or beating upon, the bars of her caged apartment, the contracted size of which afforded space only for increasing accumulations of filth, — a *foul* spectacle ; there she stood, with naked arms and disheveled hair; the un- .

washed frame invested with fragments of unclean garments ; the air so extremely offensive, though ventilation was afforded on all sides save one, that it was not possible to remain beyond a few moments without retreating for recovery to the outward air.   Irritation of body, produced by utter filth and exposure, incited her to the horrid process of tearing off her skin by inches ; her face, neck, and person were thus disfigured to hideousness.

"Is the whole story told ?   What was seen is ; what is reported is not.   These gross exposures are not for the pained sight of one alone ; all, all, coarse, brutal men, wondering, neglected children, old and young, each and all, witness this lowest, foulest state of miserable humanity. And who protects her, that worse than Pariah outcast, from other wrongs and blacker outrages ?

" Some may say these things cannot be remedied ; these furious maniacs are not to be raised from these base conditions.   I *know* they are ; could give *many* examples ; let *one* suffice.   A young woman, a pauper in a distant town, Sandisfield, was for years a raging maniac.   A cage, chains, and the whip were the agents for controlling her, united with harsh tones and profane language.   Annually, with others (the town's poor) she was put up at auction, and bid off at the lowest price which was declared for her.   One year not long past, an old man came forward in the number of applicants for the poor wretch ; he was taunted and ridiculed.   What would he and his old wife do with such a mere beast ?'   'My wife says yes,' replied he, 'and I shall take her.'   She was given to his charge ; he conveyed her home ; she was washed, neatly dressed, and placed in a decent bedroom, furnished for comfort and opening into the kitchen. How altered her condition !   As yet the *chains* were not off.   The first week she was somewhat restless, at times violent, but the quiet ways of the old people wrought a change : she received her food decently ; forsook acts of violence, and no longer uttered blasphemous or indecent language.   After a week the chain was lengthened, and she was received as a companion into the kitchen. Soon she engaged in trivial employments. 'After a fortnight,' said the old man, 'I knocked off the chains and made her a free woman.' She is at times excited, but not violently; they are careful of her diet, they keep her very clean; she calls them father and mother. Go there now, and you will find her 'clothed,' and though not perfectly in her 'right mind,' so far restored as to be a safe and comfortable inmate."

"Groton. A few rods removed from the poorhouse is a wooden building upon the roadside, constructed of heavy board and plank. . . . There is no window, save an opening half the size of the sash, and closed by a board shutter; in one corner is some brickwork surrounding an iron stove, which in cold weather serves for warming the room. The occupant of this dreary abode is a young man, who has been declared incurably insane. He can move a measured distance in his prison; that is, so far as a strong, heavy chain depending from an iron collar which invests his neck permits. In fine weather, — and it was pleasant when I was there in June last, — the door is thrown open, at once giving admission to light and air, and affording some little variety to the solitary, in watching the passers-by. But that portion of the year which allows of open doors is not the chiefest part; and it may be conceived, without draughting much on the imagination, what is the condition of one who for days and weeks and months sits in darkness and alone, without employment, without object."

This unhappy being in Groton, with the chain round his neck, is alluded to again in the following conversation between Miss Dix and the keeper of the almshouse in Fitchburg : —

"Why [she there asked, speaking of a poor lunatic] cannot you take this man abroad to work on the farm? He is harmless; air and exercise will help to recover him." "I have been talking with our overseers, [was the answer] "and I've proposed getting from the blacksmith an iron collar and chain; then I can have him out by the house." "An iron collar and chain!" "Yes. I had a cousin up in Vermont, crazy as a wildcat, and I got a collar made for him, and he liked it." "Liked it! How did he manifest his pleasure?" "Why, he left off trying to run away. I kept the almshouse in Groton. There was a man there from the hospital. I built an outhouse for him, and the blacksmith made him an iron collar and chain, so we had him fast, and the overseers approved it."

"SHELBURNE. I had heard, before visiting this place, of the bad condition of a lunatic pauper. . . . I desired to see him, and, after some difficulties raised and set aside, was conducted into the yard, where was a small building of rough boards imperfectly joined. All was still, save now and then a low groan. The person who conducted me tried, with a stick, to rouse the inmate; I entreated her to desist; the twilight of the place making it difficult to discern anything within the cage; there at last I saw a human being, partially extended, cast upon his back amidst a mass of filth, the sole furnishing, whether for comfort or necessity, which the place afforded; there he lay, ghastly, with upturned, glazed eyes and fixed gaze, heavy breathings, interrupted only by faint groans, which seemed symptomatic of an approaching termination of his sufferings. Not so thought the mistress. 'He has all sorts of ways; he'll soon rouse up and be noisy enough; he'll scream and beat about the place like any wild beast, half the time.' 'And cannot you make him more comfortable? Can he not have some clean, dry place and a fire?' 'As for clean, it will do no good; he's cleaned out now and then; but what's the use for such a creature? His own brother tried him once, but got sick enough of the bargain.' 'But a fire; there is space even here for a small box stove.' 'If he had a fire he'd only pull off his clothes, so it's no use.' I made no impression; it was plain that to keep him securely confined from escape was the chief object. 'How do you give him his food? I see no means of introducing anything here.' 'Oh!' pointing to the floor, 'one of the bars is cut shorter there; we push it through there.' 'There? Impossible! you cannot do that; you would not treat your lowest dumb animals with that disregard to *decency !*' 'As for what he eats or where he eats, it makes no difference to him; he'd as soon swallow one thing as another.'"

"NEWTON. . . . Opening into this room only was the second, which was occupied by a woman, not old, and furiously mad. It contained a wooden bunk filled with filthy straw, the room itself a counterpart to the lodging-place. Inexpressibly disgusting and loathsome was all; but the inmate herself was even more horribly repelling. She rushed out, as far as the chains would allow, almost in a state of nudity, exposed to a dozen persons, and vociferating at the top of her voice; pouring forth such a flood of indecent language as might corrupt even Newgate. I entreated the man, who was still there, to go out and close the door. He refused; that was not *his place !* Sick, horror-struck, and almost incapable of retreating, I gained the outward air."

"Of the dangers and mischiefs sometimes following the location of insane persons in our almshouses I will record but one more example. In Worcester has for several years resided a young woman, a lunatic pauper, of decent life and respectable family. I have seen her as she usually appeared, listless and silent, almost or quite sunk into a state of dementia, sitting one amidst the family, 'but not of them.' A few weeks since, revisiting that almshouse, judge my horror and amazement to see her negligently bearing in her arms a young infant, of which I was told she was the unconscious parent! Who was the father none could or would declare. Disqualified for the performance of maternal cares and duties, regarding the helpless little creature with a perplexed or indifferent gaze, she sat a silent, but oh, how eloquent. a pleader for the protection of others of her neglected and outraged sex! Details of that black story would not strengthen the cause; needs it a weightier plea than the sight of that forlorn creature and her wailing infant? Poor little child, more than orphan from birth, in this unfriendly world, — a demented mother, a father on whom the sun might blush or refuse to shine!"

Such are brief selections from some of the extreme instances of misery and barbarity to which Dorothea L. Dix now called public attention through her Memorial to the Legislature of Massachusetts. Perhaps even more pitiful was the situation of the long catalogue of those whose reason, less wholly overthrown, left them (like the poor young woman to whom Charles Sumner so pathetically alludes) more sensible of their forlorn condition. The Memorial concluded with an impassioned appeal for adequate asylum provision against the continuance any longer of so foul a blot on the fair fame of the Commonwealth : —

"Men of Massachusetts, I beg, I implore, I demand, pity and protection for these of my suffering, outraged sex. Fathers, husbands, brothers, I would supplicate you for this boon — but what do I say? I dishonor you, divest you at once of Christianity and humanity, does this appeal imply distrust. . . . Here you will put away the cold, calculating spirit of selfishness and self-seeking. lay off the armor of local strife and political opposition; here and now, for once, forgetful of the earthly and perishable, come up to these halls and consecrate them with one heart and one mind to works of righteousness and just judgment. . . . Gentlemen, I commit to you this sacred cause. Your action upon this subject will affect the present and future condition of hundreds and thousands. In this legislation, as in all things, may you exercise that wisdom which is the breath of the power of God. Respectfully submitted.

". D. L. Dix.

"85 Mt. Vernon Street, Boston,
    "*January,* 1843."

CHAPTER IX.

INEVITABLY a Memorial such as that now described struck and exploded like a bombshell. It was carrying the war into Africa. It was the arraignment not of a local evil here and there, but of the state of things prevailing more or less in every township throughout the Commonwealth of Massachusetts. " Incredible! incredible! " was the first natural outcry of humane people. " Sensational and slanderous lies ! " was the swift and fiery rejoinder of selectmen, almshouse keepers, and private citizens in arms for the credit of their towns. Everywhere the newspapers bristled with angry articles. " There are some," this was the tone too often adopted, " and Miss Dix may be one of them, who are always on tiptoe, looking forward for something more marvelous than is to be discovered in real life ; and because the things themselves will not come up to this pitch of the imagination, the imagination is brought down to them, and has a world of its own creating."

All in vain had the memorialist sought to make it plain that it was a system, and not individuals, she arraigned, and that to put the pauper insane under the practically uncontrolled authority of ignorant and passionate persons, not only destitute of due knowledge, but destitute of any fit appliances for the treatment of the most terrible of human visitations, was the straight way to insure a hell on earth. Carefully and circumstantially had she written to the sheriffs all over the State, and received from them detailed replies substantiating her position that nothing better could be looked for from such a system. But on those more immediately arraigned all this made no impression. Such people felt themselves pilloried before the public gaze as fiends in human shape, and naturally made frantic efforts to declare the statements of the Memorial a tissue of lies.

" Did you never [says, in his 'Autocrat of the Breakfast-Table,' Dr. Oliver Wendell Holmes, in words so picturesquely descriptive of the situation that the temptation to quote them is too strong to resist], did you never, in walking in the fields, come across a large flat stone, which has lain, nobody knows how long, just where you found it, with the grass forming a little hedge, as it were, all round it, close to its edges, — and have you not, in obedience to a kind of feeling that told you it had been lying there long enough, insinuated your stick or your foot or your fingers under its edge and turned it over, as a housewife turns a cake? . . . What an odd revelation, and what an unforeseen and unpleasant surprise to a small community, the very existence of which you had not suspected, until the sudden dismay and scattering among its members was produced by your turning the old stone over ! Blades of grass flattened down, colorless, matted together, as if they had been bleached and ironed ; hideous crawling creatures, some of them coleopterous or horny-shelled ; . . . black, glossy crickets, with their long filaments sticking out like the whips of four-horse stage-coaches ; motionless slug-like creatures, young larvæ, perhaps more horrible in their pulpy stillness than even in the infernal wriggle of maturity ! But no sooner is the stone turned, and the wholesome light of day let upon this compressed and blinded community of creeping things, than all of them which enjoy the luxury of legs — and some of them have a good many — rush round wildly, butting each other and everything in their way, and end in a general stampede for underground retreats from the region poisoned by sunshine.   *Next year* you will find the grass growing tall and green where the stone lay ; the ground-bird builds her nest where the beetle had his hole ; the dandelion and the buttercup are growing there, and the broad fans of insect-angels open and shut over their golden disks, as the rhythmic waves of blissful consciousness pulsate through their glorified being."

Very soon, however, was it to become clear to intelligent men and women that they were now called upon to deal with one who was at the last remove from a sensationalist ; with one, on the contrary, endowed not merely with a sensitive heart, but with a statesmanlike grasp of mind.   She had raised no wild, feminine shriek of horror, when first the abyss of evil had opened up before her, but had patiently explored the depths of the inferno, sternly shutting her lips till she should come out again to the light of day, to report what her own eyes had seen.

Exception might be taken to a particular shade of statement here or there, but to the main truth of her arraignment none.   Soon there rallied to her side a band of able men, of whom such names as those of Dr. Samuel G. Howe, Dr. William E. Channing, Hon. Horace Mann, Rev. John G. Palfrey, and Dr. Luther V. Bell, of the McLean Asylum, proved a tower of strength.   And so to the fierce and insulting comments of selectmen or almshouse keepers, as of Groton for example, she needed no more conclusive reply than the quiet publication of letters like the following from Dr. Luther V. Bell, a man who, for humanity, science, and sound practical judgment, carried irresistible weight : —

McLEAN ASYLUM, *February* 15, 1843.

MY DEAR MISS DIX, — On recurring once more to your Memorial, for which I pray that you may have a reward higher than the applause of this world, I thought I would make you a short statement touching a case of a young man in the poorhouse at Groton, referred to on page nineteen.

Various coincidences led me to suppose this individual to be one James Gilson, such as the fact of having been at "the hospital," the peculiar blacksmith work for his restraint, etc.

I extract a part of the history of his case, as recorded at the time by my assistant, of course with no expectation on his part of its being seen or published beyond the ordinary records of cases.

"1840, *December* 15.   Mr. James Gilson, Groton, aged 30, single ; town pauper.   About nine months since, whilst at work in Lowell, his derangement came on, and soon after he was sent to the house of correction, in East Cambridge ; there he remained till last June (1840), when he was removed to the poorhouse in Groton, and confined in the following revolting manner : A *band of iron*, an inch wide, went round his neck, with a chain six feet long attached.   This was used for the purpose of securing him to any particular place.   His hands were restrained by means of a *clavis* and *bolt* (of iron), appropriated to each wrist, and united by a padlock.   In this bondage, this iron cruel bondage, talking incoherently to be sure, but without any exhibition of violence, was he brought to the Asylum *in the morning, after having been chained up the night before in a barn, like a wild animal, to spend its dreary hours.*   His shackles were immediately knocked off in the presence of his keeper, his swollen limbs chafed gently, when the delighted maniac exclaimed ' My good man, I must kiss you,' etc."

So little was this man a subject for personal restraint during his residence with us that he never even injured his clothes, ate at a common table with knives and forks with a dozen others, slept in a common bedroom, and was considered as a pleasant patient filled with delusions. After a short interval, curative means were employed, and, as we judged, with most obvious and encouraging advantage, until on the 23d day of April, that is, after a little over four months' trial, when the overseers of the poor, without previous notice, sent for him, while under the most energetic use of remedies which required a gradual discontinuance. My assistant's record closes with saying, "Reluctant to go, for fear they will again chain him."

"The occupant of this dreary abode is a young man," you observe in your Memorial, "who has been declared incurably insane." Alas! he may be so now; two years of chaining, doubtless, has extinguished forever his hope of recovery; but when he was removed from this place, I declare it as my opinion that he was not only not incurably insane, but was on the path to recovery; in every respect a promising case. So fully was I impressed with this that I urged the messengers to return till I could advise the town of his prospects; but this was declined.

How much now, my dear madam, do you suppose the charge to the large and thriving town of Groton was for this poor man under the care of this department of the Massachusetts General Hospital? Precisely three dollars a week for every expense of support, care, and comfort; perhaps a third or a half more than his present cost.

Very truly yours,   LUTHER V. BELL.

Equally encouraging letters from other prominent men now came to Miss Dix. "I have felt," wrote Horace Mann, "in reading your Memorial, as I used to feel when formerly I endeavored to do something for the welfare of the same class, — as though all personal enjoyments were criminal until they were relieved." Dr. Channing, who had printed an eloquent notice of her Memorial in the "Christian World," wrote her of this notice: "I only wish it were more worthy. Such as it is I give it to you with my best thanks for your great work of humanity." Lucius Manlius Sargent sent word: "I trust you will not suffer a moment's disquietude from the consideration that there is a morbid sensibility abroad which may question the propriety of such an investigation by one of your sex."

At the present day of such pronounced ideas on the whole issue of woman's sphere and woman's work, such a letter as this last would only provoke a humorous smile. It is questionable, however, whether many of Miss Dix's letters gave her more real satisfaction. Lucius Manlius Sargent was himself a very knightly specimen of a man, and one whose chivalrous salute any woman would have taken pride in; while Miss Dix's own ideas of feminine propriety, rooted and grounded in a select young ladies' boarding-school, were of an exacting and old-fashioned order. No doubt she read the letter over several times, and rejoiced that in the eyes of so courtly a gentleman she had not "unsexed" herself in venturing to plead for her poor unsexed sisters.

Very shortly after its first presentation to the Massachusetts Legislature, the Memorial was referred to a committee, of which Dr. S. G. Howe was appointed chairman. The committee made a report at once strongly indorsing the truth of Miss Dix's statements, and fortifying them with other instances of like outrages on humanity, the report closing with an eloquent appeal for immediate legislative action. The entire

provision for the insane in the State — in the State
Hospital at Worcester, in the McLean Asylum, and
in the hospital at South Boston — was, it was asserted,
not adequate to the care of quite 500 patients, while
there were in the Commonwealth 958 pauper insane
and idiotic persons, to say nothing of about 800 at
private charge.   A resolution was introduced, recom-
mending "that the Trustees of the State Lunatic
Hospital at Worcester shall erect additional buildings,
adjoining or near the existing buildings of said hospital, sufficiently large for the addition of 200 insane
patients more."

A capital piece of good fortune was it that at this
juncture a man of the courage and indomitable
humanity of Dr. S. G. Howe should have been in
the Legislature, ready and eager to engineer the bill
through.   All along had he stood by Miss Dix, and
encouraged her efforts.   Now, as the debate went on,
he continually sent her short, stimulating letters.

" I presented [he says in one of these] your Memorial this
morning, indorsing it both as a memorial and a petition.
Your work is nobly done, but not yet ended.   I want you
to select some newspaper as your cannon, from which you
will discharge often red-hot shot into the very hearts of the
people; so that, kindling, they shall warm up the clams and
oysters of the house to deeds of charity.   When I look back
upon the time when you stood hesitating and doubting upon
the brink of the enterprise you have so bravely and nobly
accomplished, I cannot but be impressed with the lesson of
courage and hope which you have taught even to the strongest men. . . . You are pleased to overrate the importance
of my efforts.   I can only reply that if I *touch off* the piece,
it will be you who *furnish the ammunition*."

A little later on, as the inevitable delays to any

work of reform presented themselves, Dr. Howe wrote
less hopefully : —

"I do not like to indulge in feelings of distrust, but have
been irritated by the cold, pecuniary policy of these men.
A friend overheard one of those very men who talked so
pathetically to you, say, 'We must find some way to kill
this devil of a hospital bill!' Speaking about these traitors,
another friend, and one versed in the wiles of politicians,
said to me, 'Doctor, never mind : there is a hell; these
fellows will find it.' But God soften their hearts, and enable them to realize the sad condition of the insane, and
turn and do otherwise."

Happily, the feeling of discouragement expressed
in this last letter proved needless. So profound had
been the sensation throughout the Commonwealth
awakened by the frightful details and impassioned eloquence of the Memorial that the obstructions and delays of politicians were swept away before a steadily
rising tide of public indignation. The bill for immediate relief was carried by a large majority, and the
order passed for providing State accommodations at
Worcester for two hundred additional insane persons.
At once Dr. John G. Palfrey wrote congratulatingly to
the happy woman, adding, "I did not tell you, what
you will have understood, that Dr. Howe managed
the business admirably, — to say like an old stager
would be doing him injustice, — like a man of humanity, energy, and abundant resources, as he is."

Thus was ventured and won Miss Dix's first legislative victory, the precursor of such numbers to follow
through the length and breadth of the United States
that their repetition year by year, the enormous sums of
money they involved, the magnitude of the structures
they led to the building of, the range of the field they

opened out to advancing medical science, and the vast numbers of poor wretches transferred from stalls and chains to a comparative heaven of asylum comfort, fairly startle the imagination. It was a legislative victory which illustrated the peculiar characteristics of her mind. Two years, as has been seen, of patient, concentrated work had preceded any word of appeal to the public. In these two years she had gained the training of accurate observation and indomitable will so indispensable to any one who will probe to the bottom great evils, and then resolutely steer the way through the obstruction, deceit, and wrath, always aroused by insistence on radical reform. Sternly repressing the native intensity of an emotional nature, instinctively on fire at the sight of wrong and cruelty, she had acquired at last a dignity and repose of manner that carried with them the peculiar power always exercised by restrained emotion. Jailer or almshouse-keeper, no man, however cunning or however brutal, could henceforth think to wave her aside or refuse her entrance. Something formidable was there now about her, to which inferior natures irresistibly submitted; but the presence as of a higher power thus manifested came " not in the wind, nor in the earthquake, nor in the fire, but in a still, small voice."

Indeed, to this day, the oldest living friends of Miss Dix never weary of speaking of the wonderful quality of her voice. It was sweet, rich, and low, perfect in enunciation, and its every tone pervaded with blended love and power. Quiet but always tasteful in the style of her dress, her rich, wavy, dark brown hair brought down over the cheek and carried back behind the ears, her face lit with alternately soft and brilliant

blue gray eyes, their pupils so large and dilating as
to cause them often to be taken for black, a bright,
almost hectic glow of color on her cheeks, with her
shapely head set on a neck so long, flexile, and graceful as to impart an air of distinction to her carriage,
— all the accounts which have come down from this
period of her career call up a personality preëminently
fitted to sway those brought into contact with her in
her higher moods of inspiration.

Apart, moreover, from this training in self-control
and power to set aside alike wile or violence in the
attempt to block her way, Miss Dix had learned another lesson through this her first experience in dealing
with a legislative body. It was the lesson of concentrating effort on the work of leading the leaders.
Personally, she never cared to appear in public. It
was thoroughly distasteful to her to do so. She made
no addresses, she gathered no meetings. To come
to close quarters of eye, conscience, and heart with
impressionable and influential minds, to deliver her
burden as from the Lord to them, and let it work on
their sensibility and reason, — this was her invariable method. Dr. Howe had hit the centre when he
said, "If I touch off the piece, it will be you who
furnish the ammunition." For the public éclat of the
explosion she cared little; for the quality and quantity of the gunpowder and the penetrating power of
the ball, everything. Practical relief brought to the
outcast and miserable, the enlisting in their behalf
every possible order of ability, philanthropic, political,
judicial, religious, — this was her grand object.

One farther lesson, however, the greatest and most
far-reaching of all, had Miss Dix learned from her experience in Massachusetts. While there pursuing her

investigations, she had again and again crossed the border into other States, notably into Connecticut and Rhode Island. The conviction thus steadily and irresistibly forced on her was that *all over the United States*, from Maine to Florida, from the Atlantic to the Mississippi, the same appalling story held true of the wretched fate of the pauper insane. Everywhere, "insane persons confined in *cages, closets, cellars, stalls, pens ; chained, naked, beaten with rods, and lashed into obedience!*" The piteous words of her own Memorial came back to her, echoed and reëchoed from every side. But, God be praised, not to depress or daunt her, not to make her cry in despair, " What, in the way of relief, is one little drop in such an ocean of misery ? " No, but only to challenge the heroic temper of her mind, and start the thrilling thought, " If one legislature can thus be besieged and carried by storm, why not another, and another, and another ! "

Now first broke upon her the length and breadth of the mission to which she felt herself divinely called. Resolutely and untiringly, State by State, would she take up the work ; first exhaustively accumulating the facts and " preparing the ammunition," and then investing and besieging the various legislatures, till they should capitulate to the cry of the perishing within their borders. In deliberately planning, as she did thus early in her career, so vast a campaign, was revealed the greatness and compass of her mind. The splendors and audacities of moral genius now flashed out in her. Far more than simply a good and merciful woman was here. Here was a woman with the grasp of intellect, the fertility of resources, and the indomitable force of will that go to the make-up of a great statesman or a great military commander.

CHAPTER X.

IT was during the two years, 1841–43, in which
Miss Dix was diligently pursuing her investigations
in Massachusetts, that her leisure time was first sys-
tematically devoted to the study of the most advanced
methods in the humane and scientific treatment of insanity. Dr. Woodward of the Worcester Asylum,
Dr. Luther V. Bell of the McLean, and Dr. John S.
Butler of the newly erected Lunatic Hospital of Boston were her chief teachers. With Dr. Butler, in especial, she was brought into very intimate relations.
Himself a man of great natural benevolence, he had,
in 1833, when beginning the practice of medicine in
Worcester, come in contact with that remarkable pioneer in the American history of insanity, Dr. Woodward, and witnessed at his hands what seemed to him
such miraculous triumphs in the restoration to sanity
of violent madmen as to feel that a new and brighter
day was dawning on the world. "Doctor, if Llewel-
lyn can be cured," he said of a seemingly desperate
case brought under his observation, and which later
on was cured, " it will be next to a revelation in medicine to me ! "

The strong attraction always exerted over original
and experimental minds by demonstrations of a new,
positive force to deal with, now took such hold on Dr.
Butler as to convince him that this was the true field

for him to enter. Appointed, in 1839, superintendent of the Lunatic Hospital of Boston, he very soon
brought to bear such tact and skill, such courage and
patience, such power of sympathy and personal magnetism, as to work changes in the condition of his
patients as marked as those wrought by Pinel, Tuke,
and Conolly.

Speaking of this institution in 1842, the " North
American Review " says, in an article on Insanity in
Massachusetts: —

" Its patients are wholly of the pauper class. Its inmates
are of the worst and most hopeless class of cases. They are
the raving madman and the gibbering idiot, whom, in the
language of the inspectors of prisons, hospitals, etc., for Suf-
folk County, we had formerly seen tearing their clothes
amid cold, lacerating their bodies, contracting most filthy
habits, without self-control, unable to restrain the worst
feelings, endeavoring to injure those that approached them,
giving vent to their irritation in the most passionate, profane, and filthy language, fearing and feared, hating and
almost hated. Now they are all neatly clad by day, and
comfortably lodged in separate rooms by night. They walk
quietly, with self-respect, along their spacious and airy halls,
or sit in listening groups around the daily paper, or dig in
the garden, or handle edged tools, or stroll around the
neighborhood with kind and careful attendants. They attend daily and reverently upon religious exercises, and make
glad music with their united voices."

Eminently fortunate, then, was it for Miss Dix that
she was thus enabled to become the pupil of Dr. Butler, and to witness with her own eyes the actual transformation of the raging madhouse of the past into
the humane retreat of the present, — a transformation
which is unquestionably the most marvelous triumph
ever won by the moral reason of man over brute

chaos. "Look on this picture and on this!" thus became the more than Hamlet cry of her heart.

Already has it been stated that, while engaged in her special investigations in Massachusetts, Miss Dix had frequently crossed the border into other States. In Rhode Island had she struck upon scenes of misery to which she made, haste to call the attention of benevolent minds. Prominent among these friends of humanity was Thomas G. Hazard, who wrote at this time to a friend: —

"In the course of her investigations she has ferreted out some cases of human suffering almost beyond conception or belief, — one case in a neighboring town to this, of which I was yesterday an eye-witness, — which went beyond anything I supposed to exist in the civilized world, and which, without exaggeration, I believe was seldom equaled in the dark ages, the particulars of which she will describe to you."

The case to which Thomas G. Hazard alluded was that of Abram Simmons, confined in a dungeon in Little Compton, R. I. To it Miss Dix later called public attention, in the "Providence Journal" of April 10, 1844, in an article entitled "Astonishing Tenacity of Life." The article illustrates the intensity of feeling and the vigor of style characteristic of her efforts at this period to shake the apathy of the public mind. It is not written over her own signature. When possible, she always preferred to keep herself in the background, and to refer to the testimony of others, — in this instance to that of Thomas G. Hazard.

"ASTONISHING TENACITY OF LIFE.

"It is said that grains of wheat, taken from within the envelope of Egyptian mummies some thousand of years old, have been found to germinate and grow in a number of instances. Even toads and other reptiles have been found alive in situations where it is evident that they must have been encased for many hundreds, if not thousands, of years.

"It may, however, be doubted whether any instance has ever occurred in the history of the race where the vital principle has adhered so tenaciously to the human body under such a load and complication of sufferings and tortures as in the case of Abram Simmons, an insane man, who has been confined for several years in a dungeon in the town of Little Compton, in this State.

"The writer accidentally met a gentleman this morning from that town, who recounted the following facts, with leave to publish them, and there can be no doubt that they are correct.

"He stated that he visited the cell of Abram Simmons during the past winter. His prison was from six to eight feet square, built entirely of stone, — sides, roof, and floor, — and entered through two iron doors, excluding both light and fresh air, and entirely without accommodation of any description for warming and ventilating. At that time the internal surface of the walls was covered with a thick frost, adhering to the stone in some places to the thickness of half an inch, as ascertained by actual measurement. The only bed was a small sacking stuffed with straw, lying on a narrow iron bedstead, with two comfortables for a cover. The bed itself was wet, and the outside *comfortable* was completely saturated with the drippings from the walls, and stiffly frozen. Thus, in utter darkness, encased on every side by walls of frost, his garments constantly more or less wet, with only wet straw to lie upon, and a sheet of ice for his covering, has this most dreadfully abused man existed through the past inclement winter. . . . His teeth must have been worn out by constant and violent chattering for such a length of time, night and day,

"'Poor Tom's a-cold!'"

"Should any persons in this philanthropic age be disposed, from motives of curiosity, to visit the place, they may rest assured that traveling is considered quite safe in that part of the country, however improbable it may seem. The people of that region profess the Christian religion, and it is even said that they have adopted some forms and ceremonies which they call worship. It is not probable, however, that they address themselves to poor Simmons' God. Their worship, mingling with the prayers of agony which he shrieks forth from his dreary abode, would make strange discord in the ear of that Almighty Being, in whose keeping sleeps the vengeance due to all his wrongs."

Later on, in a public document of her own, Miss Dix gives the narrative of her first visit to Little Compton. As it throws farther light alike on the courageous mercy with which she went about her work, and on the character of the persons in whose charge such poor wretches were placed, it seems needful to give it. After investigating carefully the condition of two or three miserable beings confined there, and being warned not to attempt to go into the cell of Simmons, as he would surely kill her, she proceeds as follows with her narrative : —

"'Your other patient, — where is he?' 'You shall see; but stay outside till I get a lantern.' Accustomed to exploring cells and dungeons in the basements and cellars of poorhouses and prisons, I concluded that the insane man spoken of was confined in some such dark, damp retreat. Weary and oppressed, I leaned against an iron door which closed the sole entrance to a singular stone structure, much resembling a tomb, yet its use in the courtyard of the poorhouse was not apparent. Soon, low, smothered groans and moans reached me, as if from the buried alive. At this moment the mistress advanced, with keys and a lantern. 'He's here,' said she, unlocking the strong, solid iron door. A step down, and short turn through a narrow passage to the right, brought us, after a few steps, to a second iron door parallel to the first, and equally solid. In like manner, this was unlocked and opened; but so terribly noxious was the poisonous air that immediately pervaded the passage, that a considerable time elapsed before I was able to return and remain long enough to investigate this horrible den. Language is too weak to convey an idea of the scene presented. The candle was remote from the scene, and the flickering rays partly illuminated a spectacle never to be forgotten. The place, when closed, had no source of light or of ventilation. It was about seven feet by seven, and six and a half high. All, even the roof, was of stone. An iron frame interlaced with rope, was the sole furniture. The place was filthy, damp, and noisome; and the inmate, the crazy man, the helpless and dependent creature, cast by the will of Providence on the cares and sympathies of his fellow-man, — there he stood, near the door, motionless and silent; his tangled hair fell about his shoulders; his bare feet pressed the filthy, wet stone floor; he was emaciated to a shadow, etiolated, and more resembled a disinterred corpse than any living creature. Never have I looked upon an object so pitiable, so woe-struck, so imaging despair. I took his hands and endeavored to warm them by gentle friction. I spoke to him of release, of liberty, of care and kindness. Notwithstanding the assertions of the mistress that he would kill me, I persevered. A tear stole over the hollow cheek, but no words answered to my importunities; no other movement indicated consciousness of perception or of sensibility. In moving a little forward I struck against something which returned a sharp metallic sound; it was a length of ox-chain, connected to an iron ring which encircled a leg of the insane man. At one extremity it was joined to what is termed a solid chain, — namely, bars of iron eighteen inches or two feet long, linked together, and at one end connected by a staple to the rock overhead. 'My husband,' said the mistress, 'in winter rakes out sometimes, of a morn-

ing, half a bushel of frost, and yet *he never freezes;* ' refer-
ring to the oppressed and life-stricken maniac before us.
' Sometimes he screams dreadfully,' she added, ' and that is
the reason we had the double wall, and two doors in place
of one ; his cries disturbed us in the house.' ' How long
has he been here?' . ' Oh, above three years; but then he
was kept a long while in a cage first ; but once he broke his
chains and the bars, and escaped ; so we had this built,
where he can't get off.' Get off ! No, indeed; as well
might the buried dead break through the sealed gates of the
tomb ! "

What was the first practicable step toward providing fit accommodation and care for the miserable
creatures she had found all over the State of Rhode
Island ?   There already existed a small asylum in the
city of Providence, conducted on wise and humane
principles.   But it was totally inadequate to the demands made on it.   Still it furnished a good foundation, and an appeal to the wealthy and humane for
means toward its immediate enlargement seemed the
wisest present course.

In this juncture was it that the extraordinary power
of Miss Dix to reach the heart and purse of those
whom every one else failed to move showed its first
proof.   Among the list of persons to whom she had
resolved to make appeal was Mr. Cyrus Butler, a
man of large business capacity, who ultimately left
an estate of $4,000,000, but who, like so many men
absorbed in the pursuit of wealth, had contracted a
passion for accumulation that rendered it well-nigh
impossible to persuade him to give a dollar away.
People smiled significantly when Miss Dix announced
her intention of calling upon him, and expressed the
usual sentiment about getting " milk out of a stone."

"But none of these things moved her." Her faith in human nature, if only strongly and wisely enough appealed to, was invincible.

Accompanied, therefore, to the house of Mr. Butler by Rev. Edward B. Hall, D. D., of Providence, who left her at the door, she made the momentous visit. It was a singular interview. For some time, through sheer force of lifelong habit, Mr. Butler sought to put her off by diverting the conversation to the familiar but rather unprofitable topic of the weather. So great is the variety of weather in Rhode Island, as well as in her sister State of Massachusetts, that whole days might thus have been spent without exhausting the subject. Preserving her temper and self-control, Miss Dix pleasantly adjusted herself to the humor of the scene, until finally, feeling that the thing had gone far enough, she rose with commanding dignity, and said: "Mr. Butler, I wish you to hear what I have to say. I want to bring before you certain facts, involving terrible suffering to your fellow-creatures all around you — suffering you can relieve. My duty will end when I have done this, and with you will then rest all further responsibility." Then, quietly, clearly, and with suppressed emotion, she told the pathetic story of what she had seen with her own eyes. She told it as though, there in that parlor, were standing for judgment two accountable beings before the tribunal of poor Simmons' avenging God. Mr. Butler listened spellbound till she was through, and then abruptly said, "Miss Dix, what do you want me to do?" "Sir, I want you to give $50,000 toward the enlargement of the insane hospital in this city!" "Madam, I'll do it!" was his answer.

While a signal spiritual triumph to Miss Dix, such

an interview reflects honor on both parties. Underneath the hard crust induced by a life of ceaseless addiction to accumulation, it showed the beating of a genuine human heart, prompt to respond to the pleading of such an angel of mercy. The parting with $50,000 by a purely business man, to whom it might mean a prospective million, involves a mental wrench of which few can appreciate the intensity. Probably there was not another woman in the land who could have commanded such combined power of cogent statement and impassioned fervor as thus, in an hour, to reverse all the deeply rooted habit of a lifetime. The feat attracted great attention at the time in Providence, and afterwards gave rise to many exaggerated stories which went the rounds of the newspapers, — stories, some of which Miss Dix was at pains publicly to contradict in the press. Indeed, she always spoke of Mr. Butler with sincere respect, and felt most gratefully his service to the cause she had so close at heart.

The name of the asylum was now changed to that of the " Butler Hospital," — the hospital in which for long years Dr. Isaac Ray proved so invaluable a helper to every shape of mental disease. Later on, farther handsome endowments were made to it by Mr. Alexander Duncan, who had married the niece of Mr. Butler, the heiress to his great fortune.

Thus was secured Miss Dix's second asylum victory. In two States already, Massachusetts and Rhode Island, had she been the instrument of prospectively transferring from loathsome dungeons and inhuman treatment to fresh air, freedom from chains, and wise and kindly supervision, several hundred wretched creatures, and in awakening a public sentiment that was the pledge of a better order of things in the future. The "Look on this picture and on this!" was taking tangible shape in a way to gladden her benevolent heart.

Little time did she now waste in denouncing the inhumanity of jailers and almshouse keepers in their treatment of the insane. That average human nature should finally grow exasperated over such shapes of perversity; that ordinary and ignorant men and women, rendered sleepless by midnight yells of profanity and indecency, or kept in terror of fire or violence, should finally give way thoroughly to the "wild-beast theory," and feel that cellars, out-houses, and iron cages were the only safe places in which to chain up the more desperate cases, was no more than what was rationally to be expected. The only relief lay, she clearly saw, in multiplying institutions, presided over by men of the science, elevation of character, and exceptional endowment of patient insight requisite for exorcising such seeming demoniacal possession.

CHAPTER XI.

SUCCESSFUL, however, as Miss Dix had been in providing for the immediate exigency in Rhode Island through an appeal to private charity, she soon saw with increasing clearness the utter inadequacy of such measures to afford relief on the scale that was imperatively demanded. The farther she pushed her investigations, the vaster and more wide spread was discovered to be the evil to be coped with. Comparatively few of the States of the Union had as yet any State asylums. The power of *public taxation*, on a scale adequate to the work to be accomplished, must now, she felt, be evoked; more even than this, the people of the States must be wrought to a pitch of enlightenment and mercy at which they would feel willing and glad to be taxed.

It was in the State of New Jersey, and with the foundation of the asylum at Trenton, that Miss Dix began this, her far larger and more characteristic work, — the work no longer of *supplementing* the deficiencies of institutions already existing, but of *creating* institutions *de novo* and out of nothing. There, in Trenton, was it that she went through the travail of bearing beneath her heart what she ever after characterized as her " first-born child," owing its whole life to her as mother. There, forty-five years later, was she herself, worn out with toil, age, and

disease, to die, in apartments gratefully tendered for
her free use by the trustees of the institution ; and
there, in those last days of weariness and pain, was it
that, when one morning her faithful friend and physician, Dr. John W. Ward, the superintendent of the
asylum, came into her room with the joyful intelligence that he was father of his first-born child, she
broke out, " Yes, and born under the roof of my first-
born child I "

As the work of Miss Dix in first breaking ground
in the State of New Jersey, in creating there a new
and effective public sentiment, and in finally getting
this sentiment embodied in positive legislative action,
was, alike in its tactics, its courage, its persistence,
and its power of moral ascendency, the same which
she repeated so marvelously in a whole round of
States, it seems best to treat this as a typical instance
of her constant rule of action, and to go somewhat
circumstantially into the story of the nature of the
helps and hindrances she there, as everywhere, encountered. To attempt the same of all the great public institutions of which she was, single-handed, the
founder, would be to fill many volumes. One example, vividly conceived, will suffice the reader for all.

First and foremost, she went forth quietly and
alone. No trumpet announced that a distinguished
philanthropist was about to probe to the bottom the
moral condition of the State, to champion the oppressed, and to prove a terror to evil doers. Here
was no excitable novice in hunting, noisily scaring
up the game before the piece was charged and the
finger on the trigger, ready to shoot. In truth, few
knew, or so much as suspected, the fact that a quietly
dressed woman was moving about from county to

county, taking notes of the condition of every jail and almshouse. Thus, foul secrets that would have been carefully hidden away from regularly appointed committees — stopping first tumultuously to dine and wine at the public tavern, — were contemptuously exposed to this unheralded, supposedly uninfluential woman. Meanwhile, nothing escaped her trained eye, and before people dreamed what she was doing she had gathered her statistics, and was master of the position. She had now her fulcrum and her Archimedes lever, through which she felt she could lift a world of moral apathy.

This preliminary work done, and thoroughly done, the second resort of Miss Dix was always to her power of direct personal influence over the leaders of the social and political world. A born leader herself, her instinct for detecting the gift of leadership in others was well-nigh infallible. " Her insight into character," says of her Dr. P. Bryce, superintendent of the asylum at Tuscaloosa, Alabama, " was truly marvelous; and I have never met any one, man or woman, who bore more distinctly the mark of intellectuality." For large numbers of self-supposed men of weight and influence, she entertained a quiet, well-disguised contempt. Well disguised, however, it always was ; they never found it out. She was careful to make no enemies whenever she could help it; for so thoroughly did she identify herself with her cause, as to feel that enmity to her would mean enmity to it. Many and many the humble country member of the legislature, a man of few words, but those words rocks, who was recognized by her, if for no other quality but honest stubbornness in maintaining a position once taken, as in reality a more important factor to be reckoned with than a score of noisy, bustling politicians. Especially among the plain Quakers of New Jersey, men and women, did she recruit stanch supporters, who, once enlisted, never deserted the ranks.

From the moment, however, when it became the question of practically engineering a bill through the legislature, then it was another matter, and she imperatively insisted on putting the full management into the hands of men of first-rate political ability, — men humane, indeed, and sincerely interested, but men abreast with every device and trick of the enemy. Her Memorial once written, charged to the cannon's mouth with grape and canister, and, behind it, the explosive fulminate of her own latent passion, then the question of who should " touch off the piece," to recur to Dr. Howe's apt figure of speech, — whether some one who would aim at nothing and hit nothing, or some one who should discharge it straight into the thickest ranks; — was to her an issue, as all important as, with Napoleon or Nelson, that of who should handle his artillery or point his broadsides.

Just here, in the profound influence she exercised over many of these leaders, and in her consequent power to secure from them the most chivalrous service, lay one marked secret of Miss Dix's unexampled success. By a sure instinct of compassion, she speedily found her way into the heart of every household where affliction was on hand. There was, it might be, an invalid wife in the home, or a young daughter wasting away with disease, or a promising son blighted on the threshold of life by threatened or actual insanity. Into these households she stole, an angel of consolation, her sustaining power in all hours of darkness and pain a marvel to those uplifted by it. At last came the day when this was remembered in some memorable act. Let a single example of how remembered suffice. The especial case here instanced was communicated to the writer of this biography by Dr. Eugene Grissom, superintendent of the Insane Asylum at Raleigh, North Carolina, and, though occurring in another State than New Jersey, still illustrates a frequently repeated experience in Miss Dix's efforts at passing her hospital bills.

"The first appropriation bill looking to the erection of an asylum in North Carolina was defeated. Mrs. Dobbin, wife of Hon. James C. Dobbin, of Fayetteville, afterwards Secretary of the Navy, was very sick at Raleigh. Her husband was a member of the House. On her death-bed she expressed to Miss Dix her deep gratitude for the tender care that noble woman had given her in her own illness, and, almost with her dying breath, begged her gifted husband to repay her own debt of gratitude to Miss Dix by another effort to pass the asylum bill.

"Almost as soon as the last sad services of interment were ended, Mr. Dobbin entered the House, clad in the deepest mourning and broken with sorrow. He entered at once on the fulfillment of the duty he owed to the pious dead and the afflicted living. Feeling keenly his own bereavement and cherishing sympathy for the woes of others, sustained by the profound sympathy that moved every bosom, he redeemed nobly his last promise to a dying wife by a speech which made a great impression at the time, and the tradition of which has descended to this generation. . . . All was favorable to the orator. His own nature was moved to its very depths. His heart was softened and made tender by a distressing bereavement. Gratitude to Miss Dix, deep sympathy for the smitten of God, a yearning desire to help the unfortunate, all moved the gifted and generous North Carolinian, and he rose to the great demands of the occasion and the height of the argument, producing an oration rarely equaled. All opposition disappeared under the power of the eloquent and pathetic pleader, and the bill passed by an overwhelming vote."

Almost from the start of Miss Dix's career in her work of carrying the State legislatures, so profound was the impression made by her exceptional personality that an especial room, or separate alcove in the library, was habitually set apart for her, in which to be visited by the members. There she studied with eager scrutiny the list of the representatives in the Assembly, endeavoring to find out as far as possible the character of each for humanity or self-seeking, courage or servility to public opinion. Before very long she knew them thoroughly, many of them far more thoroughly than they ever knew themselves. She did not, however, herself enter the halls of legislation, nor seek interviews of the members in their homes or in the lobbies. Always she laid great stress on preserving her womanly dignity, and saw plainly how easy it was to vulgarize alike a cause and its representative by a pushing and teasing demeanor. Members of either house were brought in by influential friends to her own room or alcove, and there she wrought on them in every way of cogent argument and eloquent entreaty. The only exception to this, of a slightly more public nature, was her habit of inviting into the parlor of her boarding-house from fifteen to twenty gentlemen at a time, for conversation and discussion.

When once her Memorial had been read to the legislature, and then, through the medium of the newspapers, had been brought before the general public, she next worked with energy the instrumentality of the press, writing for it innumerable articles herself, and enlisting in the same service all who wielded eloquent pens. ⌐To rouse all over the State a powerful public opinion was an aim she never lost sight of, no one knowing more clearly the subserviency to it of politicians. ⌐

⌐To return now, from these more general statements of Miss Dix's methods, to the immediate case of the passage of the New Jersey bill, which ushered into the world her first-born asylum child.⌐

It was first on January 23, 1845, that her Memorial to the legislature of New Jersey was presented to the Senate by Miss Dix's stanch supporter, Hon. Joseph S. Dodd. Like all her public papers, it was written with great ability, and embodied a judicious blending of pathetic appeal with strong rational argument. Less nakedly terrible than the Massachusetts Memorial, it was more tender in its spirit; fuller, indeed, of the comforting hope of the redeeming Purgatorio than of the despair of the rayless Inferno. Gleams of light are thrown on the gratitude in the hearts of the poor sufferers for the smallest attempts to alleviate their miseries, as will be seen in the following extracts: —

"One whom I was so fortunate as to have removed to a situation of greater comfort, and to supply with some of the common necessaries of common life, said, raising his trembling arms reverently, 'God's spirit bids this message to you, saying it is His work you are doing; lo, it shall prosper in your hands!' ... Another, a female, whose scarred limbs bore marks of the cankering iron worn for many weary years, said, 'I could curse those who chain me like a brute beast, and I do, too, but sometimes the *soft voice* says, Pray for thine enemy, and this it *sings* often while the sun shines on the poor mind; but darkness comes, and then the thoughts are evil continually, and the soul is black!'"

How, farther, all classes, rich as well as poor, highly intellectual as well as feeble-minded, are exposed alike to the visitation of this fearful scourge was strikingly illustrated by instances of which the following gives a touching example : —

"On a level with the cellar, in a basement room, which was tolerably decent, but bare enough of comforts, lay, upon a small bed, a feeble, aged man, whose few gray locks fell tangled about his pillow. As we entered, he addressed one present, saying, ' I am all broken up, all broken up!' ' Do you feel much weaker, then, *Judge?*' ' *The mind,* the mind is going, — almost gone,' responded he, in tones of touching sadness. ' Yes,' he continued, murmuring to himself, ' the mind is going.' This feeble, depressed old man, a pauper, helpless, lonely, and yet conscious of surrounding circumstances, and not now wholly oblivious of the past, — this feeble old man, who was he? I answer as I was answered ; but he is not unknown to many of you. In his young and vigorous years he filled various places of honor and trust among you. His ability as a lawyer raised him to the bench. As a jurist, he was distinguished for uprightness, clearness, and impartiality. He also was judge of the orphans' court. He was for many years a member of the legislature. His habits were correct, and I could learn, from those who had known him for many years, nothing to his discredit, but much that commends men to honor and respect. The meridian of an active and useful life was passed ; the property, honestly acquired, on which he relied for comfortable support during his declining years was lost through some of those fluctuations which so often produce reverses for thousands. He became insane, and his insanity assumed the form of frenzy ; he was chained ' for safety.' "

The Memorial, once presented to the Senate, as above stated, by Hon. Joseph S. Dodd, was followed by him with the immediate preamble and resolution : —

"Whereas the expediency of erecting a State Lunatic Asylum having been at various times under the consideration of the legislature of this State, and it appearing by the facts now before us in relation to this subject that we greatly need such an establishment, therefore

"Resolved, by the Senate and General Assembly of the State of New Jersey, that the time has now arrived when it is the duty of the State to enter upon the execution of this work by the adoption of the necessary measures for that purpose during the present session of the legislature."

This was read and ordered to lie on the table for the present.

The next day Mr. Dodd saw it to be necessary to modify the previous resolution by calling for a joint committee of both houses for farther consideration of the subject. The resolution was passed, and Messrs. Dodd, Wurts, and Willets were appointed on the part of the Senate, and, later on, Messrs. Evans, Bond, Pierson, and Fort on the part of the House of Assembly.

By February 25 the joint committee made their report. They declared it unnecessary for them to occupy farther time, as they could " only repeat what is better said in the Memorial of Miss Dix, . . . which presents the whole subject in so lucid a manner as to supersede the necessity of farther remark from us." The report concluded with the following fervid appeal : —

" Is then our path any longer doubtful? Have we not every indication by the facts in our possession that the time has now arrived for entering at once upon this enterprise, so dear to the philanthropist, the Christian, and the patriot, and inseparably connected with the welfare of those for whom it is designed ; an enterprise whose beneficent operation will be felt not only by this, but by generations to come after us, and, as we hope, through all future time ; an enterprise that will reflect more lasting honor on the State, and tell more upon human happiness, than all our legislation for the last half century? We are behind the movements of the age and the spirit of the times. Let us be up and doing ; we are behind our sister States. Many of them have already moved forward in this field of humane exertion with a zeal and liberality that do them honor ; and shall we, Jerseymen, who are proud of the name, be left far in the distance or not move at all, sitting still, with our arms folded in inglorious sloth, satisfied if we can reap, though partially, the benefit of their labors, rather than provide for ourselves those privileges for which we are now dependent on them ?''

In Miss Dix's habitual experience in dealing with State legislatures, so thoroughly had at this stage of the proceedings the preliminary work been done that, as a rule, the higher-minded members of both Houses and the more enlightened portion of the community might now be relied on as genuine converts to the measure. Just at this point, however, usually began the real tug of war with another class of minds. After the first outburst of generous enthusiasm, a reaction was sure to set in. However pitiful the hearts of constituents, still every bill involving inevitable increase of taxation is sure to search those acutely sensitive nerves that have their terminal peripheries in the pocket. Now comes the chance of the demagogue, eager to make capital out of his championship of the interests of an already overburdened

public; now the day of fear and quaking to the timid
member, who feels his chance of reëlection at stake,
should he venture to vote for the proposed measure.
" By the way," said, at a later date, to Miss Dix, a
friend with whom she was talking, " a gentleman of
the House told me that the biggest gun that was leveled to defeat his reëlection, was the fact of having
voted to publish your Memorial." " What did he answer ? " " Why, that he would have been proud of
such a defeat ! " But large numbers were of a more
lowly frame of mind, and felt no such lofty pride in
the prospect of political martyrdom.

Here, then, was the crisis in which Miss Dix always
found the severest and most unremitting work imposed
upon her. She was up every morning before sunrise,
writing letters and editorials ; through all the hours of
the session she was holding private interviews with
members; in the evenings, as often as possible, she
was arguing with and entreating a company of fifteen
to twenty specially invited to her parlor, — generally
the most obstinate cases to deal with. Only at midnight did she seek her pillow. It was exhausting
work, for on her individual power to ray out light
enough to illuminate ignorant minds, and to radiate
heat and glow enough to kindle the apathetic, turned
the whole issue. A glimpse into her own hours, alike
of depression and of joy, is caught in the following
letter of this date to her friend Mrs. Hare, of Philadelphia : —

" I must write to you, I must have your sympathy. How
I long for your heart-charming smile ! Just now I need
calmness ; I am exhausted under this perpetual effort and
exercise of fortitude. At Trenton, thus far, all is prosperous, but you cannot imagine the labor of conversing and

convincing. Some evenings I had at once twenty gentlemen for three hours' steady conversation. The last evening, a rough country member, who had announced in the House that the 'wants of the insane in New Jersey were all humbug,' and who came to overwhelm me with his arguments, after listening an hour and a half with wonderful patience to my details and to principles of treatment, suddenly moved into the middle of the parlor, and thus delivered himself: 'Ma'am, I bid you good-night! I do not want, for my part, to hear anything more; the others can stay if they want to. *I am convinced;* you've conquered me out and out; I shall vote for the hospital. If you'll come to the House, and talk there as you've done here, no man that is n't a brute can stand you; and so, when a man's convinced, that's enough. The Lord bless you!'—and thereupon he departed."

No doubt Miss Dix went to bed that night in a happy and grateful frame of mind. In these individual victories, constantly repeated, lay the hidingplace of her power. But there remained always a plenty of material needing conversion, and, quite as likely as not, she would wake up the following morning only to read, in the newspaper report of the debate of the preceding day, a speech from an " unterrified " member, like the following: —

" Sir, I shall not trust the estimate of these commissioners, who have devised the plan of this Egyptian Collosheum. New Jersey has hitherto acted well. She has kept clear of a national debt, which some folks call a national blessing. Let us husband our resources. I had rather spend the money in educating the children of the State, . . . qualifying them to act their part well in life, and preparing them for eternity. . . . There 'll be a day of account, and it 's not far ahead. I have seldom prophesied on this floor but it turned out correct. True, I missed it last year. I do believe that if that Miss Dix had been paid $500 or $600, and escorted over the Delaware or to Philadelphia, or even $1,000, and taken to Washington city, and, if you choose, enshrined in the White House, it would have been money well laid out. Now, I should like the whys and wherefores for a building 487 feet long and 80 feet wide, for, may be, twenty lunatics. I believe that the best thing we could do, would be to appropriate $200 or $300, to fill up the cellars and sow them over with grass-seed, so that the spot may not be seen hereafter. You could n't do a more popular act!"

Unquestionably, the report of a speech like this was read with as lively satisfaction by an elect class of its author's constituents, and was as highly applauded for its combination of soaring imagination with a strict eye to business, as the honorable member could himself have desired. But this was not the kind of oratory, nor was this the type of man, of whom Miss Dix stood in any sort of fear. A few solid words from the plain country member, who the night before had said, "Ma'am, you 've conquered me out and out; I 'll vote for the hospital," would, she knew, dispose effectually of a full hour of such "spread-eagle" eloquence.

The man, however, of whom she did always stand in dread was the man of great natural flux of sentimental speech, who from the outset insinuated himself into the minds of his audience as the friend and champion of all the world's disinherited ones, never failing, likewise, to make effusive allusion to herself as that "Heaven-sent angel of mercy," and yet who forthwith proceeded to insist that now, alas! the exigency had arrived when it was the stern dictate of duty to control such sensibilities, even though with bleeding hearts they should feel obliged to vote against the bill before them.

It may be well, therefore, in commenting on these various legislative experiences to which Miss Dix had to adjust herself, to give a specimen of the kind of speech and the kind of man she always felt to be most dangerous. The speech in question was not delivered before the New Jersey Legislature, but at another period and in another State. Still, it is one of those clear-cut, polished gems of eloquence which perfectly illustrates the case in hand.

"SENATORS. — 'The liberal man,' saith Solomon, 'deviseth liberal things, and by liberal things shall he prosper.' To this sentiment I respond, and hold it to be true no less of States than individuals. None, sir, is a firmer friend than myself to this charity. . . .

"But, sir, my experience, limited as it is, has taught me that the same law governs in the moral as in the physical world, and that premature development is attended by premature decay. . . .

"It becomes us, therefore, to be borne away by no child-like sensibility, no generous enthusiasm, no over-zeal nor haste to accomplish an acknowledged good. . . .

"Under these views and feelings, therefore, I am constrained, Mr. President, at this time, to oppose this project under every aspect it may now assume before us. . . .

"In conclusion, I should do injustice to my feelings if I omitted this occasion to express my unlimited admiration of the distinguished zeal and ability with which this measure has been prosecuted by the remarkable lady who, it is but due to her to say, has been its chief promoter and friend. . . .

"Woman, Mr. President, is ever lovely, and when she assumes the rare and sacred office of disinterested philanthropy she becomes indeed an angel!"

To be called an angel, and in the same breath have her bill for the relief of the outcasts of the earth voted

down, was a strain of celestial compliment for which
Miss Dix never manifested a trace of feminine relish.
Much more delicately did she appreciate the testimonial of a rough-and-ready proposition to "raise $500
or $600 to escort her over the Delaware or to Phila-
delphia, or even $1,000 to enshrine her in the White
House ; " for this proved demonstratively that she was
making so strong an impression that low-minded men
felt it was worth "thirty pieces of silver " to get rid
of affording her any further chance to "deceive the
people."

To conclude now this full and detailed account of
the passage of the bill for the establishment of the
New Jersey State Lunatic Asylum, — an account
which, as before stated, must serve for a typical instance of the helps and hindrances encountered by
Miss Dix in all her widespread and marvelously successful legislative work ; —

By March 14, 1845, the Act of Authorization was
taken up and read for the last time, and the proposition to postpone farther action till the next session of
the Legislature voted down in the Senate : ayes 2, nays
16. Upon the question, " Shall this bill now pass ? "
ayes 18, nays none. March 20, certain amendments
were proposed by the House of Assembly, to which,
March 24, the Senate agreed. Then, March 25, the
reëngrossed Bill passed: 18 ayes, nays none. The
victory was absolute ; the State had covered itself
with glory. Immediately, Hon. Joseph S. Dodd sent
in word to Miss Dix, anxiously yet confidently awaiting intelligence in her room : —

"SENATE CHAMBER, N. J.

" I am happy to announce to you the passage unanimously
of the bill for the New Jersey State Lunatic Asylum."

It was in her "mind's eye" alone that Miss Dix
could as yet see the full meaning of this vote. So far,
only "a castle in the air" was it at whose ideal
foundations and superstructure she had thus been
working. The stately buildings; the ample and
beautiful grounds, with their grass-slopes, trees, flowers, and sparkling fountains; the quiet, home-like
wards; the wise and tender care that were to take
home to their arms so many of the friendless and
wretched, — all these benedictions, which were to
spring from the victory she had won, had as yet neither a "local habitation nor a name." But she was
one of those highly favored ones who believe without
seeing; nay, one of that exceptional class of consecrated workers for humanity who are permitted to
behold their most high-wrought "visionary" ideals
finally materialized before their eyes in a correspond-
ing real and actual. The day was drawing on when,
in twenty different States, she was to see with the bodily eye such an outward and tangible witness of the
power of her own inner life as is rarely given to a
mortal to behold. " Verily, thou wast a mighty builder
before the Lord ! " is the exclamation involuntarily
wrung from the mind of any one who, following her
footsteps from State to State, enters, one after another, the beautiful parks, and traverses the halls and
wards of the immense structures, she, with the Alad-
din's lamp of her own moral genius, summoned into
being. Very easy is it then to appreciate the enthusiasm with which her friend, Dr. S. G. Howe, wrote to
her from Boston, on July 15 of this year, 1845 : —

" As for you, my friend, what shall I say to you to express my feelings respecting your course since I have seen
you personally ? Nothing, for words would fail me ; and,

besides, you want not words of human praise. I look back
to the time when the whisperings of maiden delicacy made
you hesitate about obeying the stern voice of conscience. I
recollect what you were then, I think of your noble career
since, and I say, God grant me to look back upon some
three years of my life with a part of the self-approval you
must feel! I ask no higher fortune. No one need say to
you, Go on! for you have heard a higher than any human
voice, and you will follow whither it calleth. God give you
as much strength as you have courage, for your mission!"

CHAPTER XII.

IN the letter of Dr. S. G. Howe, quoted at the conclusion of the last chapter, wondering allusion was
made by him to the range and multiplicity of Miss
Dix's labors during the previous three years. Of the
actual extent of these labors no due notice has as yet
been taken, as it seemed wiser for the time to concen-
trate attention wholly on her work in New Jersey, and
to emphasize it as an illustration of the methods she
habitually adopted.

In reality, only a portion of the years 1843–45 had ·
been spent by her in New Jersey, either while engaged
in collecting from county to county her statistics, or
while laboring with members of the Legislature. Often the Legislature was not in session, often it was
engaged on other business, often matters were in such
promising train that she could safely leave them in the
hands of able friends.

Meanwhile, she was at work with equal zeal in the
neighboring State of Pennsylvania, conducting at
Harrisburg, the capital, quite as arduous a campaign,
and one destined to prove as successful. Thus it happened that the date of the passage of a bill for founding an entirely new State institution at Harrisburg,
Penn., corresponded very closely with the passage of
the Bill for the foundation of that at Trenton, N. J.,

— two equally great trophies of humanity won in a single year. Only constructively, therefore, as in the parallel human case of the birth of twins into the family, can the term "first-born child," the term always so dear to the heart of its fostering mother, be applied to the Trenton Asylum. Indeed, so rapidly did these asylum children now begin to follow one another into existence all over the land as to drive a bewildered biographer to the conviction that, unless distinguishing marks in the way of red, green, or blue ribbons shall be tied around their infant wrists, hopeless confusion will erelong ensue as to natal hours.

One capital sign of a mind capable of accomplishing great results had now become evident in Miss Dix. She knew when she had done enough in a given place or at a given period, and was haunted with no misgivings that, unless her own hand were perpetually on the wheel, in the immediate act of steering, the ship would surely be run on to a reef. There was a time for her to be taking her observations, working her reckoning, studying her charts, and laying out the course of the whole broad India voyage. No less a subject than the immensity of the work called for by the condition of the insane in a large majority of the States of the Union, as well as in the British Dominion of Canada, had now taken full possession of her. Accordingly, in these actual two years in which she achieved her great successes in New Jersey and in Pennsylvania, she is to be found making long and arduous journeys all along the wide stretch from Nova Scotia to New Orleans, and mastering the conditions of the problem before her. A letter or two, of widely differing dates, will serve to bring before the mind the extent of these "circumnavigations of charity." The letters were written to her friend, Miss Heath.

"LEXINGTON, KY., *December* 22, 1843.

" I left Boston in September, as you know ; visited *en route* the prisons on Long Island and in the city of New York, also those of New Jersey, and duly reached Philadelphia. There and at Harrisburg I was detained a fortnight. Proceeding to Baltimore, I visited prisons there, and so on as far as Pittsburg west. Thence to Cincinnati, where I arrived the last of October.

The first of November I came to Kentucky, and have been laboriously traveling through the counties, collecting facts and information ever since, except a week which I took in Tennessee. The Legislature being in session in Nashville, I desired to do something for the state prison. This effected, I crossed the country by a rapid journey to Louisville, traveling by stage two days and nights. I proceed to-morrow to the northeast counties, if well enough. I have engaged lodgings in Frankfort, Ky., for January and February, and shall probably go to the Southern prisons after the Legislature rises in this State."

" AT SEA. STEAMER CHARLESTON, FROM SAVANNAH TO CHARLESTON, — A STORM. LYING TO. *March* 31, 1845.

" A temporary quiet induces me to use the only writing materials I have now at hand. . . . I designed using the spring and summer chiefly in examining the jails and poorhouses of Indiana and Illinois. Having successfully completed my mission in Kentucky, I learned that traveling in the States referred to would be difficult, if not impossible, for some weeks to come, on account of mud and rains. This decided me to go down the Mississippi to examine the prisons and hospitals of New Orleans, and, returning, to see the state prisons of Louisiana at Baton Rouge, of Mississippi at Jackson, of Arkansas at Little Rock, of Missouri at Jefferson City, and of Illinois at Alton. . . . I have seen incom-

parably more to approve than to censure in New Orleans.
I took the resolution, being so far on the way, of seeing the
State institutions of Georgia, Alabama, and South Carolina.
Though this has proved excessively fatiguing, I rejoice that
I have carried out the purpose."

It is by a vigorous exercise of the imagination alone
that even a faint idea can be conceived of the difference between the fatigue and peril involved in jour-
neying such thousands of miles as far back as 1845,
and the speed, ease, and luxury with which the same
distances can be accomplished to-day. Comparatively
nothing then existed of the enormous network of railways which, at this date, enables the traveler to penetrate at will every nook and corner of the immense
area of the United States. Steamboats on the rivers,
and, by land, a few lines of coaches and the hire of
private conveyances, were then the main dependence.
The craziest of vehicles, the most deplorable roads,
and taverns whose regulation diet of corn bread and
"bacon and greens" would have undermined the digestion of an ostrich, were, in the South and West,
the rule, and not the exception.

Those too, were the reckless racing times on the
Ohio, Tennessee, Mississippi, and Missouri rivers, the
exuberant days of the earlier national effervescence,
when, — to fall back on the picturesque expressions of
the period, — the moment a rival steamboat hove in
sight, the heaviest man on board was commissioned
to sit on the safety-valve, while the excited planters
flocked round the captain, eager to dedicate their last
ham on the freight-bills, or side of greasy bacon, to
feeding the fury of the rival furnace fires. Death by
explosion counted little against the glory of victory.

Safe escaped to land, however, discomfort or posi-

tive peril merely assumed a different shape. From
the setting in of the autumn rains to the heat and
dryness of the ensuing spring, the endless stretches of
the clay lands of the South and West became a continent of seemingly bottomless mud. Few bridges
spanned the creeks and rivers, which were passable
only at certain fords, often swollen by rains, and, by
the force of the current, rendered dangerous to the last
degree. Frequent inundations submerged the country
for miles back of the watercourses; and where the
actual roads were not pure and unadulterated mud,
axle-deep and as tenacious as India-rubber, they were
largely a "corduroy" of logs, alternately rotted out,
over which the vehicle thumped and then bounded
into the air with a force which left every bone and
muscle bruised and sore. The drivers, as a rule, were
careless, happy-go-lucky negroes, or "poor whites"
fortified with whiskey enough to lift them into a realm
of serene unconsciousness of risks. Malarious fevers
were widely prevalent, and, in years of cholera or
other epidemics, the lack of medical skill and the general recklessness in the habits of life insured their
rapid spread.

Now, the very nature of the work Miss Dix was thus
opening up involved that she, a lone and unprotected
woman, should penetrate every quarter where an almshouse was to be inspected or an abuse ferreted out.
When not stopping over at any State capital during
a session of the legislature, she must keep herself indefatigably at her task of massing an amount of eye-
witness evidence, at once so exact that none could
gainsay it, and so moving in its appeal for redress
that the most hardened and selfish alone could resist
it. Of the large number of Memorials she was to

write and bring before various legislatures, — Memorials, to the ability, eloquence, and judgment of which no less a man than the celebrated Chancellor Kent paid the highest tribute of praise, — each had to be a separate work, with its own local coloring. Kentucky did not concern itself with the state of things in Tennessee, nor Tennessee with that in Kentucky. The States were sovereign. Thus, in the presence of each new legislative David must she stand up with the commanding authority of a fresh Nathan, to point the finger and cry, " Thou art the man!"

Of course, the amount of labor, physical, mental, and emotional, involved in conducting these campaigns — and no other word but "campaigns" can adequately characterize them — was enormous. And so, the question of her habits, and manner of economizing her forces becomes a highly interesting one, as always in the case of those who accomplish great results.

Miss Dix was one more illustration of the so common saying that " the work of the world is done by its invalids." Like all such sayings, this especial one has truth enough in it to make it worthy of serious thought. Again and again in the world's history has it turned out that it is the General Wolfe, consumed with the hectic fever of the last stages of consumption, who scales the Heights of Abraham and takes Quebec; the Dr. Elisha Kent Kane, who, sentenced to death by his physicians, but resolved to " die in harness," goes farther than any of his day toward penetrating the ice barriers of the North Pole; the Darwin, economizing his intervals of ten minutes' relief from suffering, who leads the van of the naturalists of Europe in solving the problem of the origin of species. Nor is the reason — a high endowment of ability once

allowed for — so far to seek. It is as simple, in fact,
as the question why an engine of ten horse-power,
its piston-rod packed tight and its valves fitting with
precision, is capable of as much work as an engine
of twenty horse-power, its draught choked with soot
and its cylinders leaking steam at every joint. The
superb dower of physical life, nine tenths of which
a giant, like Daniel Webster, uses up in digesting
enormous dinners, washed down by copious draughts
of wine, and in the excessive amount of outdoor exercise requisite to enabling him to accomplish the feat,
is found in the end to yield no more available working force than these careful invalids, consecrated to
arms, science, or humanity, manage to wrest from the
wreck of their lungs, nerves, or digestion.

This lesson of the wise economy of her strength
Miss Dix had now mastered, as far as it ever is mastered by natures consumed by such passion of self-sacrifice. She suffered no social engagements to divert
her from her chosen object. Her business habits were
prompt and accurate, and no arrears of correspondence were allowed to accumulate. Relief from overstrain of sympathy, in such constant familiarity with
misery and degradation, she sought in an unfailing
delight in nature, in the keen interest she always kept
up in botanical study, as well as through that habitual
devout communion with God which was to her perpetual invigoration and peace.

Thus, while her friends were in constant fear of her
succumbing in some lonely place, she always contrived
to go to the very verge of self-destruction, without
falling over the edge; illustrating in her own peculiar way the words of St. Paul, "as dying, and
behold we live." Somewhere in her constitution there

must have been a most tenacious fibre. Again and again, in those days, was she attacked with hæmorrhage, again and again prostrated with malarial fever. Indeed, as her lifelong friend, Dr. Charles H. Nichols, of the Bloomingdale Asylum of New York, said of her, " her system became actually saturated with malaria." And yet her brain never yielded. Throughout her long life she never knew the meaning of a headache. Meanwhile, she exercised a certain prudence of her own. Whenever, in the midst of her most exacting labors, she found herself in a position where the force of flood or washout proved too much even for her indomitable resolve to press forward, she would take continuously to her bed, and store up sleep enough — sometimes thirteen to sixteen hours on a stretch — to tide her over the next two or three nights of jolting in wretched vehicles over corduroy roads. Indeed, these chance opportunities of indulging in protracted sleep she seems always to have regarded in the same light in which devout Roman Catholics look upon the " superfluous merits of the saints," namely, as a sacred storehouse on which to draw for the benefit of the shortcomings of many an evil day and night.

The excellent military practice of always carrying along with each piece of artillery an extra wheel, together with a due store of subsidiary traces, linchpins, rammers, and repairing tools, was, moreover, one which — as far as was possible in the case of a lone woman, with a limited supply of hand-baggage — Miss Dix now sedulously adopted on all her journeys. Southern roads were then well nigh as destructive to wheels and harness as the average fire of an enemy's battery in time of war. Many the occasion of wrench

or break befalling her wagon, on which she was forced
to dismount into deep mud and under a drenching
rain, only to find that her shiftless negro driver was
without the simplest means of repairing the damage.
Extra wheels and axles, indeed, it was beyond her
power to supply from her private stores, but, one or
two such experiences encountered and laid to heart,
she ever after made a practice of carrying with her an
outfit of hammer, wrench, nails, screws, a coil of rope,
and straps of stout leather, which under many a mis-
hap sufficed to put things to rights and enable her to
pursue her journey.

It could be wished that more incidents illustrative
of these ventures by flood and field had been preserved
for record. An invincible reticence on the part of
Miss Dix prevented her talking about herself, and she
was, moreover, too constantly worn out with her work
to have freshness enough left for picturesque narration. Her letters of this period to friends are largely
simple itineraries to acquaint them with her where-
abouts, and are written by snatches on steamboats
and trains, in stations and post offices, or while sitting
on a stump awaiting repairs on a broken carriage, with
tools furnished out of her own workshop. Here there
is a brief record, " Cholera on board;" here a letter
headed "Stuck fast on a mud-bar ten miles below
Vicksburg;" here another, "Up again from malarial
fever; off for Jackson, Miss., to-night." At times,
perhaps, she will condescend to enlarge more fully on
a river ford, — a natural phenomenon for which, no
doubt on sufficient grounds of chills and fever, she
seems to have entertained an especial aversion, as in
the following extract: —

" I have encountered nothing so dangerous as river fords. I crossed the Yadkin where it was three fourths of a mile wide, rough bottom, often in places rapid currents ; the water always up to the bed of the carriage, and sometimes flowing in. The horses rested twice on sand-bars. A few miles beyond the river, having just crossed a deep branch two hundred yards wide, the axletree of the carriage broke, and away rolled one of the back wheels."

One highly interesting incident, however, has been preserved, which would no doubt serve as an example of many another experience, not in all probability alike in kind, but still quite as illustrative of her courageous character. The version of it here given first appeared in print in the Greenville (S. C.) " Patriot," and as it was sent, in slip, by Miss Dix to her bosom friend, Miss Anne E. Heath, has thus her own indorsement. The date of the occurrence was unquestionably several years later than the period of her career, we are now engaged on, but, while describing the nature of her lonely and exposed journeyings, this seems the most appropriate place in which to introduce it : —

"AN INTERESTING INCIDENT.

" The other day, in conversation with Miss Dix, the philanthropist, during her visit to Greenville, a lady said to her, ' Are you not afraid to travel all over the country alone, and have you not encountered dangers and been in perilous situations ? '

" ' I am naturally timid,' said Miss Dix, ' and diffident, like all my sex; but in order to carry out my purposes, I know that it is necessary to make sacrifices and encounter dangers. It is true, I have been, in my travels through the different States, in perilous situations. I will mention one which occurred in the State of Michigan. I had hired a carriage and driver to convey me some distance through

an uninhabited portion of the country. In starting, I discovered that the driver, a young lad, had a pair of pistols
with him. Inquiring what he was doing with arms, he said
he carried them to protect us, as he had heard that rob-
beries had been committed on our road. I said to him,
"Give me the pistols, — I will take care of them." He
did so, reluctantly.

" ' In pursuing our journey through a dismal-looking forest,
a man rushed into the road, caught the horse by the bridle,
and demanded my purse. I said to him, with as much self-
possession as I could command, "Are you not ashamed to
rob a woman? I have but little money, and that I want to
defray my expenses in visiting prisons and poorhouses, and
occasionally in giving to objects of charity. If you have
been unfortunate, are in distress and in want of money, I
will give you some." While thus speaking to him I discovered his countenance changing, and he became deathly pale.
"My God," he exclaimed, "that voice!" and immediately
told me that he had been in the Philadelphia penitentiary
and had heard me lecturing to some of the prisoners in an
adjoining cell, and that he now recognized my voice. He
then desired me to pass on, and expressed deep sorrow at
the outrage he had committed. But I drew out my purse,
and said to him, " I will give you something to support you
until you can get into honest employment." He declined, at
first, taking anything, until I insisted on his doing so, for
fear he might be tempted to rob some one else before he
could get into honest employment.'

"Had not Miss Dix taken posession of the pistols, in all
probability they would have been used by her driver, and
perhaps both of them murdered. That voice was more
powerful in subduing the heart of a robber than the sight of
a brace of pistols."

When it is recalled that, no farther back than
March, 1841, Miss Dix's friend, Rev. John T. G.
Nichols, had expressed serious fears of a person in

such feeble health so much as taking charge of a Sunday-school class in the East Cambridge jail, the results accomplished before the close of 1845 seem well-nigh miraculous. In a letter to Mrs. Rathbone, of Liverpool, they were summed up by her in the following words : —

"I have traveled more than ten thousand miles in the last three years. Have visited eighteen State penitentiaries, three hundred county jails and houses of correction, more than five hundred almshouses and other institutions, besides hospitals and houses of refuge. I have been so happy as to promote and secure the establishment of six[1] hospitals for the insane, several county poorhouses, and several jails on a reformed plan."

It seems only natural, then, that her happiness should find such expression as in the following extract from a letter, written on board a steamboat on the Ohio River, to her friend, Mrs. Hare, of Philadelphia : —

"I have had some of the most delightful evidences of good accomplishing, and to be done, the past week. I am very happy, and wonder, while such holy rewards reach me

---

[1] The six insane asylums to which Miss Dix refers were the Worcester, Mass., Asylum, greatly enlarged; the Butler Asylum, in Providence, R. I., practically refounded; the Trenton and the Harrisburg Asylums, her own outright creation; the Utica, N. Y., Asylum, doubled in size.

To these is to be added the name of another, outside the territory of the United States, in Toronto, Canada West. As early as 1843, she had memorialized the "Provincial Parliament of Canada East and West Assembled," and had enlisted the energetic interest of the governor and other leading authorities in her scheme. Sir Charles Metcalfe wrote her that, but for her efforts and labors there, "Canada West would still have long needed a hospital for the insane." Of her work, also, in procuring the reformation of jails and almshouses, Horace Mann said that it would make as wonderful a record as her more especial work in behalf of the insane.

for effort and sacrifice, I should ever find myself faltering, or sighing for the life of repose, which, in the distance, seems to me so attractive."

And yet, as this narrative proceeds, it will be seen that this was as yet but the "day of small things" with her.

CHAPTER XIII.

"VENI, VIDI, VICI!"

THE campaign, or rather series of campaigns, which, for the next nine years, were to engage Miss Dix, promised to call for all her resources. They involved nothing less than carrying the legislatures of Indiana, Illinois, Kentucky, Tennessee, Missouri, Mississippi, Louisiana, Alabama, South Carolina, North Carolina, and Maryland, besides the establishment of two entirely new asylums in the British Provinces, — the one at Halifax, Nova Scotia, the other at St. John, Newfoundland. Fortunately, there have been preserved letters of various dates during those nine years, which will help to illustrate the spirit and success of her undertakings.

• Nothing, it is said, tends to develop so swiftly in reluctant minds a sense of personal responsibility as boldly and suddenly thrusting responsibility on them. Certainly, of this kind of tactics a striking instance is given in the ensuing letter of Miss Dix to Mrs. Hare, of Philadelphia : —

"RALEIGH, N. C., *November* 27, 1848.

"They say, 'Nothing can be done here!' I reply, 'I know no such word in the vocabulary I adopt!' It is declared that no word will be uttered in opposition to my claims, but that the Democrats, having banded as a party to vote for nothing that involves expense, will unite and silently vote down the bill. A motion was made to order

lighting the lamps in the portico of the Capitol, and voted
down by the Democrats. 'Ye love darkness because your
deeds are evil!' said a Whig, in great ire; and a voice
from the gallery responded piously, 'For ye are of your
father, the Devil!'

"This morning after breakfast several gentlemen called,
all Whigs, talked of the hospital, and said the most discouraging things possible. I sent for the leading Democrats;
went to my room and brought my Memorial, written under
the exhaustion of ten weeks' most fatiguing journeys and
labors. 'Gentlemen,' I said, 'here is the document I have
prepared for your assembly. I desire you, sir, to present
it,' handing it to a Democrat popular with his party, 'and
you, gentlemen,' I said, turning to the astonished delega-
tion, 'you, I expect, will sustain the motion this gentleman
will make to print the same.'

"They took leave, I do sincerely think, fully believing in
a failure, but I thought I could not have canvassed the
State for nothing. So the result proved. The Memorial
was presented; the motion to print twelve extra copies for
each member was offered and passed without one dissenting
vote. These steps are, then, safely and successfully made.
The deep waters are yet to pass, but

> 'My heart is fixed, and fixed my eye,
> And I am girded for the race;
> The Lord is strong, and I rely
> On his assisting grace.'"

Deep waters were there always to pass before bills,
demanding such large appropriations, present and
prospective, could be carried triumphantly through.
To persuade a party so bent on illustrating its tender sympathy with its constituents' hatred of tax-bills
as to forbid so much as lighting the lamps in the portico of the State Capitol, — to persuade such a party
of the wisdom and mercy of the act of lighting, and
feeding forever after with costly oil, a lamp of sacri-

fice which has ever since burned with such beneficent
ray as the Raleigh Insane Asylum, was no task to be
accomplished without a world of anxiety and toil.
Towards this great feat she was effectively helped by
the eloquent plea of Hon. James C. Dobbin, made, as
has already been stated, in response to the entreaty of
his dying wife that he would champion the cause of
the woman who had so tenderly cared for her. By
the close, therefore, of December, 1848, Miss Dix
could enthusiastically write to her friend, Mrs. Hare :

"Rejoice, rejoice with me! Through toil, anxiety, and
tribulation, my bill has passed : 101 ayes, 10 nays. I am
not well, though perfectly happy. I leave North Carolina
compensated a thousand fold for all labors by this great
success."

The following autumn and winter of 1849 found
Miss Dix in Montgomery, Ala., arduously engaged
in trying to carry the State Legislature. There, after
a beginning made under the most favorable auspices,
a series of delays and disappointments set in, finally
brought to a climax by the conflagration of the State
Capitol. A panic in favor of retrenchment at once
ensued, and the year's work seemed lost. Sadly, but
courageously, she was forced to write to her friend,
Miss Heath : —

"My affairs were in full tide of prosperous action, when
the disastrous conflagration of the State Capitol threw everything into indescribable confusion. I have determined, as
an adjournment is had till New Year, to save time by going
at once to fulfill some objects at Selma, Mobile, New Orleans, and Jackson, Miss. I have recollected amidst these
perplexities that God requires no more to be accomplished
than He gives time for performing, and I turn now more
quietly to my work up the Hill Difficulty. The summit is

cloud-capped, but I have passed amidst dark and rough
ways before, and shall not now give out."

By the opening of the new session, however, January
1, 1850, she was back again at her post in Montgomery.
Once again was the Hill Difficulty to prove insur-
mountable. The State was in no mood for increased
appropriations, and, though stanch friends stood by
her, the conflagration had given an impulse to the
cry for retrenchment which even her energy could not
make head against. In a weary hour she wrote her
friend, Mrs. Hare : —

"I think, after this year, I shall certainly not suffer myself to engage in any legislative affairs for a year. I can
conceive the state of mind which this induces to be like
nothing save the influences of the gambling table, or any
games of chance, — on such unlooked-for, and often trivial,
balances do the issues depend. There is just one chance in
a hundred that my bill will pass."

And yet, spite of her feeling of disappointment,
Miss Dix's faithful and untiring work had really carried the day in Alabama. Not during the session of
1850 was her bill to triumph, but in that of 1851–52
it went successfully through. Touched with her devotion, the Alabama State Medical Association now
came to the rescue, appointing a special committee to
follow up the strong impressions already made, and
placing at the head of this committee Dr. Lopez,
a man after her own heart, who labored with such
earnestness through the ensuing session that an appropriation of $100,000 was finally secured, and, after
this was exhausted, one of $150,000 more.

Scarcely a month, however, after the weary and
baffled letter in which Miss Dix had compared the

anxieties and vicissitudes of legislative affairs with the "influences of the gambling table," there came a happy turn of the wheel of fortune through the course of events in the neighboring State of Mississippi, which called out the following rejoicing letter to Miss Heath : —

"Twenty-four majority in the Senate, and eighty-one in the House, was something of a conquest over prejudice and the positive declaration and determination not to give a dime ! Therefore, to give $50,000 and 3,000,000 brick, besides the farm and foundations of the structure, is no small matter. Great was my surprise at the really beautiful vote of thanks, first by the legislature, then by the commissioners, and, finally, by the citizens. Legislature, commissioners, and citizens alike insisted on naming the hospital after me."

This last tribute of honor to her name, however, Miss Dix, on this as on so many other occasions, positively refused. The Speaker, in reply, informed her that, in deference to her views, the legislature had agreed to suspend immediate action, but added that "that was all Mississippians would concede on this point to one who belonged to the country, and was honored by all."

The letter, written from some unnamed point on the Mississippi, from which the last extract is made, contains likewise a picturesque sketch illustrative of the peculiar exposures to which travelers on river boats were in those days subjected.

"We have on our boat [she says] both cholera and malignant scarlet fever. To add to our various incidents, a quantity of gunpowder was left in charge of a raw Irishman, who was directed, at a given time and place, to load the cannon and fire a salute. One hundred miles away

from the point to be so honored, Pat, thinking the bore of
the cannon as good a place of deposit for the powder as he
could find, rammed it down. Then discovering that the
rain had wet the bore, he ran with alacrity to the furnace
and returned with a burning stick, thrusting it in after the
powder, 'to dry up the wather.' This it effected; but not
this alone, for of course the powder exploded, and certain
portions of Pat's arm and hand were sent in advance toward
the distant city."

Who took care of poor Pat and dressed his wounds
the letter does not say. Ten to one, it was Miss Dix
herself. . The last thing, with truth, that could have
been urged in her case was the so common reproach
brought against philanthropists, that, while full of
tenderness for humanity in the mass, they are indifferent toward individuals; or, as Dean Swift wittily
puts it, that, while loving the race, they do not care a
ha'penny for Tom, Dick, and Harry. Indeed, there
exists an amusing letter from her lifelong friend,
Dr. William G. Eliot, of St. Louis, in which he
comments on the unerring instinct with which, on
boarding a train or steamboat, she was sure, by a kind
of freemasonry, to detect any case of illness, poverty,
or bereavement, and before long to be found ministering to it. The letter, though written at a later date,
and at the time when Dr. Eliot was himself engrossed
in completing the endowment of Washington University, St. Louis, — that monument to his own persistency
and self-sacrifice, — certainly lights up the subject in
hand by an individual contribution to New Testament
interpretation, not to be found in any of the standard
commentaries.

"I often think [he says] of your thoughtful care of
that forlorn woman in the cars. It was a rebuke to me. I

can spend or be spent for an institution or for humanity;
but if I had seen the 'certain man between Jerusalem and
Jericho,' I should have been the priest or Levite.   Perhaps
they were at work for something on a *large scale*, and could
not see the *small;* or perhaps they had no relish for charity in detail."

In fact, while on this especial subject, it may be
well enough to note here that so numerous were the
instances Miss Dix encountered on trains and steamboats, not merely of the sufferings, but of the follies
and perversities, of human beings, that, dignified and
reticent as was her habitual demeanor, she at times
would speak her mind with a freedom that created a
marked sensation.   Once, for example, three young
ladies, dressed in the extreme of fashion, boarded the
train.   It was at that especial epoch in the natural
history of woman which may be accurately enough
described as the " wasp-waist period;" when, in humble imitation of that selected insect, to reduce to the
last degree of tenuity the slight film of connection
needful for self-preservation between the thoracic and
the abdominal regions of the human body seemed to
many young maidens the " chief end of man."   The
fashion was one Miss Dix held in peculiar abhorrence,
her own studies in physiology having apparently inspired her with an intellectual respect so profound
for the functions of heart, lungs, liver, and digestive
organs that she could no more tolerate the thought of
their cruel imprisonment in the steel cage of a binding corset than that of the outraged insane in their
own cages.   Now, it so happened that on a seat not
far from the part of the car in which the three fash-
ionably dressed young ladies had placed themselves
was a fourth young woman, whose ideas on the subject

of the human waist evidently coincided more nearly
with the antiquated and exploded notions of the Venus
of Milo. She became at once an object of ridicule to
her more advanced sisters, who talked her over with
an unrestrained freedom which excited indignation
on all sides. "Better be dead than out of fashion!"
finally exclaimed one of the three. Miss Dix could
endure their insolence no longer, and, suddenly rising,
interposed with her rich, impressive voice, "My dear,
if you lace as tight as you do now, you will not long
have the privilege of the choice. You will be *both*
dead and out of fashion."

To return, however, from this digression to the series
of campaigns Miss Dix was through those nine years
engaged with, principally in the Southern and Middle
States of the Union.

It had become her habit to work from the late
autumn till advancing spring in the South, and, when
the heat grew too overpowering, to transfer her field
of activity to more northern regions. As far to the
northeast as Halifax, Nova Scotia, and St. John, Newfoundland, do we, accordingly, in these times find her.
In Halifax especially is she now, year by year, bend-
ing all her energies toward the foundation of a cruelly
needed asylum. While zealously seconded in her efforts by the Bishop of Nova Scotia, it was, however,
to the untiring courage and devotion of Hon. Hugh
Bell that final success was chiefly due.

Among the correspondence left behind at the death
of Miss Dix, the letters of this humble-minded but, in
every fibre, noble man afford a beautiful picture of
a true friendship in the spirit. Of great practical
ability, and thoroughly versed in political matters, a
tendency, none the less, to despondency was a marked

characteristic of the man, and to Miss Dix, and the
sacred work she had put into his hands, he felt he
owed a happier trust in God and faith in human
nature.   His moral admiration for her was unbounded.
Again and again he attests how her inspiration had
made life worth living to him, through lifting it to a
disinterested aim.   She, he said, was " Minerva," he
" Telemachus."   As, therefore, one sure test of the
vitality of any mind is its power to raise up a host of
co-workers, infused with its own faith and will, it is
here to the point to present a few extracts from these
letters of Hon. Hugh Bell.   Only through the medium
of such living records can any fit idea be gained
alike of the discouragements attendant on such work
as Miss Dix was engaged on, in communities as yet
insensible to its real import, and of the nature of the
happy spiritual relations established between lofty
minds made one by a common humane aim.

" HALIFAX, NOVA SCOTIA, *April* 3, 1850.

"I am sorry to have to inform you that the result of
your efforts, and of our high expectations of the action of
our Legislature, has ended in a mere compliment to you.
However just and however sincere, the 'one thing needful' would, I am sure, have been much more satisfactory to
you. . . . I fear that even the thunders of Demosthenes
would scarce disturb our apathy and insensibility respecting
such subjects."

" HALIFAX, NOVA SCOTIA, *August* 10, 1850.

" As to the final accomplishment of our object, although
I must approve of the purpose never to abandon a post
undertaken in a good cause, I am almost like the Quaker
who said to his traveling companion, when in circumstances
of danger, ' I must go by thy faith, for mine is gone !' If
there be a final triumph, I shall, if I live, rejoice to join in
the song of victory, and to aid in weaving the chaplet around

your brows. Ridiculous as this may sound now, who can
tell what may yet be done! 'Impossible!' seems to be
now an obsolete term. We live in an age of wonders."

"HALIFAX, NOVA SCOTIA, *July* 5, 1853.

"I thank you, my noble-minded and generous friend, for
your kind, encouraging letter. Your vigorous, unwavering
faith and your firm, unflinching resolution shame away
doubt and inspire confidence. With you by my side (like
Minerva, in the shape of Mentor, by the side of Telemachus), even *I* would become courageous. We shall conquer yet! Do you not inwardly chuckle as I say *we?*
It is something like the bellows-blower's and the organist's
'Did n't we do well?' Never mind! if the *well* only
comes. No matter about the 'we'!"

"HALIFAX, NOVA SCOTIA, *August* 4, 1853.

"I called on the Admiral — or rather at the Admiralty
House — to leave my card for the Earl of Ellsmore (as in
duty bound). The old Admiral met me at the door very
cordially, shook hands, and then said, 'Where is Miss
Dix?' I replied, 'She left for home yesterday. She has
been to Sable Island and back!' He exclaimed in true
sailor style, 'She 's a gallant woman!'"

"HALIFAX, NOVA SCOTIA, ——, 1853.

"The session of our Legislature closed yesterday, and I
hasten to inform you that *something* has been done for the
object of our long and earnest effort: £15,000, equal to
$60,000, has been appropriated, with the condition that
£5,000 more be subscribed. . . . They have made me,
officially, the acting and chief commissioner. How strangely
and unexpectedly are things brought about! . . . I am
bound in gratitude to be thankful that Providence has
blessed my humble efforts in behalf of our afflicted fellow beings, but I feel myself so totally inadequate as to
knowledge of the right and best way of proceeding that I

shrink from it, and wish it were in abler hands. You see how much I need your aid. May I expect to have it? I cannot but think how much stronger your faith was than mine. You always said it would be done. I confess that I had given up hope, during my life."

A few instances like these will suffice in the attempt to record the series of moral successes achieved by Miss Dix during these nine memorable years. Tedious to the reader would it be to enlarge on them separately. Suffice it to say, that each succeeding year witnessed the original foundation of one or more State asylums, and was marked by public votes of thanks from fresh legislatures, and by letters of congratulation of the tenor of that in which Dr. R. S. Steuart, of Baltimore, wrote her, after the passage of her bill in Maryland: "Most cordially do I congratulate you on *your* success, because I am well convinced that no other means than yours could have produced this result. I am glad you have one more leaf added to the chaplet that so honorably adorns your brow."

Of a like tenor letters by the score, from governors, members of legislatures, and associations of physicians, were now continually pouring in upon her from all quarters of the Union. " We can do nothing without you! " was the universal cry. Her vitalized personality withdrawn, every movement languished; while, as soon as she was again upon the spot, the stragglers hurried back, the ranks closed up, the leaders headed the columns, and victory ensued. Confidently may it be asserted that on no other page of the annals of purely merciful reform can be read such a series of moral triumphs over apathy, ignorance, and cruel neglect as were in that space of time won by Miss Dix. Besides the memorable list of previous successes, there might now have been emblazoned on her battle flag of humanity the names of Lexington, Kentucky ; Hopkinsville, Kentucky ; Indianapolis, Indiana ; Jacksonville, Illinois ; Fulton, Missouri ; Nashville, Tennessee ; Jackson, Louisiana ; Raleigh, North Carolina ; Jackson, Mississippi ; Tuscaloosa, Alabama ; Baltimore, Maryland ; Washington, District of Columbia ; Halifax, Nova Scotia. It is easy to repeat these names, harder to make each one of them summon before the mind's eye the buildings, farms, pleasure-grounds, skilled and humane supervision of a great institution, taking into its protecting arms of mercy such numbers of the most wretched and abandoned of earth's creatures. Still, even in the case of the most sluggish imagination, it cannot be difficult to rise in partial sympathy, at least, with the enthusiasm with which, on the occasion of still another success in South Carolina, that profound and noble-minded scholar, Dr. Francis Lieber, wrote to Miss Dix from Columbia, S. C. : —

"TE DEUM LAUDAMUS!

" How do you feel ? Like a general after a victory ? Oh, no! much better. Like people after a shipwreck? You are saving thousands, and not by one act, but by planting institutions, and institutions of love. And when man does that, he comes nearest to his God of love and mercy.

"Deus tibi lux!   F. L."

Indeed, at this period, Miss Dix herself looked with a not unnatural wonder, mingled with devout humility, on the unexampled success of her career. She rarely spoke of her own achievements ; but in a letter of June, 1850, to her friend, Mrs. Rathbone, of Liverpool, England, there occur a few sentences which lift the veil of her habitual reserve and admit one within the sanctuary of her inmost feeling : —

" Shall I not say to you, dear friend, that my uniform success and influence are evidence to my mind that I am called by Providence to the vocation to which life, talents, and fortune have been surrendered these many years ? I cannot say, ' Behold, now, this great Babylon which I have builded ! ' but ' Lo ! O Lord, the work which Thou gavest thy servant ; she does it, and God in his benignity blesses and advances the cause by the instrument He has fitted for the labor.' "

After the record of such a series of achievements. and before farther proceeding with the story of the still more remarkable triumphs which awaited the subject of this biography in the future, it seems natural to pause here a moment, to try in some way to grasp the secret of her power.

Notwithstanding all her virile forces of intellect and will, the ideas entertained by Miss Dix on the subject of woman's work or woman's sphere of influence in the world were at this period, and indeed remained to the end of her life, of a character that would in these days be regarded by many superior women as decidedly conservative and of the old school. And yet in them lay the hidingplace of the peculiar power she exerted in the Southern and Southwestern States, then ruled by an ideal of womanhood which had in it many elements handed down from the days of chivalry.

Distinctly and emphatically, Miss Dix believed in woman's keeping herself aloof and apart from anything savoring of ordinary political action, as equally from every desire of material reward, whether in the way of money, place, or personal distinction. She must be the incarnation of a purely disinterested idea

appealing to universal humanity, irrespective of party
or sect ; at once a voice of tender supplication for the
outcasts of the earth and their impassioned champion,
capable of flaming with sacred fire. From large numbers of the politicians with whom she was necessarily
brought into close contact, carefully as she hid the
feeling from them, she yet shrank with a distinct
moral repulsion. "They are," she declared, "the
meanest and lowest party demagogues, shocking to
say, — the basest characters."

By nature, she herself was, as one of her truest and
most admiring friends said of her, "aristocratic in
every fibre ; " that is, in the original and more literal
signification of the word as emphasizing faith in the
divine hierarchy of intellect, heart, and conscience.
Instinctively she craved and enjoyed intercourse with
the finer and higher types of humanity, and drew back
in sensitive aversion from every shape of ugliness, vul-
garity, and self-seeking. "Anthophila," the flower-
lover, was the Greek name with which, in those days,
the eminent publicist, Dr. Francis Lieber, usually addressed her ; and the name held true not merely of
her love of flowers, but of everything characterized
by social grace and refinement, by intellectual distinction, or by beauty of manners, spirit, and character. This side of her nature she had literally to cru-
cify in a great part of her work. A Christlike sense
of compassion for human misery and of fiery indignation at the infliction of pain ; an intense intellectual
revolt from the brute irrational chaos of society which,
under the light that had now broken, permitted such
evils longer to exist, — these, together with a daily
yearning supplication, "Thy kingdom come, thy will
be done on the *earth* as it is done in heaven," were

the only powers that nerved her to tolerate perpetual contact with degraded forms of misery, and with a class of public characters, many of whom were offensive to her through and through.

The natural result of this position, early adopted and inflexibly adhered to by Miss Dix, was that, especially among the ardent and impulsive peoples of the Southern and Southwestern States, she gradually came to be regarded as a being apart from ordinary humanity. Very striking is it to turn over old files of Tennessee, Georgia, Alabama, and other Southern newspapers, and read the glowing language in which they speak of the arrival within their borders of that " gracious lady," that " crown of human nature," that " chosen daughter of the Republic," that "angel of mercy."

On issues aside from her own self-consuming passion she was careful to antagonize no one. Even on the "slavery question," then becoming ever more hotly agitated, and awakening the fiercest hatred against all who belonged to the North, she persistently held her peace. What her view and action on the subject would have been, had she been left to the natural impulses of her own merciful heart, may be readily enough inferred. But she entered the South under bonds to keep the peace, — bonds not personal and selfish, but disinterested and sympathetic. One word from her lips in the way of the mildest reproval, even, and every State south of the Susquehanna would have been sealed to her. Her word would have effected nothing; but it would have left thousands of forlorn wretches to languish, without a champion, in cells and chains, in filth and misery. No, she felt she had her own God-appointed work, so vast and far-reaching in its consequences that her feeble hands

could but grasp its outermost skirts. In a very literal
sense poor Simmons's God had become passionately
identified with her own God, and "the prayers of
agony shrieked from his dreary abode" now filled her
ears till she could hear no other cry.

A letter of Dr. Francis Lieber, written as far back
as November 5, 1846, from Columbia, S. C., gives expression to his own sense of the unique, moral, and
imaginative position occupied by Miss Dix in the work
to which she had consecrated her life.

"You as a woman [he said] have a great advantage
over us, for with the firmness, courage, and strength of a
male mind you unite the advantage of a woman. Savarin,
at the head of the French police, told Napoleon, with reference to Mad. de Cayler, that he could not master the
women. This was in a bad cause; but the same holds good
in a good. You do not excite the same opposition ; no one
can suspect you of ambitious party views, and you can dare
more because people do not dare to refuse you many a
thing they would not feel ashamed of refusing to any one
of our sex. Therefore take care of yourself!"

How strong, indeed, was the impression at this
period exerted by her personality on a mind of the
range of Dr. Lieber's, is manifest in the language
of one of his own letters to George S. Hillard, of
Boston : —

"Miss, Dix has been with us again, and leaves us to-
morrow. . . . She is greatly exhausted, and I always fear
to hear that she has succumbed somewhere in a lonely
place. What a heroine she is! May God protect her !
Over the whole breadth and length of the land are her footsteps, and where she steps flowers of the richest odor of
humanity are sprouting and blooming as on an angel's
path. I have the highest veneration for her heart and will
and head."

CHAPTER XIV.

AMONG the inevitable burdens now precipitated on
the shoulders of a woman as frail in body as Miss
Dix, no slight additional an one grew out of the fact
that so great was the confidence reposed in her practical ability that again and again, after having, at a
great tax on her strength, carried a bill through a
legislature, she was farther urged to shoulder the responsibility of selecting a fit site for the projected asylum, and of deciding on the character of the buildings
to be erected. It was a task she was unwilling to
decline, for, in the wide-spread ignorance prevailing
in those days, she clearly saw how easily the successful
working of a hospital might be made or marred by the
nature of its location or its plan of construction.

In fact, a hundred questions had to be raised and
wisely answered. Was the soil wet or dry, was it
adapted to furnish the patients with fit outdoor work,
was there an abundant supply of pure water, was
there due variety of sunshine and shade, was the location easily accessible by rail or water for the delivery
of fuel and provisions , finally, were the surroundings
attractive and the scenery of a character to "minister," through its charm, "to a mind diseased"? All
these were problems demanding careful observation, and
to the end of wisely solving them Miss Dix kept herself
in constant touch with the class of exceptionally able

experts who, as superintendents, were now steadily
evolving the plans which for a period of many years
were to make the American insane asylums the model
asylums of the civilized world.

As early as at the date, in 1845, of her success in
securing the foundation of a hospital at Harrisburg,
Penn., Mr. James Lesley had written her : —

" You may rest assured that to Mr. Trego, as to all the
other commissioners, your wishes on the subject of site and
buildings will be law. He declared that no man nor woman
other than yourself, from Maine to Louisiana, could have
passed the bill under the discouraging circumstances with
which you had to contend."

Of the delight, indeed, she at first took in the additional labor thus imposed on her she writes in a
spirit of fairly girlish exuberance to her friend, Miss
Heath : —

" My farm is much liked, and it would not be surprising if I should throw up a tabernacle inwoven with green
branches, and count the bricks as they are placed one upon
another till the fabric be complete."

To the dew and freshness of the early morning,
however, there inevitably succeeds the heat and burden of the day, and this contrasting experience Miss
Dix was destined to encounter in many trying ways as
time wore on. A site once judiciously chosen for the
real end in view, then too often began the worst tug
of war.

As a rule, real-estate transactions react hardly more
felicitously in bringing out the higher attributes of
human nature than, as is traditionally asserted, does
the trading of horses. Miss Dix naturally wanted
the best procurable site for the benefit of the patients ;

the owner of the site wanted the best procurable
price for his own benefit. Miss Dix did her best to
ignore all local questions of the town or county that
was to be pecuniarily helped by the establishment of
an asylum within its borders; the town or county,
on the contrary, did its best to have this made the
first consideration. Nor was this all. Rich proprietors of country-seats, with stronger prejudices against
" madhouses " than even against pauper burial-fields,
banded together with all the power of wealth and influence to keep every such institution out of their
neighborhoods. Thus continually was she brought
into sharp collision with some of the most distasteful
features of human nature.

In the State of Maryland, for example, she, on this
last especial score, found herself subjected to very
rude and offensive treatment at the hands of certain
wealthy land-owners. So high, however, was the respect in which she was held, and so dignified, even
while immovable as a rock, was her demeanor, that
here, as elsewhere, a reaction set in, when it was seen
how disinterestedly she stood for the cause of mercy,
while her opponents stood solely for considerations of
personal selfishness. Thus from Annapolis, Md., her
stanch friend, Hon. Thomas Donaldson, was soon able
to write her : —

"There is a soul of goodness in things evil, and you have
reason to thank the malice of your opponents for the sub-
stantial aid which they give to the cause you advocate.
The attack of ——, coming from a masked battery too, has
raised you up friends that before were opponents, and has
added the impulse of indignation to the cool convictions of
your friends. The hospital never was so strong in the
Legislature of Maryland. The letter of Teackle Wallis,

printed in the Appendix of the Report, is really admirable, and it tells with great effect here. Every sentence cuts as cleverly and as cleanly as the Saladin's sword."

At times, none the less, there grew out of these self- ish and sordid complications incidents so honorable to human nature, and so strikingly illustrative of the persuasive moral eloquence of the subject of this biog- raphy, that it is a delight to record them. Such a one is the following.

No one who has ever visited the Hospital for the Insane of the Army and Navy, at Washington, D. C., could have set foot within its grounds without exclaim- ing, "This is the ideal site for an asylum!" Situated at the junction of two broad and noble rivers, the Po- tomac and the East Branch; commanding a superb view by land and water; gently sloping on all sides from its highest elevation so as to secure perfect drain- age; and embracing within its bounds the most varied charm of wood and pasture, it seems to unite every conceivable advantage. Now, at the date of the pas- sage by Congress, in 1852, of an appropriation for founding an asylum for the insane of the army and navy, this beautiful domain was the private property of Mr. Thomas Blagden, and, in carefully examining the whole country surrounding Washington, Dr. John H. Nichols, who had labored indefatigably toward the passage of the bill, had made up his mind that there was no other site at all comparable with it. Mr. Blagden, however, turned a deaf ear to every proposi- tion on the part of Dr. Nichols to buy it. The estate had become endeared to him through the exceptional beauty of its situation, and was, moreover, the espe- cial pride of his wife and daughters. Besides, the full amount appropriated by Congress for the purchase of a site was but $25,000, and on no consideration, Mr. Blagden insisted, would he part with the property at less than $40,000.

One day, after having exhausted every personal effort, and thoroughly depressed in spirits, Dr. Nichols went in to see Miss Dix. "There is nothing more to be done!" he exclaimed; "we shall have to give the matter up; and it is the finest site for a hospital in the world!"

Miss Dix listened without excitement, and then replied, in her usual quiet tone, "We must try what can be done!" Seeking a personal interview with Mr. Blagden, so earnestly and movingly did she reason with him to surrender for the future good of thousands of his suffering fellow-creatures what was so precious, indeed, to him and his family, but to one household only, that the appeal proved irresistible, and he gave her his promise of the estate at the amount appropriated by Congress. None the less the parting with it cost him a fearful wrench; for on Dr. Nichols's calling on him, the next day, with the requisite papers to sign, Mr. Blagden was found walking the room to and fro, weeping and wringing his hands in a half-hysteric condition. "I don't want to part with it!" he kept reiterating. "It is dear to me and dear to my family! But I won't break my word to Miss Dix, — I won't break my word! I told her she should have it, and she shall have it!"

Such scenes as this do honor to human nature. Indeed, it would be hard to instance a more beautiful tribute to the power of consecrated womanhood than is embodied in the following letter, so simple, hushed, and awestruck in its tone, sent to Miss Dix by Mr. Blagden, the evening of the day on which she had thus closed in, in Jacob's angel wrestle, with his deepest nature.

"WASHINGTON, *November,* 13, 1852.

" DEAR MADAM, — Since seeing you to-day, I have had no other opinion (and Mrs. B. also) than that I must not stand between you and the beloved farm, regarding you, as I do, as the instrument in the hands of God to secure this very spot for the unfortunates whose best earthly friend you are, and believing sincerely that the Almighty's blessing will not rest on, nor abide with, those who may place obstacles in your way.

" With Mrs. Blagden's and my own most friendly regards,

" Very respectfully,

" Your obedient servant,

THOMAS BLAGDEN."

Onerous and exacting as were the responsibilities thus imposed on Miss Dix through the appeals now constantly made to her by officials of the many States in which she had secured appropriations for asylums, to assume the further task of advising with the commissioners on all matters of selection of sites and plans of construction, still, even these grave burdens were, perhaps, exceeded in weight by another class of duties soon inevitably thrust upon her.

What had she really been bringing about through this series of unexampled legislative successes? Nothing less than the actual creation within the United States of the conditions for the foundation and development of a great school of trained experts in the treatment of insanity. Before those ten or twelve years of rapid, Napoleonic victories, there had existed — except in a few scattered places — neither the call nor the opportunity for practically enlisting and de-

ploying this especial order of medical talent. Now
fast grew up a wide demand for it, a great school of
practice in which to acquire and exercise the requisite
knowledge and skill. The attention of large numbers
of able medical minds was thus turned in a new direction and solicited to a new field.

Who should be superintendents, assistant physicians, stewards, attendants, and nurses in all these
fast-springing-up asylums? On wise and judicious
appointments hung the whole success of the new undertaking. What more natural, then, than that in
these as yet inexperienced States governors and legis-
lators should turn for counsel to the woman whose
commanding moral genius had summoned into being
so many new institutions? Steadily the amount of
patronage placed in her hands grew in volume; and
here her remarkable judgment of character and capacity revealed itself in its full strength. It is the
responsible privilege of a biographer to go through an
immense mass of papers, the contents of which are of
too private a character to be made known to the public. Perfectly allowable, however, is it to say here
that a list so large could be drawn up of men, later
on achieving a national reputation as authorities on
insanity, who, in these and subsequent years, owed
their appointments solely to the recommendation of
Miss Dix, that the number and character of the names
on it would awaken wide-spread surprise.

Very rich was life now becoming to Miss Dix in human relationships which in a measure relieved the
strain put upon her by the more arduous and painful
side of her work. Her range of acquaintance with
the best men and women in all parts of the land had
grown to be immense, and, homeless herself, she was

everywhere welcomed under their roofs. She had filled life with new zest to many, who but for her leadership would have found no avenue of usefulness open to them; and as the nature of her work involved the enlistment of the largest possible number of co-workers, to help add attraction to the at first bare and unhomelike asylum wards, she suffered no chance to pass of stimulating them to contributions of all kinds.

Even on the children of the various homes she visited, she never failed to impress the idea of how much they could do in aid of the blessed cause. Old toys, puzzles, musical boxes, nodding Chinese mandarins, collections of minerals, seaweeds, pressed flowers, butterflies, eggs, birdsnests, — nothing, she showed them, would come amiss in the way of amusing poor demented patients, and turning their minds away from their melancholy broodings. Numberless the prized collections that under the spell of her persuasive eloquence were thus surrendered by little boys and girls; as, equally numberless, the juvenile tears that were shed, after the spell of that eloquence was withdrawn and the instincts of the sweetness of private ownership revived in their little breasts. Amusing stories are to this day told, by persons now well advanced in years, of the miserly eagerness with which, as boys and girls, they secreted days ahead their precious treasures, on the alarming news being revealed to them that Miss Dix was expected in the house. Indeed, it may be seriously questioned whether sometimes a deep-rooted repugnance to charity and all its works was not thus lodged in certain of their minds through demands for a pitch of self-sacrifice beyond the immaturity of view as to the sacred claims of insanity usually prevalent at the age of six or eight.

A simple impossibility was it that a character of the steady intensity and force of will, which alone rendered possible such a career as that of Miss Dix, should not at times have inspired a certain sense of awe. The pace at which great souls go takes away the breath of average mortals, and they cry out at the strain that is put on their feebler powers. And yet, in the way of illustration of how completely closer intercourse with her served to dispel this fear, the following letter from Mrs. Louisa J. Hall, widow of the late Rev. Edward B. Hall, D. D., of Providence, R. I., gives a charming picture. The letter was written in answer to a request for any recollections she might feel inclined to furnish of the far-away days when she was brought into personal contact with Miss Dix : —

"CAMBRIDGE, MASS., *May* 17, 1889.

"I think it was in 1844 that my husband came to me in the nursery, and said Miss Dix was below. I declined going down, thinking she had merely called to consult him. 'No, she had come to stay all night, and would like to see me in the nursery!' I thought it an unceremonious proceeding, did not like a woman that went about a 'self-appointed critic,' had heard that she was 'cross' when she kept school, and I was a prejudiced woman, shame to me! She made her appearance, and one look at that calm, gentle face had its effect. Then only a word of ladylike apology in a sweet, low voice, and I began to feel the *gift* she had.

"I was mending my boys' socks, and she quietly took up one and began darning with a skillful hand, talking most pleasantly of the beautiful city of Providence, and of some Boston minister we both knew. For two hours we sat together, and not one word about the insane or her 'mission,' when I had anticipated that she would talk of nothing else.

This foolish, obstinate conservative was conquered by the force of that beautiful, strong nature, shining through a genuine womanhood. After dinner, she said to my husband, 'Now I am at your service,' and he immediately took her to see some persons interested in her work. She stayed some days with us, never introducing the subject, but ready to give information, and tell us of facts that made us bless the day she was born, and the day when she. found what work the Lord had for her.

"As I am a thorough woman, you must let me speak of her dress. She traveled all over the country with a moderate valise in her hand, and wearing a plain gray traveling dress with snow-white collar and cuffs. Her trunk was sent a week ahead with the necessary changes of linen, etc., and one plain black silk dress for special occasions. Neatness in everything indicated her well-directed mind. And my acquaintance with her helped me ‾on the upward way from extreme conservatism."

These opposing sides of the impression made on others by Miss Dix — the impression on the one hand of a certain rigid inflexibility, a certain self-withdrawn and awe-inspiring element in her nature, and, on the other, of a winning sweetness when the fountains of feeling were broken up from within — were inevitably felt by all who came in contact with her, and were never to the end of life thoroughly harmonized in her nature. Sometimes the one, sometimes the other, stood out separate; on other occasions they were fused in a strong and gracious unity. Her moral will aroused and at the forefront, she was adamant. "To have Miss Dix suddenly arrive at your asylum," said the eminent Dr. Isaac Ray, of Providence, "and find anything neglected or amiss, was considerably worse than an earthquake. Not that she said anything on the spot, but one felt something ominous suspended in the very air." Then again, her sensibilities touched, she was overflowing with tenderness and compassion. Lifelong invalids testified to a power of uplifting sympathy in her — as of one over whom all the waves and billows had likewise gone — possessed by the rarest few. On the great occasions, however, when these opposing characteristics were molten together in the furnace of the sacred cause for which she alternately plead and flamed at the bar of public bodies, then truly was she irresistible. Thus one seems to be dealing with so many distinct personalities. Those who met her silent and uncommunicative, after the exhaustion of one of her legislative campaigns, passed judgment on her as self-centered and unsocial; those who felt her soothing touch in the sick-room called her a ministering angel; those who beheld her organizing victory, and riding triumphant over obstacles that would have disheartened the bravest, hailed in her a modern Joan of Arc.

This diversity of judgment, and one of the natural reasons for it, find striking expression in the following extract from a beautiful memorial tribute written for the "Home Journal," of New York, by Mrs. S. C. P. Miller, of Princeton, N. J., and first printed September 11, 1889: —

" It was a long time before I could realize that she was indeed a woman having much in common with the rest of us. I saw her only when she was strong and self-collected, and believed that to be her normal condition. But there came a day when I got a new insight into her nature. I was in Richmond, and she, on a mission farther South, halted there and sent a note for me to come and see her. I went to the hotel immediately, was ushered into her room, and there found such a Miss Dix as I had never dreamed of. Overstrain of mind and body, destroying her calm exterior and bearing away the support of her high purpose, had left her stretched upon a sofa, utterly weak, nervous, and tearful. Not a bit of the heroism was left ; only the tried woman of a type I knew full well. Amazed at her condition, I bent over her with a tenderness before unknown, and a new bond of sympathy was established between us ; so strange is it, yet so true, that tears bring all women to the same level."

And yet, when at the lowest point of physical prostration, Miss Dix could herself write to a friend : " I shall be well enough when I get to Kentucky or Alabama. The tonic I need is the tonic of opposition. That always sets me on my feet."

Among the many persons of distinction with whom, at this period of her career, Miss Dix came in intimate contact, was the once famous Swedish novelist, Frederika Bremer, then on a visit to the United ·States. Herself suffering from exhaustion brought on by overwork and on the edge of utter collapse, Miss Bremer felt strongly drawn to the especial type of ministering angel whose life had been consecrated to the victims of nervous wreck. Of the various letters she addressed from point to point to her American friend, there are two or three which throw such light both on the impression made on her by the personality of Miss Dix, and on the nature of the far-reaching schemes of benevolent action, outside of her own country, already engaging the ardent mind of the latter, as to be well worthy of introduction here : —

" CONEY ISLAND, near NEW YORK, *August*, 1850.

" There now she comes, heaping burning — not coals, but flowers — on my guilty head ! Alas, dear Miss Dix ! not so guilty as poor in carrying out by the hand what the heart and thought dictate. . . . I am now about to start for my Western journey, and am full of gratitude for the delightful memories that I have gathered both in the North and South from both man and nature. Not the least delightful of these is that of a moonlight evening on the shores of the Patapsco and the Chesapeake Bay, where I heard the story of a simple life beginning, as the river before me, from a little stream born of a heavenly fountain, and widening, widening, as it ran forth through the valleys and fields and cities, to a large, rich water, opening to mingle with the waters of the ocean, and blessing and bearing fruit to every shore as it went along in the still night, looked upon alone by the clear light of heaven. That life and the river in the moonlight have become one image in my soul, and a bright and blessed spot it remains there, to be looked upon, to be enjoyed, many a time during the flying and trying years of life."

In a second letter, however, written by Miss Bremer, November 2, 1850, from Cincinnati, Ohio, a cloud has come across the fair sky, and the writer is found taking decided stand against a project already shaping itself in Miss Dix's mind, — the project, namely, that when she should have finished her immediate work in America through the successful foundation of asylums in the various States, she would seek a new field of labor in Europe, and especially in those parts of it where the treatment of insanity was in the most backward condition. To Frederika Bremer, the idea of any good being effected, in the way of awakening the people of Sweden to a sense of their duties toward any class of their own population, by a foreigner, and above all a foreigner entirely ignorant of the language, seemed wholly romantic. Her national pride took offense at the bare proposition, as equally did that of the Swedish Nightingale, Jenny Lind. Feebly, however, did she measure the heroic spirit and range of mind of the woman whose later career was so marvelously to illustrate the truth that God has made of " one blood all the dwellers on the earth," and that faith and love find easy flight over every barrier of sea, mountain, language, race, or religious creed. Still, Frederika Bremer's sensitiveness was natural enough to average, restricted humanity. Only she forgot that the " Chinese Wall," to which she will be found alluding, dated back to an antiquated order of military defenses, regarded by her invincible friend as only fit to keep out Tartars: —

"CINCINNATI, OHIO, *November* 2, 1850.

" Sweden lacks neither goodwill nor means. What is wanted there is energy and impulse of will; and *that*, a foreigner unknown in the country, and herself not knowing its language and forms of government, could not give. Jenny Lind is right in that opinion. As things now stand, it would be easier for you to climb the Chinese Wall than to work any good *personally* for the unfortunate insane in Sweden. But believe me, dear Miss Dix, what you have done, what you are doing in America, will, when properly disclosed, — as it ought to be, and must be, to Sweden, — work more for a bettering of the insane asylums there than a gift of ten millions could in their behalf. The power of the Idea, and the power of example, are the great movers of our time, and go from heart to heart, from land to land, with electric shock.

" Most thankful am I, dear Miss Dix, for the interest you express for me and my health. Thank God, I am very well now. You certainly need more to take care of your health than I now of mine. But you are as a general on a battlefield, and cannot care for life till the battle is over and victory won. May it be soon for you! "

In Miss Bremer's third letter, written the following

year from the Island of Cuba, she makes ample
amends. All wounds of aggrieved national pride are
now healed, and in a realm of free imagination, from
which all prosaic obstacles of alien languages and
forms of government are eliminated, she creates for
Miss Dix an ideal Utopia over which she shall be in-
stalled as queen : —

"St. Amelia Estate, Cuba, *March* 17, 1851.

" If I had rule on earth, Cuba — this beautiful Antille —
should be transformed into a great Maison de Santé, a home
for the sickly and feeble. There they should sit in their rock-
ing-chairs under the palms and the tamarinds, and breathe
the delightful air of this island (which I cannot think was
better in Paradise), be caressed by the soft, loving breeze,
and drink in it, as in Olympian nectar, new health, new life.
And you should be the queen here, and have a cabinet of
ladies, kind and beautiful, such as I know several in the
United States, who should chiefly officiate as nurses for the
sick, as noble Valkyrias and healing goddesses for those
slain or wounded in the battle of life."

Not unlikely the majority of readers of this last letter would set down Frederika Bremer as a far more
imaginative woman than Dorothea Lynde Dix. So
widely is genuine constructive power of imagination .
confused with the activity of a mere dreamy fancy,
that the number is legion who think a more vigorous
exercise of the " faculty divine" demanded for the
creation of an airy ideal Utopia like this, than for
first summoning before the mind's eye, and then sub-
stantializing in massive buildings and wide-ranging
farms, parks, and gardens, the actual " Retreats "
from a harsh and cruel world, which Miss Dix provided for such hosts of sufferers. In reality, the
" noble Valkyrias," of whom Frederika Bremer speaks,

" healing goddesses for those slain or wounded in the battle of life," were far more profoundly conceived, than by herself, by the heroic woman to whom she wrote. She knew, out of stern experience, that the true Valkyrias are fateful and awful powers, who must first stride the blast and sweep to the rescue through the din and shrieks of the battlefield, before they can think to reach, and bear off in their arms to the Valhalla of rest, the fallen warriors trampled in dust and blood.

CHAPTER XV.

A LETTER of Miss Dix, already quoted in Chapter XIII., will be recalled, in which, in an hour of weariness, she wrote: "I think, after this year, I shall certainly not suffer myself to engage in any legislative affairs for a year. I can conceive the state of mind which this induces to be like nothing save the influences of the gambling table, or any games of chance, — on such unlooked-for, and often trivial, balances do the issues depend."

The stakes for which she had now for years been playing were indeed pecuniarily enormous, involving in the case of each separate asylum from fifty to two hundred thousand dollars at the start, not to speak of the further appropriations for permanent expenses and for enlargement that must inevitably ensue. They were stakes, moreover, on the winning or losing of which hung the devout thanksgiving of a merciful heart at relief now close at hand for cruel shapes of human misery, or the silent torture that the old, sad story must go on unchanged.

In comparison, however, with the far vaster stake she was now about to play for, — no longer in the halls of State legislative assemblies, but on the arena of the Senate and House of Representatives of the United States, — these previous ventures involved but trivial issues.

To set the subject here to be entered on in a clear light, it will be necessary to go back several years in the story of Miss Dix's career. So manifold were the operations she was in the habit of carrying on, at the same time, that there is no other feasible way but to set apart certain of them and treat them as distinct episodes.

Already, at as early a date as 1848, had she memorialized Congress for a grant of 5,000,000 acres of the public domain, the proceeds of the sale of which were to be set apart as a perpetual fund for the care of the indigent insane; the sum total of the fund to be divided, in proportion with their respective ratas of population, among the thirty States of the Union. Partial failure in her first attempt to secure this grant had only acted on her in the way of that especial tonic which she declared always set her on her feet — the tonic of opposition, — and so led her, at a subsequent session of Congress, to raise the amount of her plea to the colossal sum of 12,225,000 acres.

It is easy to write down the numerals which stand for 12,225,000 acres of land. A far harder thing is it to stretch the imagination to the point of conceiving what they really imply. They mean nearly 20,000 square miles of territory. They mean an area nearly three times the size of the State of Massachusetts, an area more than a third as large as England, with Wales included. Could she carry this great measure, Miss Dix felt that the work of her life in her own land would be permanently crowned. A steady income, growing in volume with the growth of population in the country, would thus be secured in perpetuity for the most wretched of the children of earth.

To bring the actual situation clearly before the
mind, a short explanation is here needful of the relations borne by the Federal Government of the United
States to the disposition of the enormous areas of the
public lands.

The original thirteen Revolutionary States, stretched
along the Atlantic seaboard, — the States which had
fought for and achieved the independence of the
United States, — had always maintained a claim to
share severally in the vast areas of unoccupied lands
lying to the westward, which they had individually
ceded to the Federal Government.   Through subsequent purchase and conquest, this area had grown to
continental proportions ; and as new territories were
from time to time formed into States, and admitted as
integral members of the Union, the same claims were
fully accorded to them.   Under the condition of a
public treasury overflowing with revenue from sales
of the public domain to settlers, the representatives in
Congress had, every now and then, deemed it wise to
distribute this money surplus among the several
States.   Further, to the new States almost exclusively,
immense tracts of land, reaching in 1845 an aggre-
gate of 134,704,982 acres, had been granted for the
purpose of rapidly developing a system of general
education and of internal improvements.   And yet
there still remained unassigned more than one thousand millions of acres of the public domain.

In the main, the disposition thus far made of the
public lands had been judicious, and, especially, had
laid the foundation of an excellent school system
in the newly formed and thinly populated States.
The immense prizes, however, thus opened up to the
schemes of private speculators, internal improvement

companies, and projectors of new lines of railway, had finally inflamed the cupidity of thousands. Congress was besieged for grants of land, demanded on an incredibly lavish scale.

It was the sight of this pushing horde of greedy adventurers, assailing Congress through the Representatives of their various States, that first inspired Miss Dix with the thought, " Why cannot I too go in with this selfish, struggling throng, and plead for God's poor and outcast, that they shall not be forgotten ? " From the outset, she felt that the undertaking was to be a most formidable one. She had nothing to offer in the way of material reward, no vote to barter, no place to promise, no self-interested schemers to enlist in bolstering up her project, — nothing to fall back on but the plea for mercy from a woman's lips.

It was on June 23, 1848, that her first Memorial was submitted to Congress. Already had she taken such precautionary steps and secured such influential friends among leading Representatives from the various States in which her name had now become a household word, that the Memorial was at once referred to a select committee, and five thousand copies of it were ordered to be printed for the use of the Senate. Her prayer thus far was for a grant of 5,000,000 acres for " the relief and support of the indigent insane in the United States."

Greatly to the advantage of the effect produced by this new Memorial was it that now Miss Dix addressed herself, not to the legislature of a single State, but to the Congress of them all. She was thus enabled to focus in a single appeal the whole dire story of her investigations throughout the length and breadth of the land.

" Present hospital provision [she declares] relieves (if we do not include those institutions not considered *remedial*) less than three thousand seven hundred patients. Where are the remainder, and in what condition? More than eighteen thousand are unsuitably placed in private dwellings, in jails, in poorhouses, and other often most wretched habitations. . . . I have myself seen *more than nine thousand idiots, epileptics, and insane in these United States, destitute of appropriate care and protection ;* and of this vast and miserable company, sought out in jails, in poorhouses, and in private dwellings, there have been hundreds, — nay, rather thousands, — bound with galling chains, bowed beneath fetters and heavy iron balls attached to drag chains, lacerated with ropes, scourged with rods, and terrified beneath storms of profane execrations and cruel blows ; now subject to gibes and scorn and torturing tricks, now abandoned to the most loathsome necessities, or subject to the vilest and most outrageous violations. These are strong terms, but language fails to convey the astonishing truths. I proceed to verify this assertion, commencing with the State of Maine."

Every State is then, seriatim, arraigned. The amount of eye-witness testimony piled up is appalling. And it strikes home all round. The member from Georgia cannot turn superiorly on the member from Rhode Island, and, quoting the case of Abram Simmons, cry, " This, then, is the state of civilization and humanity in your benighted region ! " Swiftly the member from Rhode Island could retort : " Go on a few pages farther, and see how edifying is the example set by your enlightened State ! " Let us look over the shoulder of the member from Georgia, reading with him the following case in his own State, and then ask how far he would have felt inclined to protract the sectional controversy : —

" It was an intensely hot day when I visited F. He was confined in a roofed pen, which inclosed an area of about eight feet by eight. The interstices between the unhewn logs admitted the scorching rays of the sun then, as they would open the way for the fierce winds and drenching rains or frosts of the later seasons. The place was wholly bare of furniture, — *no bench, no bed, no clothing.* His food, which was of the coarsest kind, was pushed through spaces between the logs. ' Fed like the hogs, and no better!' said a stander-by. His feet had been frozen by exposure to cold in the winter past. Upon the shapeless stumps, aided by his arms, he could raise himself against the logs of his pen. In warm weather, this wretched place was cleansed out once a week or fortnight; not so in the colder seasons. ' We have men called,' said his sister, ' and they go in and tie him with ropes and throw him on the ground and throw water on him, and my husband cleans out the place.' But the expedient to prevent his freezing in winter was the most strangely horrible. In the centre of the pen was excavated a pit, six feet square, and deep ; the top was closed over securely : and into this ghastly place, entered through a trap-door, was cast the maniac, there to exist till the returning warm weather induced his care-taker to withdraw him ; there, without heat, without light, without pure air, was left the pining, miserable maniac, whose piteous groans and frantic cries might move to pity the hardest heart."

Fortifying, through the testimony of leading experts on insanity in America and Europe, her own insistence on the impossibility of coping with these terrible evils except by the establishment of scientifically conducted asylums, Miss Dix concluded her Memorial with a few strong words of appeal : —

" Should your sense of moral responsibility seek support in precedents for guiding present action, I may be permitted

to refer to the fact of liberal grants of common national
property made, in the light of a wise discrimination, to
various institutions of learning ; also to advance in the new
States common school education, and to aid two seminaries
of instruction for the deaf and dumb, viz., that in Hartford,
Connecticut, and the school at Danville, in Kentucky, etc.
But it is not for one section of the United States that I
solicit benefits, while all beside are deprived of direct advantages. . . . I ask relief for the East and for the West, for
the North and for the South. . . . I ask for the people that
which is already the property of the people, but possessions so holden that it is through your action alone they
can be applied as now urged. . . . I confide to you the
cause and the claims of the destitute, without fear or distrust.   I ask, for the thirty States of the Union, 5,000,000
acres of land, of the many hundreds of millions of public
lands, appropriated in such a manner as shall assure the
greatest benefits to all who are in circumstances of extreme
necessity, and who, through the providence of God, are
wards of the nation, claimants on the sympathy and care of
the public, through the miseries and disqualifications brought
upon them by the sorest afflictions with which humanity can
be visited.   Respectfully submitted,

" D. L. D.

"-WASHINGTON, *June* 23, 1848."

All omens at the start looked auspicious, as finds
expression in the two following letters of Miss Dix to
her cherished Philadelphia friend, Mrs. Robert Hare :

" WASHINGTON, D. C., *July* 5, 1848.

" For more than three weeks I have been ill with in-
fluenza.   While unable to go out, I wrote my Memorial to
Congress.   I can only say it embodies facts ; as a literary
effort it is open to severe criticism.   Five thousand extra
copies ordered to be printed.

" I expressed my wish for a *Select Committee.* They
said it was unusual.   I urged, and finally said, I must at

least be suffered to propose it. I wrote out my list and carried my measure entirely, — Mr. Benton, Mr. Dix, Mr. Harnegan, Mr. Bell, and Mr. Davis, of Massachusetts, — of course naming a Democratic majority. Mr. Benton promised me all his influence in the outset, and was to have been chairman, and to have presented the Memorial, but was not well, and it passed into the hands of one of my new partisans, a man of good abilities and much influence. I really think, if Congress does not suddenly adjourn, I shall pass the bills, one asking for 5,000,000 acres of the public surveyed lands for the curable and incurable indigent insane, and the other praying for 2,000,000 acres for the blind and the deaf and dumb. Shall I not be happy, if I get all this ! "

To Mrs. ROBERT HARE.

" WASHINGTON, *July* 21, 1848.

" You who understand me, you who always sympathize with my anxieties and rejoice in my successes, will be glad to know that my whole committee, even the impracticable Colonel Benton, concurred in my 5,000,000 acre bill, and it was read this morning in the Senate. . . .

" The greatest difficulty in the Senate is already surmounted. I feel gratified beyond expression for this much. The new Democratic movement in the Northern States has threatened the safety of the whole measure. Colonel Benton was giving me much anxiety. I went to him ; he put me off with promises to do for *me* all that was feasible under the circumstances. ' Sir, I have not come to ask any favor for myself, not the smallest; I ask for *yourself,* your *State,* your *people.* Sir, you are a Democrat, and profess above all others to support the interests of the people, the multitude, the poor. This is the opportunity of showing the country how far profession and practice correspond. Reject this measure, you trample on the rights of the poor, you crush them ; sustain it, and their blessings shall echo round your pillow when the angel of the last hour comes to call you to

the other life of action and progress!' 'My dear Miss Dix,
I will do all I can!' 'Then, sir, the bill and the measure
are safe!'

" I found last week my strength sinking under my anxieties. I, you know, am never sanguine, and feel confidence
only when a bill passes into an act, and is sealed by Governor or President."

Alas! the great undertaking on which Miss Dix
had now embarked was destined to be a long and
baffling one. Her usual sagacity had been displayed
in the fear she had expressed, " The new Democratic
movement in the Northern States has threatened the
safety of the whole measure." This especial movement, so dreaded by her, was a rising popular agitation
to arrest the hand of Congress in the free disposition
it was making of the public domain, and embodied a
war- cry sure to tell with electric effect. There still
remained unsold a thousand million acres of the public
lands, and the cry raised was that these vast areas must
be sacredly held for the present and prospective benefit of the poor man. It was robbery of the poor to
deed them away to railroad, canal, or general improvement companies, or to let them fall into the hands of
greedy speculators who would swiftly advance their
price. The actual settler on the spot, the settler eager
to hew for himself and family a farm out of the wilderness, — he was the real one to consider, and to him
should these lands be sold at the fixed and unalterable
price of $1.25 or $1.50 an acre. Lands granted to
railroads, and lying along their lines, were sure to go
up at once to $2.50 an acre, or even more! This was
robbery of the poor to enrich the powerful!

Of course, it helped little to argue that, without the
aid of railways and canals, the land would prove of

little actual value to the settler, or, further, that without the establishment of public schools, the next generation would lapse into practical barbarism. These were too recondite thoughts for popular apprehension. It needed an orator of very moderate ability to fire the public imagination with a dramatic picture of the Hyder Ali devastation wrought over boundless regions by the rapacious invasions of corporations, while it may be doubted whether the genius of Edmund Burke would have sufficed to picture with adequate effect the spectacle of the poor man's cart otherwise stranded up to the hubs in mud, or that of his hay and corn rotting, or his butter, milk, and eggs valueless, for want of an attainable market. Land was land, wherever situated, and $2.50 an acre was a dollar more than $1.50. The power of this outcry, then, to paralyze subservient politicians was one Miss Dix fully appreciated from the moment it began to be heard.

It can readily be seen, therefore, that it was a sea of stormy passions on which she had launched her 5,000,000 acre bill. She was, so to speak, between two fires. On the one hand, the agrarian war cry which had been raised in the Eastern States would be sure to frighten a large class of Democratic politicians from incurring popular wrath by voting away another acre ; while, on the other hand, the fierce material interests of syndicates of land speculators would stimulate them to fight against the intrusion of any new measure that threatened to swell the amount of public grants they sought to confine to their own private channels.

By the courtesy of Congress, a special alcove in the Capitol Library was set apart for Miss Dix's use, and there was she daily on hand to converse with members. The thought of the scenes that must have been witnessed in that quiet alcove awakens a longing that some picturesque record of them might have been preserved. Certainly, the contrast between the common experience of a Senator or member of the House, as a party man beset on every hand by those fiercely urging political or material schemes, and tossed to and fro by alternate promises and threats of what would ensue if he did, or did not, vote in this way or that, and his experience when he found himself in the presence of this quiet, low-voiced, entreating, yet commanding woman, speaking as out of a higher realm to him to "do justice, love mercy, and thus walk humbly with his God," must have been most impressive. No wonder, then, that member after member was brought over to promise her that, in the fierce struggle going on as to the disposition of lands soon to be the future seat of empire, he would never lose sight of the piteous claims of the helpless ones for whom she was pleading.

To many of Miss Dix's friends in various parts of the Union — particularly to those who, as themselves superintendents of insane asylums, were thoroughly alive to the import of her action — it seemed an assured fact that her bill would speedily pass both houses of Congress, and receive the signature of the President. Rejoicing in the thought that her exhausting labors would soon be over, and that, after crowning them with this magnificent success in securing full provision for ages to come for the indigent insane, she would now be able to enter on a period of rest, the question had already arisen among them as to the next field for the exercise of her invaluable energies. Brief at best, they knew, would be the season of recuperation to which she would consent, for in this great cause she literally "lived, and moved, and had her being." What farther service, then, could she render it? The view taken by one large and benevolent mind will be found in the following letter from Dr. Luther V. Bell, of the McLean Asylum, Somerville, Mass. : —

"McLEAN ASYLUM, *December* 29, 1848.

"DEAR MADAM, — Your friends cannot but trust that these terribly severe labors may be nearly at a close. And so, released by the actual accomplishment or encouraging inception of your labors, how much more remains to be done, which no one but you can do! The aggregation of misery and misfortune, of which you have sounded the depths, and have done so much to alleviate, affords yet an almost boundless field of labor with the pen, if possible of more moment than any present relief through personal devotion. In a country rushing upon the crowded population, the crimes, the miseries, of the Old World with gigantic strides, cannot something be done which shall *tell* to all future time, by informing the world, at least the wise and good of the world, how these monster evils can be grappled with?

"Is not our want of fixed principles owing to our want of facts? Now, it seems to me that when you have finished the specific course laid out for yourself, if you could, in the light of all your personal experience of human suffering, take a year and sit down to the composition of a volume which should meet the emergency alluded to, you might accomplish more than in any other way. A personal narrative of your last ten years' life would contain just the needful elements, if the fair conclusions could be eliminated from it, which you alone could do.

"Accept, dear madam, our heartfelt regards and sincerest prayers.   Yours truly,
                                        "LUTHER V. BELL."

What she should turn her mind to after the passage of her 5,000,000 acre bill was, however, the last thought with Miss Dix during her protracted labors throughout the Congressional session of 1848–49. First must the bill be passed ; then would it be time enough to ask, " What next ? " She understood the working of legislative affairs far more thoroughly than did her sanguine friends. Already, January 30, 1849, had she expressed her own view of the actual situation in a letter to her brother Joseph : —

" Specially and prominently, at this particular time, I am watching and guarding the 5,000,000 bill. Through the courtesy of my friends in the Senate and House, a special committee room is assigned to my use in the Capitol. I am neither sanguine nor discouraged. I think the bill may be deferred till next session. A new difficulty is to be combated, the President [James K. Polk] having declared to his Cabinet that he will *veto* all and every land bill which does not make a provisional payment to the general government. I suppose this will be gotten over by a small premium upon every acre sold. I, fortunately, am on good terms with Mrs. Polk and the President, knowing well all their family friends in Tennessee and North Carolina. The Vice-President, Mr. Dallas, the intimate associate of many of my Philadelphia friends, is warmly in favor of the bill. I have decidedly declined the interposition of the State legislatures, preferring to rely on the 'uninstructed' deliberations and acts of the two branches of Congress. The public interest is involved for *all* the States, and those who will vote negatively do so on constitutional grounds, imaginarily involving the federal integrity."

" Neither sanguine nor discouraged ! " In this state of mind Miss Dix worked steadily throughout the session. Every day witnessed fresh accessions to the ranks of her supporters, and she no doubt had an actual majority of members of both houses with her. But many of them were halting and half-hearted. The agrarian cry had carried consternation into the ranks of the Democratic party. They must wait till the popular excitement had abated, and to this end a "masterly inactivity" seemed the policy dictated. The bill was deferred and deferred, and finally allowed to lapse. Still Miss Dix bated no jot of faith or hope. To her, this was but the first movement in a great campaign. It had suffered check. She would appear on the field again, and in more solid phalanx. A strong impression had been made, an impression so strong that but for untoward circumstances it would have resulted in decisive action.

> " What though the field be lost ?
> All is not lost."

CHAPTER XVI.

At the outset of the session of 1850, Miss Dix for the second time memorialized Congress in behalf of the indigent insane of the United States, as well as of the indigent blind and deaf and dumb. The "tonic of opposition" had acted with its usual invigorating effect, and she now came forward, not as before with a bill for 5,000,000 acres of the public domain, but with a bill for 12,225,000 acres, — of which 10,000,000 should enure to the benefit of the insane, 2,225,000 to that of the blind and deaf and dumb. A favorable report on the Memorial was at once made, and every prospect looked promising of its speedy successful passage. From the press, and from enlightened public sentiment all over the land, came strong indorsements of the measure. Likewise, at the annual conference of the "Medical Superintendents of American Institutions for the Insane" the following vote was unanimously passed: —

"*Resolved*, — That this Association regards with deep interest the progress of the magnificent project which has been, and continues to be, urged by Miss D. L. Dix on the consideration of Congress, proposing the grant of a portion of the public domain by the federal government, the proceeds of which are to be devoted to the endowment of the public charities throughout the country, and that it meets with our unqualified sanction.

"Thomas S. Kirkbride, *Secretary*."

Once again was Miss Dix in her old place in the alcove of the Capitol Library. With her the day always began at four or five o'clock in the morning, when, on rising, she sacredly set apart the first hour for her religious devotions. In the most hurried time of work or travel she would never intermit this habit, feeling that when, frayed in spirit through pressure of care, the virtue had gone out of her, she must faint and utterly fall but for refuge in this mount of prayer. "God was her present help in time of trouble." Rarely speaking of her personal religious feelings except in confidential hours, religion was yet the breath of her life. Passionately fond of hymns, and with a memory stored with them, from the early Latin hymns of the Church and onward, through those of Bernard of Cluny in the Middle Ages and the rich stores of the German mystics and later Moravians, to the hymns of Wesley, Faber, Whittier, and Bowring in more recent days, she rose on their wings into a realm of peace and thanksgiving in which, for the time at least, all the struggle and sorrow of earth were hushed.

Her hour, however, of devotion over, the late kneeling and dependent woman was forthwith another being. Once again the sense of naked moral responsibility had taken exclusive possession of her, and every nerve of action was on the stretch. Ill or well, in pain or in temporary relief from pain, on herself alone she felt it to depend whether a vast cry of misery should continue to rise and beat in vain against a brazen vault, or be heard and answered, comforted and stilled.

By the hour of breakfast, at eight o'clock, she had despatched the daily stint of her immense correspon-

dence, now embracing the needs and problems of asylums in twenty States, and ten o'clock saw her seated
in her chair in the alcove. There for four or five
hours on the stretch, often through the intolerable
heats of a July, or August, session, would she patiently reason with, instruct, and entreat the members brought in to see her. She was at this period
of life forty-eight years old, although her rich brown
hair showed scarcely a line of white, and her blue
gray eyes, so large and dilating in the pupils as often
to be mistaken for black, retained all their range
of expression from lightning-swift decision to tender
compassion. Patience and a sweet conciliatory spirit
were now the needful weapons of a nature constitutionally high-strung and imperious. Infinitely weari-
some was it, this going over the same ground a
thousand times and replying to the same stereotyped
objections. The head might throb, the old sharp pain
in the chest might pierce, the heat of 95° to 100°
might threaten collapse of brain. Still, to give way
for a moment and suffer any irritability of physical
fibre, any impatience of scorn at political subserviency
to interrupt the even flow of persuasion and entreaty,
might be to make an enemy, not of herself — this
was nothing — but of her sacred cause.

Miss Dix had studied the art of cogent statement
and vital appeal as few orators study it. It was not
by nature hers, except on the condition of the varied
and often contradictory elements of her character becoming fused in the heat of a great idea. But in
those days of impassioned activity she had mastered
this art to a rare degree. Few ever recognized more
clearly the power of a fit word than she. In her
reading, she habitually noted down every telling

phrase, till her vocabulary became full, exact, and varied. Besides, her life for now many years had been one long school of practice in dealing with every type of human character.

None the less, this sedulous cultivation of speech was, in her case, at the last remove from any trace of rhetorical display. Her nature was too intense, too forceful, too straightforward to admit for a moment of this. She studied language as the soldier grinds his sword, to make it cut. Those who heard her on the rare occasions, except on Sundays in prisons, when she ever made an address of any length, — on occasions, for example, when she would call together the attendants and nurses in a new asylum, to speak to them about their sacred duties — say they never listened to such moving speech from human lips. Her auditory would be wrought to mingled tears and exultation, as though in their merciful vocation the divine privilege of the very call of Jesus, to be eyes to the blind and feet to the lame, had descended to them from out the heavens. And yet this was the same woman, who, at times of weariness or self-concentration, would leave no other impression on many but that she was hard and unsympathetic.

The hot summer of the session of 1850 was wearily wearing away, but still Miss Dix kept up heart and hope. Her bill had actually passed by a full majority the House of Representatives, the popular branch, of which she stood in the greater fear as more sure to be affected by the immediate political passions of the day. There was to be farther deliberation in the Senate. In this body, however, she felt sure of a victory, unless in the press of business in the last days of the session her bill should be crowded out and so " deferred."

As late in the season, then, as August 29, 1850, she is found replying to a friend, — begging her to seek change and recuperation in the more bracing air of the North, — in a tone marked by the exhaustion under which she was suffering, but still full of her usual patience of resignation : —

"None can tell what a mountain will be lifted from my breast if my bills pass.   I shall feel almost as if I could say, 'Lord, let now thy servant depart in peace, for mine eyes have seen thy salvation !'   But I recollect that my times and seasons are His, and for His work.   He will do as seems to Himself good.   I ought to be ready to meet all changes, all events, but the troubles of the miserable world would, if now no way were opened for their alleviation, make the hour of death mournful to me."

Another fortnight of the "hope deferred that maketh the heart sick," and, at the close of the session, she is forced to write to the same friend these few sad words : "My bill *is deferred* to the first month of the next session, the second Monday.   Pray that my patience do not fail utterly."

Patience did not fail.   Once again, the winter session of 1851 saw Miss Dix at her post.   Delay succeeded delay in getting the bill called up.   But at last, February 11, was penned the following letter to her friend, Miss Heath.   How thrilling a picture it gives of what Miss Dix had herself characterized as the feverish spirit of the gambling table, — of a scene rather, as it rose before her impassioned mind, in which the God of Mercy and the Power of Darkness were playing for a stupendous stake of human succor or human misery.   The letter is hastily dashed off, at intervals, from her alcove in the Capitol Library.

"Washington, D. C., *February* 11, 1851.

"My dear Friend, — My bill is up in the Senate, I awaiting the result with great anxiety, but a calmness which astonishes myself.—

"A motion to lay on the Speaker's table is just lost, 32 to 14. It is said that this is the test vote. They are speaking on amendments. — The danger is from debate. — I dread Chase of Ohio. —

"Mr. Mason of Virginia sends me word the bill will pass. —

"A message from Mr. Pearce, who says the bill will, will pass — ah! if it should fail now. —

"Mr. Shields just comes to say the bill will pass. — You know not how terrible this suspense ! — I am perfectly calm, and as cold as ice.

"4 P. M. The bill has passed the Senate beautifully. A large majority, more than two to one ! — thirty-six yeas to sixteen nays."

A glorious victory gained in the Senate! At the last session she had achieved an equal one in the House of Representatives. But before a bill can become an act, it must pass both Houses in the *same* session and be signed by the President. There remained, then, the action of the House of Representatives. What will that action be ? It is the popular branch, its term of office is shorter than that of the Senate, its members are more sensitive to the temporary wind of the hour. Of the real convictions of a large majority of these members there is no question. Will they be brave enough to act on them? Their proceedings are singularly vacillating and at cross-purposes. They are letting "I dare not" wait upon "I would." Now the question of the immediate consideration of the bill is defeated by the "rigid enforcement of the rules," and now, in turn, twice are the

rules suspended by a vote of the same House, — the
first time by 105 nays to 50 yeas, the second by 108
to 70.   The opportunity is thus again on hand, but
still some subtle political fear is paralyzing action.
Each time the House proceeds to other business.   No,
it dares not face the question.   Delay is interposed
on delay, till the session is well nigh over, and the bill
will now probably lapse.

Patient, travailing martyr, gird up thy loins and
nerve thy indomitable spirit for a second cruel defeat.
It came.   And yet she never gave way to despair.

CHAPTER XVII.

NEARLY two years elapsed after the second miscarriage of her Land Bill before Miss Dix ventured to
appeal again to Congress, and then, as far as 1852–
1853 was concerned, only in a tentative way. In vain
had she exercised the spell of her magnetic personality over the minds of Representatives of all the States
of the Union. While in her presence, and under the
sway of her spirit, the superior number of both houses
had given her assurances of support ; had indeed
given her, when the test of the vote came, a large majority, though not unitedly in the same session. But
once back among their associates, and delivered over
to partisan newspapers and menacing letters from
constituents, enough were always wavering to be glad
to seize every pretext for delay, and thus imperil the
cause. She felt, then, that she must wait. Meanwhile, she was indefatigably at work in the Southern,
Middle, and Western States, winning the memorable
series of victories that have been already narrated in
previous chapters.

With the opening, however, of the session of 1854,
all the signs looked favorable for renewing the national campaign. The first fierce excitement in the
Democratic party over the land issue had in a measure
subsided, while the unexampled series of triumphs she
herself had achieved in so many States had steadily

increased in Congress the moral ascendancy of her name. Five thousand copies of her Memorial were at once ordered to be printed, and strong supporters in each house stepped to the front to champion her cause. She now worked with buoyant hope, seeing assured victory ahead. Still, she jealously watched every step, and more eagerly than ever studied the character of every Congressman, concentrating her personal efforts on those she most feared. It was the proudest and happiest year of her life, seemingly to her the crested tidal wave, lifting and bearing on in irresistible flood the cumulative results of fourteen years of toil, anxiety, and prayer.

The first signal victory came, March 9, 1854, when her bill passed the Senate by a large majority. No other record of her feeling over this triumph remains than a hasty report to her friend Miss Heath. It is brief and simple, but full of her habitual devoutness of spirit.

"Washington, D. C., *March* 9, 1854.

"Dear Annie, — Yours this morning received just when I was putting pen to paper to tell you that my bill has passed the Senate by more than two thirds majority, 25 to 12. Congratulations flow in. I, in my heart, think the very opponents are glad; and, as I rejoice quietly and silently, I feel that it is 'the Lord who has made my mountain to stand strong.'"

Still, the House of Representatives remained to be carried. There she feared the sunken rocks on which the bark of her hopes might again be shattered. Five months of protracted suspense must she linger through before at last, in August, the decisive vote came. It was victory for the bill. Once again, a brief note to Miss Heath records the fact.

" WASHINGTON, D. C., *August* 28, 1854.

" DEAR ANNIE, — As you know, my ten million acre bill (rather 12,225,000), has passed the House, 98 to 84, and is in its final passage through the Senate. My District Hospital Bill has also passed the Senate unanimously, for $100,000, for the relief of the insane of the Army and Navy, and those of the District."

It will thus be seen that, in this year-long series of congressional campaigns, twice in the Senate, and twice in the House, — both being Democratic by large majorities, — had Miss Dix carried her bill triumphantly through. This last time, happily, success had been secured in both houses in the *same session ;* and now the bill but awaited the signature of the President to become law.

Twelve million, two hundred and twenty-five thousand acres of God's earth rescued, and consecrated forever to the succor of the most sorely-afflicted and cruelly-entreated of earth's creatures ! Who can grasp in imagination the full significance of this ! None surely, even by the most distant approach, in comparison with the merciful woman who for fourteen years had traversed the dread Inferno in which these miserable wretches lay in chains and fire, and whose very dreams had been haunted by their cries. Divided among the several States, and carefully protected so as to share in the steadily augmenting value of land, this vast domain meant stately buildings rising on every hand, with every appliance to minister to the " mind diseased ; " meant all the resources of advancing science and humanity in sacred league to

" Pluck from the memory a rooted sorrow,
Raze out the written troubles of the brain; "

meant sunshine, grass, flowers, singing birds, and bab-

bling brooks in emulous accord to weave together
" the garment of praise for the spirit of heaviness."
And all this had been won by the hand of a single
frail and suffering woman.   Hers the prophetic foresight, hers the intrepid courage, hers the unwearying
patience, hers the force of angelic persuasion, through
the united power of which, " troubled on every side
yet not distressed, cast down but not destroyed," she
had wrought this triumph of mercy.

Congratulations fast flowed in.   Already in 1850,
had Dr. Thomas S. Kirkbride, that steadfast light
through the darkest hours of the history of insanity in
America, assured her, " I have full confidence your
bill will pass, and nothing but the supreme selfishness
of politicians — which is genuine insanity as to the
welfare of the country, of the very worst kind — keeps
Congress from doing some good acts which would
tend to redeem them in the estimation of the people."
But now he could rejoicingly write, " A thousand congratulations on the success of your noble, disinterested
and persevering efforts !   There is some virtue yet
in Congress, and a large hope for the Republic."

It seemed at last that the especial work of Miss
Dix in the United States was over, at once triumphant,
and dying through its very fullness of triumph.   The
letters which now poured in upon her from superintendents and philanthropic men and women were full
of the tenderest expression of a sense of relief, that
henceforth she would be freed from the necessity of
such exhausting labors.   No more need now of these
lonely journeyings, these explorations of the depths of
human misery in remote and hidden places, these
long and weary wrestlings with successive State legislatures.

She was, in truth, in a condition of extreme exhaustion when the final victory came. But now at last had arrived the day of honorable discharge from the service. She could receive it, brimful of the sense of thanksgiving, her heart filled with the "peace of God passing understanding" for all she had been permitted to do. Then, rested and recuperated, she could write out the wonderful story of her life, and, as her friend Dr. Luther V. Bell had urged upon her, make a book that would do more for the cause she so loved than any further practical action. So things looked, in that supreme hour of success, to all Miss Dix's sympathetic friends.

And now, suddenly and all unlooked for, out of the clear, radiant sky, without a cloud to presage its advent, there fell a lightning bolt. The President, Franklin Pierce, so the incredible rumor ran, *had vetoed the bill.* A stroke of his pen, and the bright vision had vanished. The principality was gone! The stately buildings, the trained service of science and humanity, the sheltering homes, everything but the poor wretches who were to have been ministered to by these, had, as by the malign stroke of a magician's wand, been changed into so many idle and empty pictures of mirage! The struggle and oft times agony of the long years of travail had aborted in nothing!

Miss Dix fairly staggered under the blow. At first, while it was merely rumor, she refused to credit it. It could not be! President Pierce, she insisted, had personally testified to her his own interest in the measure. A veto so purely arbitrary, so purely founded in individual will, a veto in the face of such great majorities where his own party was in the ascendency — no! it could not be! Had not twice in the

last four years, and after protracted debate, the bill
passed House and Senate? Here was the clear will
of a humane and enlightened people, declared through
its representatives. Impossible, that any single man
could have the wanton cruelty to stand forth now,
when Righteousness and Peace had thus kissed one
another, and cry, " I forbid the bans!" Alas! rumor swiftly passed into stern reality. *The bill had
been vetoed.*

For a few days Miss Dix bravely rallied from the
stroke. While a ray of hope remained she was all
fire of action. Swiftly calling to her side her most
powerful supporters, she pressed upon them the question of the possibility of still carrying the bill over
the presidential veto by a two thirds majority. They
sadly told her no. There were too many subservient
politicians, to whom to cross the will of the executive
would mean political death. Then she bowed her
head, doing her best to say, " Thy will, not mine, be
done!" but sinking into a state of such complete physical prostration as to feel that absolute rest and change
were the immediate question of life or death with
her. She was willing to go away now, — to go anywhere.

CHAPTER XVIII.

At the first rumor of an impending veto, letters of indignant sympathy poured in upon Miss Dix. " Is it possible," wrote Dr. Kirkbride, "that the President can really think of vetoing your bill? If he does, ought he not to expect to see the ghosts of insane people around his bed at night, as long as he lives?" This echoed the feeling of superintendents of asylums in all quarters, and of philanthropic men and women who understood the dire urgency of the case.

On the other hand, the partisan press of the Democratic party, even that portion of it that had lately been loudest in the praise of Miss Dix, now rallied round the President, and lauded his action as the acme of constitutional wisdom and sobriety. As an instance of the disgust this so evidently servile reaction awakened in the breasts of many high-minded men and women, the following extract from a letter of William Darlington, of Pennsylvania, will suffice : —

" My sympathies have been so long and so fervently enlisted in behalf of your great philanthropic enterprise — now so cruelly thwarted by the Executive — that I find it difficult to express my sentiments in reference to that procedure in terms of moderation. I have lost all patience with those narrow-souled, caviling demagogues who everlastingly plead the Constitution against every generous measure, and recklessly trample it under foot whenever it stands in the way of their selfish purposes and foregone conclusions. . . . But what has more especially excited my disgust and contempt in this connection is the course taken by the servile partisan press. During the years of your untiring efforts to get the recently vetoed bill through the two houses of Congress, the manufacturers of public opinion (so called) seized every occasion to ingratiate themselves with the humane portion of the community by lauding the objects of *Miss Dix's bill*, and heralding the disinterested services of its benevolent author and advocate. . . . Had the bill been permitted to become a law, no doubt it would have been pronounced and claimed by the despicable echoes of the presidential will and pleasure as one of the noblest acts of his administration. . . . But, whatever may be the result, no arbitrary exercise of executive power, no accident of time nor chance, can deprive *you* of the satisfaction of having nobly and faithfully performed your part toward alleviating the miseries incident to our fallen race."

The objections taken by President Pierce to the 12,225,000 Acre Bill were, as duly set forth in his veto message, partly constitutional and partly grounded in expediency. Beginning with an earnest declaration that he had " been compelled to resist the deep sympathies of his own heart in favor of the humane purposes sought to be accomplished " by the bill, he then went on to unfold the reasons that had dictated his action. To these reasons powerful rejoinders were made in the Senate and the House of Representatives by Hon. John M. Clayton, of Delaware, Hon. Albert G. Brown, of Mississippi, Hon. Mr. Badger, of North Carolina, and other prominent members.

Congress, the President declared, had power to make provisions of an eleemosynary character within the limits of the District of Columbia, but nowhere outside of it. This single district was under the especial rule of government, and so furnished the one exception to an otherwise inflexible law. At the same time, he insisted on the right of Congress to grant lands on a lavish scale for schools, colleges, railroads, and various objects of internal improvement. Whenever, however, Congress had ventured to cross this line, as on two previous occasions it had done, in Kentucky and in Connecticut, in favor of the indigent blind and the indigent deaf and dumb, then it had transcended its power, and set up unsafe precedents, examples to be avoided rather than followed. "If Congress have power," he then proceeded, "to make provision for the indigent insane *without the limits of this district*, it has the same power to provide for the indigent who are not insane, and thus to transfer to the federal government the charge of *all the poor in all the States.*"

"The charge of all the poor in all the States!" Here was the alarmist argument driven to the last extreme. The fact that a power may be abused is conclusive reason why it ought not to exist. To this it was pertinently replied, "Because Congress has the power to order six steam frigates to be built, shall this power be abrogated for fear it may order sixty? Because Congress may rightly declare war against Spain, shall this power be taken away because war might be declared against England, France, Italy, Germany, and Russia, combined? A measure of common sense must be allowed for."

"The fountains of charity," continued President Pierce, "will be dried up at home, and the several States, instead of bestowing their own means on the social wants of their own people, may themselves become humble suppliants for the bounty of the federal government, reversing their true relation to this Union."

To this it was answered by Hon. Albert G. Brown, Senator from Mississippi : —

" I have a better opinion of the States than is here indicated. In my opinion, ' the fountains of their charity' are not more likely to be 'dried up' by grants of land for the benefit of the insane than is their passion for learning to be extinguished by similar grants for school purposes; nor is a State more likely to become 'an humble suppliant for the bounty of this government,' when she receives a small quantity of land for the relief of suffering humanity, than she is when she receives a larger quantity for internal improvements and other purposes. We have seen that grants of land for school purposes have not 'dried up' the passion for learning, but have stimulated it, and caused it to flow in a steadier and a broader stream."

" To my mind, this is the first land bill ever brought forward in the true spirit of the deeds of cession. It is the first bill that ever proposed to divide the lands among the States having in them a common interest, share and share alike.[1] . . . I am a new State man, and I am a just man. And I now say to the new States, You have no right to take from the common fund for colleges, for schools, for railroads, for swamp drainage, and for other special purposes of your own, and then say to your older sisters, You shall have no part for any purpose of yours. Can we receive for our schools, and deny to the old States for their asylums? . . . Unless it shall be shown that it is unconstitutional to

---

[1] Out of the, in round numbers, 135,000,000 acres of the public domain which had up to this date been granted by Congress, practically the whole had gone to measures for the rapid development of the new States, while the original thirteen States had received scarcely anything.

endow a lunatic asylum *per se*, it will follow that if you can give to a college in Alabama from the common fund, you may give to an asylum in Delaware from the same fund."

Pursuing the argument of his veto message, President Pierce next assumed the position that all previous grants of portions of the public domain had been for "value received," and therefore were not outright gifts. By this he meant that when conferred for educational purposes, railway and canal construction, etc., the value of lands remaining to government was thereby doubled in value, and thus a *quid pro quo* secured. To this, it was very sensibly replied: —

"Value received from whom? Not from the grantees. To them, the grant was a naked, unqualified gift; they paid nothing, did not promise to pay anything. They were gifts in the broadest, fullest, and most comprehensive sense of the term. . . . The fact that one section of land is doubled in value by giving away another section may be a very good argument to justify the use of an actual existing power. But if I have no power to give one section, it is useless to tell me how much the gift will enhance the value of the next section."

As though half conscious how indistinct a line could really be drawn between the educational and other purposes, to the furtherance of which he admitted the right of Congress to grant lands, and the charitable purposes, in respect of which he denied the existence of any such right, President Pierce now boldly faces the issue by taking ground that, in the matter of the disposition of the public lands, Congress is to be regarded as nothing more than the administrator of an estate, and is to be governed by precisely the same considerations as would act on the mind of any other "prudent proprietor" in the administration of

his own property. But now as to the question oi the
President's consistency in the view he takes of what is
wise and what is foolish action on the part of his supposed " prudent proprietor " !

"Let us suppose [continues Senator Brown] that the
President was the prudent proprietor of a million of acres
of land in Wisconsin, and that he had appointed my friend,
the Senator from that State (Mr. Walker), his trustee, with
power to dispose of the lands as a prudent proprietor would
dispose of his own estate. The Senator sells a part at auction and some at private sale, and the President approves
his acts, saying, ' That was prudent ; you had the power to
do that ! ' He gives some to a railroad, and the President
approves that. He gives some to a college, some to common schools, some to build a court-house, and some to drain
swamps. The President looks over the whole, and says,
' This is as a prudent proprietor would have done with his
own estate. You had the power to do all this, and I approve it.' Then the Senator gives a little to an insane asylum. The President says, ' I must *resist the deep sympathies of my heart in behalf of the humane purposes of this
gift.* It is not as a prudent proprietor would have managed
his own estate ; I disapprove it ! ' "

Indeed, very pertinently here might even the most
" prudent proprietor " have asked, in the name of the
insane, what poor old Shylock asked in the name of
his tribe: " Hath not a Jew eyes? hath not a Jew
hands, organs, dimensions, senses, affections, passions? " Do not five hundred insane patients in an
asylum, with their medical superintendents, nurses,
stewards, and cooks, eat, drink, and wear clothing?
Do they not. mean an impulse at once given to opening quarries, burning brick, and hewing timber ? Do
not they create an immediate market for the farmers'
hay, beef, milk, butter, eggs, grain, and vegetables?

Do they not furnish abundant goods for transportation by railway, and promote business activity in manifold ways? The number of "prudent proprietors" who, in the exercise of the purest selfishness, would voluntarily give away half of a tract of land to secure the establishment on it of a great insane asylum, with the sole end in view of enhancing the value of the other half, would be quite as large as of those who would do the like to secure the location on such lands of a shoe or cotton factory.

Read, therefore, in the light of the powerful rejoinders made to it, as well as in the light of the great majorities by which Miss Dix's bill had been indorsed by a Democratic Congress, the weak and vacillating argument of President Pierce's veto message makes it hard to account for his action on any other ground than that of personal idiosyncrasies of character and opinion. It is the veto more of an individual than of a great public official.

Politically, President Pierce was a man actuated by an almost virulent hatred of everything savoring of what he would term sentimental legislation. Elected President on the avowed platform of a "Northern man with Southern principles," he had, in the whole great national issue between freedom and slavery, always insisted that a deaf ear should be turned to anything but the plea for the narrowest and baldest construction of the letter of the Constitution. The slightest intrusion of humane sentiment into politics, and he was at once on the verge of panic. Very naturally, then, he flew wild on this occasion. Begin with doing anything for the indigent insane, and soon will the federal government have on its hands the support of every sick man, every vagabond, every drunkard, in the land! And so, long habituated to the painful duty of "*resisting the deep sympathies of his heart in behalf of the humane purposes*" of the antislavery agitation, he felt he must equally resist them in the case of the 12,225,000 Acre Bill; and, lest a worse evil should come upon us, veto it outright.

None the less, though thus defeated in the end by the (as she herself always bitterly felt) arbitrary act of a mere individual, the congressional achievement of Dorothea L. Dix, as narrated in the last four chapters, will always stand out among the memorable moral triumphs of history. Everything that human foresight could provide for had been provided for by her. Only, once again was to be justified the inscrutable experience, which in all ages has leveled to the dust the pride of man, "Nothing is certain but the unforeseen!"

CHAPTER XIX.

MISS DIX now resolved to seek entire rest and change. Her forces seemed for the time being utterly spent. She would sail for Europe, and once there — well, let Providence determine for her, for she was too weary to plan for herself. At least she would once again see her dear old English friends, the Rathbones of Liverpool, whose devotion had, eighteen years before, lifted her from the brink of the grave. As strength permitted, she would visit the asylums of Europe, to learn from them whatever might be of future service at home. Along with these undefined projects, there floated in her mind a vague hope that she might get to Palestine. Religion, in her mind, largely took the form of fervid personal love for him who "went about doing good," and who revealed through his own life that the "greatest of all is he who is the servant of all;" and she always yearned to tread the soil once pressed by his blessed feet. But beyond these vague purposes, all lay undetermined.

"Man never goes so far as when he knows not whither he is going," was a maxim born of deep personal experience in the at once mystical and practical mind of Oliver Cromwell. In one shape or another, this maxim has always expressed the deepest conviction of natures in the same breath self-reliant and God-reliant. None know more clearly the limits of finite ability ; and so, inevitably, are they led to look upon the part they are called on to play in life, as the stout ship captain looks upon his in working his vessel across the Atlantic. His to man the rudder, trim the sails, and follow the compass. But beyond these personal duties lies the whole incalculable realm of calms and gales, of unseen currents, of head winds and fair winds, of fogs blotting out headland, sun, or stars. On these must he patiently wait, meeting each as it comes, and wrestling out of each the best furtherance he can . wring from it. Once again was the devout maxim to justify itself in the case of this worn and well-nigh heart-broken woman, who knew no more than that, with a mind ever eager to do good as she found opportunity, she was perforce dropping her sacred work in her native land, and vaguely reaching out after rest and recuperation abroad.

Early in September, 1854, Miss Dix set sail for Liverpool on the steamship "Arctic," the ill-fated ship that, on the return voyage, went down with nearly all on board. A touching incident connected with her leaving home is narrated as follows, in the "New York Daily Tribune" of September 11 of that year :

"I happened to be in the office of the American steam packets when Miss Dix called to pay her passage. The clerk handed her a receipt, but declined the money, saying that Mr. E. K. Collins (the chief owner of the line) had directed him to request her acceptance of the passage. With much emotion, Miss Dix acknowledged her obligation to Mr. Collins, adding that the sum thus returned to her would enable her to carry out a plan she had much at heart.

"On board the ship, Miss Dix learned that she had yet more for which to thank Mr. Collins. He had ordered

that no one else should be put in her stateroom, thus presenting her with two passages. He was on board when
she arrived. She approached to tender her thanks, but,
taking her hands in his with an emotion that did him
honor, he said, 'The nation, madam, owes you a debt of
gratitude which it can never repay, and of which I, as an
individual, am only too happy to be thus privileged to mark
my sense.'

" Miss Dix could only reply with tears, for, as was evident to all who saw her, her nervous system is completely
prostrated. Could we expect it to be otherwise, in view of
her immense labors and her grievous disappointments ! "

In connection with this appreciative act of Mr.
E. K. Collins, it may be well here to record that for
many years now it had been the habit of railway companies all over the Union to send Miss Dix yearly
passes, and of express companies to forward, free of
charge, all the multifarious matter she was unceasingly collecting for prisons, hospitals, and insane
asylums.

There remains, of the correspondence with her friend
Miss Heath, a letter of Miss Dix, written on board
the "Arctic," which throws light on the ruling passion
of her life, while at the same time furnishing an
amusing comment on the old Latin adage, "Cœlum,
non animum, mutant, qui trans mare currunt." A
favorite poem of hers — one, indeed, that she copied
hundreds of times, and sent to friends all over the
United States — had always been the little gem beginning,

" Rest is not quitting the busy career."

That it had again been floating through her mind
during the voyage across the Atlantic, seems evident
enough from the tenor of her letter.

"STEAMSHIP ARCTIC, *September* 11, 1854.

" DEAR ANNIE, — Thus far, by the good providence of God, we are safely on our voyage. I am now free from sea-sickness, and, but for the roughness, I could easily employ myself pretty constantly. I pass the time with such a measure of listlessness as affords but few results that will tell for others' good. However, I give you an example of my success. I had observed on Sunday several parties betting on the steamer's run. I waited till the bets were decided, and then asked the winner for the winnings, which I put into the captain's care for 'The Home for the Children of Indigent Sailors' in New York. To-night I am going to ask each passenger for a donation for the same object, as our thank offering for preservation thus far on our voyage. I shall, I think, get above $150, or perhaps but $100.

"I still regard my plans as doubtful. I have not the slightest interest in going into France, or even Italy. In contrast with the aim of my accustomed pursuits, it seems the most trivial use of time. I should like to have some person take my place who would fancy it, if I could receive in exchange a good amount of working strength."

The incident of Miss Dix's thus quietly diverting from the pocket of the winner the sum total of the bets on the steamer's run, and transferring it into the till of the Home for the Children of Indigent Sailors, affords opportunity for a brief allusion to a charge often brought against her, namely, that she followed too literally the Apostle's injunction to be " instant in season and *out* of season." From the variability of human standards of judgment, it will inevitably follow that here is a text which will always be differently interpreted, whether by divines or laymen. " It is entirely *out* of season," the winner of a dozen bets will no doubt say, — " it is entirely *out* of season to come to me just when I have pocketed enough to buy a whole box of cigars, and disagreeably remind me of the wants of the children of indigent sailors, who are not my lookout. I bet to win and smoke, not to relieve human suffering!" No doubt his friends would to a man be of a like opinion. Meanwhile, the result of an appeal to a higher tribunal, which should impartially weigh in the scale the claim to peace and comfort of the successful better against the sore needs of the children of shipwrecked sailors, might be a reversal of the verdict.

For a month or six weeks after her arrival in Liverpool, Miss Dix seems really to have sought rest and change through seeing old friends and by various excursions into interesting parts of the country. Still, within a very few days of her setting foot on English soil there were ominous signs of what would before long inevitably follow. Thus to her friend, Miss Heath, she writes as early as September 22: —

"I am still here with dear friends, much occupied with charitable institutions and the meetings of the British Scientific Association. All this tires me sadly, but I shall take things easier in a week. It is my purpose to go to Scotland to see the hospitals in ten days."

Perhaps, to the average reader, the strict logical connection between "taking things easier in a week" and "going to Scotland to see the hospitals in ten days" may not seem so obvious as apparently it did to the writer. In reality the Scotch visit was to involve Miss Dix in one of the most arduous undertakings of her life. For a few weeks, however, it was deferred, and the intervening time spent in a run through Ireland, one delightful incident of which is described in a letter to Mrs. Rathbone, in Liverpool : —

"BALLINASLOE, IRELAND, *October* 25, 1854.

"MY DEAR FRIEND, — I could not sleep to-night before writing a line to tell you how much I have wished you with me the last fortnight, but especially for the past nine hours, from seven last night to four this morning. I reached Parsontown yesterday at two P. M. Sent a note of introduction to the Castle, to Lord Rosse, asking permission to see his telescope. In half an hour received an invitation to dinner at seven P. M. ; and almost immediately his assistant, Mr. Mitchell, arrived at the Parsontown Arms, to say that Lord Rosse had sent him to conduct me to the Castle, in order that the instruments might be seen by day, and the machinery. I reserve all details till we meet, simply saying that I was swinging in mid-air, sixty feet from the ground, at two in the morning, yesterday, — Lord Rosse, Captain King, Mr. Mitchell, and Mr. Tirn, — on a massive gallery, by turn looking through the most magnificent telescope in the world."

To this Irish visit, and to the pleasure she was equally enjoying in the scenery and society of England, Miss Dix refers in a subsequent letter to Miss Heath, of Boston, Mass. : —

"LIVERPOOL, *November* 16, 1854.

" DEAR ANNIE, — I am lately arrived from a tour over Ireland, which consumed four entire weeks; a period which I shall always recall with lively interest. . . . Having no great desire and no urgent motive to cross the Channel to the Continent, I shall not do so except the climate here prove too severe. . . . Few traveling parties would suit my tastes or habits, and I as little should suit theirs. In fact, the institutions of England *do* interest me, both literary, scientific, and humane, and in becoming familiar with them I shall acquire much to remember with pleasure and advantage during the year I propose to complete this side the Atlantic.

" Nothing can be more distressing than the news from the seat of war [the war in the Crimea], where violence and the plague seem to spend their force on both armies. The affliction of families where kindred are so exposed is most painful, and leads to a distress involving serious consequences, and increasing demands on hospitals for the insane. There is little prospect of the soon coming of the kingdom of heaven on earth, and the peace which is of Christ and his doctrines.

" Romanism and Church of Englandism are waging as hot a spiritual war as is maintained in the Crimea by physical force, and the heart of pity is petrified under the assaults of bigotry and dogmatism. Social intercourse is interrupted by religious animosities; but where these disturbing influences do not penetrate, society is full of life and interest. Conversation, rather than talking, engages thought and measures time. One feels that something is gained on parting with one's friends, which remains to supply new aliment for reflection long after the circle which supplied it is dissolved."

Delightful, however, to Miss Dix as was this season of change from the protracted labors of so many years, and keenly as she enjoyed the opportunity of giving a free breath to her intellectual nature through contact with superior men and women, with something worth hearing to say, it was a season of change destined to be of short duration. Of her, emphatically held true those words of Martineau : " High hearts are never long without hearing some new call, some distant clarion of God, even in their dreams ; and soon they are observed to break up the camp of ease, and start on some fresh march of faithful service." The visit to Scotland was soon to bring to her lips the

old familiar cry, " While such suffering remains unre-
dressed, perish in me every thought of personal ease
or social delights ! "　And yet, before proceeding to
narrate the great results which came of that visit to
Scotland, once again it becomes necessary — as on a
previous occasion — to turn back, and treat in distinct
episode another work of mercy Miss Dix had been
engaged in, the happy outcome of which now first saw
the light of day.　Within a couple of months of her
landing in Liverpool, there came letters from home
which brought to her rejoicing heart the news of a
glorious success, the preparations for which she had
been laying in the past two years.　The nature and
extent of this success will be unfolded in the next
chapter.

CHAPTER XX.

OF a letter from Hon. Hugh Bell to Miss Dix, dated Halifax, August 4, 1853, the following words may be recalled by the reader: "I called on the Admiral — or rather at the Admiralty House — to leave my card for the Earl of Ellsmere (as in duty bound). The old Admiral met me at the door very cordially, shook hands, and then said, ' Where is Miss Dix?' I replied, 'She left for home yesterday. She has been to Sable Island and back!' He exclaimed in true sailor style, ' She 's a gallant woman! ' "

How gallant a woman the sequel to this visit was to prove her not even the hearty old Admiral dreamed. It so happened that while Miss Dix, in June, 1853, was engaged in asylum work at St. John, Newfoundland, there occurred a fearful storm, attended by appalling shipwrecks which left a lasting impression on her mind. She had gone through some perilous experiences of her own on these exposed coasts, but from a letter to her friend, Miss Heath, describing the fury of the elements on this especial night, it was evident that her whole nature had now been wrought to the pitch of a fixed resolution to devise some efficient practical means for the rescue of those at the mercy of such terrible gales. Hence her visit to Sable Island, so fitly named "The Graveyard of Ships." The familiar maxim, "It is an ill wind that blows nobody any good," was now destined to receive a fresh commentary.

.Sable Island, jutting far out into the western Atlantic, lies in latitude 43° 56' north, longitude 60° 3' west, some thirty miles southward from the easterly end of Nova Scotia. It is a waste of desolate, windswept sand hills, fringed with everlasting surf, harborless and shelterless on every side.

."The whole region for leagues around is a trap and a snare. One sunken bar stretches sixteen miles away to the northeast, another twenty-eight miles to the northwest. The embrace of these long arms is death, for between them lie alternate deeps and shoals, and when the sea is angry it thunders and reverberates along a front of thirty miles, extending twenty-eight miles to seaward. No lighthouse throws its warning gleam beyond this seething death-line, for stone structures will not stand upon these ever shifting sands, and wooden ones of sufficient height could not withstand the storms. The mariner drifts to his grave through total gloom. The whole island bristles with stark timbers and the débris of wrecks. Thus like the monster polypus of ancient story, it lieth in the very track of commerce, stretching out its huge tentacles for its prey, enveloped in fogs and mists, and scarcely distinguishable from the gray surf that unceasingly lashes its shores." [1]

Official records set the number of known wrecks on the island, occurring between 1830 and 1848, at sixteen full-rigged ships, fourteen brigs, and thirteen schooners. Besides these, the loss of large numbers of unknown vessels, engulfed and never surviving to tell their fatal story by more than a floating spar, would have vastly farther swollen the tragic list.

The first authentic mention of Sable Island dates

[1] "The Secrets of Sable Island," *Harper's New Monthly Magazine*, December, 1866.

from the surviving companions of the ill-fated Sir Humphrey Gilbert, the gallant and devout courtier of Queen Elizabeth, who added so heroic a name to the proud list of England's worthies. The occasion of his search for the island, with his little fleet of three vessels, is thus described in " Hakluyt's Voyages " : —

"Sabla lyeth to the sea-ward of Cape Brittan, about 45 leagues, whither we were determined to go upon intelligence we had of a Portingall, during our abode in St. John's, who was himself present when the Portingals about 30 years past did put into the same island both neat and swine to breed, which were since exceedingly multiplied. The distance between Cape Race and Cape Britton is 100 leagues, in which navigation we spent 8 days, having the wind many times indifferent good, but could never attain sight of any land all that time, seeing we were hindered by the current. At last we fell into such flats and dangers that hardly any of us escaped, where nevertheless we lost the [ship] Admiral with all the men and provision, not knowing certainly the place.

"Contrary to the mind of the expert Master Coxe, on Wednesday the 27th August they bore up towards the land, those in the doomed ship, the Admiral, continually sounding trumpets and drums, whilst strange voices from the deep scared the helmsman from his post on board the frigate. Thursday the 28th the wind arose and blew vehemently from the south and east, bringing withal rain and thick mist, that we could not see a cable length before us, and betimes in the morning we were altogether run and folded in amongst flats and sands, amongst which we found flats and deeps every three or four ship's length. Immediately tokens were given to the Admiral to cast about to seaward, which, being the greater ship and of burden 120 tons, was performost upon the beach, keeping so ill watch that they knew not the danger before they felt the same too late to recover it, for presently the Admiral struck a-ground, and had soon after her stern and hinder parts beaten in pieces."

Thus beginning the record it has ever since maintained, such was the disastrous reception given by Sable Island, August 28, 1583, to Sir Humphrey Gilbert, who with great difficulty escaped with his two remaining vessels, only soon after himself to founder in the terrible gale off the Grand Banks, in which, "standing at the helm, sorely wounded in one foot, and Bible in hand," he cheerily shouted to his companions on the sole surviving vessel, "We are as near to heaven by sea as by land!"

Later on, in 1598, Sable Island was made a penal colony for convicts from the French settlements in Arcadia, forty of them having been landed there by the Marquis de la Roche, and left to their fate. It was found seven years later that only twelve had survived to tell the story of their sufferings. Later, as increasing commerce added to the tale of wrecks, the island became the abode of desperate men, who as piratical wreckers gave it such a name that it was reputed better for mariners to be swallowed up by the sea than to escape only to be murdered on land. Finally, in 1802, after the wreck of the British transport, Princess Amelia, "having[1] on board the furniture of Prince Edward, with recruits, officers, and servants to the number of two hundred, all of whom perished, — though it is supposed that some reached shore, and were murdered by the pirates," — the Provincial Legislature took action. A relief station was established, the wreckers were driven off the island, and a superintendent, with a crew of four men, placed

---

[1] *Sable Island*, by J. Bernard Gilpin, B. A., M. D., M. R. C. S. Halifax, 1858.

in charge. From step to step, these humane provisions were increased, until in 1836 the annual fund
was raised to £2,000, stanch buildings were erected,
and new apparatus added. Such, then, is the ill-
omened, though gradually ameliorating, history of
Sable Island in the past.

It is certainly a striking commentary on the change
that has come over the world on the subject of "woman's sphere" and "woman's appropriate work,"
since the days when Iago summed them up in such
unflattering terms, that now an overtaxed and suffering representative of the sex should see it in the light
of imperative duty to make a voyage to this so dreaded
island, to study on the spot whether something more
effective could not be devised for the safety of those
exposed to such frightful perils. Why her imperative duty? Were there not the home government
and the provincial government; were there not ad-
mirals and captains in plenty; were there not the rich
shipping merchants of Halifax, Liverpool, New York,
and Boston, whose argosies lay stranded at every
point of those storm-lashed shores? And she herself?
Surely, with hospitals to look after in twenty States,
12,225,000 Acre Bills to engineer through Congress,
and two new asylums actually in hand in Nova Scotia
and Newfoundland, might she not guiltlessly have
washed her hands of Sable Island? No, thither must
she go, to study the problem on the spot, to examine
into every detail of the life-saving apparatus used,
and to leave behind her, as she scoured every part
of the island on one of the ragged little wild ponies
that breed there, "the character of an intrepid horse-
man."

Making Sable Island, landing there for a stay of

several days, and then getting away again, is an undertaking always involving a certain amount of risk. There is no harbor, and even on the north, the more sheltered shore, vessels have to lie off at a considerable distance, ready at the first sign of an unfavorable change of wind to put out to sea. Fortunately for the purposes Miss Dix had in view, her visit occurred at a time especially good for her, though ill omened for others. It so chanced that a wreck actually occurred during the two days of her stay on the island, — that of a fine new vessel, the "Guide," with a cargo for Labrador. She went ashore on the south side; no storm, but a dense fog prevailing, in which she became bewildered till she found herself within the fatal arms of the sand polypus.

As the weather remained calm, all lives were saved by the surf boats. The wreck, however, enabled Miss Dix to secure a vivid object lesson of what could and what could not be done by the force of men and character of apparatus on hand. Oddly enough, moreover, an incident occurred which united in a kind of dramatic unity a romantic blending of her old mission in behalf of the insane with her new in behalf of the sailor. It is thus described in a letter from Mr. E. Merriam, of New York, who later on rendered invaluable service to her scheme for equipping the island with proper lifeboats and appliances.

"The ship, was abandoned by all but the captain. He had become a raving maniac, and would not leave. Miss Dix rode to the beach on horseback, as the last boat landed from the ill-fated ship, and learned the sad fate of the commander, who, the sailors said, was a kind-hearted man. She plead with them to return to the wreck and bring him on shore, and to bind him if it was necessary for his safety.

They obeyed her summons, and soon were again on the beach, with their captain bound hand and foot. She loosened the cords, took him by the arm and led him to a boathouse built for the shipwrecked, and there by kind words calmed his mind and persuaded him to thank the sailors for saving his life; she trusted that rest and nourishing food would restore him to his reason."

Scarcely back in the United States, Miss Dix set to work with her usual energy. She had found the boats and the life-saving apparatus at Sable Island far behind the requirements of the day. There was no mortar for throwing a line across a wrecked vessel, no provision of cars and breeches-buoys. Above all, the boats were clumsy and unsafe, utterly incapable of the perilous services demanded of them. Applying at once to her friends among the merchants of Boston, New York, and Philadelphia, she was quickly provided with funds for building boats of the most approved modern construction and ordering a full equipment of the newest inventions in apparatus.

August 20, 1853, on reaching Boston, Miss Dix at once sought communication with such experts in nautical matters as Captain Robert B. Forbes, — then chairman of the Humane Society of Boston, — who quickly responded to her appeal. Captain Forbes was a notable instance of that noble breed of American sailors and merchants, who at one period carried the fame of their country for courage, enterprise, and sagacity all round the globe. Full of public spirit, he had on a previous occasion taken command of the " Jamestown " when she was sent out laden with corn for the relief of famine-stricken Ireland, as equally he had founded the Sailors' Snug Harbor for disabled seamen in Quincy, Mass. Nothing bearing on the

questions either of building stanch ships, or caring
for the welfare of their crews, or lighting exposed
points for their guidance, or saving their lives when
the hour of disaster struck, failed to appeal to his intelligence and humanity.

The letter Miss Dix addressed to Captain Forbes,
immediately after arriving in Boston, bears the mark
of a certain breathless haste, as though no time were
to be lost : —

"BOSTON, *August* 20, 1853.

"Miss Dix's compliments to Mr. Forbes, and wishes to
consult him on several questions relative to marine interests,
wherein his superior judgment and assistance can assist her
own aims. Will Mr. Forbes oblige Miss Dix by calling at
the residence of Charles Hayward, Esq., No. 9 Franklin
Place, at the earliest hour his convenience will allow, on
Wednesday morning, August 21st?"

It is not surprising, accordingly, to find in Captain
Forbes's journal, as early as September 16, an entry
to the effect : —

"Trying experiments with life-preservers and boat. I
went into the river with a neighbor to show Miss Dix how
to capsize and how to right a boat. We invited her to throw
herself over, and permit us to save her, but, as she had no
change of clothes, she declined."

By the middle of November matters had gone at
such a pace that, after personally superintending the
building of the " Victoria " in Boston, Captain Forbes
was able to write as follows of this boat and of the
others that had been constructed in New York : —

"MISS D. L. DIX, —

" *My dear Lady :* — Your several notes are received.
The last bears date, Buffalo, 12th inst., and, as far as I can

make out (you do write a hard hand for a business woman [1]), asks for an answer to New Jersey and Trenton. Here it is. "The boat is in Boston, and being fitted with her floats, some of which being smaller than ordered, I am putting in copper air-tight cases. All will, I trust, be ready for shipment in four or five days.

"Do not, I beg of you, say anything about obligation to me. It is me, and the rest of us merchants, whom you have laid under obligations. I made a long journey to Williamsburg, where your New York boats are lying in the shop of Francis. They are good boats, though rather heavy, and I predict that the 'Victoria' will be the queen of the fleet."

"I am very truly yours,

"R. B. FORBES."

By the 25th of November the boats and outfits were completed, the three boats built in New York being publicly exhibited on Wall Street, and attracting great attention by their beauty and strength. It was Miss Dix's desire to forward the entire little fleet by a sailing vessel to Halifax, thence, as opportunity offered, to be transferred to Sable Island. To this plan Captain Forbes strongly objected as "putting too many eggs in one basket," and insisting on sending the Boston boat, the "Victoria," to Halifax by a Cunard steamer. She was accordingly thus forwarded, accompanied by the following letter from Miss Dix: —

---

[1] Miss Dix's handwriting was at once the amusement and the despair of her correspondents, who were often driven to their wit's ends in vain attempts to decipher it. The trouble began back in her school-keeping days, when overstrain added writer's cramp to her numerous disabilities. Things grew worse in this respect when so vast a correspondence was thrust upon her by her asylum work. Indeed, her biography could hardly have been written without an amount of serious preliminary study of her manuscripts, fairly equal to that of Champollion in his preparation for deciphering the hieroglyphics of Egypt.

"New York, *November* 28, 1853.

"To His Excellency, Sir John Gaspard Le Marchant, *Lieut. Governor of Nova Scotia, etc., K. C. B., etc.*

"I have the honor and pleasure of consigning by this writing to your excellency a lifeboat, 'The Victoria of Boston,' for the use of Sable Island, and which with its appendages is a gift to me for this sole purpose from Hon. Abbot Lawrence, Hon. Jonathan Philipps, Col. T. H. Perkins, Hon. William Appleton, R. C. Harper, R. B. Forbes, and G. N. Upton, Esq., all of Boston.

"To Mr. Forbes, who for courage and knowledge in nautical affairs has a wide reputation, I am especially obliged, since his judgment and experience have assisted me in effecting the completion of my wishes in this business in a satisfactory manner. . . .

"I have the honor to be your Excellency's sincere friend, with sentiments of respect and esteem,

"D. L. Dix.

"P. S. The Boston boat will very soon be followed by the New York and Philadelphia boats, with the outfits."

The brig "Eleanora," destined to carry the New York boats, sailed November 27th. On her were shipped by Miss Dix two surf boats, one lifeboat, two boat wagons, one life car, the mortar, with fit ammunition, coils of manilla rope, etc. The following letter accompanied them, a letter that shows the varied nature of the interests in behalf of Sable Island, with which Miss Dix's mind was filled: —

"New York, *November* 29, 1880.

"His Excellency Sir George Seymour, *K. C. B., etc.*

"When I was in Nova Scotia last summer, an opportunity occurred of visiting Sable Island. I found it deficient in libraries, opening a source of amusement and instruction to isolated mariners, stationed there, and that there was neither a lighthouse for warning, nor lifeboats for rescue in

the event of perilous shipwrecks. The first and last deficiencies I was confident I could by myself and my friends
at home supply, but the second — the lighthouse — I could
only hope to see established through your Excellency's influence, met and sustained by the gubernatorial authority of
Sir Gaspard le Marchant. . . . The opinions of civilians
differ, but as they suffer none of the exposures and encounter none of the dangers of maritime life, I presume
they will concede the decision to those who unite prudence
with courage, and who, while they unshrinkingly meet
perils, do not despise aids for avoiding destruction. I shall
regard elaborate argument unseasonable in presenting this
subject to your excellency for cordial support; and, in the
confidence which your reputation for humanity and energy
inspire, leave this work in your hands for early accomplishment.

"I may inform you that a library of several hundred
volumes, the joint gift of some of my friends and several
liberal booksellers in Boston, has already been forwarded
to Halifax, to constitute a Mariner's Library for Sable
Island.

"In view of supplying lifeboats to meet a necessity, in
a spirit of 'neighborly good will and fraternal kindness,' I
asked of a few of my mercantile friends in the cities of
Boston, New York, and Philadelphia, a sufficient subscrip-
tion for four first-class lifeboats, a life car, with mortar,
cables, trucks, harnesses, etc. . . . I have named the Philadelphia boat, 'The Grace Darling,' the New York boats,
severally, 'The Reliance,' and 'The Samaritan,' the car,
'The Rescue,' and the Boston boat, 'The Victoria of Boston.' . . . I shall be gratified if you will do me the honor
of inspecting them. I already have seen them conquer the
breakers in a stormy sea. . . .

"I have, your excellency, the honor to be with sincere
respect and high appreciation, your excellency's friend,

" D. L. DIX."

Alas! the warning of Captain R. B. Forbes, in regard to "too many eggs in one basket," was destined to prove prophetic. For a long time nothing was heard of the brig "Eleanora," till at last came a letter to Miss Dix from her stanch friend in hospital work, Hon. Hugh Bell, which brought sad tidings.

"HALIFAX, *January* 10, 1854.

"DEAR MADAM, — Perhaps before this reaches you, tho newspapers or the shippers will have informed you of the fate of the lifeboats. The brig 'Eleanora,' on board which they were shipped, was driven ashore, in the tempestuous weather we have lately had, at a place called Cranberry Head, about nine miles from Yarmouth, and is a total wreck. I telegraphed to Yarmouth to ascertain respecting the boats. The reply is, 'One totally lost (went to sea), one badly broken, other, in hold, uncertain, — buoys, etc., I believe, saved.' Thus your benevolent intentions, and those of your generous friends, are for the present frustrated."

The disappointment was a sad one to Miss Dix, who constitutionally liked to see everything doing its own appointed work, and did not at all enjoy the reversed situation of a life-saving outfit that needed to be saved itself. However, she at once gave directions to have the two broken boats, as well as the one that had gone to sea and was later picked up, together with all the accoutrements, sent back to New York for thorough repair; at the same time issuing orders that "The Victoria" should remain in Halifax till the whole little fleet should be ready. Long delays in receiving and reshipping ensued, so that it was not until the ensuing October that, in two detachments, the entire outfit was landed on Sable Island.

Now, in a romantic drama to be entitled "The

Grace Darling," and sensationally worked up to thrill the spectators, and emphasize the sure reward of virtue, the writer would no doubt extemporize a shipwreck to glorify, within twenty-four hours of its advent, so humanely-sent a means of rescue, and to give it a chance to make immediate display of its heroic quality. Not always, however, is poetic justice confined to the stage. Strange to relate, in the night of October 27 — within a few days only after the arrival of the first three boats, and a day only after that of "The Reliance," which proved the real hero of the scene — a shipwreck, and a frightful one, did occur. It was that of the ship "Arcadia," Captain William Jordan, from Antwerp, for New York, with one hundred and forty-seven passengers on board, and a crew of twenty-one men.

The first tidings of the behavior of the little fleet were sent Miss Dix — then, as has already been seen, in England — by Hon. Hugh Bell, of Halifax, N. S.

"DEAR MADAM, — The very day after the arrival of the largest lifeboat (the 'Reliance') at Sable Island, the others having been, together with the attached cars and wagons, previously forwarded, a large American ship from Antwerp, with upwards of one hundred and sixty passengers, men, women, and children, was cast upon one of the sandbanks off the northeast end of the island, and lurched so that the sea beat into her and rendered all chance of escape by the efforts of the people on board quite hopeless. The sea was so heavy, and the weather so boisterous, that none of the island's boats could live in it. To reach the wreck from the station was over twenty miles ; your wagons thus came into use. Your 'Reliance' rode over the waves, as the sailors said, like a duck, and with her and two of your smaller boats, the 'Samaritan' and the 'Rescue,' the whole of the passengers were safely landed ; poor things, almost in a state of nudity, not being able to save anything from the ship. Will you not rejoice at this result of your bounty? Including the crew, one hundred and eighty human beings were saved by the means thus opportunely, and may I not add providentially, furnished through your care.

"I am very truly your friend and obedient servant,

"HUGH BELL."

This letter from Hon. Hugh Bell was, a few weeks later, followed by a letter to himself from Capt. M. D. McKenna, Superintendent of the Relief Station at Sable Island, which gives farther particulars.

"SABLE ISLAND, *December* 6, 1854.

"DEAR SIR, — The 'Arcadia' struck on the S. E. side of the N. E. bar of this island at 6 P. M., on the 26th inst., in a dense fog, and the wind blowing strong from S. S. W. As soon as we got the report on the following morning, we started at once for the wreck with the largest lifeboat, and found the ship lying about two hundred yards from the beach, head to the southward, settled deep in the sand, and listed seaward with her lee side under water, main and mizzen masts gone by the deck, and a tremendous sea running and sweeping over her bows. . . .

"We immediately launched the Francis lifeboat 'Reliance,' when the boat's crew took their stations, and with the mate started for the wreck, and after contending for some considerable time with tremendous seas, strong currents, and high winds, they got alongside the wreck, and during the afternoon made six trips to the wreck, and brought on shore about eighty persons, large and small. Two other attempts were made to reach the wreck, but the oars and thole pins were broken by the violence of the sea, and the boat had to return to the beach. An attempt was made to send a warp from the ship to the shore, but the current ran at such a rate that it could not be accomplished. When night came on, and we had to haul up our boat, the cries from those left on the wreck were truly heart-rending. In the hurry of work, families had been separated, and when those on shore heard the cries of those on the wreck at seeing the boats hauled up, a scene was witnessed that may be imagined, but cannot be described. I walked slowly from the place, leading my horse, till by the roaring of the sea, the whistling of the winds, and the distance I had traveled, their doleful cries could not be heard. . . .

"Next morning, we launched the lifeboat as soon as it was clear enough to see how to work her, and by 10 A. M. we had both crew and passengers safely landed. . . . The ship was broken in a thousand pieces on the night of the 29th, and only a few packages of cargo and some small things of ship's materials are saved. Captain Jordan was knocked down by a sea and very severely cut and bruised, while our boat was making her second trip, which deprived us of his advice and assistance. The mate, Mr. Collamore, acted nobly throughout the whole business. . . . The Island men exerted themselves to the utmost, and the boat's crew nobly stuck to their boat, and declined accepting the offer of the mate to give them a spell with some of the ship's crew. The Francis metallic lifeboat 'Reliance' has done what no other boat could do, that I have ever seen. It was a fearful time, yet the boats' crews each took their stations readily, and soon showed that they felt the 'Reliance' to be worthy of her name.

"I am sure that our benevolent friend, Miss Dix, will feel herself more than compensated for her great exertions in behalf of Sable Island Establishment, when she becomes acquainted with what we have already done through the means she furnished, and we, with many others, have reason to thank God that her good works have been felt on Sable Island. For my own part, I shall think of her with feelings of gratitude while memory lasts.

"Your obedient servant,   M. D. McKenna.

"To the Honorable Hugh Bell,
    Chairman, Board of Works, Halifax."

Congratulatory letters from home friends, and friends in England, now came thick and fast to Miss Dix, among which one has been preserved, which gives so sprightly and amusing a picture of international rivalry in acts of mercy, as to make it quite as worthy of record as the majority of the public reports of international rivalries in yacht racing or even in pugilistic prowess. The letter was written by Miss Anna Gurney of the well known Quaker family, illustrated in the annals of philanthropy by such names as those of Elizabeth Fry, John Joseph Gurney, and Sir Fowell Buxton. To bring out its point, a few words in relation to Miss Gurney are necessary.

Miss Anna Gurney — says the "Gentleman's Magazine" in an obituary of her written several years later — was a life-long invalid.

"At ten months old, she was attacked with a paralytic affection, which deprived her forever of the use of her lower limbs. She passed through her busy, active, and happy life, without ever having been able to stand or move. As her appetite for knowledge displayed itself at an early age, her parents procured for her the instruction of a tutor whose only complaint was that he could not keep pace with her eager desire and rapid acquisitions. She thus learned successively Latin, Greek, and Hebrew; after which she betook herself to the Teutonic languages, her proficiency in which was soon marked by translation of the Anglo-Saxon Chronicle, printed in 1819.

"After the one irreparable loss to her of the sister of Sir Fowell Buxton, in 1839, she continued to inhabit her beautiful cottage of Northrepps, near Comer, finding consolation and happiness in a ceaseless round of beneficence. She had procured, at her own expense, one of Captain Manby's apparatus for saving the lives of seamen on that most dangerous coast; and in case of great emergency and peril, she caused herself to be carried down to the beach, and, from the chair in which she wheeled herself, directed all measures for rescue. We cannot conceive a more touching and elevating picture than that of the infirm woman, dependent even for the least movement on artificial help, coming from the luxurious comfort of her lovely cottage to face the fury of the storm, that she might hope to save some from perishing."

Surely, then, if ever a brave-hearted woman was entitled to her fair share of men, women, and children snatched from the maw of the devouring sea, Miss Anna Gurney was that woman! And now there had suddenly loomed up a rival American sister, who had secured one hundred and eighty at a single haul of the net. The virulence of Miss Gurney's envious feelings will be readily perceived from the following letter : —

" MY DEAR MISS DIX, — I congratulate you *intensely !* I never heard of such a success, and to have it exactly the day after your boats arrived! I can only tell you, I have been on the look-out these thirty years, and tolerably sharp, too, I hope, and never got so much as a pussy-cat to my own share of a wreck, though I have had plenty to do with crews and dogs and cats, too. But I never had really the joy of being the instrument of deliverance, as you may truly feel yourself. . . . Once, indeed, my servant threw a rocket-line over a stranded vessel, and my gang of fishermen were very indignant that the men would not give me the honor and glory of letting themselves be *dragged through the breakers* upon the sand, but would wait to come ashore *comfortably*, in a lifeboat, which just then came in sight. So, in fact, I have had no luck at all, though, as I say, I have been gaping for it like an oyster these five and thirty years."

Immediately on receipt of the news of the rescue of the passengers and crew of the " Arcadia," Miss Dix acted with her usual thoughtfulness in calling the attention of the Mariners' Royal Benevolent Society to the gallant conduct of Captain McKenna and his men, and in procuring for them, by unanimous vote, the gold medal of the corporation for the chief, and the silver medal for each of those serving under him. The vote of the Royal Benevolent Society bears date August 8, 1855, though it was not until October 1 that Miss Dix received and forwarded to Sable Island, from Vevay in Switzerland, the medals. They were accompanied by a letter full of the admiration of a heroic woman for brave and self-sacrificing men.

"VEVAY, SWITZERLAND, *October* 1, 1855.

"To CAPTAIN McKENNA, *Sable Island :* —

"*Sir,* — I have the great satisfaction of communicating to you and the brave men under your command, at Sable Island, a copy of the documents which I have this week received from the secretary of the Mariners' Royal Benevolent Society, London, to whom I communicated the facts of your unhesitating performance of the sacred duty resting upon you in giving succor to all ships and persons in distress, by reason of peril through storm and wreck, upon the dangerous bars of Sable Island.

"No rewards can measure with such services, and no wages recompense them. Life is hazarded to save life, and selfish considerations are absorbed in exertions to rescue those whose sole human dependence rests on your heroism and effective action. Yet, I believe you will highly value the bestowal of the gold and silver medals of the Royal Benevolent Society, unanimously awarded, affording, as it does, evidence that your services in a lonely and desolate island are honorably estimated, and gratefully recorded. I beg you will convey to the seamen serving under you the expression of my confidence in the continued discharge of their duty, and my prayer that, as you and they in the hour which tries mens' souls have given help to the helpless, so you all in

your time of need, when more than human strength is
wanted, may find that succor which shall guide *your* Life
Boat safely into the Haven of Salvation, and land you with
joy upon the shores of Eternal Life.

"Your Friend,   D. L. Dix."

Neither Capt. William Jordan nor First Mate Dex-
ter Collamore were British subjects, and so could
not come in for their share in the distribution of
medals. But as the first of these had stood bravely
by his ship and passengers till disabled by the blow of
a wave, and the second, on taking command, had
proved himself thoroughly self-possessed, Miss Dix
constituted herself a " Royal Benevolent Society " in
their behalf, sending to each a token of her personal
esteem, and receiving from each a grateful and sailor-
like reply. Near the same date came also a letter
from the mother of one of the shipwrecked crew,
which gives a glimpse of what must have been the
spirit of thanksgiving in many a scattered household.

"CASTINE, MAINE, *March* 6, 1855.

" MY FRIEND AND BENEFACTRESS, MISS DIX, —

" You will not be surprised at this address when I tell
you that my son was one of the crew of the ship 'Arcadia,'
saved through your instrumentality. While our hearts ascend, I trust, to our Heavenly Preserver with grateful emo-
tions, it is fitting that we should express to you our thanks
and kind regards, with the hope that your benevolent efforts for elevating character and saving life may be crowned
with success, and that the blessing of many ready to perish
may come upon you.

"Affectionately,   LUCY S. ADAMS."

As usual with Miss Dix, this happy result of her
efforts in behalf of Sable Island, seems to have acted

simply as an incentive to farther activity. Indeed, the same held true of the spirit of the gallant little fleet, which again and again distinguished itself; while throughout the remainder of her own life, she kept up an unfailing interest in the life-saving stations all along the coasts of the United States, supplying them with libraries, and keeping herself ever on the alert to learn and communicate anything new bearing on their fullest equipment for their work. It is, therefore, perfectly characteristic of her to find, within a few days of the receipt in England of the glad tidings, an entry in her journal which reads: " I have been trying lifeboats and visiting ship-yards, listening to lectures on the variation of the compass, also much interested in a project for supporting light-houses in loose soils by screws that work down deep into the sands." Indeed, few persons ever indorsed more heartily than she the Cromwellian maxim, " Fear God, and keep your powder dry." Impregnable was her reliance on God, but never on a God who was not jealous of the glory of his own laws, or who would ever consent to bestow the crown of victory on saints presumptuous enough to serve the artillery of heaven with damp gunpowder. It was, then, only a piece of poetic justice, in consonance with Miss Dix's inflexible law of life, that, in the terrible gale at Sable Island it should have been the " Reliance " that " rode the waves like a duck," and proved herself " Queen of the Fleet."

CHAPTER XXI.

AFTER brief allusion to the incidents connected with Miss Dix's arrival in England, October, 1854, it became necessary, as has been seen, to turn backward for a while in order to narrate consecutively the Sable Island episode in her career, — the news of the happy success of which reached her a month or more after her landing in Liverpool. At that time we left her "sadly tired," as she confessed, but resolving to "take things easier in a week," and, by way of this, proposing in "ten days to go to Scotland to see the hospitals." Her immediate purpose, however, seems to have been changed in favor of three weeks of recuperative travel in Ireland.

Indeed, it now fairly began to look as though the overtaxed woman really intended to give herself a period of protracted rest, and would, moreover, have keenly enjoyed it, had not events soon occurred which were to awaken once again the master-passion of her nature and throw it into flaming activity. Thus, as late even as December 8, 1854, she is found writing to her friend, Miss Heath, in America : —

"I could not but smile at your idea of my visiting the prisons in Italy, an idea, certainly, that you have the sole merit of suggesting, for it had not occurred to me, for any purpose, to penetrate into those places of so many bitter memories and horrible sufferings. What should I gain, or

what would others gain, by my passage through those
dreary dungeons and under the Piombini? Where I do visit
prisons, it is where I have before me a rational object and
a clear purpose. As I write, the little birds are singing
'merrily, cheerily' below my windows, the flowers on my
table yield a sweet fragrance, the lauristinas open their buds
and flowers along the walks, and the grass is a vivid
green."

From the tenor of the above letter, it would seem
that Miss Dix's nature was imperfectly sympathetic
with the order of sensibilities which lead the average
American tourist to feel that a visit to Venice would
hardly be worth the discomforts of a voyage across
the Atlantic, unless it yielded an hour, at least, of the'
luxury of tears with poor Silvio Pellico, under the
lead roofs of the Doge's palace. True, Silvio Pellico
has now these many years been dead, and, it is
devoutly to be hoped, in bliss with the saints in
heaven. Still was he not once a poor, languishing
prisoner? This singular contrast between the immediate practical objects for which sentimental tourists
effusively explore prisons and chambers of torture,
and those which actuate the Howards and Frys in
their grim fight with groans, curses, typhus fever,
and broken idiocy, is one frequently noted between
amateurs and professionals in philanthropy.

By the 26th of February, however, it is evident
that Miss Dix is " taking things more easily " after
the wonted fashion of her last fifteen years. She has
gone to Scotland, and is yielding herself to the line of
least resistance as obediently as the gentle brook,
only, in this case, the brook is a mountain torrent that
finds the natural outlet to its heroic temper in forcing
its way through barriers of granite. The first letter

which brings this out is addressed to her friend Miss Heath. Though the letter is written from Edinburgh, not a word does it contain about the dungeon in which hapless Mary, Queen of Scots, was immured, nor, indeed, about the sufferings of any other, though long departed, historical character.

"EDINBURGH, *February* 26, 1855.

"DEAR ANNIE, — If you should visit Great Britain, recollect that no city will claim, rewardingly, so much of your time as this. I have had the good fortune to enjoy the best society here, and shall recollect so much with great pleasure that it is painful to connect with it what is very much the reverse of good, — I mean a few of the many public institutions in the city and neighborhood, which are preëminently bad. Of these none are so much needing quick reform as the private establishments for the insane. I am confident that this move is to rest with me, and that the sooner I address myself to this work of humanity, the sooner will my conscience cease to suggest effort, or rebuke inaction. It will be no holiday work, however; but hundreds of miserable creatures may be released from a bitter bondage, which the people at large are quite unconscious of. It is true I came here for pleasure, but that is no reason why I should close my eyes to the condition of these most helpless of all God's creatures."

It is clear from this letter that Miss Dix has already begun to strike upon abuses and miseries in Scotland, that fill her heart with the same distress and moral wrath inspired in her by her first encounter with the like in her native New England. This conviction settled in an hour for her all international questions. Scotland or the United States! What matter in which of the two, outcast wretches were shivering in chill, dripping cells, chained to walls, beaten with

clubs. To what end, she vehemently argued, did
Christ tell the story of the Samaritan stranger and
the wounded Jew, if every effort to obey his call, " Go
thou and do likewise," was to be paralyzed by the
modern travesty of the old, hard-hearted Jewish
maxim, " The Scotch have no dealings (of mercy
even) with the Americans " ?   It was the Martin
Luther spirit once again to the front : " Here I stand,
God help me, I cannot otherwise ! "

Remonstrances from all sides now came from loved
and honored English friends. Some told her plainly
she could do no good, and that her action would be
regarded as impertinent interference on the part of a
stranger and outsider. Others reasoned with her as
though she were under the spell of mere nervous restlessness. Still others deplored that, in her state of exhaustion, she should allow anything to interfere with
needful rest, and so endanger her prospects of future
usefulness. Among the last was her venerated friend,
Mrs. William Rathbone, to whom she replied in a letter whose underscored words witness the vehemence of
her feeling in the matter.

To Mrs. William Rathbone.

" I am not so very ill, only very variable, and, I assure
you, do not work the more for being tired. I am not *naturally* very active, and *never do* anything there is a fair
chance *other* people will take up. So, when you know I am
busy, you may be sure it is leading the forlorn hope, —
which I conduct to a successful termination through a certain sort of obstinacy that some people make the blunder of
calling zeal, and the yet greater blunder of having its first
inciting cause in philanthropy. I have no particular love
for my species at large, but own to an exhaustless fund of
compassion.

" It is pretty clear that I am *in* for a serious work in both England and Scotland. I do not see the *end* of this beginning, but everybody says, who speaks at all on this question, that if I go away the whole work will fall off. So I pursue what I so strangely commenced."

Almost of the same date, February 20, is another letter to Mrs. Rathbone, which shows what rapid progress she is making in gaining adherents, and how utterly indifferent is now to her the question whether the work of mercy she is engaged in shall chance to fall within the boundaries of her own country or those of a country not her own.

" Edinburgh, *February* 20, 1855.

" My Dear Mrs. Rathbone, — The procession of my fate still holds me here. I expected this night to have lodged in Newcastle, but I am fairly in for reform of the establishments at Musselburg, and have consented under advice and request of Mr. Comb, Sir Robert Arbuthnot, Lord Irving (Senior Judge), the Lord Provost, Dr. Lincoln, and others, to delay another week. I fear the next move connected with this may be to London, but possibly not. Lord Teignmouth and Sir Walter Trevelyan are numbered with my allies. Your excellent friend Dr. Traill is earnest in this business. I have asked him to check the idea that some might naturally adopt that I *came* here to take up this measure, than which nothing was ever farther from my thoughts. Dr. Simpson, in his earnestness, introduced me to a party the other day as ' our timely-arrived benefactor and reformer.' This thought will kill my plans outright. So I gave Dr. Traill the commission to set others right. Unfortunately, everybody is very busy, and all say I can do what citizens cannot. The Sheriff and the Procurator Fiscal are in great perplexity.

" I have written a great deal about myself, but do not suppose, therefore, that I am self-engrossed. Tell Mr. Rath-

bone, with my love, that I can bear a little, or a great deal,
of opposition and misapprehension in such a cause as I am
pressing here, and that it is a *question of conscience* with
me, not a self-indulging and indulgent pursuit. . . . But I
really do not want to create any additional discussion of this
question. I have here at all events ' passed the Rubicon,'
and retreat is not to be thought of."

What now, it becomes pertinent to ask, was the justification — the dire necessity, she herself would have
said — of Miss Dix's thus heading the " forlorn hope"
and throwing herself into the breach, in the determination to bring to a sense of their accountability before God and man the people of another nationality
than her own? The justification can in no way be
made clearer than through the direct statements and,
generally, express words of Dr. Daniel Hack Tuke,
one of the most prominent alienists of Great Britain.
In his " History of the Insane in the British Isles," [1]
Dr. Tuke devotes a long section of his work to the
gradual steps toward amelioration taken in Scotland,
and emphasizes at length the obligation the whole
country lay under to Miss Dix for a work at once so
humanely conceived and so brilliantly executed, as actually to *revolutionize the Lunacy Laws of the land.*
This writer is a lineal descendant of the great-hearted
Quaker, William Tuke, who shares with Pinel the beneficent glory of ushering in the Age of Humanity in
the treatment of insanity. Moreover, as an eye-witness of the work of Miss Dix, in Scotland, and most

[1] *Chapters in the History of the Insane in the British Isles,* by Daniel
Hack Tuke, M. D., F. R. C. P., President of the Medico-Psychologi-
cal Association, Joint Editor of the *Journal of Medical Science,* and
formerly Visiting Physician to the York Retreat, London. Kegan
Paul, Trench, & Co., 1 Paternoster Square, 1882.

efficient sympathizer with it, his testimony carries additional weight.

"Judging from the records of the past [says Dr. Tuke], as given or brought to light by writers like Heron, Dalyell, and Dr. Mitchell, no country ever exceeded Scotland in the grossness of its superstition and the unhappy consequences which flowed from it. When we include in this the horrible treatment of the insane, from the prevalent and for long inveterate belief in witchcraft, we cannot find language sufficiently strong to characterize the conduct of the people, from the highest to the lowest in the land, until this monstrous belief was expelled by the spread of knowledge, the influence of which on conduct and on law some do not sufficiently realize. The lunatic and the witch of to-day might aptly exclaim, —

> "'The good of ancient times let others state:
> I think it lucky I was born so late!'

"Passing [continues Dr. Tuke] over two centuries, I must observe that in 1792, Dr. Duncan, then President of the Royal College of Physicians of Edinburgh, laid before that body a plan for establishing a lunatic asylum in the neighborhood of Edinburgh. . . . but enough money was not raised to start the project in a rational way. . . . First, in 1807, a royal charter was obtained, and subscriptions were raised, not only from Scotland, but England, and even India, Ceylon, and the West Indies. Madras, alone, subscribed £1,000. . . . From the beginning, the teaching of mental disease to students was considered, as well as the cure and care of the inmates. The management was a wise one.

"Next came an Act regulating madhouses in Scotland, passed in the year 1815 — that important epoch in lunacy legislation in the British Isles. . . .

"On the 3d of February, 1818, a bill for the erecting of district lunatic asylums in Scotland for the care and confinement of lunatics, brought in by Lord Binning and Mr. Brogden, was read for the first time. A few days after, a petition of the noblemen, gentlemen, freeholders, justices for the peace, commissioners of supply, and other heritors of the County of Ayr, was presented against it. Persistent obstruction triumphed, and the act was rejected.

" How much legislation was needed at this period is well shown by the description by a philanthropist (Mr. J. J. Gurney) of the condition of the lunatics in the Perth Tolbooth. In his investigations, Mr. Gurney was accompanied by his indefatigable sister, Mrs. Fry."

Mr. Gurney's report reads like one of Miss Dix's own to State legislatures in America: —

" Solitary confinement, dark closets far more like the dens of wild animals than the habitations of mankind, cold and nakedness, no resident in the house to superintend these afflicted persons, poor demented wretches, *treated exactly as if they had been beasts.*"

" Scotland south of Edinburgh and Glasgow [continues Dr. Tuke] had not, until 1839, any retreat or place of confinement for the insane, except six squalid stone cells attached to the public hospital of Dumfries. Violent or vagrant lunatics were physically restrained in their own houses, allowed to roam at large, or incarcerated in prisons or police stations."

It was not, however, till 1848, that legislation striking at the root of the worst evil was really undertaken. Excellent asylums there were now in several quarters of Scotland, some of them conducted on the most advanced system. But there was no sort of provision for the indigent insane. Now, at length, a bill designed, not merely to regulate existing asylums for the well-to-do, but to *establish asylums for pauper lunatics,* was brought in by the Lord Advocate (Lord

Rutherfurd), Sir George Grey, and the Secretary of War. Alas! The old, cruel story was repeated. "Petitions against it poured in from almost every shire in Scotland, and the bill had unfortunately to be withdrawn. Undaunted, the Lord Advocate made another attempt in the following year, but with the same result." The failure of this humane bill was frequently deplored in the debates of succeeding years. Still, it was a brave attempt, which, as Dr. Tuke says in a private letter, "no doubt to some extent prepared the way for the victory Miss Dix achieved."

"It is not necessary [goes on the 'History of the Insane in the British Isles'] to dwell longer on the condition of the insane, or the legislation adopted on their behalf, till we come to the year 1855, which proved to be the commencement of a *new departure* in the *care taken of them by the State*. Unfortunately, in spite of legal enactment, the state of the insane in Scotland at this time, outside the asylums, was as bad as it could be, and even in some asylums it was deplorable. At this period a well-known American lady, Miss Dix, who devoted her life to the interests of the insane, visited Scotland, and the writer had the opportunity of hearing from her own lips, on her return from her philanthropic expedition, the narration of what she saw of the cruel neglect of the pauper lunatics in that country. She caused so much sensation by her visits and her remonstrances, accompanied by the intimation that she should report what she witnessed at headquarters in London, that a certain official in Edinburgh decided to anticipate 'the American Invader,' as Dr. W. A. F. Browne called her. Miss Dix was, however, equal to the occasion, and hurriedly leaving the scene of her investigations, she took the night mail to London, and appeared before the Home Secretary on the following day, when the gentleman from Edinburgh was still on the road, quite unconscious that the good lady

had already traversed it. The facts she laid before the
Home Office were so startling that they produced a marked
effect, and, notwithstanding counter allegations, the conclusion was very soon arrived at that there was sufficient *prima
facie* evidence to justify an inquiry. A Royal Commission
was appointed, dated April 3, 1855, to inquire into the
condition of lunatic asylums in Scotland, and the existing
state of the law of that country in reference to lunatics and
lunatic asylums."

Such, then, in brief outline, is the history of lunacy
legislation in Scotland up to the date of Miss Dix's
arrival there late in January, 1855. Seven years before, in 1848, as has been seen, the memorable struggle
in Parliament, led by Lord Advocate Rutherfurd,
Lord Ashley, Sir James Graham, Mr. E. Ellice, Mr.
Stuart Wortley, and Mr. H. Drummond, to secure
humane provision for the pauper lunatic, had been
cruelly defeated through the flood of selfish protests
against the bill poured in from almost every shire in
Scotland. The bill had finally been abandoned in
despair, and no farther courage was left to lead the
"forlorn hope." And yet by April 9, 1855, a little
more than two months after the arrival there of a
single-handed woman, and she a suffering invalid and
a foreigner, the following Order of Commission was
issued by Queen Victoria: —

" WHITEHALL, *April* 9, 1855.

" The Queen has been pleased to direct letters patent to be
passed under the seal appointed by the Treaty of Union, to
be kept and made use of in place of the Great Seal of Scotland, appointing,

" William Gaskell, Esq., Fellow of the Royal College of
Surgeons : William George Campbell, Esq., Advocate, Sheriff
of the Shire of Fife : Alexander Earle Monteith, Esq., Barris-

ter at Law : and James Coxe, Esq., Doctor of Medicine : to
be her Majesty's Commissioners for the purpose of inquiring into the state of the Lunatic Asylums in Scotland, and
also into the present state of the law respecting Lunatics
and Lunatic Asylums in that part of the United Kingdom."

In all this, the simple facts of the case tell their own
story, — perhaps more impressively than with any
added comment. Still, if a certain local light and atmosphere can be thrown around the naked facts, they
will appeal more vividly to the imagination. This will
be attempted in the ensuing chapter. Fortunately,
there remain a number of private letters and narra-
tives, which render it possible to do this. Enough
now and here, to say that alike in its inception, in the
masterly manner in which it was conducted, and in the
enthusiasm with which devoted noblemen, statesmen,
philanthropists, and men of the highest medical authority were inspired to rally under its banner, the
whole achievement was the work of a single woman.
On all sides was the entire credit of the feat generously and unreservedly given to Miss Dix. No trace
of envy or of national jealousy intervened to deny her
the full meed of praise. At the most, it was deplored,
as by Sir George Grey on the floor of the House of
Commons, that the inauguration of so needed a reform
should have been left to the initiative of "a foreigner,
and that foreigner a woman, and that woman a dis-
senter." Perhaps, this frank avowal cannot be more
implicitly stated than in the following extract from
the speech of Mr. Ellice, M. P. : —

"The Commission was entirely due to Miss Dix's exertion. After visiting the lunatic asylums of England, she
proceeded to Scotland, where her suspicions were aroused
by the great difficulty she experienced in penetrating into the

lunatic asylums of Scotland; but when she did gain access, she found the unfortunate inmates were in a most miserable condition. She came to London and placed herself in communication with the Secretary of State for the Home Department and with the Duke of Argyll, and at her instance and without any public movement on the subject, a Royal Commission was appointed to inquire into the state of the lunatic asylums of Scotland. No one, we feel sure, could read the Report of the Commission without feeling grateful to that lady for having been instrumental in exposing proceedings which were disgraceful to this or to any civilized country." [1]

[1] *Parliamentary Debates*, vol. cxiv., p. 1025.

CHAPTER XXII.

TOWARD the attempt in this chapter to revive the memory of some of the local incidents connected with Miss Dix's Scotch experiences, in 1855, the writer of this biography is under great obligation to Dr. Daniel Hack Tuke for a letter, dated Hanwell, England, August, 1888, embodying his own memories of those exciting days. Other letters, partly of Miss Dix herself, and partly of friends who were eye-witnesses of all that was going on, will follow.

"My reminiscences of Miss Dix's visit to this country, in 1855 [writes Dr. Tuke], during which visit she was for some weeks our guest at York, are exceedingly vivid as to the general impression left upon the memory, but I regret to say, that the lapse of time — about three and thirty years — has to some extent obliterated the details, interesting and fruitful in result as they were, in the cause of the insane which she had so much at heart.

"She was very much out of health, and indeed was confined to bed for some days, but the indomitable energy with which she pursued her mission was extraordinary. She visited most of the institutions for the insane about York, and I remember that on our driving in a hired vehicle to one of them, she showed that her sympathies were not restricted to the insane by remonstrating with the driver for his treatment of the horse. . . .

"It was during Miss Dix's sojourn at York that she determined to ascertain the condition of the insane in Scotland.

That country was justly famed for its excellent chartered asylums,[1] the result of philanthropic endowments, and maintained by the payments of a certain number of higher class patients. Miss Dix, however, knew full well from her experience of her own country, that such might be the case, and yet a great mass of poor lunatics be altogether neglected and shamefully treated. And so it proved. Her intrepid raid upon the dwellings where lunatics and idiots were stowed away, her visits to workhouses and to some asylums in which paupers were confined, confirmed her worst misgivings, and her revelations took many of the Scotch themselves by surprise.

" It would have been more fitting had members of the medical profession in Scotland ascertained and protested against this deplorable condition of things, and it is not surprising that when this terrible reformer, yet gentle lady, came from the other side of the Atlantic to set their house in order, the Scotch doctors were disposed to resent the intrusion. To some of these very men it proved, however, a boon, for when an inquiry was instituted, and a Lunacy Commission was established in Edinburgh, they were placed on the Board. At the present day, there is not a doctor in Scotland, interested in the welfare of the insane and in the splendid asylums now in operation in that country, who would not acknowledge the profound debt of gratitude due to Miss Dix for her courage, her pertinacity, and her judicious advice. . . .

" One amusing and characteristic incident of Miss Dix's exposure of the treatment of the insane in some parts of the country will no doubt be referred to in her biography, the sudden departure of the Lord Provost of Edinburgh to London, in order to forestall the American lady's representations to the Home Secretary. Although this was before the racing of rival trains between Edinburgh and London, wit-

---

[1] I speak of them as a class. I am aware that some were not in a creditable state, and that all are at the present time in a vastly improved condition.

nessed at the present moment (August, 1888), the two actors
in the scene did undertake an exciting race to the English
capital, with the result that the lady beat the gentleman,
although by a very short space, interviewed the Secretary
of State, and produced an impression upon him too powerful to be removed by the assertions of the Lord Provost.
Fresh from her great exertions, she returned to York, much
exhausted, but sanguine as to the ultimate success of the
mission she had so bravely undertaken. . . .

"You ask me to indicate the salient features of Miss
Dix's character as they struck me when I knew her. It
seems to me that what I have now written is really the best
answer I can give to your request, but I may add a few
words. What she told me of having in the early part of her
life intended to live mainly to herself, to enjoy literature and
art without any higher aims, and of having discovered that
this was a fatal mistake, and resolved to devote her energies
to the good of man, seems to me the pivot on which her
future career revolved. The lines of one of her countrywomen might seem to have been especially composed to
describe the change which came over Miss Dix : —

> "'I slept and dreamt that life was beauty,
>   I woke, and found that life was duty.'

In complete accord with the same idea, I may mention that
on the fly-leaf of her own Bible, presented to me when she
left our house, she had written Wordsworth's 'Ode to
Duty.'

"Her long sustained exertions, undertaken from the highest motives, mark the untiring and irrepressible energy and
fortitude which more especially struck me during our personal acquaintance. That these qualities must have exerted
enormous influence in inducing others — especially young
physicians — to engage in the humane treatment of the
insane can easily be understood. . . .

"The refinement and intrinsic gentleness of Miss Dix
had much to do with the esteem and affection entertained

for her, because they disarmed the criticism and opposition
which were not unnaturally excited when a woman entered
the public arena, and was expected to commit injudicious
and emotional acts, however well-intentioned they might be.
But Miss Dix's enthusiasm was based on actual facts and
undeniable abuses, while the remedies she proposed were
those which commended themselves to the best men engaged
in the treatment of the insane in the United States.

" I will only say, in conclusion, that in whatever other department Miss Dix may have earned the gratitude of mankind, in that of the proper care and humane treatment of the
insane (not the so-called nonrestraint system which she did
not accept) she ought to be regarded as the patron saint of
every hospital for this class established through her instrumentality, as an angel of mercy, not only in her own, but in
other lands, and therefore held in everlasting remembrance
on both sides of the Atlantic as one worthy of double honor.

" D. HACK TUKE.

"HANWELL, *August*, 1888."

In preceding extracts, allusion has more than once
been made to the exciting railway race from Edinburgh
to London between Miss Dix and the Lord Provost of
Edinburgh, each bent on first gaining the ear and
prepossessing the mind of the Secretary of State, Sir
George Grey. The result of the race was one more
illustration of Napoleon's favorite sayings that "the
rarest kind of courage is two o'clock in the morning
courage," and that he " had always noticed that these
odd fifteen minutes determined the fate of the battle."

The Lord Provost stopped to have his trunk packed,
and to journey comfortably by day. Miss Dix grasped
a hand-bag and boarded the night train. How much
the whole issue of the reform which revolutionized the
lunacy legislation of Scotland turned on the twelve
hours start thus effected by Miss Dix's lightning-swift
decision, it is of course impossible to say.

One important point gained is, however, certain. The hot haste with which she traveled secured for her the opportunity for another of those interviews at close quarters, in which her commanding personality reached the culmination of its power. Already has it been seen how one of those memorable interviews, that with Mr. Cyrus Butler, of Providence, Rhode Island, secured the foundation of the Butler Asylum; and how another, that with Mr. Thomas Blagden, of Washington, D. C., led to the immediate surrender on his part of the magnificent site at present occupied by the Army and Navy Lunatic Asylum. The third is now on the eve between herself and Sir George Grey. Later on, a fourth is to be witnessed in Rome, with Pope Pius IX. What depths in the heart were reached in those exceptional hours, and how abiding was the impression wrought, can now be judged only by the momentous results which followed, or, here and there, by a brief expression like that in Mr. Blagden's letter: " Regarding you, as I do, as the instrument in the hands of God to secure this very spot for the unfortunates whose best earthly friend you are, I sincerely believe that the Almighty's blessing will not rest on, nor abide with, those who may place obstacles in your way."

Fortunately, there has been preserved a more than ordinarily long letter of Miss Dix herself, — to her friend, Mrs. Samuel Torrey, of Boston, Massachusetts, — in which the flying trip to London, and the great results it led to, are circumstantially detailed. The letter is here subjoined : —

"LONDON, 18 GLOUCESTER SQUARE, *March* 8, 1855.

" MY DEAR FRIEND, — I am here only on business, and for a short time at present, intending to return to Edinburgh in a few days. . . . While in Edinburgh, I had discovered eleven Private Establishments for the Insane, to which licenses had been given by the Sheriff of Mid-Lothian (who exercises the function of Chief Justice in the High Court of the County) without regard to the *special qualifications* requisite. People of the lowest grade of character, and very ignorant, had been accepted upon their application for liberty to open houses for all classes of patients.

" The *Public* Institutions for the treatment of Insanity are good, *very* good. I have visited all these, namely, Dumfries, Marston, Glasgow, Perth, Dundee, Aberdeen, and Edinburgh, besides thirteen private houses, some of which have several hundred patients. But as I was saying, those at Mussellburgh, six miles from Edinburgh, were so very ill ordered, and the proprietors so irresponsible for all they did, or did not do, that I took decisive steps. calling the attention of the Lord Provost, Dr. Traile, the Chief Justices, and other influential citizens to their condition.

" The law is singularly defective, allowing, without consent of the proprietors, no admission to these places, except in the person of the Sheriff of Mid-Lothian, who may take a physician of the Medical College on his *semi-annual* visitations. The semi-annual visits of medical men, employed by the proprietors, were not likely to control the direction of the parties. The law required them to report abuses, if abuses existed ; their pecuniary interests urged them to pass them in silence ; in fine, the proprietors had the thing all their own way, and they were intent on making money.

" The Sheriff, when I appealed to him as really the sole authority, trifled, jested, and prevaricated. I could not excuse this. The weather was *very cold*, the poor patients by hundreds suffering. I consulted the Justice, three physicians, Mr. Comb, and Mr. Mackenzie, Sir Robert Arbuthnot, and several besides. The conclusion was that nothing would do but to demand of the Home Secretary, Sir George Grey, in London, a Commission for Investigation. But who was to go ? One was an invalid, a dozen had urgent professional business. *I* — why could not *I* go? said one and another. It was clear to me that if I would see this done at once, which was so much needed, I must go.

"I looked into my purse, and counted time, and considered my health, — for I had not felt so strong for some days as I could desire, — but my conscience told me quite distinctly what was my duty. I took, then, my carpet-bag, and wrapping about me my warm traveling garments, called a cab, and at a quarter past nine P. M. put myself into the express train direct for London, expecting to arrive in twelve hours, four hundred miles. I first telegraphed to Lord Shaftesbury, asking an interview at three P. M. the following day, and naming the King's Cross Station as my point of arrival. I did not sleep, but was comfortable. An accident at nine A. M. detained the train till eleven A. M., which should have arrived an hour and a half earlier.

"I had never been in London, knew *not one location.* I stepped from the royal mail carriage, and a gentleman in a moment asked if I was Miss Dix, and announced a messenger from Lord Shaftesbury, accepting my appointment at the C—— office, 19 Whitehall Place.

"I looked at my watch. It was only an hour to twelve. I had not time to dress for presentation, took a cab, and asking the distance to Kensington, where I had learned was the residence of the Duke of Argyle (for I could reach that point in an hour), threw off my traveling cloak in the cab for a velvet I had in my hand, folded a cashmere shawl on, and believe I did not look so much amiss as one traveling so far might look.

"The clock struck twelve. I was at Argyle Lodge on C—— Hill, Kensington. The bell was rung; a servant answered. I sent in my card; was introduced; found the Duchess and two others in the library with the Duke; opened my subject; asked of his Grace immediate communication on his part in behalf of Scotland with the Home Secretary. An hour and a half settled matters. His Grace would call for me at Whitehall Place at three and a half, to go to Downing Street.

"I was to proceed to the former place at once; found myself there at two and a half. Happily, Lord Shaftesbury anticipated his time, and I found all the Board in session. We talked the whole subject over; settled that no time ought to be lost in urging the usually *tardy* Secretary. His Grace the Duke arrived and reported Sir George Grey summoned to a council at Buckingham Palace, but said, 'You shall see him yourself, but I shall now meet him at the palace, and will state what you have said.'

"It was now 4 P. M. I could do no more till the following day, so sent for a cab, and drove to 38 Gloucester Square to my banker's (Mr. Morgan), asked for a basin of water to wash my neglected face and hands, a cup of tea, and bed, all of which Mr. Morgan's prompt orders secured. In the evening I got a note from his Grace, saying that Sir George doubted his authority to order a commission for Scotland, that the Lord Advocate must be consulted. This I did not wish, for I knew social and political interests would hinder the right action of Lord Moncrieff. In the morning I drove again to Argyle Lodge. His Grace said that Sir George expressed willingness to comply, but hesitated to act. He would see him again. I saw, then, Lord Shaftesbury and got forward some affairs respecting the English hospitals.

"The next day a note from the Duke informed me that the Home Secretary had written to the Lord Advocate at Edinburgh. I took a carriage and determined to see Sir George myself, drove to Downing Street, sent up my card with a written request for a personal interview in the reception room of the Home Department; was ushered up with some state, and received courteously by his Lordship; stated my wishes. Sir George said he had already consulted the Lord Chancellor, and he doubted his power to issue warrants without the concurrence of the Lord Advocate ('to whom I have telegraphed,' added Sir George, 'and who will forthwith come to London. He may be here on Monday.') Next I received the thanks of the Home Secretary for my efforts, thanked him in return for his early attention to the subject and unprecedented alacrity in the annals of public affairs here, and proceeded to see Sir James Clark, the Queen's physician. He entered cordially into my plans, and so I waited.

" Monday the Lord Advocate did not come. Tuesday still not heard from, nor Wednesday. Thursday he arrived, and sent a note appointing to call the following day. We had a long conference. I got the promise from him that the Commission of reform for all Scotland should at once be formed. Sir George Grey had taken orders to that effect, with his concurrence, the Lord Chancellor approving. To-day I have all business closed. I have two Commissions, one of inquiry, one of investigation in Mid-Lothian. This assures, first, reports into the condition of all the insane in Scotland. Next the *entire* modification of the Lunacy laws, the *abrogation* of all *Private* establishments ; the establishment of two or three new general hospitals, etc. My odd time I have spent chiefly in securing the interest and votes of members of Parliament for the Bill soon to be introduced, and now I go back to Edinburgh to-morrow to report this to parties interested, and to rest if I need it, which is more than probable. In two weeks I shall go to Walsington, the seat of Sir Walter-Calverley Trevelyan, who has with Lady Trevelyan invited me there, and they will do the honors of Northumberland. I cannot write more now.   Yours truly,

"D. L. DIX."

Two other brief notes of Miss Dix, to her friend, Mrs. Rathbone, of Liverpool, — the first expressive of amazement at the opportunities for concealment afforded the Private Insane Asylums of Scotland, and the other indulging in the freest strictures on certain of the Scotch officials, — are all that remain of her correspondence from London.

"LONDON, *February* 27, 1855.

"Sir George Grey has consulted the Lord Chancellor, and, strange as is the fact, it is doubted if any official party in England has the right to authorize the inspection of any *private* madhouse of whatever capacity in Scotland. The question is now under debate."

"LONDON, *February* 28, 1855.

"The Sheriff is a bad man, wholly despotic, and ridicules the entire idea of reform; the Procurator Fiscal is not, like the Sheriff, a dissipated man, but a member and elder of Dr. Guthrie's church, but tied with red tape to the Sheriff; the Lord Advocate is crowded with business and is a selfish man, so that I have an odd sort of work on my hands. But ultimately good will result from this. I certainly hold myself much better occupied in doing this work than in strolling about Rome or Florence."

Her task in London thus successfully ended, Miss Dix as soon as possible went back to Scotland, to mass farther material for a report to be submitted to the Royal Commission, which should start and keep them on the real scent. By native instinct and years of training she had long since become master of the art of tracking to their hidden lairs, and dragging out to the light of day, the sullenest and most secret shapes of human deceit and cruelty. All in vain was it to seek to throw her off the scent. Keen-sighted, and tireless as an American Indian hunter, when once she had struck the trail of duplicity and greed, she followed it relentlessly through thicket, defile, or swamp, till she had come up with poor wretches hidden in the Cave of Despair to which it led. A sort of terror, as of the terror of vermin before nobler creatures of the hunt, inevitably set in upon the objects of her pursuit. Thence the impression she made on all the friends of reform in Scotland; and thence their insistence that, should she draw back, everything would relapse into the old state of apathy and despair. She, a foreigner and a woman, was besought to go to London to bring the whole issue before the highest tribunal of the United Kingdom, simply because it was instinctively felt that no one else could do it with such commanding authority of knowledge and character.

Setting to work on the trails opened to them by Miss Dix, the members of the Royal Commission soon thoroughly indorsed the fidelity of the revelation of shame and cruelty she had so impressively made. By May 14, Dr. James Coxe, of the Commission, wrote her : —

"We came home yesterday from a hurried *raid* upon Perth and Dundee, and start to-morrow for Glasgow, Greenock, etc. We have seen enough already to convince us that there is ample field for work before us which cannot fail to bring a glorious harvest. Hitherto, we have scarcely scraped the ground."

Likewise, Dr. David Skae, of the Royal Edinburgh Asylum for the Insane, continually wrote her, expressing his amazement at her power to impress influential people, and insisting that she was still indispensable to the complete triumph of the good work.

Though the immediate personal share of Miss Dix in the matter of reform in Scotland was now in a month or two to end, it is of interest to pursue here the subsequent work of the Royal Commission, as well as to tell the story of the practical legislation in Parliament, which was the result of their investigations.

Not before 1857 — almost a year after the return of Miss Dix to the United States — did the Commission make its report to Parliament. Its radical character, however, when once made public, may be judged from a few extracts : —

"It is obvious [says the Report] that an appalling amount of misery prevails throughout Scotland in this respect.[1] When estimating the condition of the insane not in establishments, it should be remembered that the details furnished by us give only an imperfect *representation of the true state of matters.* They form only a part of the picture of misery; and had we been able to extend our investigations, it would, we are convinced, have assumed a much darker shade."

It is not needful here to go into particulars of the enormities encountered on all sides. The reader of this biography has already gone over precisely parallel details, of necessity presented in describing Miss Dix's early work in the United States. That, in either country, the same hard-hearted brutality characterized many of the overseers of pauper lunatics is clear enough from the testimony of one of them before the Commission, who, after admitting that numbers of the patients, men and women, were stripped at night, and huddled together on loose straw in a state of perfect nudity, went on to add, "*I consider the treatment is proper for them.*"

In short, both as regards licensed houses and unlicensed houses, the report winds up by giving a dismal picture; for as to the former, "They are crowded in an extreme degree. Profit is the principal object of the proprietors, and the securities against abuse are very inadequate;" and as to the latter, "They have

[1] Condensed from *The History of the Insane in the British Isles.*

been opened as trading concerns for the reception of a certain class of patients who are detained in them without any safeguard whatever against ill-treatment and abuse."

"The Report once fully presented to Parliament, Mr. Ellice, the member for St. Andrews, asked the government what steps they intended to take. He charged the Scotch authorities with an almost total neglect of the duties which were incumbent on them under the law, that their statements were positively untruths, and entirely deceptive, year after year, as to the real state of the lunatics in Scotland.

"The member for Aberdeen characterized the Report of Commissioners as 'one of the most horrifying documents he had ever seen. It was a state of things which they could not before have believed to prevail in any civilized country, much less in this country, which made peculiar claims to civilization, and boasted of its religious and humane principles. . . . Distressing as were the cases which he had mentioned, there were others ten times worse, remaining behind — so horrible, indeed, that he durst not venture to shock the feelings of the House by relating them.'

"Sir George Grey homœopathically diluted the blame of the Board of Supervision of Scotland, by showing that the individual responsibility was infinitesmal, and could not, therefore be detected and punished in the way it so richly merited; but promised to introduce a bill, calculated to remove the defects in the law, established by the Report. . . . The Lord Advocate rejoiced at the publication of the Report and the statements of Mr. Ellice from the bottom of his heart, because the state of things has for a long time been a disgrace and a scandal to Scotland. 'The people of that country,' he said, 'had known that it was a disgrace and a scandal, and he regretted to add that it was not the first time that statements had been made similar to those to which they had just listened. . . . That noble-minded lady, Miss Dix, went to Edinburgh and visited the asylums at

Musselburgh. After seeing them, she said there was something wrong, and she wished to be allowed to visit them at the dead of night, when she would not be expected. He had felt a difficulty about giving a permission of that kind to a non-official person, and accordingly she applied to the Home Secretary. . . . The facts were now so clearly proved that if he proposed the very remedy which was rejected in 1848, it would he adopted by both Houses of Parliament, without any important opposition.'"

"On the second reading [June 9, 1857] no serious opposition was offered to the bill. Mr. Cowan, member for Edinburgh, said that he had been requested to present a petition, signed by the Lord Provost and Magistrates of Edinburgh, seeking for delay, but he did not like to incur that responsibility, and would therefore support the second reading. . . . Mr. Hope Johnstone, member for Dumfriesshire, enforced these remonstrances by stating that he had representations made to him from every quarter in opposition to the appointment of a new board. Mr. Drummond hereupon made an observation greatly to his credit, which deserves to be remembered. He said that the question was not so much what would be the most expensive, as what would be the most efficient machinery. There were plenty of representatives of the rate-payers in that House, but no *representatives of the lunatics of Scotland.* They seemed to have no friends there, while really they were the persons who stood most in need of being represented."

Through these extracts from speeches made in Parliament, the at last fully aroused spirit of that body is clearly revealed. How changed, through the heroic fire of a single woman, the moral temper, from the days of 1848, when Lord Rutherfurd's Bill was helplessly swept away before the flood of remonstrances that poured in from rate-payers and interested parties all over Scotland! Now certain of the Scotch members did not dare so much as to present the selfish objections of their constituents. The victory was complete, and August 25, 1857, came the passage of the Act — 20 & 21 Vict. c. 71 — through which a new epoch was inaugurated in humane and adequate provision for the insane, especially the pauper insane, of Scotland. This meant nothing less than the foundation of new and humanely administered asylums in various quarters of the land, to the relief of an untold amount of human misery.

As already stated, some considerable time before the final passage of this Act, Miss Dix had returned to the United States, and was as zealously as ever at work in her old field. None the less, devoted friends abroad kept her apprised of the steady progress of the good cause. A few extracts from letters, of widely differing dates, will throw farther local light on this memorable episode in a memorable career.

" EDINBURGH, *June* 4, 1857.

" DEAR MADAM, — Some days ago, I had the pleasure of writing to announce that the Scotch Lunacy Report had broken the shell and seen the light. We are quite surprised at the sensation the Report has produced. Throughout the length and breadth of the land, the press is ringing with it. . . . At first I took what steps I could to direct public attention to the result of our labors, but soon my only fear was that the general clamor would pass beyond bounds. . . . You will see by the proceedings in Parliament, that no time is to be lost in bringing forward a remedial measure. Government is wise in this respect. Strike while the iron is hot. This is evidently their maxim, and doubtless if they waited till next session they would meet with far more opposition. I hope you noticed how cordially Sir George Grey acknowledged in the House of Commons the obligations we are under to you. What the nature of the

proposed measure may be, is not yet known, but rumor says
it is to be an extension of the English Commission to Scotland.

" With much respect,
" Very faithfully yours,
" JAMES COXE."

" EDINBURGH, SCOTLAND, *June* 20, 1857.

. . . " You will have seen from the English newspapers
that our Report has created considerable sensation, and that
the Lord Advocate has already introduced a legislative
measure into Parliament.   Already, on every side, is heard
the din of preparation for resistance.   Town councils,
county meetings, parochial boards, and the existing large
asylums, are banding together for this object, all animated
with the desire to avoid legal interference.   I have thought
the public might be made to adopt more humane and less
selfish views by showing them what you are doing in America, and how generously the Legislatures come to your aid.
I have therefore taken the liberty to send to the newspapers
an extract from your letter.

" Most truly yours,
" JAMES COXE."

In a letter from Sir James A. Clark, Physician to
the Queen, who had attended Miss Dix during a severe inflammatory attack, in London, occurs the following grateful assurance : —

" BAGSHOT PARK, SURREY, *December* 30, 1861.

" Before going farther I will give you a piece of information which I feel sure will gratify you, as the first movement in the improvement which has been effected in Scotland through your exertions.   The treatment of the pauper
insane in Scotland is now more carefully attended to than
in any other part of Great Britain, I may say.

" Sincerely yours,
" J. A. CLARK."

Finally, from her fast friend, Dr. Tuke, came the ensuing expression of congratulation : —

"FALMOUTH, CORNWALL, ENGLAND, *May* 6, 1865.

" I think you might say to the Scotch, ' You are my joy and my crown,' for they have gone on wonderfully since ' The American Invader ' aroused them from their lethargy.

" Sincerely your friend,

" D. HACK TUKE."

CHAPTER XXIII.

THE CHANNEL ISLANDS.

In order to complete the account of the action of the Royal Commission, extending as it did through a period of several years, it became necessary, in the previous chapter, to leave Miss Dix at the close of her personal share in the work of reform in Scotland. A severe inflammatory attack, brought on by the damp and chill she had exposed herself to in a hurried visit to Westminster Abbey and St. Paul's, when already overfatigued by the heavy responsibilities of her work in London, had left her little strength for the farther probing of the foul nest of evils she had agreed to prosecute on her return to Scotland. Spite of all, she persisted until, her report finally prepared for the help of the Commissioners, she now sought rest in the home of her friend, Dr. Tuke, in York, England. Not for long, however. Circumstances were soon to occur destined once again to bring to her lips the familiar refrain,

"Rest is not quitting the busy career."

The original impulse toward the new project which was before long to engross Miss Dix's mind will be found stated in a letter addressed by her, May 6, 1855, to her life-long friend and, at times, personal physician, Dr. H. A. Buttolph, then Superintendent of the Trenton Asylum, New Jersey. As written to her medical adviser, this letter contains a more detailed account of her physical disabilities than, on the matter of health, was common with one, who, in her correspondence and intercourse with her friends, so generally acted on the sun-dial maxim, " Horas non numero nisi sere-nas." The letter soon goes on, however, to give an account of the chance interview which first called her attention to the sad condition of things existing in the Channel Islands; [1] and is farther accompanied by a copy of a communication from a young Dutch alienist, Dr. Van Leuven, then temporarily resident on the Island of Jersey. With these preliminary explanations, the letters will tell their own story.

"York, *May* 16, 1855.

" My dear Friend, — You will recollect all the symptoms for which you have treated me when I have from time to time been your guest. These have never left me at any time, and, though not ill always, I have *at no* time felt well enough to justify uncertain journeys on the Continent. Counting time since I left the steamer, I find that rather more than half the period I have been either really too ill, or too languid, to do anything. The irritation of the mucous membrane of the stomach has of late affected me more seriously, and the inaction of the heart has left me feeble. . . .

" In Scotland, I felt myself giving out, but came forward to York intending to rest a day, and then see the fourteen public and private institutions for the insane in this immediate vicinity. I commenced, but gave out, and am here in a cheerful, quiet apartment. Next to mine, retiring from the labors of an active life spent in the cause of the insane, lies helpless the good Samuel Tuke, the master of this house. The Angel of Death stands at the door watching, but still the last great blessing is deferred, the entrance into the im-

---

[1] A number of islands in the British Channel, politically attached to Great Britain, but connected with France by geographical position, the largest of which are Jersey, Guernsey, and Alderney.

mortal life where no clouds obscure the thought, nor hinder the spirit's growth.

" Let me give you an instance of what, in my case, I call *leads of Providence*. So I wait a little now till returning strength comes to assist the weakened *instrument* of the Divine will. This I say most reverently and with full understanding of what I have in view.

" When in Edinburgh last winter, I *accidentally*, as it might be said, called in at Dr. Simpson's. In the drawing-room was a lady from the south of England, who, hearing my name, came immediately forward, and asked if I had ever visited the islands of Jersey and Guernsey in the British Channel. I replied in the negative, when she and her uncle proceeded to give me an account of the great abuses to which the insane were there subject, and concluded by begging that I would go there. I could not go then, but *I laid these things up in my mind.*

" Well, a few days after I was here, Dr. Tuke entered my room with some pamphlets, asked me if I read French, and said, ' Here is an interesting report from Dr. Van Leuven, of Jersey.' I read it during the day, and at the evening visit said to the doctor, ' I see a movement is made in Jersey; if it has led to no result beside employing Dr. Van Leuven to visit and report on hospitals abroad, *my* going to Jersey would be quite a work of supererogation, for which I have, I assure you, no inclination. Do write to the doctor for information.' This was done at once. The return post brought the following answer, and determined my *duty and next work*, — as soon as I am well enough. Dr. Van Leuven's letter is as follows : —

" ' Island of Jersey.

" ' My dear Tuke, — I have your welcome letter and hasten to answer you about Miss Dix's visit. Strange to say it was only last Saturday, 5th of May, three days ago, that I had a proposal from Mr. Isaac Pothecary, of Grove Place near Southampton (well known for its inhuman treatment and dealings in lunatics, see reports of the Commissioners), asking if I would give him some information and assistance in establishing a private asylum for the insane in Jersey, — he could not go on in England since the Commissioners were so severe, the laws so stringent, and the formalities for the reception of patients so embarrassing — " to escape or avoid all this nonsense in England, he intended to transport not less than twenty private patients (of whom some paid £500 and more per annum) to Jersey, where even no license is required," and "he had come here to look out for two or more fit places for their reception." "I would then," so he writes, "have you visit my asylums twice a week, and be well paid."

" 'I could not help, my dear Tuke, thinking of cattle and horses and slave-dealers, and of York asylums in 1816, and of Bethlem Hospital in 1852! What had I to do? Mr. Pothecary was decided about coming over with the poor patients next week. I could not check him. Ought I to withhold my assistance? Well, I thought, I do not assist the mercenary interests of Mr. Pothecary, but I may assist his unhappy patients. If I withdraw entirely, I leave the poor sufferers at the mercy of their *owner*, and of some of the many doctors in Jersey, who do everything for money.

" 'So the matter stands in an island whose government does not care one bit for its own pauper insane, and much less for those imported from England. Could Miss Dix persuade the English Government to admit *no* asylums in Jersey, Guernsey, or Wright, but under the same laws as exist in England? This would be the proper thing. If Miss Dix will come to Jersey, I will give her a hearty welcome, that she may counterbalance the odious *Insanity Trade* now begun. Please communicate to Miss Dix my most respectful regards. And let me hear soon.

" 'Yours very truly, D. H. VAN LEUVEN.'

"There, my Friend, this must help me get well soon!
"Adieu. Yours truly, D. L. D."

Eminently characteristic of Miss Dix, this final exclamation, " There, my Friend, this must help me get
well soon ! " In her own entirely rational way, she
was thirty-five years ago as thorough a believer in the
" Mind Cure " as are to-day thousands in their puer-
ile and superstitious way, that is, her faith in the ren-
ovating power over bodily infirmity of a great purpose, or a generous affection, was invincible. The idea,
however, that should she chance to break a leg or rup-
ture an artery, all that was needful was firmly to *believe* in a new sound leg, in order, forthwith, to walk
off safely on it, or in a new circulatory system, in order to dispense with the degrading material assistance
of a tourniquet, — this idea, reserved for certain of her
later more enlightened American sisters, — was one
which never crossed her imperfectly illuminated mind.

Indeed, this whole letter to Dr. Buttolph, with its en-
closures, furnishes a striking example of unconscious
self-revelation of character. It begins, as addressed
to a physician, with the pains and infirmities of the
poor body, the sole mortal instrument at the disposal
of a most ardent mind. The chronic symptoms, enfeebled action of the heart, irritability of the mucous
lining, involving both the digestive organs and the
lungs, and others which have not been enumerated,
are clearly and distinctly stated. But soon heart and
soul assert their ascendancy. A new inspiring project has risen before her mind. Not an allusion to
the wonderful success of the recent campaign in Scotland. That work is over and done. Now for the
next duty the Lord would summon her to ! " Let
me give you an instance of what, in my case, I call
leads of Providence ! " To her, there is no chance
in the world. No one need seek after his way in life.

It is revealed to him, if he have eyes to see and ears to hear, in the everyday events of life. God is in them, God speaks through them. The whole universe is the immediate call of God, requiring no other answer but a swift and obedient " Here am I, send me ! " " The return post determined my *duty* and *next work !* "

One all-important link in the chain of circumstances through which, as Miss Dix devoutly believed, God bound every willing soul to its appointed task, had, in this instance, been young Dr. Van Leuven, to whom allusion has several times been made. Among the French papers given her to read by Dr. Tuke was a series of letters written by this philanthropic Hollander, in which he had tried to rouse public sentiment in Jersey, in behalf of the wretched and neglected insane. An extract will show the strength and pathos with which he wrote, though it suffers through its translation from French into English : —

" Eight days after the appearance of my third article in this newspaper (June 27, 1853), a respectable Jersey farmer came to talk with me. Through his simplicity, the stamp of truth, his discourse so interested me that I feel it my duty to give it here, almost in his own words.

" ' Sir,' he said, ' I am only a poor Jersey farmer. Formerly, I knew better days, but I have been reduced these many years by an unhappy insane son. Reading your articles in the " Chronique," I wanted to express my gratitude for what you have written in behalf of the insane poor, and to say, God bless your efforts ! '

" I then asked him to tell me a little about his troubles.

" ' Yes, sir,' continued the good man, ' I have suffered greatly from this affliction which, as you say, has plunged so many families in misery. Through an epidemic of fever, which raged here sixteen years ago, my son became insane. Since that time my annual trips to England for the sale of

Jersey cows have been suspended. I was obliged to stay at home to watch over my son, for there was no one else to take proper care of him ; my wife and the other children were too exhausted, or had suffered too much while I was away ; our neighbors were afraid of him. How many times has he escaped from the house when I had to be elsewhere ; for example, taking part in the militia drill of my parish ! How many whole nights have I spent searching for him ! Often I would find him asleep, from weariness, on danger-ous cliffs, and chilled with frost ! In thus devoting myself to my unhappy son, I was obliged to neglect my trade in Jersey cows, and met severe losses. His image followed me everywhere. Before long he became so violent that I was obliged to bind him. I went to the General Hospital to see about placing him there, but I found the insane quarters utterly unfit for human beings, least of all for those insane. Finally, I was forced to resort to iron chains : yes, sir, I had to chain up my own son ! My heart was broken under such misery ! '

" Poor Jersey father, who have had yourself to chain your own child ! How bitter will this memory be when one day you will see in Jersey a special asylum for the insane, where, as in the English asylums, there will be no more frightful cells, nor iron bars, nor any shapes of mechanical constraint ! Such an asylum in this island, and your son could have been saved, and you need never to have been reduced to this poverty ! "

Still farther information from Dr. Van Leuven arrived later, to which allusion is made in the follow-ing letter from Dr. Tuke, written to Miss Dix when she was somewhere away from his home : —

" St. Lawrence Parish, *June* 23, 1855.

" I must talk to you about our excellent Jersey friend and his admirable letter of June 11th. There does indeed seem to be the most remarkable opening, and your power of doing

good in the matter appears clearly established, whether or
not you go in person to the island. Would it not be best
to send the doctor's letter to Lord Shaftesbury at once, for
perusal? Its natural and telling style would, I think, produce more effect upon him than any other agency. . . . As
I write, my conscience, however, keeps intruding with ' But
remember Miss Dix's strength ! ' "

Spite of the saving clause at the end, it would look
as though this letter were a little open to the construction of aiding and abetting an already too incorrigible
offender ; particularly as only a few days before its
author had written Miss Dix : " Now a word about
your symptoms. I don't like them. They certainly
indicate great debility of the heart (not your moral
organ !), and it behooves you to draw from them the
lesson of rest from mental excitement." Still, who
after seeing any feat superbly executed, whether by
singer, orator, or reformer, can refrain from an enthusiastic encore ! Indeed, the worst demoralization
wrought by military and naval reviews is said to lie
in the fact that the sight of such splendidly equipped
armaments is sure to inspire the minds of the spectators with the longing to see them quit holiday manœu-
vering and close in dead-in-earnest fight.

Be all this as it may, it is clear that, for now six or
eight weeks, Miss Dix's mind was steadily concentrating on a visit in person to the Channel Islands, and
that she was only waiting strength for the undertaking. How exuberant were the hopes and resolves
that filled her, finds eloquent expression in a letter to
her friend, Miss Heath : —

"YORK, EAST RIDING, ENGLAND, *June* 1, 1855.

" MY DEAR ANNIE, — It is four weeks now that I have
been quite unable to be out of the house, till a few days this

week I have gone into the garden in Lindley Murray's chair, — Lindley Murray of *Grammar* and our *child-time tearful* memories.   Mr. Tuke was one of Mr. Murray's executors, and here I see many relics, the family Bible, the garden dial, and the Bath chair.

"Let me tell you, I am now, though not strong for much exertion, able to go to Green Bank, where I am engaged to pass with my dear friends several weeks, until I am able to go to the *Channel Islands* to fulfill a duty lately made clear to me, of helping out of dismal dark dungeons those whose only crime is that they are sick — insane, — and so, feared and tantalized till they are really what the sane would call them, mad men and mad women, capable of any outbreak. I shall see their chains off.   I shall take them into the green fields, and show them the lovely little flowers and the blue sky, and they shall play with the lambs and listen to the song of the birds, 'and a little child shall lead them.'   This is no romance; this all will be, if I get to the Channel Islands, Jersey and Guernsey, with God's blessing.

"I was at a very good hotel, but my friends, Dr. and Mrs. Tuke, insisted on my removal to their nice comfortable home, where I am tended as carefully and tenderly as if I were a sister.   I have been very feeble, but not helpless, and never cheerless. . . . It is now beginning to *dawn* on me that I may not go to the United States this autumn.   I do not see any great use in getting back just as the cold weather advances, unless there is a call to labor.   If so, I dare say the strength would come for the 'daily task,' — 'daily the manna fell from heaven.'

"I should like one of your sweet nice letters now and then.   Cannot you give me so much pleasure?"

To Miss Dix's swift and decisive mind, one thing was clear from Dr. Van Leuven's letters, namely, that the hue and cry of late raised in England and Scotland over miscreants carrying on private madhouses for mercenary ends, and with nefarious and criminal

intent, had thoroughly frightened certain of them.
The country was fast getting too hot to hold them.
So far, so good! "Rats leave a falling house."
Yes, but they go elsewhere to burrow, nest, and defile.
Thither, likewise, must they be followed up, repois-
oned, and driven out of their holes. It was plain
enough what was in the wind. Mr. Pothecary would
quietly transport his chain-gang to the seclusion of
the Island of Jersey, where, happily, busy-body philanthropists did not intrude to disturb the reposeful
scene. There would he have his own paid doctor, to
wink at any little departures from the Decalogue. It
scarcely needs to be added that Miss Dix *laid Mr.
Pothecary up in her mind.* Meanwhile, her grand
aim was to seek to get measures taken, through which
the same ægis of government protection should be
extended over all, wherever they might be in the
United Kingdom.

Not until near the middle of July was Miss Dix
well enough to visit in person the Island of Jersey.
This time she went, not as she had entered Scotland,
a single-handed woman dependent upon her own resources of will and courage, but as one who now had
the ear of the Lord Chancellor and the Home Secretary, as well as the prestige of parliamentary success.
That she acted with her usual dispatch, is evident
from a hasty summary of her course of action, written
from Jersey to her friend, Dr. Buttolph, as well as
from a few flying notes to other friends. The letter
to Dr. Buttolph runs thus : —

"8 QUEEN'S TERRACE, ST. HELLIERS,
ISLAND OF JERSEY, *July* 15, 1855.

"MY DEAR FRIEND, — I now proceed to give you a
running narrative of my affairs here. Left London, Friday,

8½ P. M. . . . detained off Guernsey by fogs, just escaped
the sunken rocks, and landed four and a half hours late at
the Jersey pier, on Saturday, 5 P. M.

"Sunday, at home all day. Monday, 9 A. M., took a
carriage and drove with Dr. Van Leuven to the hospital —
found the insane in a horrid state, naked, filthy, and attended by persons of ill character committed to this establishment for vice too gross to admit of their being at large.
. . . After faithful inspection of the forty insane in the
cells and yards, I drove with my letter of introduction to
Government House; the Governor not at home. I left a
note, previously prepared, soliciting an interview at his Excellency's convenience, which I left with Sir George Grey's
letter, and proceeded to General Touzel's, they also out.
Returned to dinner at Madam R.'s. At 3 o'clock, drove to
look at a site for *the* hospital, les Moraines, the escheated
property of an insane woman who died without heirs, from
which the Crown derives a handsome annual rent. I approved it for *our* use, if it could be had a free gift. We then
proceeded to visit several insane persons in private families,
— a sad, very sad scene. During absence, the Governor and
Mrs. Love had called, also General and Mrs. Touzel twice,
the latter leaving invitation for breakfast on Wednesday,
and the Governor for dinner on same day.

"Went early Wednesday to General Touzel's, had a long
conversation wholly on business affairs. At 10 A. M. General T. went with me to see the Governor. First I presented and represented Mr. Pothecary. The Governor received my evidence in the case, summoned the Attorney
General, . . . thanked me for the information, and would
resume the subject. Next we took up the Jersey Hospital
question. I was promised all government support, but had
to *fight* my way with three dozen members of the States,
viz., twelve *rectors*, twelve yeomen, twelve chief-constables
or managers of the Parishes. The Attorney General in-
vites me to inspect with him Mr. ·Pothecary's residence,

etc. . . . I shall tell you some time about this visit. I got some *useful* information.

" Thursday, drove into the country, still surveying farms and seeing the scattered insane. In the evening some members of the committees of the States called. . . . Friday, A. M., other members called, and settled that the full Board of fifteen should be summoned to an extra meeting, if I would attend. . . . I consented to remain till the full Board reported, and *not* present the subject to the *Government at Home*, if they would do the work without. To-morrow I go with General Touzel to the Treasurer of the States at 9 A. M., at 10½ meet the Committee of Fifteen, . . . then go to Government House and report progress, and *so I will do to you* when I know what is the result.

" Yours cordially,

" D. L. Dix."

There were certain features of partial independence in the relation borne to the General Government of the United Kingdom by the local authorities of the Channel Islands, which made these authorities peculiarly anxious to keep matters in their own hands. Of this fear, on their part, of being reported for any criminal neglect, and so, perhaps, having their powers abridged, Miss Dix skillfully availed herself. So long as they would agree to a thorough reformation of a shameful condition of things, it was, as far as she was concerned, a matter of perfect indifference by what machinery it was done. In that case, she would refrain from appealing to Parliament. But either pledge themselves to do this work themselves, or be reported, was the inexorable alternative she would consent to offer. Meanwhile, that she had not forgotten one little personal matter comes out emphatically in a hurried line, addressed to Mrs. Rathbone, of Liverpool.

"8 QUEEN'S TERRACE, ST. HELLIERS, *July*, 1855.

"To-day I can only be brief. I am very much occupied. First, I have gotten Mr. Pothecary into the custody of the High Constable of Jersey, by order of the Governor and counsel of the Attorney General. So *that* business is well settled, and the laws will protect the patients he has so boldly *transported*. I have seen them. Next, I have got a farm for the hospital that I hope shall be, and the hospital I will call La Maison de l'Espérance. I shall stay in Jersey so long as will settle the question of hospital or no hospital."

One other letter of Miss Dix to Dr. Buttolph, is all that remains of her correspondence from Jersey. It is full of hope at what she feels will be the outcome of her visit : —

"ISLAND OF JERSEY, *July* 18, 1855.

"MY DEAR FRIEND, — At a full committee of sixteen gentlemen yesterday, the resolution was passed *unanimously* to build a hospital here for the insane, with the least possible delay. To-morrow, I accompany a sub-committee to search out a fit site and farm, and a structure for 100 patients is to be commenced upon a plan capable of extension at need. . . . I want hints, plans, and specifications from you, *without cost.* Let me hear by return steamer. I must push these people, or the building will not be finished till next century. . . . I expect to go to Guernsey on Friday, and to England on Monday next."

A few days more and Miss Dix is back again in England, with her friends at Greenbank, whence she writes to Miss Heath : —

"Safely arrived in the dear old home. I rest and am quiet to my heart's content. Friends are all well and in prosperity, and so I find them drawing toward the latter days in peace, doing good to all as they have opportunity. Gough, the temperance lecturer, has made a great impressicn here, and I am glad to see the impulse given to that cause is quickened and quickening. Barnum's book is vile. It has done more to dishonor Americans and the American character here than you would believe possible."

While thus quietly resting at Greenbank, Dr. Tuke writes to congratulate her on the recent work in Jersey : —

"I think you have good reason to be satisfied with the results already apparent, and, with Dr. Van Leuven left on the spot, there is probably less danger of the thing being lost sight of. There will be nothing more needed, I believe, but keeping up a brisk fire."

In concluding the account of this Island of Jersey episode in Miss Dix's career, it is here the fitting place to state that her own words, " I must push these people, or the building will not be finished till the next century," proved partially prophetic. But only partially. The "next century" still lags ten years behind, and these words were written thirty-five years ago. Still it was not till 1868, nearly thirteen years after her bringing the Jersey Islanders to a sense of their duty, that a large public asylum was finally completed for the humane and scientific treatment of the insane.

The nature and degree of the impression produced on the minds of many of Miss Dix's truest friends at this triumphant period of her life can hardly be better expressed than in the warning letter written her just before her departure for Jersey by her aged friend, William Rathbone, of Liverpool. It will be recalled by the reader that it was into Mr. Rathbone's home that she had been taken on her first visit to England in 1837, then apparently marked for early death by consumption. The last thing that could have been prophesied of her at that time was the extraordinary career that really lay before her. Indeed, to quote the recollection of one of the sons of the family, written just after Miss Dix's death, in 1887, to Dr. John W. Ward, of Trenton, N J.: " She was at this period an invalid, a very gentle and poetical and sentimental young lady, and, in the then state of her health, without any appearance of mental energy or great power of character." Through all the succeeding years of her labors in the United States, her footsteps had been followed with unfailing interest by Mr. and Mrs. Rathbone, and still they were living to witness the wonders she had accomplished in Scotland. Mr. Rathbone's letter was as follows: —

"GREENBANK, *Sunday, July* 8, 1855.

" MY DEAR FRIEND, — Not being inclined to sleep, I have thought that a quiet hour before breakfast could not be better employed than in saying, God bless my valued and loved friend, and speed her successfully in her progress, — so far as is consistent with the scheme of His inscrutable, yet ever beneficent, Providence ! He has *tried* you in the success of what you have undertaken beyond what I have ever known, or, as far as my recollection serves me, have read of any other person, male or female — far beyond that of Howard, Father Mathew, Mrs. Chisholm, or Mrs. Fry. I speak now of the entirety of the success as much as of the extent, and it has not turned your head or, as I believe, led you to forget the source from which your strength has been derived. In the most tender love, therefore, to a faithful and self-sacrificing minister to His designs, He may fit the burden to the strength, and not try you too far by allowing you to carry the *World* before you. That your head has not already been, as we say, turned by the magnitude and vast extent of your success, is, as much as the many other parts of your character, the subject of my respectful admiration. These thoughts have been suggested by the *check so far* you have met in your efforts to supply the wants of the insane in Newfoundland.[1] . . .

" Your affectionate friend,

" W. RATHBONE."

That Miss Dix's head was not fatally turned by the unexampled series of triumphs of the past fifteen years, was signal proof that her head was at once very strong and very well balanced. The testimonials so profusely showered on her had been the enthusiastic encomiums of great public bodies, — of twenty State legislatures, of the Federal Congress of the United States, and finally of the British Parliament. Self-reliance, under such unusual temptations, might read-ily enough leap all barriers and pass over into arro-gant assumption ; the sense of power might easily become inflamed into a dominating passion for the exercise of power ; the sweetness of praise might de-generate into making the pursuit of praise the end of life.

Constitutionally ambitious of distinction, as is in-stinctive with such commanding personalities, what saved her from such a fate was the intensity of her commiseration with suffering and the fervor of her religious faith. Point out to her a new field of labor, in which she could hope to alleviate the miseries of her fellow-creatures, and in a moment she was eager to turn her back on every remembrance of past achieve-ment, and plunge anew into obscurity and a life of lonely toil and pain. Then as to the essence of her

---

[1] The Asylum at St. John's, Newfoundland, the long delays attend-ant on the foundation of which had been to Miss Dix a source of con-stant anxiety and disappointment.

religious faith, and what it taught her. She was a perfectly clear-headed woman, not subject to illusions. She knew, as simple fact of nature, that she " differed from others." She knew that she could. do what not one in a million could do. How could she help knowing it ? It was so. All this, her past career had made matter of daily demonstration ; and she, moreover, self-respectfully enjoyed the tribute of competent minds to the range and value of her work.

Only passingly, however, did she allow these thoughts to engross her. The moment gaping companies sought to lionize her, she flung the attempt off as offensive insult. Habitually there was a deeper depth in her being, retiring into the sanctuary of which, she communed with the momentous question of St. Paul : " Who maketh thee to differ from another, and what hast thou that thou hast not received ? Now, if thou didst receive it, why dost thou glory as if thou hadst not received it." This was to her the divine voice "casting down imaginations and every vain thought that exalteth itself against the knowledge of God." Downright before man, nay, often terrible to him, when she found him the callous oppressor of the helpless, she was, before God, lowly and self-abnegating, an unprofitable servant. Then, once again, some cry of distress would fall upon her ear, and, in an instant, "forgetting the things that were behind, she was pressing toward the mark for the prize of the high calling" embodied to her in the word : " Inasmuch as ye have done it unto one of the least of these, ye have done it unto me ! "

Quite impossible is it, however, for any one who sanely estimates the frailty of human nature at its best, to read the private letters and public resolutions which, at this period, were showered on Miss Dix, without tremblingly recurring to the words of warning from her aged friend, William Rathbone: "God has *tried* you in the success of what you have undertaken beyond what I have ever known, or, as far as my recollection serves me, have read of any other person, male or female." It is well, therefore, to note from how high and varied quarters these seductive "trials" came. Thus only can a due conception be formed of how much she was really subjected to in that most subtle and dangerous of all forms of temptation, the praise of man.

First, she had touched the spring of patriotic pride in her own countrymen and countrywomen, then abroad; how intensely, may be judged from this brief extract from a letter, to a friend in England, of Mrs. E. H. Walsh, wife of the American ambassador to France: —

"VERSAILLES, *June* 3, 1855.

"Pray remember me to Miss Dix. If with you, tell her I kiss the hem of her garment, and bless God that our country has produced such a noble heart. She will see the honorable mention of her services by the Earl of Shaftesbury in Parliament, and Mr. Walsh is about to add his testimony to her immense worth, in his correspondence. He regrets very much not having made the acquaintance of Miss Dix. He is right. Such a woman is to be worshiped, if anything human could be worshiped."

Again, by the Annual Convention of the Association of Superintendents of American Insane Asylums, held in the summer of 1855, Miss Dix was addressed in terms of honor and love like these: —

"*Resolved*, That the Secretary of the Association be directed to request Miss Dix to favor us at our next meeting

with an account of her observations and investigations in the
countries she is now visiting, the same to be read in private
session and be deemed strictly confidential, if in her judgment or wish such a course is expedient.

"Our Association has never met without many grateful
recognitions of your invaluable services to humanity, and
though, at the late meeting, you and ourselves were much
more widely separated than ever before since we became an
organized body, I can assure you that you never held a
higher place in our most respectful consideration. And
while on the one hand we felt much fraternal solicitude on
account of your continued feebleness, it on the other afforded us the liveliest satisfaction to learn that our mother-
countrymen have received you with that eminent consideration and personal kindness which are so fully accorded to
you everywhere at home.

"We all miss you from the country, and especially do
those of us miss the great benefits of your personal encour-
agement and coöperation, who are the immediate masters of
those 'many mansions' of beneficence, which owe their existence under Providence to the extrordinary success of your
appeals to humanity in prosperity in favor of humanity in
adversity. We pray for the renewal of your health and
strength, and shall hail with gladness your return to the
scenes of your widest and most fruitful labors." . . . .

"I am, dear Madam, with the highest esteem,
    "Your friend and servant,
        "J. H. NICHOLS, *Secretary.*"

Finally, let the two following extracts from the
letters of superintendents of large asylums in America,
suffice as evidence of the peculiar honor in which alike
her sound judgment and personal approval were at
this period held. The names of the writers, long at
the head of great institutions, are, on grounds of delicacy, withheld, though in all probability they would
give glad permission to have them used.

The first extract confines itself to remembrances of past services of Miss Dix, when on one of her visits to an asylum : —

"It is not, however, by any such visible tokens as books and pictures that your visit will be remembered. Your clear and unmistakable showing of what our defects are, is the greatest boon that you could have conferred. I did not misunderstand those criticisms, so delicately administered to others, and, at the same time, so applicable to us. Not only has every observation been carefully treasured up in my memory, but every word which could be remembered has been made the text for suggestive commentaries of my own."

The extract which follows is in a vein rarely adopted by an eminent professional man to a woman, with no other diploma but the diploma of a strong brain, a wide experience, and a great heart : —

"Thus you see that I have not been idle during your absence from the country of upwards of six months, but have diligently striven to do what was demanded of my position, and what I thought you would approve, — always feeling a responsibility to your prospective approbation in carrying on a work which is so rightfully yours. If you can say ' Well done ! ' to what is already done, I shall be glad. Your confidence and friendship are a well of pleasure and a tower of strength to me. I think I appreciate them. I hope they are not misplaced.

"I am not unaware of your noble and extraordinary achievements in view of the amelioration of the condition of the insane of Scotland. I know that this is a secondary consideration with you, but I think the narrative of that achievement will make one of the brightest pages in the history of the progressive ameliorations of the sufferings of humanity."

CHAPTER XXIV.

IN a letter, already quoted, to Miss Heath, of date, East Riding, England, June 1, 1855, there occurs the first intimation of an intention on the part of Miss Dix to prolong her stay in Europe, and visit the Continent. She is, as she says, "very feeble, but not helpless, and never cheerless," and goes on, "it is now beginning to dawn on me that I may not go to the United States this autumn. I do not see any great use in getting back just as the cold weather advances, unless there is a call to labor. If so, I dare say the strength would come for the daily task, — 'Daily the manna fell from heaven.'"

Accordingly, as the summer advanced, a cordial invitation from the Rathbones, then in Switzerland, to join them as their guest and see the Alps, brought matters to a final decision with her.

Naturally anxious to do everything for her health and comfort, her kindly friends had strongly urged upon her that, before setting out from England, she should secure the services of a capable woman as maid, — a proposition which called from Miss Dix the following characteristic and rather amusing reply:

"You desire that I should have some one with me, a maid, to save me fatigue and prevent my *feeling desolate* when alone. A maid would be only in the way, with nothing to do; and, for feeling desolate, I never felt desolate in my life, and I have been much alone in both populous and thinly-settled countries. . . . You are quite right in saying I cannot rest in England any more than in America, now that I know how much suffering calls aloud for relief. I must turn a deaf ear to the cries, and go beyond the reach of the sound of the many afflicted ones, till I have gathered up force to renew — should it please God that I work longer — the work whereunto I am called."

To the reader of this biography, already familiar with Miss Dix's habits of travel on her lonely and hazardous journeys through the former comparative wildernesses of the southern and western regions of the United States, — journeys on which she always carried with her a private outfit of hammers, screws, wrenches, leather straps, and coils of rope, to be ready for repairs in event of accident, — it will easily be conceived that the proposed relation, however kindly suggested, between Miss Dix and a maid would hardly have proved a happy one for either party. Miss Dix would have been distressed for fear of the maid "feeling desolate," while the maid herself would have been frightened out of all propriety at having to stand by and see the thousand and one things her mistress could do for herself, beyond anything it had ever entered her humble imagination to conceive.

The Swiss visit proved to Miss Dix one of the most delightful holiday seasons of her active and crowded life. In after years, she never tired of talking about Chamonix and the Bernese Oberland. Once "beyond the reach of the sound of the many afflicted ones," she seems to have freely yielded herself to the spell of the magnificent spectacle daily before her eyes. Easily rising, as was constitutional with her, to a state of high spiritual exaltation, she speaks of

the "snow-clad peaks, mantled with their regal robes
of pasture and forest, as a sublime cathedral anthem
to God." Along with this, her vivid interest in all
natural phenomena — next to compassion the strongest impulse of her nature — here found a fruitful field
of exercise. The glaciers, the Arctic flora, the geo-
logic forces in such active operation, now supplied her
with data at least, which in all later years made her
an eager and appreciative reader of the studies on
these subjects of men like Agassiz, Lyell, and Tyndal.
Even, in the midst of the distraction and suffering of
the later Civil War, she writes, in 1862 : —

"Your thoughtful care for my gratification in planning
that pleasant journey to the Continent has enriched my life
for all time. I never find the glorious views of the Alps
fade from my mind's eye. A thousand incidents recall and
repeat the memory of those grand snow peaks piercing the
skies."

Moreover, the rest and recreation of spirit thus
afforded had acted so beneficially on her physical
condition that she at last felt justified in carrying out
the plan she had for some time been revolving, of an
extended tour of observation of the hospitals, insane
asylums, and prisons of Europe, including those of
Turkey, with, possibly, the accomplishment of the
yearned-for visit to Palestine.

Accompanying the Rathbones on their way back to
England, Miss Dix shortly after parted with them and
set out for France. She was now once more alone,
and, as she liked to be when engrossed in her work,
left to her sole individual resources. How meagre in
one important respect were these resources, could not
but awaken a half-compassionate, half-amused smile

in her devoted friends. Apart from English, she
spoke no other language but a little very rudimentary
French; and here she was proposing to face undaunted the linguistic problems of Italy, Greece, Turkey, Sclavonia, Russia, Germany, Norway, and Holland, and that, too, before the days of the " royal
road " to philological knowledge later opened by the
introduction of polyglot waiters into every inn. Not
unlikely, however, in her fondness for heroic stories
and her keen sense of their pith and marrow, she had
called to mind the legendary account of the mother of
St. Thomas à Becket: how, deserted in Syria by her
husband, an English crusader, the poor yearning wife
had set out from the East, traversed all Europe on
foot, and finally rejoined him in his own land on the
strength of the two sole words of his language she
knew, " à Becket " and " England." Surely, if a
lone Moslem woman was equal to such a feat, why
might not an American woman, mistress of a little
rudimentary French, hope to penetrate the secrets of
Greek insane asylums, Turkish bagnios, and Russian
prisons.

Fortunately there remain a number of letters by
the help of which Miss Dix's footsteps can be traced
through a part of the long journeyings, to which she
was now to devote nearly a full year. Those from
France are few and unimportant, but as she makes her
way to Italy, Greece, and onward to Constantinople,
they become more frequent and more eventful : —

To MRS. RATHBONE.

"METTRAY, NEAR TOURS, *September* 3, 1855.

" Arrived at Rouen at 4 P. M. Visited hospitals for aged
men and women, and establishment for juvenile offenders

at Quilly, five miles out of Rouen, at St. Yon another. Then Paris, then Orleans, then Blois, then Tours, then Mettray.   Go next to Nantes, return to Paris."

To Mrs. RATHBONE.

"PARIS, *September*, 1855.

"Yesterday, and only till then, I became possessor of a full Police and Magisterial Sanction under seal, — for which nine official parties were to be reached, — for entering all the prisons and hospitals of Paris, without exception."

To Mrs. SAMUEL TORREY, BOSTON, U. S.

"PARIS, *November*, 1855.

"I am still entirely occupied in seeing the charitable institutions of this city and environs, which I hope to have done by two weeks more. The very short days and the very dull weather unite to make this slow work. I am obliged to take much rest ; it seems to have become absolutely the condition on which I do anything in the pursuit of my vocation. The vast multiplication of all sorts of hospitals for all sorts of complaints and infirmities, and for all ages, tells of the different condition of family life from that we are used to observe. I quite comprehend the turbulence and crimes of revolutionary periods, especially those movements in which women have been conspicuous for trampling on all laws human and divine."

To DR. BUTTOLPH, TRENTON, U. S.

"PARIS, *December* 3, 1855.

"I should say that *all* the charitable institutions of Paris, liberally supported as they are by government, possess in a large measure great excellencies, but two radical universal defects, at least, strike the most casual observer. The want of ventilation is the chiefest ill, and quite explains the amazing mortality, apart from the well - known *experimental* methods of treatment by the *Internes*, — resident students. In *all* these establishments, associated with other employees, are found Sisters of Charity, and nuns of various orders. Some of them are very self-denying, not many. They are never over-tasked, except possibly in some period of serious epidemic. As for the priests, they should for the most part occupy places in houses of correctional discipline, and enlightening cultivation."

It was not until the second week in January that Miss Dix, after completing her examination of the charitable institutions of France, was ready to leave for Italy. The first letter from there bears date, Genoa, March 3, 1856 : —

To Mrs. Rathbone.

"Genoa, Italy, *March* 3, 1856.

"This morning I spent in the hospital for the insane, and find much to commend, with some things to disapprove ; but after seeing that at Rome, I regard all other institutions in this country with comparative favor. . . . I left Naples, Rome, and Florence with regret that I could not have had leisure to observe the works of art, ancient and modern, which have great attraction, but I saw a good deal, considering the claims of hospitals and the short time I spent in each place. I get daily news from Constantinople which moves my sympathy for the poor insane of Turkey. Innovations in usages are now fast going on there, so we may hope the hospitals will share in the advance of civilization."

Three days later, the above letter is followed by one to Mrs. Samuel Torrey, in which a backward glance is thrown by Miss Dix over the objects that had engaged her since her arrival in Italy : —

To Mrs. Samuel Torrey.

"Genoa, *March* 6, 1856.

"I left Marseilles so suddenly for Italy the second week of January, and since have been so wholly and fatiguingly occupied, that all letter-writing is very seriously interfered with. . . . I was but thirteen days in Naples. The bad weather which I had experienced during all the autumn in France followed me there. I found at Rome a hospital for the insane so very bad, that I set about the difficult work of reform at once, and during the fourteen days I was there, so far succeeded as to have Papal promises and Cardinal assurances, etc., of immediate action in remedying abuses and supplying deficiencies. I have promised some of the Roman citizens and some of the physicians to return there in two months, if no advance is made in the object of my late efforts, so that coming to the United States in June is, I fear, quite set aside. I also wish a new hospital in Florence. This has been contemplated by the Commune of Florence, but the onerous taxation consequent on the Austrian invasion has impoverished the city. You need not be much surprised to hear of me in Constantinople. I have for a long time felt distressed at the horrid stories of suffering in the prisons and hospitals there; and yet, till quite lately, I have not had a thought of personally undertaking anything in that quarter; but recent political and social changes, joined with information had from Sir Charles and Lady Hamilton, recently returned from the East, have led me to believe that something might be commenced in the way of reform. . . . My work seems to me to be indicated by Providence, and I cannot conscientiously turn away from attempting, as far as possible, to alleviate miseries wherever I find them."

Only a day after the dispatch of the preceding letter, Miss Dix writes as follows, from Turin: —

To Mrs. Rathbone.

"Turin, Italy, *March* 7, 1856.

"I left Genoa at 11 A. M. and arrived safely after a very pleasant journey. . . . It is just as easy traveling alone here as it is in England or America. I now regret I had not sooner tried it."

Next day : " The General Hospitals here, as in Italy at large, are very good, but that in this city for the insane is so bad that I feel quite heart-sick. I drove to the hospital in the country, — very bad. Then I drove to the hospital within the walls, made an appointment with the chief doctor for to-morrow, and with the Protestant minister, shall try to represent the importance of entire change for the patients. I do not think it will do much good, but it is my duty to try. I shall appeal in writing to the king. Leave for Milan to-morrow."

Later : " My plans appear to be about as stable as spring breezes. After the meeting touching hospital affairs yesterday, and which only served to establish my opinion of the melancholy defects of the institutions in question, I was invited to visit to-day the five prisons of Turin, and to join in my application for hospital reform some remonstrance against the pernicious arrangement of these establishments. I have not to convince officers of government alone, but to make stand against the *priests*, who interfere with everything that is done or to be done. I never felt anything more difficult than this work in Italy. In Rome I found government and the priestly office united, and the very *shame* of foreign and Protestant interposition quickened them to action or *promise* rather than humanity ; but in Florence, Genoa, and here, it is a fact that changes are coming over the old rule, and one must wait a little where so much is doing and to be done. I will now make no more plans for going or returning, so many things constantly occur to change or hinder my intentions."

From the above letters it is evident that in Rome itself Miss Dix felt she had struck upon a worse condition of things in the treatment of the insane than anywhere else in Italy. Even in Naples, and under the rule of King " Bomba," she had found an asylum worthy of warm tributes of praise ; but here, under

the very shadow of the Vatican, the condition of the
lunatic was so hopelessly wretched as to convince her
that this must be her field of immediate energetic action.   As it will be necessary to enlarge to some extent
on the work she accomplished in Rome, it is a satisfaction to find a letter, expressive of her personal feeling
on the subject, addressed by her from Florence to her
friends, Dr. and Mrs. Buttolph, of Trenton, N. J.

To Dr. and Mrs. Buttolph.

" Florence, Italy, 1856.

"In Naples I did nothing for hospitals ; indeed, strange
as it is, I found a better institution there for the insane than
has been founded in all southern and central Italy.   In
Rome things were quite different.   6,000 priests, 300
monks, 3,000 nuns, and a spiritual sovereignty joined with
the temporal powers had not assured for the miserable
insane a decent, much less an intelligent, care.   I could not
bear to know this, see this, and do nothing.   An appeal to
the Pope which involved care, patience, time, and negotiation has secured promises.   Land is bought (at least I had
the assurances of the officers of state that it was that day
purchased), and plans are prepared.   Now if these *are not
carried out*, I do *not return* to the United States but go to
Rome and stay till they do that which is needed. . . . Since
coming to Florence five days ago, I find a bad hospital here,
and mountains of difficulty in the way of remedy for serious
ills.   I have the idea of removing these mountains, and seeing if Protestant energy cannot work what Catholic powers
fail to undertake."

It will readily be seen that it was a work of a very
delicate nature which Miss Dix now found on her
hands.   She was a foreigner, a Protestant, and a
woman; and yet, with all these serious disabilities, she
now saw it in the light of inexorable duty to seek an

audience of the Supreme Pontiff of the great Roman
Catholic Church, and, in a way not to offend his sensibilities, but graciously to win his favor, clearly to
apprise the "Anointed Vicar of Christ on Earth,"
that in the light of modern knowledge and humanity,
the insane asylum of the Holy City was a disgrace
and a scandal. The audience must be, moreover, no
mere ceremonial interview, with graceful interchange
of bows and genuflections, but a direct encounter between the two grand rival Infallibilities confronting
one another in the Nineteenth Century, — the Infallibility of Rome, and the infallibility of Enlightened
Reason. That in the realm of the new revelation of
the humane and rational treatment of insanity which
had now broken upon the world, she stood a divinely-
commissioned champion of Moral Reason, and was
backed by an authority of science so irresistible that
" whatsoever it should bind on earth, should be bound
in heaven," — of all this she felt no more question
than Pope Hildebrand, when at Canossa he confronted
the imperial power of Henry IV. with the sacerdotal
power embodied in his own personality. No such
thing was there, no such thing could there be, as an
infallibly-good bad insane asylum.

At the same time, there could be no employment
here of Hildebrand tactics. The weapons of the
modern warfare of humane science are not of the flesh,
but of the spirit. They demand no trophies in the
shape of humiliated defiers of their dogmas. But
they do demand, with more than Papal authority,
absolute and unconditional submission, and that their
"Yea shall be Yea, and their Nay, Nay," in "sæcula
sæculorum." So now, if a new triumph for the outcast and miserable was to be won, it could come alone

of convincing the judgment and touching the heart of Pope Pius IX.

As Miss Dix herself wrote, "The appeal to the Pope involved care, patience, time, and negotiation." Fortunately, early in her attempts she had secured the powerful assistance of Cardinal Antonelli, who entered warmly into her scheme, and whose clear-cut intellectual force made a life-long impression on her. Alike as an astute diplomatist, and as almost the last survival of the old regime of cardinals, who contrived to unite the freedom from earthly ties of the celibate state with a large family of children, perhaps too openly permitted to avow their parentage on the Corso, Cardinal Antonelli has come in for his full share of censorious criticism. But it is a curious fact that, to the end of her days, Miss Dix — whose standard in such matters was inexorable — would never in her presence suffer a word to be said against him. He was the most enlightened, humane, and merciful man, she insisted, she had found in Rome, a man who spared himself no pains to urge the plea of the wronged and suffering.

Unfortunately, no letter or paper of any kind remains that might serve to recall the particulars of the interview Miss Dix ultimately obtained with Pope Pius IX. That it was one which, from the circumstances of the case, — the supreme spiritual authority of the Pontiff, the beautiful benignity of the man, and the far-reaching consequences it might entail, — must have called out her full resources, there can be no question. All that can be gathered to-day to illustrate the scene must come from the memories of certain of Miss Dix's still surviving friends, to whom, in those rare hours of intimacy in which she suffered her habitual reticence about herself to be broken through, she told the story.

She found Pius IX. benignity itself. Happily at home in English, nothing of the power of the plea was lost by having to pass through the medium of an interpreter. He listened with fixed attention to her recital, and was painfully shocked at its details, promising her immediately to make a personal examination and appointing a second audience at a later date. A day or two after, he drove unannounced to the insane asylum, and taking its officials unawares inspected the wards himself. Then, at the second audience granted Miss Dix, he freely acknowledged his distress at the condition of things he had found, and warmly thanked her, a woman and a Protestant, for crossing the seas to call to his attention as Chief Shepherd of the Sheep these cruelly-entreated members of his flock. " And did you really kneel down and kiss his hand ? " were wont to ask some of her ultra-Protestant and Quaker hearers. " Most certainly, I did," she would reply. " I revered him for his saintliness."

And yet. impressive, and perhaps entirely unexpected, as this scene and its sequel may appear to the majority of Protestant readers, their naïve surprise is simply a measure of their ignorance of the grand tradition of the Roman Catholic Church. Through all the centuries of Christendom, has that marvelous religious organization known how to interpret, utilize, and open a career to exceptional women, after a fashion that Protestantism has never yet mastered. That, for example, the " Babylonian Captivity " of the church was brought to an end, and the restoration of the Papacy from Avignon to the Eternal City finally effected, by the clear insight and passionate pleading

of a woman, Catherine of Siena, is something which the
Roman Catholic Church has never hesitated proudly
and gratefully to avow. Such rare and exceptional
combinations in women of mystical fervor of faith with
commanding practical ability, it has not only known
how to avail itself of for founding new and im-
mensely effective religious orders in all lands, but, after death, it has canonized the representatives of them
as saints ; thus dowering them with a supernatural
power over generations to come greater even than the
natural power they exerted over their own generations.

In point of fact, a woman of precisely the same
stamp was standing there before Pius IX. in the Vatican, February, 1856. Had she been born in 1515 in
still mediæval and imaginatively-religious Spain, instead of in 1802 in rational, practical New England,
then, just as inevitably as in the case of St. Theresa,
would she have founded great conventual establishments in a Malaga, Valladolid, Toledo, Segovia, and
Salamanca, as she in reality did great asylums for the
insane in a Baltimore, Raleigh, Columbia, Nashville,
Lexington, or Halifax. Equally too would she have
ruled them as abbess. Precisely the same characteristics marked her, the same absolute religious consecration, the same heroic readiness to trample under
foot the pains of illness, loneliness, and opposition, the
same intellectual grasp of what a great reformatory
work demanded.

St. Theresa was nourished from childhood on the
miraculous legends of the saints, and breathed all her
life an atmosphere of supernatural marvel and por-
tent. Dorothea Lynde Dix was nourished on the devout humanitarianism of Channing, and breathed the

quickening air of a time just awakening to enthusiastic faith in the amelioration of human misery through
the beneficent discoveries of science. And so, very
curious, historically, is it to notice, in the parallel of
these two kindred founders of great institutions, the
change of view time works in religious faiths. The
acute pain in the side which through life clung to each
of them, and which came in each instance of pulmonary weakness, was in the first case believed to have
been a stroke delivered by an angel who pierced her
with a lance tipped with fire, and in the other — though
equally tipped with fire — devoutly accepted as the
ordained action of those immutable physical laws of
God, through which He works out the eternal counsel
of His will.

Very great, then, was the mistake made by a woman
of such genius as George Eliot, when, in her attempt
in Middlemarch, to portray the inevitable fate in this
shallow, material Nineteenth Century, of a modern
St. Theresa, she selected as the type of such a nature,
a sentimental woman like Dorothea Brooke, and as the
pitiful outcome of all such soaring aspirations, evolved
the story of her marriage with the acrid bookworm
Casaubon, whom she had fancifully mistaken for a profound scholar and a man of sublime aims. " Dorothea," comments George Eliot, " with all her eagerness
to know the truth of life, retained very childlike ideas
about marriage. She felt sure that she would have
accepted the ' Judicious Hooker,' if she had been born
in time to save him from that wretched mistake he
made in matrimony ; or John Milton when his blind-
ness had come on ; or any of the other great men
whose odd habits it would have been glorious piety to
endure."

Now, retrospective visions on the part of gentle and aspiring young ladies of the blissful changes that would have been wrought in the fate of departed men of genius, had they themselves only happened to be Mrs. Richard Hooker or Mrs. John Milton, are no doubt very charming and, had they come in time, would have spared much domestic misery. Still, such romantic visions are at the last remove from any kind of proof that the young ladies in question have the attributes of a St. Theresa. " A new Theresa," says George Eliot, " will hardly have the opportunity of reforming a conventual life, any more than a new Antigone will spend her heroic piety in daring all for the sake of a brother's burial; the medium in which their ardent deeds took shape is forever gone." " No, the medium is forever here ! " say the real St. Theresas. " In one age, it assumes one shape ; in another, another. He that has eyes to see, let him see ! "

To return, however, to the audiences granted Miss Dix in the Vatican by Pope Pius IX. The first outcome of them was most assuring to her. And yet, though confident the Pope would remain faithful to his own pledges, and relying on Cardinal Antonelli as a tower of strength, she still read with perfect clearness the character of the ecclesiastical bureaucracy of Rome, and understood how many an interest of ignorance, superstition, and private greed would lift its outcry against every shape of innovation. She therefore stood ready — as has already been seen in previously quoted letters from Florence and Genoa — to return at any moment to Rome, and renew the battle. It was, however, a great relief before long to learn that an especial physician had been sent to France to study the methods of the best asylums there, and that a tract of land near the Villa Borghese had actually been purchased, — as well as, still later on, to be assured by an American friend in Rome, Dr. Joseph Parish, that "preliminary steps had already been taken by the Pope toward the erection of a new asylum on the most approved plan." An account of a visit to this subsequently-erected asylum, written Miss Dix many years later, by Mrs. J. P. Bancroft, is here subjoined : —

"NAPLES, *February* 7, 1876.

"MY DEAR MISS DIX, — I have always remembered with lively interest the accounts you gave us, many years ago, of the efforts you made in Rome to reach the insane, and improve their condition. This recollection gave me more than ordinary desire, while in Rome, to see the asylum which was erected by Pius' IX., and which' perhaps your efforts may have originated in his mind. So I devoted a day to a visit at the Institution.

"I found ready access to the principal Medical Director, and joined him in a circuit of all parts of the houses and grounds. It is a department of the General Hospital, San Spirito, and has gone under the control of the Italian Government since the occupation. . . . There are 650 patients, made up of paying patients and dependents, the latter being far the larger number. . . . From what I saw I believe the management is inspired by the spirit of the times. But in the realization of results, two obstacles are in the way, poverty and lack of the best experience. While these exist, we can never expect the conditions found in English and American Asylums. . . . I think their ideas and demands as to personal tidiness and cleanliness are much more lax than among the English-speaking peoples. . . . I was not so much surprised at the manner in which I saw them take their meals, when I observed along the streets the poorer class eating in their homes. . . . Italy is fearfully poor, and the people are taxed to the last extreme ; and, with this and all the expense of the military system she feels obliged to keep up, I cannot see how very great improvement can be looked for at present in the management of their public institutions of charity. . . . There can be no question that a great revolution in the care and treatment of the insane was effected by the organization of this present Institution, in comparison with former methods. The superintendent manifests great interest in his work, and I could not but regret his lack of means to make the house as pleasant and inviting as money might make it. . . .

" Very cordially your friend,
"J. P. BANCROFT."

CHAPTER XXV.

ONCE away from Italy, which she left early in March, 1856, the first traces of Miss Dix on her travel eastward, are met in two time-stained letters, the first addressed to Dr. Buttolph, in the United States, the second to Mr. William Rathbone, in England. Written while her steamer was lying at anchor in the harbor of the Island of Corfu, they furnish glimpses of the diligence with which she was pursuing her appointed work.

To DR. H. A. BUTTOLPH.

" You will not be more surprised than I am that I find traveling *alone* perfectly easy. I get into all the hospitals and all the prisons I have time to see or strength to explore. I take no refusals, and yet I speak neither Italian, German, Greek, or Sclavonic. I have no letter of introduction, and know no persons *en route.* I found at Trieste a very bad hospital for the insane. Fortunately a physician attached to the suite of the Archduke Maximilian has promised the intervention of government at Trieste and assured me that all the institutions of Austria shall be open to my visits if I come to Vienna." . . .

To MR. WILLIAM RATHBONE.

" ISLAND OF CORFU, *March* 27, 1856.

" I have just time, since running on shore to see the prisons and hospitals, to report myself briefly to you and Mrs. R. Providence graciously protects me, and I am in no respects thus far impeded in my great objects of seeing the prisons and hospitals. By rare good fortune, I had an introduction to the physician of the Archduke Maximilian at Trieste, and made a move for a reform and renewal of the hospitals for the insane in that part of the Austrian Dominions; also had the promise of the entrée to all the institutions of the Empire, if I went to Vienna. When the boat arrived last night, I went on shore as early as I could do anything, took a cab and drove to the Greek institutions; — *saw all!* "

Five days later, as she sits awaiting the arrival of a steamer at Piræus, the port of Athens, another glimpse is caught of the traveler, and of the way in which she has been spending the intervening time. Within close sight of Athens, and still, in her letter, not the most distant allusion to the Acropolis or the Parthenon, or Phidias, nor even to the imperative need of raising money for the exhumation of statues which would reveal a new ideal of the glory of the human form! And yet never a soul that breathed, more passionately bent on the exhumation, from beneath the accumulations of ages of cruelty and neglect, of the divine archetypal idea of man as created in the image of God!

As an illustration of the power of a dominating purpose in the case of one whose mind was naturally so active, this absence of any reference to places, events, and personalities, with whose inspiring story she had been familiar from childhood, and the bare hope of ever standing on whose soil would, under other conditions, have intensely excited her, is certainly very striking. "I must work the work that is given me to do, and how is my soul straitened until it be accomplished," was unquestionably her feeling, as it was equally the feeling of John Howard. Like him, she stood resolutely on her guard against the intrusion of all side issues, however fascinating. Embarked on a mission of mercy, her limited store of strength must be wholly consecrated to that. And yet those who in later years listened to her, on those rare occasions on which she talked of her travels, said that her eyes seemed to have been ever on the alert and to have taken in everything.

To MRS. WILLIAM RATHBONE.

"PIRÆUS, GREECE, *April* 2, 1856.

"I am waiting for the arrival of the steamer which came around the Peloponnesus. I came by the Isthmus that I might land at Ancona and the Ionian Islands to see the hospitals. I reached Athens at dark last night; left at noon to resume my sea voyage. The weather is intensely cold. Mt. Parnassus is as white as Mt. Blanc. . . . This hour arrives a French steamer with the blessed news of Peace.[1] . . . . We give devout thanks that the hours of warfare are ended, but how long it must be before the wounds which have been inflicted on social and domestic happiness are healed or forgotten. . . . I hoped after crossing the Isthmus to visit Corinth, but the captain would not consent to my leaving the protection of the powerful guard of one hundred soldiers, which surrounded the transport carriages. As the danger was shown to be *real*, I readily gave up my previous wish. A fierce band of robbers attacked the carriage twenty days since, and succeeded in getting all the luggage and money, of which a large sum was being conveyed for paying the soldiers at Athens. So in each carriage sat an armed soldier, while at the side, in close file, rode a bodyguard who looked quite able to protect a much more valuable company. By way of adding interest to the scene, videttes were gal

[1] The end of the Crimean War.

loping hither and thither, and hidden in the bushes at intervals were parties of soldiers. And yet these precautions
are declared to be necessary for ordinary security. . . . I
have no idea how long I shall be in Constantinople, but
everywhere I hear the most sad accounts of the insane
there, on all the islands, and in Asia Minor. I see if I can
only secure something for Constantinople, it is all I ought
to attempt, and of that I am not sanguine at all. I feel
that Miss Nightingale will have a great work still in the
East. God bless her efforts ! "

By April 10, Miss Dix had reached Constantinople,
and in a letter of that date gives her first impressions
on landing.

To Mrs. William Rathbone.

" Constantinople, *April* 10, 1856.

"I made most of the landings *en route.* At Smyrna I
found a good English hospital for sailors, and also one for
the Dutch and Greeks. I found my way to these by no-
ticing the flagstaffs before landing, and on the way visited several Greek and Armenian churches and the chief
mosque. . . . The officers on the steamship were civil.
My only associates were two physicians, — one an Italian
belonging to the ship, the other an Austrian from Vienna,
highly educated, and of most benevolent disposition. He
was on his way to Jerusalem, to execute the will of a lady
in Vienna, who had given 50,000 florins to establish a
school for poor children in the Holy City.

"Taking a boat, I was rowed to a landing at Pera, or
rather Galata, and toiled over or through streets that seemed
only opened to serve as public drains. . . . After breakfast,
I stepped into a caïque with two rowers, — speaking the
words 'Hospital! Scutari!' — and in half an hour landed
at the wharf of upper Scutari. I paid and discharged the
boatmen, and, inquiring of an English sailor the way to the
nurse's quarter, proceeded thither. Miss Nightingale was

absent, having been a month at Balaklava, where there is much sickness of the English and French troops. I went over the chief hospital, which was in excellent order, and chiefly filled with convalescents. There was another large establishment, but I could not walk to and over it, for by this time my feet had become too painful to allow of further exercise. I shall proceed to see the hospitals for the insane as soon as possible. Meanwhile, I do not allow my hopes to rise. . . . I see the first difficulty is the want of persons to *execute* the *trusts* of an institution. But time must show."

As it was with sad forebodings of finding in Constantinople a state of unexampled neglect and misery in the condition of the insane, that Miss Dix had journeyed there, it is cheering in her next letter to read how happily, in some instances at least, she was on personal inspection undeceived. The visit occurred shortly after the close of the Crimean War. It had been her ardent desire to come into intimate relations with Miss Florence Nightingale, then completing her work of mercy in the East. But neither in Constantinople, nor later, on the return to England, was it granted to those two kindred spirits to see one another face to face.

To MRS. WILLIAM RATHBONE.

"CONSTANTINOPLE, *April* 29, 1856.

" I was greatly surprised and much gratified to find in Constantinople a very well directed hospital for the insane in the Turkish quarter, and I failed to discover in either Stamboul or its suburbs any examples of abuse and barbarous usage of this class, so I proceeded to the Greek and Armenian-Christian hospitals, in which, I regret to say, I found very mistaken supervision of all the patients, — chains, neglect, and absence of all curative treatment.

"I think the means I took for the remedy of these abuses will avail to correct them generally in the vicinity of the Turkish Capital, but in the provinces I apprehend that great evils will long exist. . . . The insane of Constantinople are in a *far better condition* than those of Rome or Trieste, and in some respects better cared for than in Turin, Milan, or Ancona. All the patients were Turks, fifty-two men, twenty women, eighteen servants and attendants, three physicians, one resident director, and night watchmen. The hospital was founded by Solyman, the Magnificent, and the provisions for the comfort and pleasure of the patients, including music, quite astonished me. The superintendent proposes improvements. I had *substantially* little to suggest, and *nothing* to urge ! ! !

"D. L. D."

All that remains in Miss Dix's handwriting in the way of narrative of her visit to Constantinople has now been given. It is a satisfaction, however, to be able to supplement her own too meagre account with the personal recollections of this now far-away time, embraced in a letter to her biographer from Dr. Cyrus Hamlin, D. D., LL. D., then President of Robert College, Constantinople.

"LEXINGTON, MASSACHUSETTS. *August* 7, 1880.

"I regret to say that I have found nothing of my valued correspondence with Miss Dix in 1856 and at other times. I can therefore only give you my impressions of her and her work. She remained a part of the time a welcome guest in my house during her visit to Constantinople, in 1856. My residence was too far from the great city to make it always convenient, but she came and went at pleasure. She had two objects in view, the hospitals and prisons. To these she seemed wholly devoted, although her conversation and her interest embraced a vast variety of subjects. She had

traveled extensively, knew very well the official world and its peculiarities, and was acquainted with ~~men and things.'~~
She often entertained us with the peculiarities of certain officials with whom her work led her to have intercourse.

" The most annoying to her were the indifferent. The least annoying were the gruff. She could generally come round that. But the excessively polite she had learned to fear. Her criticisms were always in a kindly spirit, and she clearly saw the humorous as well as the sorrowful in human life.

" She visited, I think, all the prisons and hospitals of the great city. These are very numerous, as every nationality, the Armenians, Greeks, Catholic-Armenians, and Turks, has its own. I obtained admission for her to the great Greek hospital of Ballocli, under very favorable circumstances. She was treated very politely. Also in the great Armenian hospital. In both these she found departments for the insane, with the management of which she was not pleased. The English prison called forth the severest criticism. Dr. Hayland, who had the medical care, was not pleased with her intrusion. She thought to find it the best, and she pronounced it the worst.

" I think with the exception of the Turkish penal prison, the Bagnio, she gained access to all the institutions she wished to visit. The Turkish debtors' prison she found nauseous for filth and want of ventilation. But her great surprise was the Turkish insane hospital. The treatment of the Turkish insane was once one of the horrors of Constantinople. Travelers . generally tried their rhetoric upon it without any aid but their imaginations. Miss Dix had read these high-wrought descriptions of expelling the devils of insanity by alternate tortures and generous treatment, and was prepared for anything.

" She found, instead, order, cleanliness, light, ventilation, clothing, diet, which left nothing to be desired. Employments also and diversions were equally admirable. She came home at night joyful. She said ' I have found one

institution in Constantinople the very best, where I thought
to find the very worst.'

" The explanation is this: A young Turk of wealth and
station was educated at Paris. While there, he became interested in the famous French Hospital for the Insane. He
studied the system. He was admitted into every part of
the great establishment, and was kindly aided to prepare
himself for what he felt to be his ' mission,' to establish the
like for his own people. This is the only instance I have
known of a young Turk's preparing himself for usefulness
by a Parisian education. In every case she addressed a
communication to the heads and managers of the institutions, pointing out what seemed to her desirable changes,
and giving them reports and pamphlets containing much
useful information for their consideration.

" Miss Dix made the impression at Constantinople of a
person of culture, judgment, self-possession, absolute fearless-
ness in the path of duty, and yet a woman of refinement
and true Christian philanthrophy. I remember her with
the profoundest respect and admiration, and regret that all
my correspondence with her is lost. She was equally worthy with Elizabeth Fry to be called the ' female Howard.'

" Very sincerely yours,
"Cyrus Hamlin."

On leaving Constantinople, Miss Dix took passage
up the Danube to Pesth and Vienna. It is while the
steamer, " Franz Joseph," is making a landing in Assora, Hungary, that she writes the following letter to
her friend Miss Heath : —

" Assora, Hungary, *May* 9, 1856.

" My dear Annie,— Look on your map of Europe, and
you may trace my route from Venice, whence I last wrote,
to Trieste, Ancona, Molfetta, Brindisi, Corfu, Cephalonia,
Zante, Patras, Missolonghi, Mycenæ, Corinth, Piræus,
Athens, Syra, Teos, Sangras, Mytilene, Gallipoli, Marmora,
Constantinople, Bosphorus, Varna, Saluna, mouth of the

Danube, Galatz, Balaka, Assora, whence the boat is bound up this grand river to Pesth and Vienna. Why I have made this long route would now occupy too much time to relate, but I hope to meet you face to face, and speak of these and many more subjects.

" I have the strong hope that I shall not need to return to Rome, for a letter received from my banker there acquainted me that the Pope has listened to my remonstrance and intercession, and restored Dr. Guildini to the charge of the hospital, which augurs well for the residue of my petition, and the fulfillment of the distinct assurances I received before I left Rome. I have as far as at present practicable effected the objects of my visit to Constantinople, but it has opened to me work for the future. So far as the Christian hospitals are concerned, those of the Mahometans are *better*, to my great surprise.

" I do not see anything to hinder my embarking for the United States within three months. I am likely to be at Vienna two or three weeks, for the Government has very courteously given me beforehand the entrée of the prisons and the hospitals, and if I do not see much to mend, I may discover something to copy for application at home.

" I find traveling here alone *no more difficult* than I should do in any part of America. My usual experience attends me. People are civil and obliging, who are treated civilly. I am afraid I shall be *obliged* to write a book, a sort of narration of what I have seen during my long absence. I am the sole representative of England and America on the boat. There are, besides, people of many tribes, and persons of far distant English possessions, affording a singular association of oriental costumes and occidental attire. As for speech, Babel is not illy illustrated. You will wonder that I give so meagre descriptions of persons and places, but if one is busy in examining, while pausing for a few days or hours in a city, there is little time for putting on paper in an interesting manner details worth sending so far.

" I have resisted the very great temptation of going to

Palestine, which I desired more than anything besides, because I could not afford the expense, though only twelve days distant from Jerusalem. All my life I have wished to visit the Holy City and the sacred places of Syria. As yet, I have confined my journeys to those places where hospitals, or the want of them, have called me. I trust my observations may be applied to some good uses.

" The impression of the loss of the ' Arctic ' is painfully fresh in my recollection. I do not fear at sea, but I never for an hour forget the vicinity or the presence of danger, and, in the event of accident, the almost certain loss of life. *To be ready* is the lesson we should learn, so that if the call be heard on the sea or the land, by day or by night, we may be glad to go home, where our limited capacities may more fully expand, and immortality perfect what time has rightly planted."

Little more is left to record than the bare fact that, after completing her examination of the hospitals of Austria, and while in Vienna, pressing the subject of the promised new asylum in Dalmatia, on the eastern coast of the Adriatic, Miss Dix visited successively Russia, Sweden, Norway, Denmark, Holland, Belgium, and a part of Germany, returning by way of France to England. Day by day, she patiently explored the asylums, prisons, and poorhouses of every place in which she set her foot, glad to her heart's core when she found anything to commend and learn a lesson from, and patiently striving, wherever she struck the traces of ignorance, neglect, or wrong, to right the evil by direct appeal to the highest authorities, and by the distribution of books and reports, embodying clear information as to the best methods of hospital or prison construction and modes of treatment. How much she thus effected in the way of correcting abuses and stimulating the minds of earnest workers for humanity, will be known only when the secrets of all hearts are revealed. Of the strength, however, of the impression produced by this quiet, sweet-voiced, yet strangely authoritative woman who had come from a land thousands of miles across the sea, and whose unerring eye and immense experience enabled her at a glance to see just where to praise and where mercifully to blame, something may perhaps be judged from a single chance instance, revealing the memory she left behind her in Prague, Bohemia.

Ten years after her return to America, there was sent her a large box of highly-polished wood, inlaid with the metallic inscription on the top " To Miss D. L. D. From the American Club of Bohemian Ladies." The club consisted of " ladies interested in the condition and elevation of the women of Bohemia, of the poorer classes, or wherever a good deed can help a human being." Inside the box were a brief biography of Miss Dix in the Bohemian language, translations of Bohemian poems by Professor Wratislaw, of Christ's College, Cambridge, England, an illustrated quarto of Bohemian National Songs, an album of views of historical interest, and another of photographs of distinguished Bohemian women, statesmen, soldiers, etc., the last bearing an inscription on ivory, " To Miss D. L. Dix, this album is dedicated as a token of the affection and admiration of the Bohemian Ladies' American Club, Prague, 1868."

One sure result of these arduous journeys and patient explorations lay in the fact that now Miss Dix had put herself abreast with the worst and the best Europe had to show on the subject that engrossed her mind, and had come into direct personal contact with the ablest authorities on insanity in their respective countries. That she was often cheered as well as depressed by what she saw, is clear from the only additional note in her own handwriting that still remains:—

"In Russia I saw much to approve and appreciate. As for the insane in the hospitals in St. Petersburg and at Moscow, I really had nothing to ask. Every comfort and all needed care were possessed, and much recreation secured, — very little restraint was used. Considering I do not speak the language, I get on wonderfully well, and *see* all that time allows."

Thus, then, was completed this long and detailed "circumnavigation of charity." Alike in its motive, and in the fidelity with which it was executed, how literally it recalls the often quoted, but never hackneyed words of the tribute of Edmund Burke to Howard, the philanthropist:—

"He has visited all Europe, — not to survey the sumptuousness of palaces, or the stateliness of temples; not to make accurate measurements of the remains of ancient grandeur; not to form a scale of the curiosity of modern art; not to collect medals, or collate manuscripts; — but to dive into the depths of dungeons; to plunge into the infection of hospitals; to survey the mansions of sorrow and pain; to take the gauge and dimensions of misery, depression, and contempt; to remember the forgotten, to attend to the neglected, to visit the forsaken, and to compare and collate the distresses of all men in all countries. His plan is original; and it is as full of genius as it is of humanity. It was a voyage of discovery; a circumnavigation of charity."

CHAPTER XXVI.

SEPTEMBER 16, 1856, Miss Dix set sail from Liverpool to New York on the steamship " Baltic." Two full years had now gone by since she had set foot on English soil, then seeking recuperation from the exhausting labors of her previous fourteen years, and from the overwhelming blow of the veto of her 12,225,000 Acre Bill. Of the dreamy, lotus-eating way in which, during the intervening time, she had surrendered her tired body and mind to the luxury of rest, enough has been detailed in previous chapters. It remains only to give an instance or two of the spirit of congratulation and blessing that now found vent in farewell words from English friends. No more touching illustration of this can be presented than the following brief good - by letters from Dr. .D. Hack Tuke, and from the venerable Dr. John Conolly, — the peer, perhaps in the history of insanity, of Pinel and Samuel Tuke : —

" YORK, ENGLAND, *September* 14, 1856.

" MY DEAR FRIEND, — I have pretty much given up the pleasing illusion of seeing you before sailing. . . . I am inclined to envy you the feelings which you must have in the retrospect of what you have been enabled to do since you set foot on British land. I cannot doubt that the day will come when many, very many, will rise up to call you, Blessed. Blessed to them, who, until they have been relieved from their bodily infirmities, cannot thank you for

all you have done, and the yet more you have longed to be
able to do, for them.

　　　　　" Your truly attached friend,
　　　　　　　　　　" Daniel H. Tuke."

　　　　　　　　"Hanwell, England, *August* 19, 1856.

　" My dear Madam, — . . . Your words of approbation, dear Miss Dix, are very precious to me; for I honor
you and your great labors for the benefit of your fellow-
creatures in many ways. . . . God bless you, my dear lady.
I trust that there are regions where, after this world, all
will be more congenial to such spirits, and to those who
sympathize with you, and share your good and noble aspirations.　　　　　　Ever faithfully yours,
　　　　　　　　　　" J. Conolly."

Happily, the home voyage proved continuously
smooth and sunny. The one only trace of physical
fear that can be detected in Miss Dix's courageous nature was fear of the sea. Embarked on it, she confessed herself always haunted with an undefined
sense of apprehension. In the loss, on the return
voyage, of the " Arctic," — the ship on which she
herself had crossed over to England, — several dear
friends had perished, and the shock of this had added
to the constitutional feeling of dread with which she
had always regarded the Atlantic. This time, however, all went so prosperously that she was able at the
very close of the voyage to write back to England :
" We are still getting on well, and already land birds
come to the vessel for food and rest. They are very
familiar, and eat from our hands. One came into the
open window near me while at dinner to-day, rested
on the table by the captain's plate, picked up some
crumbs, and, finally satisfied, flew away, — perhaps for
the distant land, fifty miles off."

From the insistent urgency of the appeals for renewed work which, from various quarters of the
United States and of Canada, forthwith greeted Miss
Dix on her return to her native land, one can only
wonder that the birds, of which she so tenderly speaks
as alighting on the table of the " Baltic " to pick up
crumbs, were not in reality seriously-minded carrier-
pigeons, each with a momentous little billet under its
wing from Halifax, or Nashville, or Columbia, addressed " D. L. D. Immediate Delivery." All were
of one tenor : we need fresh extensions, we must have
another hospital in another part of the State, we must
get large appropriations this coming winter, everything missteers when your hand is off the helm.

In exact contrast with all this, it had been the hope
of many of Miss Dix's old asylum friends that she
would now be able to devote herself to writing a book,
in which she should carefully digest the results of her
immense range of observation in Europe and in the
East. But she was then fifty-four years old, and the
habits of a lifetime are not to be altered. Her whole
soul was bent now on fruitfully applying what she had
seen and learned to the actual needs of the present,
rather than on sitting quietly down to formulate general principles.

Indeed, it becomes ever clearer as Miss Dix's work
is carefully studied into, that, in the actual founding
of the many asylums she so fondly called her children,
her labors were destined to bear about the same pro-
portional relation to the coming toils demanded for
their extension and full development, as does the
travail of the actual mother in bringing her little ones
into the world, to the subsequent nursing, training,
watching over, and educating them, till they shall

have reached the full estate of manhood or womanhood.

A great feat it no doubt was ·to carry a bill for the
establishment of a new asylum through a State legislature. And yet here lay but the first triumph over
ignorance and apathy. To get the institution well
manned ; to help the asylum to endear itself to the
community through the cures effected, or the chronic
misery relieved ; to raise up friends for it who would
always bear in mind its first estate of bareness and
destitution, and try to make it homelike and supply it
with means for industrial occupation and amusement;
to get ready for the day of needed enlargement; all
these cares and anxieties the fond and thoughtful
asylum-mother bore perpetually on her mind.

In truth, it was with a literal "godly jealousy" that
she watched over these young institutions, yearning
to see the physicians and attendants a consecrated
band, martyrs, if need be, in a sacred cause. On
them, she felt it rested to win for the cause full reverence and support. Never sparing herself, the ideal
of absolute devotion she illustrated in action, far more
than preached by word, is touchingly shown in the following extract from a letter written her, so late as the
advanced age of seventy-one, by Dr. J. M. Cleaveland
of the Hudson River State Hospital : —

"Your devotion to duty in starting off in that pitiless
Monday's storm touched all our hearts. The lesson it in-
culcated was more than a chapter of moral maxims, and I
hope we may never forget it."

No, she could not stop to write a book. The cry
from so many quarters, " Come over and help us ! "
was too loud and continuous. Accordingly, it is

simply what was to be expected, to find her before the close of the year writing from as far north as Toronto, Canada West: —

"It is truly sorrowful to find so much suffering through neglect, ignorance, and mismanagement, but I hope for better things at no distant time. The weather has been severe and stormy, but in proportion as my own discomforts have increased, my conviction of the necessity of search into the wants of the friendless and afflicted has deepened. If I am cold, they are cold ; if I am weary, they are distressed ; if I am alone, they are abandoned."

There now lay before Miss Dix, — until the breaking out in 1861 of the great Civil War which imperatively turned her energies in a new direction, — more than four years of unremitting activity. They were the years of her life marked by obtaining larger appropriations of money, for purely benevolent purposes, than, probably, it was ever given to any other mortal in the old world or the new to raise. The United States has earned the somewhat dubious fame of being "the land of millionaires," and the rivalry is growing ever faster and more furious who shall pile up the most fabulous amount, — set down to his own private credit. Unquestionably, under this last proviso, Miss Dix must humbly yield precedence to the Astors, Vanderbilts, Jay Goulds, and others of the plutocratic hierarchy. None the less will the faithful historian have to record the fact that of the "millionaires of charity," she easily heads the list. These were the years of the enlargement of nearly all the asylums she had founded, as well as the years marked by the foundation of a number of new ones.

To condense, therefore, the narrative of this period within any fairly readable limits, there is but one possible course to pursue. It is to omit, and omit, and omit. All that can be done in this and the succeeding chapter is to present a limited selection of letters and memoranda, and let the reader multiply at will their main tenor.

The internal history of the personnel of a great insane asylum is, to any one who has been privileged to read so immense a mass of correspondence as Miss Dix left behind her, one of the most curious, baffling, and often tragic it is possible to conceive. From the sheer necessity of the case, the feeling of a superintendent and of his assistant physicians must often be that of men who are sleeping over a powder magazine. Outside is a jealous public swift to conceive dire suspicions. Inside is a mass of disorganized human nature, the prey of wild hallucinations and shapes of degraded passion, — cunning, deceitful, and unable to distinguish between fact and fancy. Pass through the wards, and forthwith will rational-seeming men and attractive women stop you, and with streaming eyes begin to tell you such stories of the brutality to which they have been subjected by the violence or sensuality of the superintendent — a man, perhaps, of the elevation of character and consecration of life of a Bell, Woodward, or Kirkbride, — as would for a moment stagger the faith of Abraham, so quietly, logically, and movingly are the stories told.

Nor is this all. There are, besides, scores of nurses and attendants, as well as a great department, sometimes under its own separate head, of cooks, scullions, and workmen. A quotum of these are inevitably persons of ill-regulated character. Often they have to be discharged for unfaithfulness. Then comes their day of revenge. They have their mates, some of them likewise discontented. How easy, then, out of such a storehouse of inflammable material, to start a story that will run like wildfire, and which can be supported before a committee of investigation by the evidence of two or three, perhaps beautiful, women, who tell so circumstantially their piteous story and are so heart-moving in their appeal for redress, that the reputation of the most revered superintendent in the land can hardly hold its own in the minds of the directors of his own institution. Soon the outside public has got hold of the terrible revelation of what is going on behind the bars of the asylum, and furious factions are formed, as deaf to the voice of reason as any of the inmates within.

In cases like the above, Miss Dix was appealed to again and again, and often her clear judgment and thorough knowledge of the workings of insanity enabled her to disabuse the minds of committees who had been made to harbor unjust suspicions of the purest and most devoted men. Though her decisions entailed upon her much abuse, she never shrank from doing her duty. As an instance, therefore, of her religiously-exalted self-reliance when she felt herself to be in the right, the following short extract from a letter to her friend, Miss Heath, is of interest. There had been trouble in the internal working of the asylum in Worcester, Mass., a conflict of authority between matron and steward, as to which Miss Dix, on appeal, had taken decided ground. The two belligerent parties had carried their grievance to the outside public of Worcester, one faction of which had betaken itself to that palladium of modern liberties, the press, and had there roundly abused Miss Dix.

"*March* 24, 1857.

"My dear Annie, — Do not take too much to heart that which mistaken people say in Worcester; it is as the weight of a feather to me. I am *right*, what harm can these do me? 'The Lord is the strength of my life, whom should I fear; the Lord is my defense on my right hand, of whom should I be afraid?' I am steadfast in His might."

Six months later, there occurs a passage in a letter to Mrs. Rathbone, of Liverpool, throwing light on another species of annoyance with which Miss Dix was constantly beset, — the annoyance too familiarly known in the United States as that of the importunity of office seekers. For years had she been exposed to it in her own land, but now the reputation she had gained in Scotland, and the number of desirable positions that would be opened up through the creation of new county asylums, had, it seemed, acted on aspiring Scotch medical minds very much as it would have on the minds of the brethren in America, — thus demonstrating once again how "one touch of nature makes the whole world kin."

"I have had letters from abroad," she now writes, "urging me to commend various parties to official places in regard to the insane. I, of course, decline such interference, considering it out of my line of activity." On this point, at least, of refusing, even on local Scotch solicitation, to reënact the now popular part of "The American Invader," Miss Dix was inexorable. Meanwhile, at home, her power of patronage was constantly growing larger and larger. No one else in the country — and that at the appeal of high public officials throughout the south and west — exercised to such an extent the "right of investiture," or had so

many medical "livings" at command. But no man
ever helped his cause by personal solicitation of her
influence. Her own sense of fitness for the post decided her action, and, a recommendation given, she
sought to have it kept an inviolable secret. So strong,
indeed, was this feeling with her, that, — as personally
told to the writer of her biography by Dr. John W.
Ward, of Trenton, N. J., — on the occasion of his
learning from his trustees some years after his appointment as superintendent that he owed it to the
emphatic recommendation of Miss Dix, and then in-
cautiously proceeding to thank her, she turned sharply
on him and denounced it as a betrayal of confidence
that he had ever been permitted to know the fact. It
is easy to imagine the devoutness of the exclamation,
"O sancta simplicitas!" with which such an account
would be read by the average American Senator or
Member of the House of Representatives.

July 21, 1857, finds Miss Dix beginning a letter in
Cleveland, O., to Mrs. Rathbone, and finishing it in
Zelienople, Penn. An entirely new asylum to be
founded near Pittsburg, an institution on the plan of
the Rath House near Hamburg, Germany, to be studied, and a zealous attempt to be made to "confer a
real benefit on the stagnant life" of a dying community by affording it an opportunity to contribute to
the prospected hospital, are here the visible straws
which show the swift and strong set of the current.

To Mrs. Rathbone.

"Cleveland, Ohio, *July* 21, 1857.

"I am here only for a few days, and proceed to Zelienople, and 'thence to Pittsburg, where I hope to complete
what I have begun and advanced there. I have induced the

managers of the proposed benevolent Institution to sell the farm which had been purchased, and which is not well situated, and take a magnificent location for a hospital on a fine elevated site which I found on the Ohio River, eight miles from Pittsburg, and which is both salubrious and cheerful, joined with outlooks of rare beauty associated with some elements of grandeur.

"ZELIENOPLE, PENN., *August* 10. I was broken off from my writing more than a fortnight since. Here at Zelienople, I am both looking for a farm well situated and well watered, and studying an Institution having chiefly the features of the celebrated Rauhe Haus at Horn near Hamburg. It is a new Reformatory, erected by a noble-minded clergyman of the German Lutheran persuasion, — one of those men of rare power, Fénelon-like spirit, and Apostolic self-sacrifice whom we occasionally see rising up to show the astonished world how much one man can do through the force of moral power without riches save the riches of a sanctified spirit. . . .

"I proceed to-morrow to Economy, hoping to secure from the followers of that singular man Rapp, the Suabian peasant, who emigrated with his family to the United States more than fifty years ago, a contribution for hospital uses. . . . The large wealth accumulated by singular skill and industry, before the death of their leader and founder, Rapp, is stored in secret, and no doubt before many years will escheat to the Commonwealth. They have no longer hopes or expectations. The prophetic declarations of their Founder are falsified, and now a handful remain where once their name was ' Legion.' One seeks of them charities as conferring on their stagnant life a real benefit. Lately they gave $500 to the new hospital."

The above quoted extracts must suffice for furnishing glimpses of the indefatigable worker in 1857. The new year of 1858 may well enough open with a letter of date, Oneida, N. Y., January 25.

To Mrs. Rathbone.

"Oneida, N. Y., *January* 25, 1858.

"Snow two feet deep, thermometer 27° below zero, gas-burners easily lighted by the spark transmitted by the finger. Thus it is not difficult to realize the severity of the cold so often described by Arctic voyagers. Do you hear anything of Mrs. Chisholm, that woman of transcendent worth? I have often wished I could do something that would show her how much good hearts in this Western world appreciate her and her works. How is Miss Carpenter succeeding? I have great faith that the school and discipline on the Ackbar will finally succeed. Our work of Reform seems gigantic, and most discouraging if the whole field is taken at once; but if each does his or her part, we may hope for final success. . . .

"I saw the announcement of Father Mathew's death with a sense of thankfulness that the good man was released from the infirmities which have so increased upon him as to arrest his usefulness, and make life now for many months a burthen and a source of anxiety to himself and friends. Blessed be his memory! The sudden death of Hugh Miller is distressing in its manner, but while all who knew and appreciated him will regret him and his abridged usefulness, they will feel that he is released from a heavy dispensation, viz., the total loss of his reasoning faculties, a danger which I fully perceived and which I knew he dreaded two years since. He was a remarkable man, and will not be forgotten.

"Your steadfast friend, D. L. Dix."

This last letter concludes with a sympathetic description of the burial of a dear friend, Rev. Samuel Gilman, D. D., the Unitarian minister of Charleston, S. C., a man characterized by such sanctity of spirit that his funeral services were reverentially attended by Catholic priests, Jewish rabbis, Episcopalian rectors, and Baptist, Methodist, and Presbyterian minis-

ters. Only a few years before his death, Dr. Gilman
had paid Miss Dix the two lines of reverential tribute,
which are here subjoined : —

"To D. L. D."

" One pain alone thy visit gives — our shame
To live so far beneath thy own great aim."

Evidently the year 1859 was a very congenial and
happy one to the subject of this biography. The earlier part of it was spent in Texas. In that far-away
and before unvisited section of the Union, where naturally she had expected to find herself an entire
stranger, she was overjoyed at the cordiality of her
reception.

Very pleasant is it, therefore, after wading through
endless files of letters that are bare itineraries or dis-
cussions of hospital issues, without a word of personal
revelation, to light upon a few in which free expression is given to the natural delight in manifestations
of outspoken sympathy and admiration which must
have and ought to have yielded keen pleasure.

The first of these letters to intimate friends in
which she expresses her delight in the exuberant testimonials of kindliness she now encountered, is to Mrs.
Hare, of Philadelphia, and bears date, Austin, Texas,
March 28, 1859. In it, after giving a vivid account
of two days and nights of staging experience, exhausting and dangerous to a high degree, she goes
on : —

" You ask, perhaps, how I occupied myself under these
adverse circumstances. Why, meditated how poor, sick,
insane people were to live in being transported such distances over such roads! I am thankful I have come, because I find much to do, and people take me by the hand as a

beloved friend. My eyes fill with tears at the hourly heart-warm welcome, the confidence, the cordial good-will, and the succession of incidents, proving that I do in very truth dwell in the hearts of my countrymen. I am so astonished that my wishes in regard to Institutions, my opinions touching organization, are considered definitive. A gentleman in the State Service said to me, ' You are a moral autocrat ; you speak and your word is law.' People say, ' O, you are no stranger. We have known you years and years.' "

A second letter of like tenure was written in reply to one from Mrs. Samuel Torrey, who had addressed her thus : —

" I have been desired by Mr. Gannett to inform you that a man called upon him a few days ago, and put into his hands $100 for you from the mother of a shipwrecked seaman who had been saved by one of your lifeboats when wrecked off the coast of Newfoundland. Mr. Gannett questioned the man, but could not elicit any information respecting the woman. The money was to be employed to assist poor seamen."

Miss Dix's reply runs as follows : —

" BATON ROUGE, LOUISIANA, *April* 7, 1859.

" MY DEAR FRIEND, — Mr. Torrey can hold the $100 on interest till I can find leisure to apply it advantageously. I shall be glad to increase its amount a little by adding something to it myself. I can build another lifeboat which I want. . . . I have been needing lifeboats myself in the Gulf of Mexico, last month. We just escaped foundering. In fact, for twenty-four hours the captain did not leave his station on the deck. . . .

" In Texas everybody was kind, obliging, and most attentive. I had a hundred instances that filled my eyes with tears. I did not imagine anybody would know me there, but on the contrary, I was claimed and acknowledged as a

dear friend in such wise as has made a lasting impression
on my heart and mind. I was taking a dinner at a small
public house on a wide, lonely prairie. The master stood,
with the stage way-bill in his hand, reading and eyeing me,
I thought, because I was the only lady passenger, but, when
I drew out my purse to pay as usual, his quick expression
was, ' No, no, by George ! I don't take money from you ;
why, I never thought I should see you, and now you are in
my house ! You have done good to everybody for years
and years. Make sure now there 's a home for you in every
house in Texas. Here, wife, this is Miss Dix! Shake
hands, and call the children.'

" Don't think me conceited in relating this incident. It
is one of a hundred in Texas, one of a thousand this winter
all through the South. I am constantly surprised by spontaneous expressions of the heartiest good-will, and I may
well be careful what I demand for hospitals, etc., for my
work is unquestioned, and so I try to be very prudent and
watchful."

Yet another letter, to her friend Miss Heath, written
December 8, 1859, from Columbia, South Carolina,
bears witness to the same enthusiastic gratitude testified to her by the people of another State.

To Miss Annie Heath.

" I arrived here Saturday night greeted and welcomed on
all sides by private friends and public authorities. I have
really been quite astonished at the public expressions of welcome. . . . I am very happy in knowing I am much beloved by my fellow-citizens in this part of the Union. ' We
will prove our regard for you by our acts in behalf of those
for whom you plead,' said a Senator who spoke as the representative of the body. I could not measure half the
pleasant words uttered. ' Our State will always welcome
you as to a home, and so will we at our firesides among the
wives and children.' ' Yes ! yes ! that we will,' sounded

forth spontaneously from all who were present. I have
sent you egotistical lines, Annie; keep them to yourself."

It is a matter for congratulation that the friend to
whom the above letter was addressed did not "keep
these lines to herself," but carefully put them away in
a safe place from which some day they should emerge
to the light of day. Why should not the subject of
such demonstrations of enthusiastic love openly rejoice in them? Truly, they had been bought with a
price. But a few days before this hearty reception in
the hall of the South Carolina House of Representatives, she had written from New Orleans: —

"I have traveled out of ninety-three days and nights
past thirty-two days and nights, and this of necessity, so
that I lie down now and sleep any hour I can, to make up
lost time, and to-day I am feeling a good deal refreshed.
I am bound from this place to Baton Rouge, and thence by
land to Jackson, La., next to Bayou Sara, to Vicksburg by
river, thence by railroad to Jackson, Miss., after that to
Memphis, thence to St. Louis, thence up the Missouri to
the State Hospital at Fulton, returning to Jacksonville,
Ill., and to Springfield:" to all which she adds from Jackson, Miss., "So far as I can see a favorable impression is
made, and there is a probability that I shall get an appropriation of $80,000. I ask this winter in different States
more than a third of a million."

It was at this period of her exacting career that the
new invention of the sleeping car — that "sweet oblivious antidote" to the weary leagues of American
railway travel — was first brought into practical use.
Naturally enough it might have been prophesied that
of all the women of the land to welcome the blessing,
Miss Dix, who had sat bolt upright through such an
infinity of nights, would have led the van. Amusing

is it, however, in this present year of 1890, to read her first aghast impressions of these whirling dormitories, and to see how strongly they shocked that delicate sense of feminine propriety which was so marked a characteristic of her nature : —

"Shall be here [she writes Miss Heath from Jackson, Miss.] till the 30th, when I go to Columbia, S. C., a journey of three days and three nights. I *saw* some sleeping cars. That was enough. Nothing would induce me to occupy one of them, they are quite *detestable.* I did make one night's experiment later, between Pittsburg and Cincinnati ; that will suffice for the rest of life. I cannot suppose that persons of decent habits, especially ladies, will occupy them, unless some essential changes are made in their arrangements and regulations."

One farther letter will fitly conclude the narration of this fruitful year, 1859. It contains the fullest detailed description Miss Dix has left behind of any of her brilliant dashes of energy and courage. Written in a vein of humorous enjoyment of the scene, it unconsciously furnishes a striking exhibition of that lightning-swift dispatch with which — however over-weighted with other cares — she stood ready to turn instantly aside to right a wrong appealing from any new quarter.

To Mrs. William Rathbone.

"Did I write you an account of my affair with, or in connection with, some kidnapped Indians? If it is briefly recapitulated no harm will come, but you must have thought it singular, at least, — if you saw the New York papers,[1] —

---

[1] Several New York papers had given highly sensational accounts of the attack of the rescuing party as led by Miss Dix in person.

that my name was in such odd juxtaposition with street riots and acts of violence endangering life.

" While in Albany, in the State Library last month, several persons being with me consulting on pending questions, a white man and an Indian entered, and the former said, ' There is Miss Dix ; come, tell her your story ! ' It was this : Near Syracuse, in Central New York, is an Indian settlement of five hundred souls. A company of circus riders and strolling players, visiting Syracuse, thought it might be a good speculation to entice some of the Indians from this village to New York, three hundred miles distant, embark with them for Europe, and make a show of the Aborigines for their own profit.

"To this end they proceeded to the Indian village, selected their dupes, — six lads of about fourteen, and several squaws, with one or two infants. Promising them fine shows and sights in Syracuse, they induced them to go there. This excited no other attention than a little feeling of envy amongst those who could not witness the promised exhibitions. After the plays were over, the above-named Indians were persuaded to get on a night train of cars and 'take a little ride.' This little ride ended only in the city of New York, and still held by blinding promises they were taken to a remote tavern on the outskirts of the city, and there strictly watched till the vessel was ready in which the company designed to embark.

" Meanwhile, one of the boys managed to escape and found his way to his own people, reporting the captivity of his companions. The father of two of the boys, a chief, hastened to the city, but the journey consumed his little stock of money, and, however bold and at home in the forests, the mighty city of New York, and the people with whose language he was so little familiar thronging everywhere, yet unheeding his perplexities, made him fearful and troubled. He came up the river again as far as Albany, saw a man on the street he knew, and related his troubles.

This man, a doorkeeper at the State Capitol, brought him to me, and after a few minutes' consideration I, taking with me the Indian, proceeded to the office of the Regent of the University and asked the professor to attend me to the Executive Chambers. They were crowded, but the Governor was my friend and my host, for I was at that time a guest at Government House. At once I stated the case, asking authority to send to the city for the release of the captive Indians. The State attorney was sent for, but not being particularly prompt, nor giving in the sequence any very lucid opinion, I turned away. The Governor gave the Indian sufficient money to pay his expenses back by cars to New York, one hundred and thirty miles.

" I took leave, and sent a page to the Senate Chamber for one of the city Senators. That body was specially engaged. I repeated my message urgently, and Mr. Spencer came. I stated the case. He wrote an order to the Chief of Police, directing him to make search for the missing parties and deliver them to the chief, and by all means prevent their embarkation. I then addressed a letter to the District Attorney of New York, and now it wanted but ten minutes to the departure of the cars south. I bade the Indian run to the station, — an Indian can always run, — giving him the sealed packages, and to say, on arriving in the city, to the conductor of the train that he wanted a policeman to guide him to the captain's office — being there to deliver the papers and wait the result.

" It appears all went well thus far. The Chief of Police detailed a party of policemen, and the 'Show Company' were found occupying a low tavern in the suburbs, and concealed in a back room where they watched their Onandaga captives. The five boys were immediately taken, though some opposition and a show of fight were made. The next day a second party went out to take the remainder of the Indians, and now thirty or forty partisans of the company, rowdies of the baser sort, being collected, a fight commenced. The police were assailed with stones, knives, and blows, but eventually carried their point, besides arresting some of the leaders of the affray and the landlord.

"The Indians were all conveyed to the North River Station, free passage given to Albany, and dispatched to the Seat of Government with a letter to Governor King, and the next day some news-scavenger threw into the columns of a newspaper a history of the affair with embellishments, and — using my name as chief patroness of all people in adversity or otherwise oppressed, — so oddly mixed up the story as to make it look very much as if I were not content with the more quiet part of the performance, but had heroically led the attack, not by pen, but by armed force.

"I send this hastily written letter off without looking to see what is so carelessly put together. I invite myself to be your guest five years from now, all of us surviving that period, and I trust you will live many long and good years.

"God bless you and yours,

"Truly yours,

"D. L. Dix."

CHAPTER XXVII.

THERE remained now but little over a year before the outbreak of the great Civil War, which was to put an end, in Miss Dix's case, to all especial asylum work, until the vaster question was settled in blood whether the American Union was to be rent in twain or reëstablished on the rock of universal liberty. Few knew the real spirit of the South so thoroughly as she, few were so full of well-grounded apprehensions. But though her heart was painfully distressed with sad forebodings, the whole interval was filled with ceaseless activity.

There are several letters of this especial year, 1860, which throw a clear, revealing light on the deepest-seated characteristic of the subject of this biography, namely, the well-nigh awful intensity of will with which she closed in life-and-death grapple with every shape of wrong inflicted on the class of miserable beings to whose championship she believed herself called by the immediate voice of God. Spite of the wonderful results wrought through her campaign in Great Britain, and in the very press, moreover, of ceaseless work in America, her mind is none the less found going back to the old country still haunted with distressing memories of abuses there, piteously demanding redress. How inevitably, in reading the following letter to Mrs. Rathbone, does the outcry of a previously quoted letter from Toronto, Canada, recur to the mind : " If I am cold, they are cold ; if I am weary, they are distressed; if I am alone, they are abandoned." Inevitably, too, recur the characterizing words of Dr. Tuke, " that terrible reformer, but gentle lady."

"HARRISBURG, PA., *March* 18, 1860.

" MY DEAR FRIEND . . . I wish much that I could see you again. This idea will not give way even when I see how much one can find to do, ever laboring with constant diligence. *Should* I recross the ocean, I should greatly desire to do something for the *Private Houses*, hospitals they cannot be called, for the hapless insane, whose greatest calamity is in being cast within their imprisoning walls. This horror haunts me like an ill dream, or a fearful remembrance of what it is actually, a *series of most dreadful facts.* I cannot excuse or forgive the English Commissioners of Lunacy. They surely should know their duty, if they do not : but their dull eyes and sluggish, far-separated visitations have revealed something of the dreary horrors of those heathen receptacles sustained by a Christian people. They are too indolent to exert the influence their official station gives to remedy, at least in a measure, what their criminal sufferance makes them participants in maintaining. If I could have *author-ity*, I would not let one circling moon pass her changes, before I was again upon that field of toil, — and neither time nor thought should be spared in the service. But I must turn from this subject, on which I never allow myself to think at all, if I can help it."

A striking illustration of the range of outlook characteristic of Miss Dix is furnished in this same year, 1860, in a letter from Wisconsin, while on the way to Minnesota. Since first she had begun her work of caring for the outcasts in the many States of the Union, how marvelous had been the unceasing creation out of previous wilderness of ever new States, each covering the area of what would constitute a kingdom in Europe! What a spectacle the American continent was thus presenting of a vast tidal wave of civilization steadily and irresistibly sweeping from the Atlantic to the far-away Pacific! A Sioux Indian uprising, say in Minnesota, accompanied by wide-spread massacre of the scattered settlers, and then, in a seeming trice, a fresh onrolling of the momentarily baffled tide of immigration, which meant enormous new areas of cultivated land, thriving manufactories, compact cities, schools, colleges, and libraries! Yes, and it must mean equally institutions of mercy for the helpless and miserable! was Miss Dix's invincible resolve. The pioneer in charity must keep abreast with the pioneer of material civilization.

To Mrs. WILLIAM RATHBONE.

"PRAIRIE DU CHIEN, WISCONSIN, *August* 27, 1860.

"I am writing at a side table in a telegraph office, waiting for a boat to La Crosse, after which I shall push up the Mississippi to St. Paul, Fort Snelling, and St. Anthony. I miss your letters so pleasant and refreshing, often cheering me by the way as I am seated in the cars, passing from one place to another.

"I expect to be in the Northwest, in this wonderful country of vast prairies, wide, deep, ocean-reaching rivers, and lakes that deceive you into the idea that you are where the Atlantic rushes in upon the resisting shores of the Eastern States. . . . The country is packed with luckless foreigners. Well, the world at present is large enough for all. If all would do their part for the general good, how would the earth become as 'the Garden of the Lord.' The German and the Norwegian element is making a mark here, and their people in the main are industrious, saving, and orderly, except a remnant of the former who are in life and character very coarse and brutal, and singularly addicted to wife-tyranny, — beating and often killing the poor drudges of the household. The insane of this class of Germans and of the South of Ireland people are rarely cured, and so they go to swell the amount of those who crowd the incurable wards of hospitals."

With the coming of colder weather in the same year, 1860, the customary legislative activity was transferred farther South; with what cheering results may be gathered from the following extract from a letter to Mrs. Rathbone, of date, Columbia, South Carolina, November 9 and December 19, 1860 : —

" I made a rapid journey hither by railroad from Jackson, Miss., traveling without stopping a half hour three days and three nights, and arriving to find all hospital business not at a standstill merely, but looking very unpromising. I had no time to lose, and at once saw the Senate and House Committees, reasoned, explained, persuaded, urged, till I secured a unanimous report from these parties to their respective bodies in favor of an extension by new wings, etc., of the State Hospital for the Insane. Thus the work is fairly commenced.

" *Dec.* 19. My Bill [1] has passed both Senate and House by almost unanimous vote, and I go hence to attend to some hospital interests at Charleston, S. C. Providence seems leading me on, and He, by whose mercy I am preserved, blesses all my labors for the afflicted. . . Whether we are

[1] Miss Dix's bill in South Carolina was for $60,000 for support of the asylum toward the foundation of which she had worked from 1852 to 1858 ; $5,000 for repairs; $10,000 for back debts, and $80,000 for new extension. This same winter she had carried through a Bill in Tennessee for an entirely new hospital in Knoxville, as well as raised a large appropriation for the old one she had founded in Nashville. These amounts, together with over $100,000 secured in Pennsylvania, represent a portion only of the work of the year.

permitted to meet again is doubtful. I do certainly indulge the hope. At present I have much that *must* be undertaken here."

It need, then, hardly be wondered at that the year 1860 closed on the part of Miss Dix with devout thanksgiving, and that with the opening of 1861, she should write to her friend Miss Heath in the following rejoicing strain : —

"FRANKFORT, KENTUCKY, *March*, 1861.

"DEAR ANNIE, — All my Bills have passed. My winter has been fully successful. I have had great cares, greater fatigues, many dangers, countless blessings unmeasured, preserving mercies, and am joined to all occasions for thanksgiving — well, and still able to work very satisfactorily. . . . God spare our distressed country ! "

CHAPTER XXVIII.

NOTWITHSTANDING the imminence of a bloody issue between South and North in the United States, Miss Dix, as has been seen, kept on steadily at her accustomed work. The election to the presidency of Abraham Lincoln would, she was entirely persuaded, precipitate war. For years had she been brought into close personal contact with the majority of the powerful leaders of public opinion in the South, and understood their ideas and spirit as did few Northern people. Wholly devoted to her self-chosen work, and feeling that a word from her on the slavery question would, through vast sections of the country, destroy in an instant her power to do anything farther for the insane, she had for years maintained a rigid silence on the whole issue. It was an instance of the inevitable sacrifice of one cause of humanity for another. As has been already said, she was under bonds to hold her peace, — bonds not of self-interest, but of merciful compassion.

Work, constant work, was now her refuge from distressful thought about her country. Thus, February, 1861, we find her writing from Illinois to her friend Miss Heath : —

"I thank God, dear Annie, I have such full uses for time now, for the state of our beloved country, otherwise, would crush my heart and life. I was never so unhappy but once before, and that grief was more selfish perhaps, viz., when the 12,225,000 Acre Bill was killed by a poor, base man in power."

It will readily be remembered by the reader that on the sudden and startling call of President Lincoln for 75,000 volunteer troops to defend Washington, Massachusetts was the first to respond, with two regiments, the Sixth and Eighth. The possibility of such instantaneous promptitude had been due to the ardor and foresight of Governor John A. Andrew, who mainly of his own personal initiative had provided the needful accoutrements and ammunition.

The regiment the first to leave Massachusetts got safely through to Baltimore, where, in marching through the streets to the Washington Station, it was assailed by a furious mob, and a number of its soldiers were massacred. The main body, however, made its way across the city, boarded the train, and reached the National Capital the same evening.

At once the Secession element in Baltimore gained the upper hand, and before the following morning parties were sent out to burn the railroad bridges between the city and Philadelphia, — two of these bridges each a mile or more in length. Thus was railway communication cut off between Washington and the North, and the possibility of holding the National Capitol, surrounded as it was by a fiercely hostile population, seriously imperiled. Everything depended on the rapidity with which troops could be thrown into the city. To effect this by rail, farther than to the north bank of the Susquehanna River, was now an impossibility ; but from this point water communication could be had by way of the Susquehanna and of Chesapeake Bay to Annapolis, Md., from whence it was a march of scarcely twenty miles to Washington.

Fortunately, the President of the Philadelphia and Baltimore Railroad, Samuel M. Felton, was a man capable of taking in the full peril of the situation. Instantly seizing the steamboats on the river, he collected them on the north shore, provisioned and coaled them, and had all in readiness for a start as soon as the arrival on the following day of the second contingent of the Massachusetts troops under General Benjamin F. Butler. Thus by a masterly move was the flank of infuriated Maryland turned, and, not improbably, Washington saved.

The peculiar part played by Miss Dix in the preparations instituted to meet this critical juncture is known to but few, though it was a part always recognized with gratitude and admiration by President Felton. Indeed, in a letter to the writer of this biography, he states that he " again and again besought Miss Dix to permit him to make known how much the country owed to her, but that she had always given a point-blank refusal to have any use made of her name." Years later, however, President Felton wrote out on his own responsibility a full narrative of the episode. It furnishes one more example of Miss Dix's practical grasp of an emergency, and of her singular power of impressing her convictions on others. Extracts from President Felton's personal letter run as follows : —

"PHILADELPHIA, 1026 WALNUT ST., *May* 8, 1888.

" DEAR MR. TIFFANY, —. . . I send you the inclosed extract from a paper which I prepared some twenty years ago, at the request of Mr. Sibley, then Librarian of Harvard University, detailing the part which I took in the beginning of the War of the Rebellion. In that are my recollections of Miss Dix, showing the part she took in those early days . . .

" Early in the year 1861, Miss Dix, the Philanthropist,

came into my office on a Saturday afternoon. I had known
her for some years as one engaged in alleviating the sufferings of the afflicted.   Her occupation in building hospitals
had brought her into contact with the prominent men South.
She had become familiar with the structure of Southern society, and also with the working of its political machinery.
She stated to me that she had an important communication
to make to me personally.

"I listened attentively to what she had to say for more
than an hour.   She put in a tangible and reliable shape by
the facts she related what before I had heard in numerous
and detached parcels.   The sum of it all was, that there
was then an extensive and organized conspiracy through the
South to seize upon Washington, with its archives and records, and then declare the Southern Confederacy de facto
the Government of the United States.   At the same time
they were to cut off all means of communication between
Washington and the North, East, and West, and thus prevent the transportation of troops to wrest the Capital from
the hands of the insurgents.   Mr. Lincoln's inauguration
was thus to be prevented, or his life was to fall a sacrifice.
In fact, she said, troops were then drilling on the line of
our own road, the Washington and Annapolis line, and other
lines of railroad.   The men drilled were to obey the commands of their leaders, and the leaders were banded together to capture Washington."

So profound was the impression produced on the
mind of President Felton by this interview as to lead
to the immediate inception of measures which revealed
the full extent of the peril of which Miss Dix had
given him such startling information.   Detectives
were hired, who managed to enlist as volunteers in
the various squads of men secretly drilling along the
lines of railroad from Harrisburg and from Philadelphia to Baltimore and Washington, and who thus be-

came at home in their schemes. That it was the intention to assassinate Abraham Lincoln, on his way to the Capital to be inaugurated as President, became increasingly clear to Mr. Felton. Thence the masterly move by which he averted this appalling danger, and secretly smuggled the President - Elect through to Washington. Certainly it is a noteworthy fact that, in the days when the wits of most men were utterly at sea, the keen insight and military decision of mind of a woman should have lighted on the precise point where the greatest peril to the nation lay, and that the power of the warning she gave should have been so impressive as to have led to the decisive measures through which in all probability the name and fame of Abraham Lincoln were preserved to the country, and, not unlikely, Washington itself saved.

It so happened that, at the time of the wild excitement which broke out as soon as it was known that the Sixth Massachusetts was on its way from Boston to Washington, and that other regiments from various States were to follow, Miss Dix was with her old friends, Dr. and Mrs. Buttolph, at the Trenton Asylum, resting there from a recent arduous tour through the West. Taking in the situation in an instant, she felt that Washington, where camp disease and wounded men would soon be the order of the day, was now her post of duty. Accordingly, only three hours after the massacre in Baltimore, and while all was still frightful tumult, she reached that city, and with great difficulty making her way through the thronging streets, managed to board the last train that was permitted to leave for Washington. The call for volunteers had brought her as a volunteer, — to report for nursing duties. A hurried line from her to her friend Miss Heath tells the story.

"WASHINGTON, D. C., *April 20*, 1861.

" DEAR ANNIE, — Yesterday I followed in the train three hours after the tumult in Baltimore. It was not easy getting across the city, but I did not choose to turn back, and so I reached my place of destination. I think my duty lies near military hospitals for the present. This need not be announced. I have reported myself and some nurses for free service at the War Department and to the Surgeon General."

Thus, through the promptitude with which she was first on the ground, had Miss Dix manifested her old-time spirit. Perfectly naturally, then, did it come about that she should at once be appointed " Superintendent of Women Nurses, to select and assign women nurses to general or permanent military hospitals, they *not* to be employed in such hospitals without her sanction and approval, except in cases of urgent need." Orders to this effect were at once issued by Simon Cameron, Secretary of War, and D. C. Wood, Acting Surgeon General.

The literal meaning, however, of such a commission as had thus been hurriedly bestowed on Miss Dix — applying as it did to the women nurses of the military hospitals of the whole United States not in actual rebellion — was one which, in those early days of the war, no one so much as began to take in. A fatal delusion possessed the mind of the North that in two or three months at most the war would be over. Indeed, thousands severely blamed the President for ordering out such a host of three-months' men. At any rate, the 75,000 volunteer troops would soon sweep everything before their irresistible mass and valor. That a four years' deadly struggle confronted the nation, that before it was settled more than a mil-

lion of men would be arrayed on either side, this no
imagination was prophetic enough to grasp. Such
a commission, then, — as the march of events was
before long to prove, — involved a sheer practical
impossibility. It implied not a single-handed woman,
nearly sixty years old and shattered in health, but
immense organized departments at twenty different
centres.

Up to the time of the Civil War, the United States
had maintained an army of but from 20,000 to 25,000
men. Except in the exceptional case of the Mexican
War, no mind in the country had ever coped with the
problem of dealing with the medical care of forces
larger than those of the few regiments quartered in
widely distant parts of the Union. To help, through
non-military volunteer service, to meet the dire demand now suddenly sprung on the nation, the men
and women of the North were working night and day;
pouring out unstintedly treasures of money, and accumulating and forwarding enormous stores of clothing,
bandages, and delicate foods for the sick and wounded
in the hospitals.

What agency, then, should prove itself competent
to handle and promptly distribute these vast stores?
No agency, it was soon found out, short of powerful
organizations like the Sanitary Commission, and, later
on, the Christian Commission, — organizations with
immense sums of money at their disposal, storehouses
at a hundred different points, trains of army wagons
in the field, department divisions presided over by
able administrative minds, with a little army of efficient subordinates. Women nurses, moreover, were
volunteering by the thousands, the majority of them
without the experience or health to fit them for such

arduous service.   Who should pass on their qualifications, who station, superintend, and train them?

Now, under the Atlas weight of cares and responsibilities so suddenly thrust on Miss Dix, the very
qualifications which had so preëminently fitted her
for the previous sphere in which she had wrought
such miracles of success began to tell against her.
She was nearly sixty years old, and with a constitution
sapped with 'malaria, overwork, and pulmonary weakness.   She had for years been a lonely and single-
handed worker, planning her own projects, keeping
her own counsel, and pressing on, unhampered by
the need of consulting others toward her self-chosen
goal.   In all this, her towering idealism, and thirst
after perfection of organization and discipline had
proved the precise qualities needed.   Nowhere else in
the world is there demanded such wise selection of
officials, such sleepless vigilance, and such exercise of
perpetual self-control, as in a well ordered insane
asylum.

But in war — especially in a war precipitately entered on by a raw and inexperienced people — all such
perfection of organization and discipline is out of
question.   If a good field hospital cannot be had, the
best must be made of a bad one.   If a skillful surgeon is not on hand, then an incompetent one must
hack away after his own butcher fashion.   If selfish
and greedy attendants or physicians will eat up and
drink up the supplies of delicacies and wines for the
sick, then enough more must be supplied to give the
sick the fag-end of a chance.   It is useless to try to
idealize war.   While it calls out all that is heroic
and consecrated in one class of men, it calls out all
that is selfish and base in another.

All this, however, Miss Dix could not bring herself to endure. Ready to live on a crust and to sacrifice herself without stint, her whole soul was on fire at the spectacles of incompetence and callous indifference she was daily doomed to witness. She became overwrought and lost the requisite self-control. That pathetic sympathy with human suffering which had been the mainspring of her long and wonderful philanthropic career, now, when she was brought face to face with such massive misery she could not relieve, served only to unnerve her. Inevitably, then, she became involved in sharp altercations with prominent medical officials and with regimental surgeons. She tried to stand over the sick and wounded soldiers as the avenging angel of their wrongs. Many and many an abuse did she ferret out and get redressed. Still, it is the clear opinion of her best and most judicious friends that she pitched her demands impracticably high, and failed to take due account of such poor material as average human nature, and so to work with it to the best advantage. She tried to insist on her women nurses being at least thirty years old, and to establish standards of pure consecration to duty which were out of the range of any but a few exceptional natures like her own. Moreover, to meet the constant inpouring into Washington of hundreds of tons of hospital supplies, she had no adequate provision of storehouses nor of the needful machinery of distribution. The lone worker could not change her nature. She tried to do everything herself, and the feat before long became an impossibility. At length she came to recognize this, again and again exclaiming in her distress, " This is not the work I would have my life judged by ! "

Still, partially at least, her life will have to be
judged by this work, — the life of a woman of nearly
sixty, broken by the strain of years, upon whom had
suddenly devolved an entirely new burden of responsibilities too great for any single mind to cope
with; and the verdict will have to be that, while in
personal devotion no portion of her career surpassed
this, still in wisdom and practical efficiency it was
distinctly inferior to her work in her own great sphere.
Of its consecration of purpose there can be no question. Through the four long years of the war she
never took a day's furlough. Untiringly did she remain at her post, organizing bands of nurses, forwarding supplies, inspecting hospitals, and in many a case
of neglect and abuse making her name a salutary
terror. Especially in the early days of the war, before the Sanitary and Christian Commissions assumed
their later immense proportions, her labors proved the
means of relieving a large amount of suffering and
saving many a valuable life. From the outset her reputation and wide range of acquaintance had rallied to
her side many of the most efficient nurses in the land,
while the trust reposed in her by humane and patriotic
minds had led to there being placed at her disposal
immense stores of invaluable supplies. No doubt,
farther, through the very height of the demand she
made for absolute devotion to the cause of the soldier,
and the fiery zeal with which she joined battle with
all that fell below the mark, she helped to raise the
standard. This unquestionably made her very unpopular with many; to which she would no doubt
have replied, " Woe unto you when all men speak
well of you!"

In dealing with the question of popularity, — especially in democratic America where this especial virtue outranks faith, hope, and charity, — it is always hard to hold the balance of praise or blame strictly even. What seems to have been the fault of Miss Dix's administration of her responsible office, namely, an overwrought zeal precipitating her at times into intemperate action, and thus impairing that singular balance of faculties through which her previous successes had been achieved, has, perhaps, been sufficiently dwelt on.

In summary, however, of the impression left by her at this period of her career on minds kindred to her own in absolute devotion to duty, no higher testimonial can be offered than in the following extract from a letter of one whose services to the sick and wounded in the war won the admiration of all, Dr. Caroline A. Burghardt : —

" She was [writes Dr. Burghardt] a very retiring, sensitive woman, yet brave and bold as a lion to do battle for the right and for justice. She was very unpopular in the war with surgeons, nurses, and any others, who failed to do their whole duty, and they disliked to see her appear, as she was sure to do if needed. . . She was one who found no time to make herself famous with pen and paper, but a hard, earnest worker, living in the most severely simple manner, often having to be reminded that she needed food. . . To those of us who were privileged to know her, her memory is, and ever will be, very dear. Every day recalls some of her noble acts of kindness and self-sacrifice to mind. She seemed to me to lead a dual life, one for the outside world, the other for her trusted, tried friends."

One massive character was there, however, in Washington, the great War Secretary, Edwin M. Stanton, on whom no outcry of unpopularity against Miss Dix could produce any effect. Accustomed himself to do

his duty at all risks, unpopularity reaped in doing it
was in his eyes a commendation of fidelity rather than
a reproach. So high was his sense of the country's in-
debtedness to the woman, who had been first on the
ground and was last to quit the post of duty, that at
the close of war, he appealed to her to know in what
shape it would be most agreeable to her to have her
services officially recognized. A great public meeting
presided over by the highest officials, or a vote of
money from Congress were proposed. These Miss
Dix absolutely declined. What, then, would she like?
was asked. "The Flags of my Country," she replied,
never deeming that her request would be granted.
A beautiful pair of the national colors were specially
directed by government to be made for her, and the following order was issued from the War Department: —

"WAR DEPARTMENT, WASHINGTON CITY,
"*December* 3, 1866.
"*Order in Relation to the Services of Miss Dix.*

"In token and acknowledgment of the inestimable services
rendered by Miss Dorothea L. Dix for the Care, Succor,
and Relief of the Sick and Wounded Soldiers of the United
States on the Battle-Field, in Camps and Hospitals during the
recent War, and of her benevolent and diligent labors and
devoted efforts to whatever might contribute to their comfort and welfare, it is ordered that a Stand of Arms of
the United States National Colors be presented to Miss Dix.
"EDWIN M. STANTON, *Secretary of War.*"

January 14, 1867, the execution of the above order
was communicated in the ensuing letter: —

"WAR DEPARTMENT, ADJUTANT GENERAL'S OFFICE,
"WASHINGTON, *January* 14, 1867.
"MISS D. L. DIX, *No. 2 Pearl St., Boston, Mass.*

"MY DEAR MISS DIX, — I have the pleasure of sending
by express this day, in obedience to an order of Mr. Stan-

ton, Secretary of War, a box containing a Stand of the United States Colors presented to you by the Secretary. I trust they will arrive safely.

" With great respect, your obedient servant.

"E. D. TOWNSEND."

To these communications Miss Dix made reply : —

To GENERAL E. D. TOWNSEND.

" ALBANY, N. Y., *January* 25, 1867.

" DEAR SIR, — I am just in receipt of your letter of the 14th, and acknowledge with the deep emotion of a patriotic heart my sense of the honor conferred by the presentation through you from the Secretary of War of a Stand of the United States Colors. No greater distinction could have been conferred on me, and the value of this gift is greatly enhanced by the quiet manner in which it is bestowed.

" Respectfully,   D. L. DIX."

To HONORABLE EDWIN M. STANTON.

" ALBANY, N. Y., *January* 25, 1867.

" SIR, — I beg to express my sense of the honorable distinction conferred on me by the Secretary of War, in the presentation of a Stand of United States Colors received by order through Assistant Adjutant General Townsend. No more precious gift could have been bestowed, and no possession will be so prized while life remains to love and serve my country.

" Very respectfully and with well-grounded esteem,

" D. L. DIX."

These beautiful flags were bequeathed by Miss Dix to Harvard College, where, in the noble Memorial Hall dedicated to the Sons of Harvard who died for their Country in the War for the Maintenance of the Union, they to-day hang, suspended over the main portal.

CHAPTER XXIX.

BUILDS A MONUMENT.

WITH the close of the war came honorable discharge from the service to hundreds of thousands of soldiers, officers, surgeons, and nurses. "Home, Sweet Home!" was now the rejoicing air struck up by the regimental bands. To a nature like Miss Dix's, however, this could not be. She had no home. She was a stranger and a pilgrim on the earth. She asked no discharge this side the grave. For her, then, another, but still a martial strain, must be taken up by drum and trumpet, set to the words of her favorite hymn,

> "A soldier's life, from battles won
> To new commencing strife,
> A pilgrim's, restless as the Sun,
> Behold the Christian's life."

Almost inevitably had it come about, through her duties as superintendent of women nurses that she should have assumed an immense number of commissions from soldiers dying in hospitals under her charge, commissions which involved large correspondence with their families. Moreover, for hundreds who had been wounded and had ultimately recovered, as well as for large numbers of nurses, who had become invalided in their work and were left poor and unprovided for, had she undertaken the rôle of volunteer pension agent. All this crowded her with work for eighteen months to come. Her authority with the

War Department here rendered her services to great numbers of the humble and uninfluential, invaluable.

No long time went by, however, before her ardent sympathies became enlisted in another work, — the work this time of erecting an enduring monument to the memory of the thousands of brave men who lay, sleeping their last sleep, in the newly-established National Cemetery, at Hampton, Virginia, near Fortress Monroe. On this, to her hallowed ground, had she received too many dying messages from the soldiers she so loved, not to make the work seem to her a consecrated duty.

The first idea of such a monument had been conceived by others, who, either wearying in the task of raising the necessary funds for it, or, unequal to doing it, felt that they must transfer the burden to the shoulders of this overtasked woman, who swiftly and gladly took it up. To her it seemed a disloyal outrage that so devout a memorial should not be erected. Few shared so strong a sense of the duty of a nation's enduringly commemorating in bronze and stone its obligation to its martyrs to liberty, as the very woman who always refused point-blank to have her own name connected with any of her great works. It is a seeming inconsistency not uncommon with the order of minds to which she belonged. No doubt John Howard would have subscribed most liberally to a monument for any other philanthropist, while leaving behind, in far-away Cherson, the strict order, " Bury me where I die, and let me be forgotten."

The first allusion to any personal connection of Miss Dix with this projected monument is found in a letter to Mrs. William Rathbone, an extract from which will attest the depth of the feelings that had moved the writer to undertake the work.

"MY DEAR FRIEND, — . . . Lately I have collected in a quiet way among my friends $8,000, with which to erect a granite monument in a cemetery at Fortress Monroe where are interred more than 6,000 of our brave, loyal soldiers. . . . I had especial direction over most of these martyred to a sacred cause, and never forget the countless last messages of hundreds of dying men to fathers, mothers, wives, and children ; never forget the calm, manly fortitude which sustained them through the anguish of mortal wounds and the agonies of dissolution. Nothing, in a review of the past four years' war, so astonishes me as the uniformly calm and firm bearing of these soldiers of a good cause, dying without a murmur as they had suffered without a complaint. Thank Heaven the war is over. I would that its memories also could pass away."

Once making herself responsible that the monument should, and so, necessarily, would, be built, Miss Dix set to work with her usual energy. She was by nature a builder, and always happier in dealing with those reliable and tangible servants of God, stone and iron, lime and hydraulic cement, rock foundations, than with the hay, wood, and stubble of politicians. She meant that, as a structure, this should be a monument that would tell its story of self-sacrifice for generations to come. With this end in view, weeks were spent by her in visiting quarry after quarry along the sea-coast of Maine, till she should find a granite of such imperishable quality as fitly to symbolize to her the granite in the character of the men whose name and fame it was to repeat to their children's children. " It promises to stand for centuries unless an earthquake should shake it down," was her own word of happy congratulation when at last the structure stood completed.

Contributions now flowed in rapidly in response to the appeals she made, and by December 11, 1867, all was in such state of forwardness that she could write to her friend Mrs. Torrey : " Reaching Washington, I proceeded at once to the Ordnance Bureau to see Major General Dyer, wrote a letter to General Grant, which was signed 'approved' by General Dyer, asking for 1,000 muskets and bayonets, 15 rifled guns, and a quantity of 24-pound shot, with which to construct my fence. I am rather gratified that every bill has been paid as soon as forwarded." So energetically was the work then pushed that early in May, 1868, the completed monument was handed over to the care of the United States Government, and the following letter received from Secretary Stanton : —

"WAR DEPARTMENT, WASHINGTON CITY, *May* 12, 1868.

" DEAR MADAM, — Inasmuch as by the Act of Congress the National Cemeteries are placed in charge of the Secretary of War, and under his direction, I accept with pleasure the tender of this memorial to our gallant dead, and return the thanks of the Department to the public-spirited citizens who have furnished the means for erecting it ; and to yourself for your arduous, patriotic, humane, and benevolent labors in bringing to a successful completion such a noble testimonial to our gallant dead who perished in the war to maintain their government and suppress the rebellion.

" Yours truly,

" EDWIN M. STANTON, *Secretary of War.*"

In another and less ceremonious vein, now humorously writes to Miss Dix his felicitations, her dear old asylum friend, Dr. Isaac Ray.

"I congratulate you [he says] on the completion of your Monument. With so much stone and iron on your shoulders, I do not wonder you got sick. Pray, do take a lighter load the next time you undertake to shoulder other people's burdens."

In the National Cemetery in which this memorial stands, there sleep to-day, under the shade of the magnolias and cedars, more than twelve thousand Union soldiers, to whose ranks each year contributes its fresh quotum from the fast-vanishing inmates of the great Soldiers' Home close at hand. The monument itself is an obelisk of syenite rising to a height of seventy-five feet, and resting on a massive base twenty-seven feet square. It is inclosed with a circular fence of musket-barrels, bayonets, and rifled cannon set in heavy blocks of stone. The impression it makes on the mind is simple, dignified, and martial. On it is set the inscription, "In Memory of Union Soldiers who Died to maintain the Laws." The first object visible over the low level of the peninsula to vessels coming in from sea to the Roads, it stands the reverential tribute of a heroic woman to the heroic men she honored with all her soul.

CHAPTER XXX.

HER last duties connected with the war at an end, Miss Dix, now sixty-five years old, took up once again her old asylum work, never relaxing in the fidelity with which she pursued it, till, at the age of eighty, she retired incapacitated for further service, to the shelter gratefully tendered her by the Board of Managers of the Asylum in Trenton, N. J., her "First-born Child."

That the impoverishment wrought by war in the Southern and Southwestern States must have left all institutions of charity in a deplorable condition, she was clearly enough convinced. But the old glad welcome with which she had once been cheered in her work there, was it not over forever, love turned to hate, blessing to reviling and cursing? Fully had she herself shared the consuming wrath with which sensitive natures were in those days inflamed, and unsparingly had she denounced what had seemed to her the wanton wickedness of the action of the South. When, in the course of her duties as superintendent of nurses, she had had to receive back and care for great bodies of Union soldiers just released from the Southern prisons, starved to skeletons and idiotic with the misery they had undergone, it had seemed to her, in the bitterness of her soul, that she could never again shake hands with those she had once so warmly loved.

Great, then, was her surprise and delight at finding that in her case at least an exception was made to the vindictive feelings inevitably engendered by war. The old memories of love and admiration had survived as fresh as ever, and the old sense of grateful depend- ence on her for services no one else could render found immediate, imploring expression just as in by- gone days. Yes, the condition of things was deplor- able, all told her, but to whom could they look for help but to her !

From the large number of beseeching letters· that now came to her, limitations of space forbid more than the selection of a single typical example, — an example, however, which pathetically illustrates the grief felt by devoted friends of the insane over the ruin that had been wrought in the South, and which at the same time testifies to the yearning of heart with which their old-time benefactor was looked to for aid. The extracts given are from a letter of Mr. Alfred Huger, of Charleston, S. C. Though not written till the beginning of 1870, the letter shows the thankful- ness awakened in so many minds by the bare fact that Miss Dix was now once more on the field.

"CHARLESTON, S. C., *January* 31, 1870.

" MY DEAR MADAM, — I have just heard of your arrival at Columbia ! The Past, the Present, and the Future, are by this announcement grouped before me. It is the instinct of the afflicted to be aroused and encouraged when your name is mentioned. Ruin and desolation hold their court among us. Our poor little State is sinking under a weight of calamity and of woe, our temples are draped in mourning, and our hearts are in the dust. Still, we flock to the altar when the High Priestess is there. ; . . .

" I was one of the founders of the lunatic asylum.

Everywhere and at all times I have watched its progress. During the war I was in daily, almost hourly, interchange with our valued friend, Dr. Parker, and with that household of wounded minds over which he presides, and, as we believe, doing so with a holy purpose. Dr. Parker is the father, brother, and friend, the very 'shield and buckler' of our stricken brethren.

"We have heard, like a summons to meet death, of his possible removal, and we have heard also of your providential advent. If the authorities that rule over us select this man as a victim, or if Dr. Parker himself can endure his surroundings no longer, then there is an agony upon us, and may we not appeal to *you* for succor and for help. . . . We look to you both as the vicegerents of 'Our Father who is in Heaven,' and we cannot look in vain, and we must not look in vain, and we will not look in vain! Dr. Parker has no equal in our State for the position he occupies. You have no superior, with your mission signed in the High Chancery of Heaven, and witnessed by angels who do justice and love mercy.

"In this hour of our trial, a word of information or of consolation from you would be a boon and a blessing."

"Faithfully and with profound respect,

"ALFRED HUGER."

To appreciate the desolation of spirit that finds vent in the above letter it is necessary to call to mind the actual condition of things then prevailing in South Carolina. The State was under the control of a legislature packed almost solid with brutal plantation negroes. The influential leaders who swayed them were largely "carpet-bag" politicians from the North, the picturesque title then given to a class of rapacious adventurers, whose worldly possessions, consisting solely in an extra shirt and a pair of socks, could hardly as yet aspire to the dignity of a trunk. Later,

indeed they meant to have one, and to have it packed
full. What would be the inevitable policy of such a
legislature and such leaders toward a State Insane
Asylum can readily be conceived. It would be to put
in some ignorant, thievish black as steward, some
greedy, half-educated white doctor as superintendent,
and in the same way to dispose of the rest of the
legitimate spoils of office. The condition of things
was worse in South Carolina than in the other Southern States. Still, something analagous to this was in
danger of prevailing in them all.

No wonder, then, that in the misery of his position,
Dr. Parker should have written vehemently to Miss
Dix in reply to a letter from her counseling patience.
Patience! patience! The regents of his asylum were
half or two thirds negroes. They had apparently got
wind of certain of the ways of Europe and had made
the happy discovery of a new official genus, hitherto
unknown, called the " pluralist ; " on the strength of
which discovery they had bestowed three offices in the
asylum on a single person totally unfit to discharge the
duties of any one of them. On Dr. Parker's reporting
the delinquencies of the man, the culprit had defiantly
written to the regents : " Everything will go on well,
if you (the regents) can have your own way, but not
if the superintendent is to have his." Happily, one
negro regent had the good sense to administer, in his
own peculiar vernacular, the following sound rebuke :
" Well, Dr. H., the superintendent is the man to have
his way ; he is boss, and we will not have two bosses."
At the close of his letter, Dr. Parker says, " If any
one can save our cherished institution from ruin, you
are the person."

Now already in the previous two years of 1868 and

1869 had Miss Dix been at work with her old success in the Northern and Middle States. Spite of war the national population had been steadily growing. The demands, moreover, on such institutions as the Army and Navy Asylum in Washington had advanced a hundred-fold through the vast increase of the military and naval forces. To help to meet all these new exigencies, her energies were taxed to the extreme, and at times there comes from her a cry of agony and despair. Resuming once again her old inspection of almshouses and jails, she finds the melancholy condition of things to which she had at the outset called such effective attention, renewing itself through the inadequacy of existing institutions to cope with the growth of population and the tide of immigration. " It would seem," she breaks out in sadness to her friend Mrs. Torrey, "that all my work is to be done over so far as the insane are concerned. Language is poor to describe the miserable state of these poor wretches in dungeon cells. I did not think I was to find here in this year 1868 such monstrous abuses."

Still encouraging results continued to cheer her. Thus, May 6, 1868, Professor Silliman writes her from New Haven, Conn. : —

" It is just two years this month since you came here to move this matter, and now the first patients are in the New Hospital building. How much we all owe you for your timely aid, courage, and energy, without which this noble work would not have been undertaken, certainly for many years ! And it was all done so quietly ! The springs of influence were touched in a way which shows how possible it is to do great and noble things in public assemblies without a lobby or the use of money."

Equally in Washington does she meet a like success, while of Pennsylvania she can write : —

"Tomorrow I go to the Northeastern district of the State to find a farm of 300 acres for the third hospital, for which I have got an appropriation of $200,000.

It was well that the encouraging stimulus of yearly success should thus come to the woman nearing the age of seventy, on whose shoulders such a burden rested. One by one, she now took up the cause of the many asylums she had founded, laboring indefatigably toward their restoration and enlargement and toward infusing into the minds of new legislatures liberal and rational ideas on the whole subject of the treatment of insanity. From many an old asylum, too, in full tide of prosperity, there now came to her grateful remembrances.

" I trust [wrote to her, in 1871, Mr. John Harper, treasurer of the Dixmont Hospital in Pennsylvania] when the warm weather comes, you will visit Dixmont and see for yourself what a monument for humanity has been erected and put into prosperous operation through your foresight and exertions. Do you remember the day in my room in the bank, when you urged the establishment of a new rural hospital, and Judge —— opposed you so bitterly? The judge was a man of great eloquence and influence, but you beat him to his astonishment."

Earlier, too, on the occasion of the presentation of a portrait of Miss Dix to this same Dixmont Asylum by an unknown citizen of Pennsylvania, had Mr. Harper written the donor : —

˙ " You know, sir, in the olden time, each institution sacred to charity had its patron saint. The Dixmont Hospital, notwithstanding our Protestant and iconoclastic ideas, has a patroness whom we respect and love ; indeed who is canonized in our affections quite as strongly as were saintly ladies in the Mediæval Age. The mission of 'our Lady' is to create those noble institutions which aid in the restoration of the dethroned reason, and Dixmont Hospital is one of the jewels which will adorn her crown hereafter."

Enough has now been said to illustrate the nature of the work that was to engage Miss Dix to the end of her active days. Farther to particularize would be but to weary the reader with a bare catalogue of achievements, each indeed fraught with some shape of succor to the miserable, but as a catalogue a mere burden to the mind. From Maine to Texas, from New York to San Francisco, she is henceforth perpetually on the wing. The asylums scattered throughout the length and breadth of the land have become to her her children. How they are faring is the one thought of her heart. Everywhere, on her arrival, the keys of the wards are freely handed to her, and she is allowed to wander round alone. She is recognized as a "lunacy commission" in herself, so admirable a one, indeed, that at even so late a date as 1877, when she was then seventy-five years of age, Dr. Charles F. Folsom, of Boston, Mass., could say of her in his "Diseases of the Mind": "Her frequent visits to our institutions of the insane now, and her searching criticisms, constitute of themselves a better lunacy commission than would be likely to be appointed in many of our States."

The inevitable infirmities of age are now growing on her. She is more silent and concentrated, more abrupt and imperative, more the embodiment of habit than of the earlier spontaneity and enthusiasm which once irresistibly swept the legislatures of twenty States before her. But her intellectual perceptions are as clear and acute as ever. Nothing escapes her eye, whether to be commended as meritorious or taken ex-

ception to as faulty. No fear or favor sways her a
hair. Alike in the asylum of her earliest superintendent friend, or in that of the latest appointee, she feels
that it is the question of the best good for the stricken
and miserable that is to dominate her own mind and
the minds of all.

Inevitably was there something trying to the heads
of asylums in the sudden and unexpected visitations of
this exceptional woman and her equally sudden departures. She was the organized and embodied conscience of the highest ideals of asylum management,
with a searching power of intellect and character that
few could encounter without a lurking feeling of
dread. The older members of the profession, who for
long years·had known the inestimable value of her
services to the cause they stood for, understood that
no criticism would escape her that was not dictated by
the inmost sense of justice and kindness, and, farther,
that a vast experience lay behind it that would make
it worthy of their best consideration. But many of
the newer men in the newer States, who " knew not
Joseph," felt inclined to take exception to the quiet
but irresistible air of authority with which this woman,
of no outward official position, would arrive, see all and
judge all, and, perhaps, without a word of comment,
leave them feeling that alike the good and bad had
been weighed in the scales of even-handed justice.

A few even were there who were disposed to make
merry over this " self-constituted lunacy commission "
in the person of a single, aged woman. The story is
told of her once going into an asylum where she called
for a trial of the fire-extinguishing apparatus. It
proved to be out of order and useless, and she spoke
some words of stern rebuke. Later, it became the

habit of some of the younger doctors, of a supposedly-
humorous turn of mind, to refer to this incident as
furnishing the matter of an exquisitely funny story.
Vastly pleasant did they seem to find it to expatiate
on the consternation the "old lady" had caused by her
appalling demonstration that the whole elaborate system for saving the buildings from conflagration was
absolutely worthless.

A vastly amusing story, no doubt, and yet one can
hardly avoid charitably wishing that a select few of
such humorously minded young doctors might be
compelled to serve an apprenticeship on a Cunard or
White Star steamship. What would they witness
there? This: that the instant a certain signal is
sounded, whether in the dead of night, or at break of
day, or when dinner or supper is in full tide, every
waiter, every bedroom steward, every deck-hand, every
officer, drops on the spot whatever he is at, and runs
with lightning speed to take his appointed place at
the pumps or at the handling of the hose. Should it
then turn out — even on this mere formal review —
that the fire apparatus would not work, it is easy to
imagine the nature of the reception at the captain's
hands any responsible officer would get, who showed
a disposition to regard the miscarriage as a capital
joke. Miss Dix had had too fearful experience of insane asylums burning to the ground and of scores of
wretched victims perishing, not to feel that such a
failure ought to be branded on the spot as guilt and
crime.[1]

[1] Even as this biography is going through the press, there comes
from Montreal, Canada, the news of the total destruction by fire of an
immense insane asylum there, in which one hundred miserable victims were roasted alive. The asylum was provided with a complete

Perhaps, then, a fairer and more discriminating picture can hardly be drawn of the salutary impression left by these comings and goings of Miss Dix on minds kindred in moral earnestness with her own, than is found in the ensuing letter of Mrs. Harriet C. Kerlin, wife of the superintendent of the institution for feeble-minded children at Elwyn, Penn. : —

" Among our many visitors, there has never been one so ready to praise the good found, and so agreeably to reprove mistakes or failures. This may not always have been her characteristic, but surely we met only the gentle, considerate side of her nature, so that when Dr. Kerlin said, ' Miss Dix won't you come up to see where our teachers have rooms ? ' her reply, ' Oh, no ! doctor, I have never found any suffering among officers of an institution,' was so frankly and half-wittily spoken, it carried no offensive sarcasm.

" If she were found at 5 o'clock A. M. in an unusual place, watching the early movements of our large family, her kindly manner of telling what she had seen, right or wrong, made us feel that sympathy with the superintendence prompted her desire for as perfect management as possible, and that no spirit of pleasure in spying out wrong had caused her unexpected early walk. She never gossiped about the weakness or faults of others. Her judgment was given with consideration of accompanying circumstances. Her language, voice, and manner were thoroughly gentle and lady-like, yet so strong was she in intelligence and and womanhood that at times I ranked her alone, and above all other women."

The picture drawn in this letter of the inexorable fidelity tempered with kindness and gentleness, of Miss

fire-extinguishing apparatus. Only, as it turned out, the hose was disconnected from the pumps, and the wrench mislaid. Before connection could be made the flames had got too much headway to be arrested.

Dix, weighed in connection with the fire-apparatus story and her terrible power of rebuke, when rebuke was demanded, will serve together to call up a vivid idea of the manner of woman she was in these last years of her active life. Pleasanter it no doubt was to receive the visitation of duly appointed State inspectors, who would beam graciously and ignorantly on the excellent condition in which they found everything, take a glass of wine in the medicinal room of the establishment, and then adjourn to a good dinner. But this was not Miss Dix's way. From the hour in which the terrible abyss of human suffering had been opened to her, and a sacred voice within had summoned her to consecrate her life to the service of these miserable ones, her faith had never wavered that God had eternally ordained her for this special mission. It was to be no child's play, but a stern and awful ordeal. Every day made it clearer to her that " Eternal Vigilance is the Price " of justice and mercy toward these outcasts of the world.

CHAPTER XXXI.

THE LAST OF EARTH.

FREQUENT allusion has been make in past chapters to the eagerness with which Miss Dix seized every opportunity to extend the blessings of a rational and humane treatment of insanity into all quarters of the world. Very pleasant, then, is it to narrate one more happy result of these widespread efforts, the knowledge of which came to her as late as in 1875.

Years before, when first a chargé d'affaires was sent to Washington from Japan to represent its interests before the United States Government, had she sought his acquaintance, and held long and earnest interviews with him on the subject that lay nearest her heart. Fortunately, in Jugoi Arinori Mori she found a man of great intellectual capacity and large humanity. Readers of this biography will recall the shock produced in the minds of all true friends of Japan by his assassination a year or more ago in his own country at the hands of a fanatic. He had by that time become acknowledged as the foremost statesman in his native land. From him, came to Miss Dix, in 1875, a letter which was one more illustration of the wisdom of a favorite maxim with her, " Sow beside *all* waters! "

"TOKIO, JAPAN, *November* 23, 1875.

"MY DEAR MISS DIX, — During the long silence, do not think I have been idle about the matter in which you take so deep an interest. I have given the subject much of my time and attention, and have successfully established an asylum for the insane at Kiyoto, and another in this city is being built and will soon be ready for its work of good. Other asylums will follow, too, and I ardently hope they will be the means of alleviating much misery.

" Very truly yours,

" ARINORI MORI."

Two more asylums in far-away Japan, with others very likely to follow, were now to be added to the thirty-two she had already been the instrument of either founding outright or greatly enlarging. She was accustomed to mark each one on a map with the sign of the cross. Could all the prisons on new and better plans she carried bills for, and all the alms-houses she caused to be thoroughly reconstructed be added to these, and then all brought vividly before the mind's eye, how amazing would be the impression left!

It was noted by benevolent minds in these latter days of Miss Dix's career that, whenever any great calamity occurred like the terrible fires which destroyed such large portions of Chicago and Boston, she was sure soon to appear on the spot with sums of money she had collected from her many friends, and quietly and judiciously searching out for herself where help was most needed, or what persons already on hand could be relied on to expend the fund most wisely, would seek to do her part in mitigating the wide-spread distress. Not human beings alone, but the brute creation likewise appealed to her unfailing compassion. Thus among her other projects of relief in these days was that of setting up a drinking fountain in a densely thronged part of Boston where she had noticed that

the draught-horses were subjected to the hardest work.
It was her application to the Poet Whittier to send
her the translation of an Arabic inscription cut on the
curb of a similar fountain in the East, an inscription
the beauty of which had struck her when he had repeated it on a previous occasion, which called out from
him the ensuing letter: —

"OAK KNOLL, 18*th* 8*th* Mo., 1879.

"MY DEAR FRIEND, — I cannot recall the Arabic inscription I referred to for the fountain, and have written
one myself, taking it for granted that the fountain was to
be thy gift, though thee did not say so.

"Such a gift would not be inappropriate for one who all
her life has been opening fountains in the desert of human
suffering, — who, to use Scripture phrase, has ' passed over
the dry valley of Baca, making it a well.'

"With love and reverence thy friend,

"JOHN G. WHITTIER."

"Stranger and traveler !
  Drink freely and bestow
A kindly thought on her
  Who bade this fountain flow ;
Yet hath for it no claim
  Save as the minister
Of blessing in God's name."

Whatever the strength, however, or whatever the
power of the inspiring motive, there must come an
end to every mortal tether. In October, 1881, worn
out with fatigue, Miss Dix went for rest to one of her
hospital homes, the Trenton, New Jersey, Asylum,
which she was destined never again to leave. Previous to this, the last characteristic glimpse of her
is caught in the following account related by Dr.
George F. Jelly, former Superintendent of the Mc-
Lean Asylum.

She arrived at my house in Boston, said, in substance, Dr. Jelly, after nightfall one bitter, snowy winter evening. She seemed chilled to the marrow, and said she would go straight to bed. I offered her my assistance in mounting the staircase, but she declined every aid. The furnace draughts were opened for greater heat, a large fire was kept blazing in the grate of her bedroom, my wife piled five or six blankets on her, and I administered some warming drink. Spite of all she shivered with cold and would, I felt sure, succumb to pneumonia. She was on one of her tours of inspection, and had ordered the carriage to come for her in the early morning. Nothing could move her to change her plan, and when morning came she was up and ready to start. It was still a bitter snowstorm. I begged her at least to let me go with her to the station, for I feared she might die before she reached her destination. No! she would go alone. She was used to such things, she said, and, as soon as she had got through her work in New England, would go farther South, where she always became better soon.

Something pathetic and painful is there in such a narrative of exposure in extreme old age; something sad and hard to be reconciled to in this refusal of so much as the helping hand of a strong man in mounting the staircase on tottering feet, — the refusal, too, by one whose whole long life had been a ceaseless ministry to others. Still, the anecdote is too characteristic to be omitted, revealing, as it does, such persistence to the end of the indomitable will power that had led on to such vast achievement.

From Trenton, however, there was to be no more going forth. Those thousand-mile journeys from Halifax to Texas, from New York to San Francisco, were now over forever.

To the great credit of the managers of the New Jersey State Asylum, no sooner was it known that Miss Dix was seriously ill in the asylum, and unlikely ever again to be strong enough to leave it, than they called a meeting and passed a unanimous vote, inviting her to end her days under the roof of the institution she had founded, as its loved and revered guest. The managers of this institution had always manifested toward her singular gratitude and respect. Roomy and comfortable apartments were assigned her, where she preferred they should be, under the pediment of the great Greek portico which forms the façade of the main building, apartments commanding a superb view of the park-like grounds, the open country, and the beautiful sweep of Delaware River.

The private resources of Miss Dix would at this time have amply sufficed to maintain her in comfort during her declining years. But it was an indication of her high self-respect of character, that she should have felt the fitness of thus ending her days as the honored guest of one of the many institutions she had founded, rather than in any private house. For half a century she had had no home, but had been in every fibre of her being a public character. The asylums were her children, and that, when worn out and incapacitated for farther service, one of these children should thus take her and care for her beneath its roof-tree, seemed to her but in the natural order of family love and duty. Moreover, the passion of doing for others had become absolute in her nature. She had a large list of dependents for whose wants she was always providing, and the one luxury that remained to her was the power of being able to continue this to the end. Beyond the grave, even, stretched the longing to be still of use on earth. An intense solicitude had now taken possession of her to preserve unbroken the capital of her property, and to leave it in trust so that the income of it should be devoted in perpetuity to charitable objects. Thus the instinct of saving, which in extreme old age is the almost invariable accompaniment of human nature, assumed in her case the character of what had ever been the master passion of her life.

For more than five years Miss Dix was now destined to linger on in her hospital home. They were years of great suffering from exhaustion, and the pain of the steadily-advancing disease of which she died, — ossification of the lining membranes of the arteries. Imprisonment within the narrow walls of her rooms came doubly hard to her, as always to overpoweringly active natures. Still no complaint escaped her lips. " It was all right it should be so," she said, " it was God's will, only it was hard to bear." Life had at no period seemed child's play to her, but a stern though merciful ordeal. Her Bible and collections of sacred poetry were now her stay and comfort. In hymns, especially, the utterance of the suffering and triumphant ones of all the ages, she heard the voices that came home to her with the greatest power and peace. Never a letter she wrote to dear friends with trembling hand that did not contain some of these cherished lines.

Meanwhile, old friends did not forget her. From far places would they travel to spend an hour with her, while the older superintendents of asylums kept her duly informed of all that was going on in the world in which she had so long lived, or sent her from their annual meetings greetings of respect and love.

A few of the letters that came to her in her asylum home will serve to make vivid the nature and sweetness of the consolations that helped her through these last five years of imprisonment, weariness, and pain. They came in great numbers, alike from private and from well-known persons.

December 31, 1882, writes knightly Dr. Kirkbride as follows: —

"In three hours more, 1882 will belong to the past. May that which follows it bring to you, my most valued and honored friend, all the happiness that can come from a life devoted to good works and to the relief of the afflicted."

Shortly after, comes greeting from her once pupil and life-long friend, Mrs. John Kebler, of Cincinnati: —

"I never think of you as grown old. You always come to me as I knew you first, crowned with rich brown hair, the like of which no one else ever had. Of all your pupils I am sure none loved you as I did and do. Few days of all my life have been unblessed by loving, grateful thoughts of the gracious, graceful teacher and friend. Always shall I connect with you, if I remain longer than you, that lovely hymn of Whittier, and my prayer shall be, —

> "'Still, let thy mild rebukings stand
> Between me and the wrong,
> And thy dear memory serve to make
> My faith in goodness strong.'"

May 6, 1882, arrives a remembrance of cheer and consolation from Mr. Whittier himself: —

"OAK KNOLL, DANVERS, MASS.

"MY DEAR FRIEND, — I am glad to know that thou art with kind friends, and as comfortable as possible under the circumstances. Thou hast done so much for others that it is right for thee now, in age and illness, to be kindly minis-

tered to. He who has led thee in thy great work of benevolence will never leave thee nor forsake thee.

" With a feeling of almost painful unworthiness, I read
thy overkind words as regards myself. I wish I could feel
that I deserved them. But compared with such a life as
thine, my own seems poor and inadequate. But none the
less do I thank thee for thy generous appreciation.

" May the blessing of our Father in Heaven rest upon
thee, dear friend ! Believe me always and gratefully thy
friend,   " JOHN G. WHITTIER."

Of course so old and tried a friend, so kindred a
spirit with her own in love and sacrifice, as Rev. William G. Eliot, D. D., of St. Louis, did not forget her
now in her loneliness and pain. From his many letters, let the following short extract and accompanying
lines serve to show the loving tenor : —

" We think and speak of you very often, and in spirit I
spend many hours with you daily. Last night young Mr.
Nichols, grandson of your old friend in Portland, was here,
and we talked of you an hour. . . . After he left me, I
wrote these lines before going to bed. They are a part of
the truth, the whole of which cannot be told. . . . If love
and gratitude and prayer could save you from all suffering
and anxiety, no pain nor loneliness of feeling would ever
reach you.

" Dear Sister, in thy lonely hours of suffering and pain,
Take comfort! The ten thousand prayers cannot ascend in vain,
From hearts which thou hast comforted and homes which thou hast
        cheered,
And children, saved from ignorance, whose pathway thou hast cleared,
From loyal hearts and homes, wherever they are found,
In palaces and cottages, with peace and honor crowned.

" Dear Sister, thou art not alone, God's angels hover near;
His presence is thy sure defense, then what hast thou to fear ?

The 'good fight' thou hast nobly fought and truly 'kept the
  faith;'
The 'crown' awaits thee, Sister dear, the 'victory over death;'
Take courage then, dear friend! The 'prize' is almost won;
Hark! 'Tis the Saviour's voice we hear, 'Servant of God, well
  done!'"

  "Your Brother-friend,
  "W. G. Eliot."

Similar testimonials of love and veneration from
men and women foremost in all good works throughout the country, as well as from kindred spirits on
the other side of the Atlantic, might be indefinitely
multiplied. Let them conclude, however, with an extract from a letter of one of the younger men in the
battle of humanity, General S. C. Armstrong, a man
who, brave as the bravest throughout the war for the
preservation of the Union, as soon as peace sounded,
" beat his sword into a plowshare and his spear into a
pruning hook," and thenceforth labored with the zeal
of an apostle to make self-respecting and useful American citizens out of the ignorant and degraded negro
freedmen. In his first effort to reduce to order the
chaos and anarchy of the whole region about Hampton, Virginia, and to establish an industrial and
Christianizing school of instruction there, he had
found no stancher friend or wiser adviser than Miss
Dix.

  "You are one of my heroes," he now wrote to her in her
last retreat. "My ideal is not one who gives the flush and
strength of youth to good work, — for who can help doing
so when a chance opens! He is a traitor who declines the
chance, just as is he who does n't fight for his country when
it needs him, and he can possibly go. But you kept in the
field long past your best days. Your grit and resolve have
been wonderful. Faithfully yours,
  "S. C. Armstrong."

Two years after the death of Miss Dix, there appeared in the " New York Home Journal," of September 11, 1889, an article embodying reminiscences of her traits of character and of incidents in her career. It was from the pen of a valued personal friend of her earlier years, Mrs. S. C. P. Miller. The picture drawn in it of these last days of Miss Dix's life in her asylum home is at once so touching, and so stamped with that exceedingly rare endowment of human beings, the power to see what is actually before their eyes, as to render it a positive addition to any attempt to interpret her character.

" Accidentally meeting [says Mrs. Miller] an oldtime friend from Washington, she mentioned a recent visit to Miss Dix.

" Eagerly inquiring about her, I learned that she was a confirmed invalid, occupying apartments in the Insane Asylum at Trenton, which had been given to her by the State of New Jersey in acknowledgment of her agency in securing the erection of the building. At the earliest moment I went over to see her, sending up my card, with much misgiving as to her memory of me. Immediately I was taken to rooms in the tower. She was glowing in her welcome. ' I told them to bring you right up, for I was so impatient to see my friend that I would not wait a minute.'

" She was propped up in bed and greatly altered. She was unable to walk, and for several years had not even been carried outside of her own rooms, and to this utter helplessness were added paroxysms of intense pain. ' The doctor does not encourage me to hope that I shall ever be better,' she told me ; ' but he comforts me with the assurance that I am in no danger of ever losing my reason.' . . .

" She was curious to know whether I would have recognized her, so curious, indeed, as to embarrass me in the reply that I should not have done so in an unexpected meet-

ing. . . . I seized the occasion to say : 'You should be at
the pains, Miss Dix, to arrange that you go down to posterity in that beautiful portrait of you in the Atheneum at
Boston.' A smile of satisfaction brightened her face at the
suggestion, and I was amused to see that even the good
and great, and strong and old, possessed, in common with
their weaker sisters, a keen relish of a gentle insinuation of
personal beauty.

"It was evident to me that her helplessness did not extend either to her head or hands, for soon I saw that her
warmest interest was still flowing in its long-accustomed
channel, and that from her sick room lines of communication ran in every direction to the outside world. She spoke
of the gift made to her of her rooms with much gratification. Her sense of home seemed wholly centered in them.
The cosey little bedroom opened into a small, bright parlor,
from the windows of which was an exquisite view of the
grounds and distant landscape. . . .

"'Are you strong enough,' I asked her on one occasion,
'to use your pen as in former times?' Summoning the
nurse she had some loose sheets handed to me, saying, 'I
wrote these and had them printed by the Indian boys at
Hampton; but, ——, I can't hold lines long in my memory.'
They were short hymns,[1] and her difficulty was to frame a
verse and hold it in mind until she could get it on paper
either by her own hand or that of another. . . .

"She was unfeignedly interested in good work done by
other hands, and her manner in discussing it, that of the
fellow-laborer, not of the master-workman. I never de-
scried the faintest soupçon of such assumption, nor did I
ever detect any personal ambition in her great work. She
never sought notoriety. Not even in the seclusion of her
last years, when it would have been so natural for her to entertain me with the exciting scenes of her previous history,

---

[1] A favorite occupation of Miss Dix throughout life was the writing of hymns. They were devout, heroic, pleading, and submissive;
but she possessed in no marked degree the lyric faculty.

did she ever drag in her past enterprises and successes. Present work seemed to fill her mind, not her former triumphs.

" Of course her friendliness extended to my family. I took my daughters to see her, and under the impulse of her ruling passion she inquired what schemes of usefulness entered into their young lives. One of them detailed to her the effort she was making to benefit the children in her church. On a subsequent visit, months afterward, she asked how it went on. I pictured its progress with some warmth, she listening sympathizingly and now and then nodding approvingly, when she suddenly exclaimed, with a beaming smile, ' I know S—— would like to have her fingers in my purse ; now would n't she ? ' I promptly declined any gift, telling her she already had objects enough of her own to prosecute ; but she would not be denied, and a crisp, new note, so large that I protested against it, was sent with the message, ' that of all the agencies of charity the school was the most hopeful.'

" It is a mistake that age has power to cast out the evil instincts of human nature. It often intensifies them. Anger and bitterness scowl along the twilight of many a brilliant career, as the dark clouds gather upon the evening horizon of some exquisite day. With Miss Dix this was not so ; her heated, excited day merged into a quiet, peaceful close. In the full tide of work she had been called imperious and arbitrary. These traits may have been necessary ; certainly, they were powerful aids in the accomplishment of her splendid designs ; but as the night drew on, her character mellowed, and all that was most lovable in her nature appeared as her life slowly faded away.

" She suffered at times agonies of pain, and her ability at self-entertainment lessened rapidly in the last year. She had become extremely deaf, her sight also was much impaired, and in her increasing bodily feebleness I imagine that her well-stored memory, from which she had drawn so largely for her comfort and refreshment, now often deserted her. Kind friends sought to aid her failing senses by the best helps that science could supply, but in vain. It was pitiful to have her say to me, ' Try to put this tube in my ear so as not to pain, and yet allow me to hear what you say.' And of her eyes, too, she said in a sort of despairing attempt at cheerfulness, ' I do not think it right to get such numbers of spectacles that nobody else can use, and which do me no good.'

" I saw her only a few months before her death, when she had become so weak as to allow me to stay only half an hour. Feeble as she was, however, with that singular thoughtfulness for others which never left her, she endeavored to entertain the daughter I had brought with me. As the interview wore on it became evident to me that she wished to say something confidential, and at her suggestion I tried to manœuver the faithful nurse out of hearing.

" Failing ignominiously, I said, ' Oh, never mind now ; tell me when I come again.' ' Ah, yes, if I am here ; if I am here.' ' Oh,' I replied, quite too warmly I feared to meet her wishes, for I thought death would be welcomed by her, — ' Oh, I hope you will be here for many a year to come.' She started up with agitated eagerness and said, with wild excitement, ' My dear friend, if you hope that, pray for it : pray that I may be here. I think even lying on my bed I can still do something.' She fell back upon her pillow exhausted, whilst I, moved and surprised beyond measure, sat down that she might have time to recover her composure. I then rose to go. She threw her arms round me, saying with unwonted tenderness, ' O darling,' and I had parted with my old friend forever.   S. C. P. MILLER.

" PRINCETON, N. J."

Constant touches throughout this narrative reveal in Mrs. Miller the genuine observer. With the second childhood of extreme old age and the diminishing power of self-restraint, almost inevitably does vanity prompt the veteran soldier, sailor, statesman or trav-

eler to give way to the temptation of rehearsing to
others the flattering story of the battles or sea-fights
he has fought or has won, the great debates or perilous adventures in which he has borne a heroic part.
Of all this no trace is found in Miss Dix. To her
when a thing is done, it is done. The present absorbs
her while it yet offers any good to do. Aged, broken,
and full of suffering, still for all her religious faith,
for all her yearning after a higher spiritual realm beyond, she does not want to die. "I think even lying
on my bed, I can still do something." The last exclamation, too, "O darling," is the one that occurs over
and over again in the broken, fragmentary letters she
at this period writes to dear friends, proving what a
world of tenderness underlay that self-controlled, ad-
amantine character with which she had fronted the
world in her long warfare for the outcast and despised.

As long as strength lasted it remained the habit of
Miss Dix to sit during the declining hours of sunlight
at her window, feasting her eyes on the beauty of the
landscape and communing with Him, of whom all this
visible glory was to her the perpetual manifestation.
There below her stretched the park-like expanse of
the grounds of the asylum, and there, sitting under
the trees or wandering along the paths in the fullest
enjoyment of liberty possible to their sad condition,
were the poor children of affliction, whose former miseries in chains and cages had first started in her the
vow of consecration never to the end to be broken.

Now, in contrast, could she look down on them ministered to by the uttermost that could be done by science, humanity, religion, and the healing charms of
nature. And yet in the hours of reverie to which this
visible scene must inevitably have led on, how equally

distinctly to imagination must there have often risen
before her mind's eye, in twenty different States
stretching over half a continent in America, from the
pines and maples of Newfoundland to the live oaks
and palmettos of Louisiana, as well as in Europe and
in far-away Japan, the repetition of the same blessed
picture. He whom she had so loved and followed,
the Son of Man who came not to be ministered unto
but to minister, — how often in those sacred hours
must she have felt the fullness of his benediction, " I
was an hungered, and ye gave me meat; I was thirsty,
and ye gave me drink; I was a stranger, and ye took
me in; naked, and ye clothed me ; I was sick, and ye
visited me; I was in prison, and ye came unto me."

The end came on the evening of July 17, 1887.
For a month she had been growing steadily weaker.
Still with her habitual fortitude, and that desire to
pass unobscured through the portal of death so characteristic of believing natures, she had begged her
dear friend Dr. Ward to avoid the use of anodynes,
and to tell her distinctly when the last hour was at
hand. This was not to be. Although Dr. Ward had
given her his pledge that he would apprise her as
soon as he saw the end near by, it came as unexpectedly to him as to her. He was sitting at the tea-
table when the nurse suddenly ran down to report
that Miss Dix was sinking away. Rapidly mounting
the stairs, on opening the door, just as his eye fell on
her, she breathed a quiet sigh and all of earth was
over.

The burial took place in Mount Auburn Cemetery,
near Boston, Mass. Occurring when, in the height of
the summer heats, so many are away at the sea-shore
or in the mountains, a few friends only, among them

Dr. John W. Ward, Dr. Charles H. Nichols, and Mr. Horace A. Lamb, stood by the grave. Communicating to her English friends the intelligence of her last illness and death, Dr. Nichols, who had been so long and intimately associated with her throughout her great career, closed with these words his letter to Dr. D. Hack Tuke : —

"Thus has died and been laid to rest in the most quiet, unostentatious way the most useful and distinguished woman America has yet produced."

CHAPTER XXXII.

SUMMARY.

A CONDENSED summary of the incidents and spirit of a career already so fully illustrated as that of Miss Dix seems hardly called for. Her story is one that tells itself as it goes along. Still, it may be well in a few words to gather in hand the separate threads, and weave them into a combined picture of the essential characteristics of her life and work.

The childhood of Miss Dix was, as has been seen, bleak, humiliating, and painful; more so, indeed, than it has been deemed needful to record. By the age of twelve, the prematurely thoughtful little girl clearly foresaw that she would have to take into her own hands the problem of her future destiny, as well as of the destiny of her two child brothers. How bitter her earliest experience was, is evident from the fact that never to her dying day would she unlock her lips on the subject to her most intimate friend.

At an age, then, when most children are carelessly living in their little world of dolls, the proud and sensitive child keenly felt that she would have to conquer for herself and others a foothold in the world. At once her inborn decision of character displayed itself. She ran away from her mortifying and belittling present that she might secure the possibility of a more promising future. Independent she would be, and master of the means of carrying out what was then the strongest desire in the heart of the premature child - mother. To fit herself to become a teacher seemed the one way to achieve her purpose. It was the New England ideal of honorable work ; it fell in with her own thirst for knowledge ; and it opened up a field for forcefully impressing herself on others, always so predominant a trait of her character. Thus from the start were the intrepidity and rational clearness of her mind revealed.

Underlying, however, this exceptional energy and ambition, there lay a temperament of extreme sensitiveness, of a sensitiveness, indeed, so acute as physically to betray itself all through her girlhood and young womanhood in a quick flushing of the face whenever she was addressed. All her views of life took on an idealistic shape. She craved the society of refined, intellectual, and morally superior people. She reveled in poetry, she was a worshiper of intellectual greatness, she was full of heart-break for affection, she drank in passionately the religious prophecies of teachers like Channing. And yet her love of knowledge, beauty, and spirituality were at the last remove from selfish absorption in the pursuit of them. Poverty, ignorance, and degradation distressed her as keenly as their opposites allured her ; and the moment she could command the means she began to gather together the children of neglect and misery, to make them sharers in a richer life.

Every ideal in her mind thus tended irresistibly to practical benevolent action, the religious fervor of her nature finding vent in enthusiastic personal love of him who went about doing good, and who yearned to make all life a perpetual feast of love and beauty to which from the highways and hedges the outcast should be invited in, the wedding garment thrown over their rags and misery.

There is, then, no way of understanding the later career of this outwardly so self-sustained and commanding woman, apart from the full recognition of the intensity of an emotional temperament pouring out the molten metal which shaped every lineament in the gradually consolidating bronze statue. This temperament was at once the exaltation and the despair of her youth, and the hidingplace of the power of her oncoming days. What kept her sane through the terrible strain of her later years was the relief she got in the passionate love and study of nature, in her power of swiftly kindling to ideal visions of what could and should be made real, and in adoring communion with God, through whose help she rested assured all things were possible. Thus even in the extreme of physical exhaustion, as after her memorable campaign in Scotland, the inextinguishable fervor of her nature leaps up into its old wonted flame, the moment she hears of a new field of promise in the Island of Jersey. "I shall see their chains off," she enthusiastically writes in a letter already quoted in a previous chapter, "I shall take them into the green fields, and show them the lovely little flowers and the blue sky, and they shall play with the lambs and listen to the song of the birds, and 'a little child shall lead them!' This is no romance, this all will be if I get to the Channel Islands, with God's blessing." The romantic ideal, "they shall play with the lambs," the splendid self-confidence, "if *I* get there," the devout recognition, "with God's blessing," — here lay the three root motive-powers of the woman.

Throughout the school-keeping period of Miss Dix's

life, the contradictory elements in her nature, intense and even perilous sensibility held down and often trampled under foot by rigid, ascetic will-power, were never really harmonized. Sensibility to ideals dictated for herself and for her pupils a height of consecration to knowledge, duty, and service beyond the possibility of realization, while inflexible will instituted rules and practices which took no count of flesh and blood, and were severe and monastic to an extreme. Periods of exhaustion and irritability, with subsequently the swift advance of threatening pulmonary disease, were the penalty she herself paid; while, in the case of the children, some looked back to their school experience with pain, and others declared that they owed to it the best they had ever been or done in life. With Miss Dix, it ended, as has been seen, in the utter collapse of her physical powers, her mind, however, proudly sustained by the feeling that no sharpness of suffering had ever moved her to flinch, that she had made a home for her younger brothers and launched them on the world, had achieved independence, and finally had set a stamp on large numbers of young lives that would be indelible for good as long as they should live.

Next follows the eighteen months of extreme illness and languishing in Liverpool, England, — the jubilee year of her life as she always termed it, the period, for all its pain and all its near prospect of death, in which she felt she had been permitted the most luxuriously to surrender herself to leisure, beauty, domestic love, and spiritual conmmunion with Heaven. It wrought a marked softening and enriching influence on her character. Still, it was destined to be followed on her return to America by the saddest and

most disenchanted period of her earthly experience.
Reaching home a feeble invalid, her career as a teacher
over, lonely and with no distinct prospect before her
for the future, she felt herself an exile in her own
land.

Now first came to her the unifying power which was
to fuse into one harmonious whole the contradictory
elements of her nature. Once she was brought into
contact with the abyss of human misery opened up in
the condition of the outcast insane in Massachusetts,
and, as she soon discovered, all over the Union, then
forthwith in the overpowering call of God to dedicate
herself to their championship, she became revealed to
herself and revealed to others. Had she stood and
simply gazed down into that abyss of woe, it would
have paralyzed so sensitive a nature. But high above
all the moaning and despair she heard the angel song
of the new gospel of glad tidings of great joy to them
that sat in darkness, revealed to the world through
the humane inspiration of such sons of consolation as
Pinel and Tuke. To the fervid apostleship of this,
to her, " new Jerusalem descending like a bride from
the heavens" would she consecrate her life. " Look
on this picture and on this," was henceforth the pole
star of her guidance.

Here, then, it at once became clear was a nature demanding a large field on which to deploy its forces,
forces which shut up to anything lesser must inevitably have preyed on herself and preyed on others.
Now could she plan great enterprises. Now could
she measure her indomitable moral will against the
apathy and selfishness of whole legislatures, and finally
kindle in their hearts the enthusiasm of humanity.
Now could she command and dispose of enormous

pecuniary resources, the outcome of public taxation. Now could she cause in twenty States vast structures to rise out of the ground, which should take into the merciful keeping of their quiet, beauty, and skill those heretofore chained, scourged, and pinched with cold. Now could she create the national conditions of a great school of insanity, and open a career to the eminent men who were destined to carry so far the name and fame of her native land. No wonder she grew happier. She was made for such happiness. No wonder she grew healthier. The caged and drooping eagle in her nature was now afloat on the great spaces in which alone it could find vigor and joy.

Then forthwith was it seen how the very powers, the excess of which had been faults in a more restricted sphere, proved the exact means to her great ends. The very persistency of will which exercised on minor matters had often been trying to others now took the leadership of the " forlorn hope," and became the assurance of victory on victory, making strong men like her friend Dr. Buttolph write her, " I have learned from you never to despair." The very self-confidence which, shut up to little things, might easily have been characterized as assumption, now inspired her to seemingly impossible feats of moral daring, which became their own splendid justification. The very asceticism which exerted in a round of trivial duties had been injurious to mind and body now became power to " endure hardness as a good soldier of Christ," the spur to " scorn delights and live laborious days." The very reticence which, in social life, had proved a barrier to closer intimacy, and often had defeated the craving for affection so intense in her self-repressed nature now enabled her to hold her own counsel, and, while the repository of the secret history of two thirds of the asylums in the land, never in a single instance to betray confidence. Finally, that very yearning to relieve misery and that passionate wrath over its longer existence, which left to themselves would either have unnerved or have consumed her, now became the reacting motive to plunge into practical work, and achieve mastership over every detail of hospital construction and hospital management.

The marvelous series of campaigns of pure humanity won by this single-handed woman, and resulting in the establishment of such a host of asylums has already been sufficiently described. Imagination is feeble to call up the extent and enduring character of this her work. It is only by one who has journeyed over the many States of the Union, and seen with the bodily eye the enormous structures and park-like grounds she, with the wand of her moral genius, made to start out of the earth, that it can be adequately conceived. Then first the beholder feels the force of the words written her as far back as 1850 by President Fillmore : —

"Accept my sincere thanks for the print of the Hospital for the Insane in Tennessee. . . . When I looked upon its turrets and recollected that this was the thirteenth monument you had caused to be erected of your philanthropy, I could not help thinking that wealth and power never reared such monuments to selfish pride as you have reared to the love of mankind."

It will be recalled from previous chapters how frequently the impression made by the absolute consecration of Miss Dix to her work had led many superintendents and private benefactors of asylums all over the land, to speak of her as "our Lady," "our Patron

Saint," — a strain of Mediævalism certainly not very common in practical, unimaginative America. Indeed, in a memorial notice written after her death by Dr. Daniel Hack Tuke, of England, the same idea recurs when, in alluding to his own visit to America, he says, " The writer has observed in at least one asylum chapel the portrait of this saintly woman on the wall where in a Roman Catholic Church the Virgin Mary would have been placed." None can doubt that had she lived in earlier ages of the world her works of mercy would have led to her actual canonization, and that, on the altar pieces of churches, her halo-crowned figure, marked by some especial symbol, would have become as familiar a sight as those of St. Catherine of Siena, or Santa Barbara. Surely, the poor dazed and broken minds of the demented could invoke from a higher realm no more merciful or prevailing spirit.

It is, however, an admirable custom in the Roman Catholic Church that, whenever its prelates are summoned to deliberate the momentous question of adding to the sacred calendar a new name, one out of their number should be appointed to enact the part of what is termed the "Advocatus Diaboli," or Devil's Advocate. His duty it is to rake out of every hidden quarter and every unguarded hour of life the worst that can possibly be urged against the candidate for canonization. A world-old idea this, one already imaginatively glorified. as far back as in the days of the Book of Job, where, before the court of God and His angels, appears Satan, the Adversary, to challenge the name of the man pronounced "perfect and upright, and one that feared God, and eschewed evil." In the light of the frailty of human nature, even at its best estate, the custom, let it be repeated, is an admirable one, and one that falls in with every natural instinct of justice; only with the needful proviso that the preternatural acuteness of the Adversary for discovering spots even on the face of the sun shall not be suffered to outweigh the entire mass of counter testimony to the fact that, after all is said, the sun remains a resplendent luminary.

The only serious faults that were ever urged against the character of Miss Dix were that in minor matters many people thought her too much inclined to take the reins into her own hands, too inflexible and dictatorial in her treatment of the judgment of others, and that at times her self-consciousness was oppressive. These were instinctive elements in her nature, manifest from childhood: in reality without the strong tap root in her being from which they sprang, she could never have achieved her enormous work. They are elements of character the praise or blame of which turns wholly on what other qualities of mind are allied with them. United with clear ideas and noble purposes they lead on to grand results; and it is only when bound up with narrow thoughts and petty personal ends that they prove morally censurable. No great character can keep always at its high-water mark. There come times of exhaustion and disenchantment when the higher qualities of the intellect and soul are in abeyance, and the automatic habit of the underlying native temperament alone asserts itself.

Emphatically, the automatic habit of Miss Dix's nature was that of imperial command, the instinct of taking into her own hands the decision of momentous questions involving the welfare or misery of thousands, and of undauntedly insisting, no matter in the face of whom, — in the face of Legislature, Congress, Parliament, or Pope, — this way, in the name of the Father of the Fatherless ! this way, and no otherwise, shall it be. For it, thousands and tens of thousands who elsewise would have continued to languish in misery had occasion to rise up and call her Blessed! That this great tidal set of a powerful nature should at times in minor matters, and when no large idea was longer present, have swept persistently on, was a fault of character of which, when the most is made, no serious detraction from her greatness remains. The older superintendents of asylums, who recognized the immense debt of obligation under which they lay to her, smiled good-humoredly at such trifling peculiarities, knowing full well what a stronghold justice and mercy ever maintained in her heart, and that it was after all a "godly jealousy" for the sacred name of the institutions she yearned over that made her so insistent that no jot or tittle should pass from their law.

The faults, then, of the character of Miss Dix belonged to the class of what have been aptly named the "faults of one's virtues," that is, they grew out of the excess of good and great qualities. The phrase is a most significant one. Not that a fault does not still remain a fault, and a virtue a virtue. And yet it would be but the barest justice to add that of all her feats of dominating obstacles, the greatest feat of them all was the success with which through long, long years she dominated the extremes of her own sensitive, fiery, and commanding spirit. Throughout her whole asylum life, it was her struggle, and almost always successful struggle, to hide the imperious element in her nature under the cover of an unfailing patience, sweet-

ness of persuasion, and utter sinking of self in the
cause of the poor outcasts for whom she was pleading.
"I perceive," wrote to her President Fillmore in 1850,
during her long struggle in Washington, "that you
feel anxious and sad. I cannot wonder at it! I wonder your patience has held out so long and that you
can speak with such equanimity. But yours is a goodness that never tires, a benevolence that never wearies,
a confident hope that never seems to desert you. None
but the most disinterested and self-sacrificing can have
such faith, or display such all-conquering perseverance."
Did then, persons at times accuse her of being interfering and dictatorial in smaller matters? Be it so!
She had come heroically by the fault, even when it
was a fault. For by what had it been bred in her?
Simply by this, that all through her long and self-
sacrificing public career of over forty years it had
been the very burden of God laid on her shoulders, *to
interfere* now with brutal almshouse keepers, now
with a low and besotted state of public opinion, now
with selfish politicians, now with narrow partisan legislatures, yes, and to persist in interfering till the voice
of justice and mercy prevailed. Surely such virtues
were resplendent enough to swallow up in their light
the few "faults of her virtues."

The prescribed limits of this biography forbid the
introduction here of the grateful and detailed tributes
paid after her death to the memory of Miss Dix, at the
annual convention of the Association of Superintendents of American Insane Asylums, as well as embodied
in the yearly reports of the many and vast institutions
she had founded. With scarcely the faintest note of
dissent they were in one vein of praise and veneration.
It was for the "judgment of the competent" that she

alone ever cared, and the seal of this was indelibly stamped on her name and work. Had she taken thought of mere personal fame and yielded to the constant appeals of governors and State legislatures, her name carved in stone would be read to-day over the portals of more stately structures than were ever from the foundation called after any private man or woman. As it was, the Dix Ward of the McLean Asylum, Somerville, Mass., and Dixmont Hospital, Penn., are the only institutions, where, except for her portrait hanging in so many of their chapels, there is anything visible to suggest her name.

Very pleasant is it, however, to round off this summary of the more public characteristics of so salient a character with the notice of a more private trait peculiarly feminine in its nature, — a straw, perhaps, but still a straw which reveals the main set of the current of a life dedicated to going about doing good.

Although herself an unmarried woman, who in early life had met a blight of her affections after an engagement with a cousin, Miss Dix retained till late in her days a romantic fondness for bringing together those she thought fitted to make loving helpmates to one another, and then leaving it to the elective affinities to complete the process of domestic attraction and cohesion. In this eager disposition of the woman who had never known the blessedness of a home of her own to enact the part of special providence in securing a happy home for others, her judgment again and again proved as clear as her heart was warm. One series of letters was there left among her papers — from a superintendent and his wife both long since dead, and whom none now living can name — that were one continuous chant of benediction to the Lady Bountiful,

who had so tenderly and delicately brought them together, and secured them nineteen years of unbroken
domestic love.

Innumerable likewise, as illustrating the purely
womanly side of Miss Dix's nature, were the letters
from sick rooms and homes of bereavement, containing
each some such endearing message as: " In this I place
a couple of Heart's-ease blossoms from our garden.
They seem to me peculiarly *your* flower."

INDEX.